NAPOLEON IV: 1943

The third book in the series

Bob Farnham, Bedfordshire, England

"From the excellent cover design (front and back) to the last chapter and the Character description ... the Glossary and the excellent Afterward, all exceed expectations. You have excelled yourself in producing a third part that far exceeds part one and two. Right from the first word I was gripped and lost in the story, in a way that only a great story can do. And the story still goes on, if it is as good as this one it **will** be a World Beating Blockbuster."

NEW BRITAIN Kz1

The second book in the series

P.D. James, Baroness James of Holland Park.

"To have it set in a fascist concentration camp in occupied New Britain in 1941 is certainly an intriguing and original idea."

Dr. Dorian Hayes, Curator, Canadian Collection and North American Literature, British Library
"I do hope you continue working on this fascinating series of publications."

Paul Swayze, Hamilton, Canada
"I thoroughly enjoyed it ... liked the research you've so obviously done and the twists and turns."

SAVING THE KING

The first book in the series

This is, as can seen from the above, an alternative history of the Second World War. This is of course not a new idea, but what I like about this one is the sheer exuberance with which it is written … Bravo!"

Paige Turner, Turning Pages Review

"…it's an engaging story."

Joanne Pedicone, Librarian

"I was blown away by this impressive first novel … It is credible, imaginative and rich in historical detail … Enthusiastically recommended."

Mark Schmidt, Curator World War II Museum, U.S.A.

"Oldham has cleverly tied in a great knowledge of World War II-era history into a very readable, interesting and unforeseen view of how events in the Battle of Britain might very well gone had certain things gone in favor of the Nazis and against the British … Touching view of the deposed and disgraced Edward and Wallis Simpson … loyal to the fatherland but fearful of life under the National Socialists; the loyal Tower of London employee; the cloak-and-dagger tactics of the British underground; the turn of events in the United States; all make this a very illuminating and thought provoking query into how things might have gone…"

GO FOR A SOLDIER

BOOK FOUR OF AN ALTERNATIVE HISTORY OF WORLD WAR TWO

ROBERT P. OLDHAM

Hamilton, Canada: Raven Press Ontario (Canada), 2009.

Published by Raven Press Ontario (Canada)
For copies of any of the books in the series please contact:
  Bryan Prince, Bookseller Ltd.,
  1060 King Street West, Hamilton, Ontario, Canada L8S 1L7
  www.princebooks.net 905-528-4508 / Fax 905-528-1877
  1-800-867-0090 (toll free in Canada/USA)
Printed in Canada

- Saving the King: Book One of An Alternative Novel of World War Two (ISBN   978-0-9690573-5-2)
- New Britain KZ1: Book Two of an Alternative History of World War Two (ISBN   978-0-9690573-4-5)
- Napoleon IV: 1943 Book Three of an Alternative History of World War (ISBN 978-0-9690573-6-9)
- Go For A Soldier: Book Four of an Alternative History of World War Two (ISBN   978-0-9690573-7-6)

Library and Archives Canada Cataloguing in Publication
Oldham, Robert, 1950-
Go for a soldier : book four of an alternative history of World War Two / Robert Oldham.
ISBN 978-0-9690573-7-6
I. Title.
PS8579.L27G6 2009   C813'.54   C2009-904805-1

Printed at Monsoon Books, Milton, Ontario, Canada
Copyright © 2009   Robert Oldham
Copyright © 2009   Cover Aubrey Oldham
Copyright © 2007   Author photo Ruth Oldham

"Go, go, go like a soldier,
Go, go, go like a soldier.
Go, go, go like a soldier
So-oldier of the Queen!"

Rudyard Kipling
'The Young British Soldier',
Barrack Room Ballads

Dedicated to
Prince William, Flying Officer William Wales RAF and
Prince Henry, Lieutenant Harry Wales, Royal Household Cavalry
and other servicemen and women of the British Commonwealth
who 'go like a soldier' to wherever they are ordered.

TABLE OF CONTENTS

FOREWORD

Thanks to all who have read my books and supported me particularly Bryan Prince Booksellers and Coles Books, Jackson Square, Hamilton; Len Dickey, Joanne Pedicone and April Windus in Canada, Bob Farnham in England; Bruce McIntyre and Nora Hayes-Stapylton in Australia and of course my wife and family.

Information provided by Thom Richardson FSA, Keeper of Armour and Oriental Collections, Royal Armouries, about a double-bladed Persian dagger that caught my interest in May 2007 was very helpful. I heartily recommend a visit to the magnificent new Royal Armouries Museum, Leeds, England. It gave me the idea for Alan's mission.

No disrespect towards any living or dead member of the royal family is intended, quite the contrary, I hope they have been depicted with the sensitivity due to an institution which I support and revere. I have to the best of my ability, made up a tale incorporating famous people and fictitious characters in an historic fantasy, based upon logically extrapolated accepted historical facts. Readers are encouraged to find out what really happened by consulting the many fascinating, excellent materials on World War Two at their local public library.

A list of characters, both historical and fictional, and a glossary of terms are given in an appendix at the end of the book.

1

INTRODUCTION

Saving the King, the first book in series, covers from 1937 through the breakout of war in 1939 until early 1941. John and Felicity became members of the Free Britain resistance movement when Great Britain was occupied by Nazi forces after the Germans successfully invaded in September 1940. John Stafford, my father, and his identical twin Alan, were born in 1920 and brought up in Hamilton, Canada by their parents, my grandparents, Colonel Rex and Winifred Stafford. In 1937 as a young man John travelled to Europe, he studied German in Munich before returning to Canada to read History at the University of Toronto. The next year on his second trip he was recruited as a spy by Lord Beaverbrook and Winston Churchill by his father's old friend and later my maternal grandfather, Colonel Meseurier a military attaché at Canada House in Trafalgar Square, London.

After adventures on the continent and on the island of Malta John returned to London to report. He began a romantic attachment with a childhood friend, Felicity, who was studying fine art conservation at the Royal Academy of Art. John and Alan enlisted in the Royal Hamilton Rifles, their father's old regiment, and were shipped with the Canadian Division to Britain at the commencement of hostilities.

John volunteered to go with the British Expeditionary Force to Norway where he won the Military Cross. After the fall of France in 1940 the Canadian Expeditionary Force came under General Montgomery's command. He was ordered to defend the south coast of England in the event of German invasion. John underwent Commando training in Achnarry, Scotland. There he met the men who would become his brothers-in-arms: Australian Lieutenant Aubrey Hunter, Scottish Sub-Lieutenant Duncan MacLeod and Nova Scotian Sergeant-Major Frances Lincoln. With invasion imminent John was promoted to acting Major commanding A Troop Ist Commandos and ordered to Windsor

Castle with his men, just in time to rescue Princesses Elizabeth and Margaret. Felicity was on hand to help since she was packing art work to protect it from bomb damage. Hitler ordered Operation Sea Lion, the invasion of Great Britain in September 1940. Despite the best efforts of the British Army, various factors, including the destruction of RAF airfields and the loss of the gargantuan battle of Hayward's Heath meant that Prime Minister Winston Churchill organized Operation Magneto the 'Great Evac' to Canada and Iceland. During the 'Great Evac' my great uncle, Alan Stafford, was a Lieutenant in the 3rd Canadian Division fighting in the rearguard withdrawing westward toward the ports of Bristol and Cardiff. He was evacuated from Bristol but John and his troop were ordered to the mountains of Wales as part of a planned resistance movement throughout the British Isles. Felicity left for Canada in the evacuation and underwent SOE espionage training before returning to join the Red Dragons. The Red Dragons freed the puppet King and Queen of New Britain, Edward VIII and Queen Wallis from the Tower of London.

New Britain KZ1, the second book in the series, deals with a concentration camp on the Isle of Wight. John and his Red Dragons along with Alan, now a Canadian Commando, ensure that an important Jewish physicist Lise Meitner is brought to North America. The third book, Napoleon IV is about French Colonel D'Allaincourt, a direct descendant of Napoleon I, after he successfully leads a coup in French Indo-China against the pro-Japanese Vichy government. His declaration galvanises pro-Allied revolts in French Syria, Algeria and Morocco. Eager to get to the front lines on his visit to General Montgomery's 8th Army in North Africa Napoleon IV and Brigadier Orde Wingate assume the roles of French paratroopers and join John Stafford's long-range attack against a German S1 rocket site in the desert. Alan recuperates from his experience impersonating an SS officer in Kz1 at a military hospital in Winnipeg and returns to the fight. In America General George S. Patton revels in fiercely engaging German, Japanese and Mexican troops defeating them in the Battle of Houston saving the Texas oil fields.

1944 was the fifth year of war. The Allies; the British Empire and Dominions including Canada, Australia, New Zealand and South Africa, with the United States and China were fighting the Axis Alliance of Germany, Italy, Spain and most of Central and Latin America. It was the 'the nearest run thing you ever saw in your life' as Wellington said of his victory at Waterloo. Franco's Spain had been promised Gibraltar, Cuba and the Philippines.

Canada was home to the British armed forces, the government-in-exile led by Prime Minister Clement Attlee and the Princesses Elizabeth and Margaret evacuated from Great Britain in Churchill's 'Great Evac' of October 1940. The Dominion was producing huge amounts of armaments and foodstuffs as the entire population of men and women over eighteen were conscripted for the armed forces or the Land Army of farm labourers, unless they were working in industrial jobs.

The United States led by President Franklin Delano Roosevelt, known affectionately as FDR, had been weakened in 1943 by fascist armies attacking California, Texas, Louisiana and Florida. Only the 6th Army in Texas led by General Patton had total success. It decimated the Axis armies which crossed the Rio Grande, saved the oil fields and pursued the enemy into Mexico. Thanks to successful germ warfare, the enemy had encircled San Diego and taken Los Angeles. To the east the enemy had penetrated inland to Birmingham. Alabama. New Mexico, southern California, Louisiana, Mississippi and Florida were occupied by Axis forces. The enemy were poised to take Atlanta, Georgia. The US Navy base at San Diego on the west coast was a ghost town due to 'Devil's Dust' unleashed by the Japanese. Only some of the docks were in use until total decontamination was completed.

Germs were sprayed over cities and farms by aircraft or placed in the water supplies by fascist agents. As a result death stalked the land from Phoenix to Nashville. A new ingredient had been added to the typhoid, anthrax, bubonic plague germs and ricin poison sprays and shells used by the enemy. It was a mutated variant of the Spanish Influenza virus that had wiped out about

5

thirty million around the world in 1918. American scientists working around the clock in laboratories across the US to find an antidote were close to a solution.

FDR galvanized the American population and industry to perform miracles in battle and on the factory floor. He promised his allies that despite being invaded America would continue to fully support its overseas campaign in Australia and keep its commitment to invade Spain. His state of the union speech with his trademark educated New York accent was also his shortest union address to Congress on 1st January, 1944. It had 80 million holding their breath listening to it on the radio on all networks in every part of the country including the occupied states. It was the most important of his many crucial

"This will be a brief but no less crucial state of the union address but the situation demands we get back to the work of winning the war quickly. Our boys and girls demand nothing less.

"No matter what happens America will keep its word to fight fascism overseas shoulder-to-shoulder with our allies in the Free Alliance of Nations. We will support the founding meeting of the Earth Government in Montreal planned for 1945. Yes, we have been invaded, yes we are hurting. But no we shall not surrender. I shall tell you what we will do. We shall fight back using every ounce of our strength no matter what color he or she is or creed he or she follows. We are as one in the direst days of our young country's history. I tell you that our greatest days are still to come.

"A cure will be found to combat the terrible weapons the enemy are employing against us in the battlegrounds of the south and our farms. The rain that nature brings is having a moderating effect upon their germ weapons as are the more sophisticated sterilization techniques that our nation is following assiduously. Our factories are working every minute of the day producing aircraft, guns, tanks and ships that are better in quality than those used by the enemy. Our fighting men and now women are well-trained and well-armed. We have raised six armies consisting of

three million men and women in combat roles and support roles that are in action as I speak. The first women sailors have seen action at sea, female pilots have shot down enemy aircraft over Colorado, women soldiers are serving in tanks and in foxholes in their own battalions by the Mississippi and fighting for Los Angeles against Japanese and Latin assaults. Yes, these are hard times but these are tremendous days that will be spoken of in centuries to come with reverence by our descendants.

"My fellow Americans, join me in asking this question every morning. What can I do for my country today? Do not ask what your country can do for you. Ask instead what you can do to help the United States of America! I thank you for all you are doing. With God's help we shall succeed."

Cameras captured him taking off his pince-nez spectacles to clean off a tear from his cheek, putting them back and flashing one of his wide warm smiles acknowledging the long moments of applause. The cameras did not record his son, Ensign Franklin Delano Jr., on-leave but in naval uniform helping his polio-stricken father leave the podium. Journalists agreed in 1932, when Roosevelt began his meteoric streak across the national political scene, that they would not depict the crippling effect of polio which weakened his legs in a cruel mid-adult attack.

Every American man and woman over sixteen was armed and trained to kill, except for nurses, doctors, foresters, farmers, oil, munitions and railway workers. The United Confederate States of America had been declared by the Japanese and a fascist government led by Air Marshal Charles Lindburgh was set up in 1941 in occupied Honolulu. At that time it was considered a joke since it seemed impossible to think that mainland America could ever be invaded. Now the UCSA had grown to include the southern-most section of the USA, except for Texas. California, Colorado, Arizona, Louisiana, Mississipi, Florida, Alabama and Georgia were ruled by Air Marshal Lindburgh and the UCS Congress in Miami. The George Washington Army comprised of right-wing Americans was in action in South Carolina against their

7

fellow Americans. But a fifth-column of American freedom fighters, including many southern blacks, was making life miserable for garrison Axis troops.

Montgomery destroyed Rommel's *Afrika Korps* in North Africa with the help of Bradley's American army. Hitler's *Festung Europe*-Fortress Europe was next. Terrific strides were being made in Hamilton, Canada and the USA in cracking enemy codes and developing computers. Allied radar systems were well ahead of Axis technology. Hitler ruled all Europe, including New Britain but, despite constant air raids, the British islands of Gibraltar and Malta in the Mediterranean were holding out. In China troops trained and led by American officers and provided with good tanks and equipment were achieving one victory after another against the Japanese invading armies. Stettin, the American industrial master mind had achieved the impossible industrialising Chiang Kai-shek country. The Burma Road had been completed to allow supplies to be sent from Rangoon to China and an airlift from India over the Himalayas to China was successfully ensuring supplies and advisors were being sent.

Singapore was under siege but the Japanese were stymied in their advance down the Malayan Archipelago by the stubborn British, Australian, Canadian and Indian defenders. They were supplied by massive transport submarines and air drops from India and Ceylon. In Australia, General Eisenhower's army of Americans and Australians was pushing back the Japanese invader. There was hope and a grim determination in the hearts of millions who realized that to lose the war would mean the end of civilization as we know it for hundreds of years if not forever.

The stage is set to tell the fictionalized true adventures of my parents, John and Felicity and their comrades in 1944.

H. G. Stafford,

Hamilton, Canada   Trafalgar Day 21 October, 2009

CHAPTER ONE   GREEN BERETS

"The war may spread to Spain and Morocco.
It may spread eastward to Turkey and Russia.
The Huns may lay their hands for a time upon the
granaries of the Ukraine and the oil wells of the Caucasus.
They may dominate the Black Sea. They may dominate the
Caspian. Who can tell?"

Winston Churchill 'Westward Look the Land is Bright'
speech 27 April, 1941

At Tangier, Africa squares off against Spain across the slim channel of the Strait of Gibraltar. Major John Stafford paused to watch a scene of frantic activity alongside the nearby airfield, home to six squadrons of USAAF and RAF aircraft. He was on his early morning walk to the officer's mess tent. The tall, suntanned Canadian walked with a spring in his step fresh from his first leave in a year. He took a fortnight in a jeep to explore south to the snow-capped Atlas Mountains then to Casablanca up the Moroccan coast to Tangier. He and his unit were part of the British, American and Canadian armies poised to invade Hitler's Europe. The thought excited him, he loved a challenge and leading his men onto a Spanish beach on D-Day was certainly that. *I shall carry my father's sword as we land* he resolved. *Must have it cleaned and sharpened.* He referred to the Wilkinson infantry officer's sword his father had worn through the Battle of Vimy Ridge in the Great War and had given to him. Officers no longer were expected to take their swords into battle but save them for ceremonial occasions but the Çommandos were not conventional troops, they were a shock-troop unit designed to take on tough amphibious assignments and audacity, self-reliance and eccentricity were lauded as character building. In the brown leather holster attached to his belt he carried the long-barrelled Webley target pistol also a gift from his father. John chuckled, knowing he was the eldest son by only five minutes and thought of his twin brother on special duties in the Middle East. *Oh well, Alan did get Dad's army regular issue Webley .38 revolver, swagger stick and Gilette shaving tackle.*

John wore the insignia of his rank of Major, a St. Edward's Crown upon each of the epaulettes of his smartly ironed open-necked tan cotton shirt. He entered the mess tent for eggs and bacon. On the right side of his shoulder upon his shirt was stitched the outline of a red dragon. The two hundred men of A Troop were his responsibility, it was unusual for someone so young to be a major but then the war threw up strange things all the time. If you had talked to him and expressed surprise that twenty-three year old, sporting a ginger military moustache without one grey whisker, could be a major, just under a colonel in rank and above a captain, he would have laughed and told you Major-General James Wolfe was thirty-three when he took Quebec. He would have added, showing his love of history, that Wolfe was commissioned in his father's regiment of marines aged fifteen, fought in the Battle of Dettingen aged sixteen and became a major aged twenty-two. He might have added for good measure that his RAF pal 'Brock' Badger knew a flying instructor in the Battle of Britain aged 18! 'Needs must' was one of John's favourite expressions that he had learnt at his mother's knee in Hamilton, Canada and that covered a multitude of sins. It was how the army functioned, one operated inside lines of accepted behaviour or made sure that that one was not caught.

John and his twin brother Alan, following in Wolfe's tracks, joined their father's regiment, the Royal Hamilton Rifles in Ontario, Canada in 1939. Both subalterns crossed the ocean with their regiment to Great Britain. John volunteered for the Commandos. Lieutenant Alan Stafford fought against the invading German army at Eastbourne and led his men to Bristol and a ship to Canada. John stayed as a Commando resistance leader.

The officers and men John commanded become a band of brothers, as Shakespeare's Henry V termed his small army of archers and knights at Agincourt. His unit wearing Red Dragon patches on their right shoulders had fought in the mountains of Wales against the fascists of New Britain then transferred to Cairo to march their way eastward across North Africa as part of Monty's Desert Rats, the 8th Army. His two platoon commanders were Captain Aubrey Hunter and Sub-Lieutenant Duncan MacLeod. Aubrey fair-haired Australian from Perth who ran away from home as a boy, sheered sheep and wandered the outback befriending the Aborigines who taught him how to survive. Aged twenty-eight he was the oldest officer in the unit. He joined the Royal Australian Artillery in 1936 and worked his way up the ranks taking his fiery dislike of artifice and privilege with him. Sub-Lieutenant Duncan MacLeod, RN was a spectacled Scot who quit his Edinburgh University studies to join the Royal Navy saw action in the North Sea on a destroyer then transferred to the Commandos where individuality was encouraged. Accordingly he wore a kilt in the Macleod tartan topped by his Royal Navy jacket and a white submariner's roll-neck jumper.

John also had support from the Bren gun wielding Sergeant-Major Frances 'President' Lincoln, a Nova Scotian descendant of a black slave brought to America who joined the British army during the American Revolutionary War and went to Canada for free land and hard pioneer life. Lincoln boxed as heavyweight once beating champion Primo Canara before enlisting in the British army and becoming a physical training instructor at Commando School. He trained hundreds including John, Aubrey and Duncan in hand-to-hand combat and ensured they ran gruelling miles over the highland moors in full-kit turning them into prime specimens of fighting men in any nasty weather Achnarry, Scotland could throw at them. He was rarely seen without his beloved 'Bertha' his Bren machine-gun, to most it was a heavy weapon but he carried it so easily it might have been a wooden toy. With invasion imminent the Commando commandant graduated John's intake a few days early, gave him a field promotion from Captain to Major and his own Commando Troop with orders to drive in convoy to Windsor Castle to reinforce the Coldstream Guards on duty protecting the royal Princesses,

Elizabeth and Margaret. John's troop lacked a senior NCO and Lincoln volunteered.

John's six-foot lean, alert frame, straight red hair and ginger moustache would have marked him out even if he wasn't an army officer with a ribbon on his battledress blouse indicating he was a holder of the Military Cross for bravery. He earned a promotion to Captain and an MC overcoming an entrenched German machine-gun nest in Norway in early 1940. When the British army was overwhelmed in the Battle of Britain, he led the Welsh Commando resistance group in the mountains of Wales hence their name, and badge, a red Welsh dragon.

His worn officer's peaked cap was emblazoned with the badge of the Royal Marines, a globe on an anchor surmounted by a crown. The brass decoration gleamed in the morning light thanks to the spit and polish polishing of John's batman, the cynical crack-shot of the troop, Corporal Williams. John squinted as he faced the early morning sun and put on the American sunglasses he bought for five Dirhams at the *medina* in Fez. It already was getting hot despite it being early in the morning but after campaigning across North Africa he was used to it.

John stood in front of long rows of sand coloured tents housing just one small part of the allied army poised to invade Spain which included the two hundred men of his Red Dragons. Parked a few miles away were ranks of USAAF B-17, Mitchell and Liberator bombers, as well as RAF and RCAF Halifaxes and Lancasters. Squadrons of USAAF Thunderbolt, Mustang and Kitty-hawk fighter planes were landing to replenish bullets, bombs and rockets after being on patrol over Gibraltar and the Bay of Biscay. So laden were they that John swore they actually waddled their way into the air. He knew that those that came back would return minus the extra fuel tanks which they would jettison over the Straits of Gibraltar when empty or, in combat dropped when full to give them more speed.

Duncan McLeod and Aubrey Hunter strode up to stand by John and take in all the early morning activity. "Brock told me the other day that his squadron came back with twigs and branches stuck in their wings and it's true I saw this lot come back yesterday just like that. They're 604 County of Middlesex Squadron." John said.

The Scot spoke in a light Edinburgh burr, "Well here we are D-Day minus five days. After months of training we are going to be part of the big show very soon. Bit of an honour."

"I never thought I would be sailing into battle in a metal box depending on sailors to get me there and no ride back, just jumping on the beach. The American paratroopers think we're crazy getting seasick or drowning as we jump off the ramp laden with heavy kit, they prefer to jump out of aircraft with a thin bit of silk to do the job," the straw haired Australian said shaking his head. "They think *we're* insane. Streuth!"

"They've got some nerve, those Yanks but that's why we want them on our side," John noted. My American Ranger pal, Dan Stannard is all steamed up ready to go with his Rangers, at one of the training sessions he positively rubbed his hands with glee when he saw the mock up of their Omaha landing beach and he was really excited to see the Rangers will take and hold that beach for the GIs on the first day. Their landing will be south of Cadiz . From there they go south to Algaricas and relieve Gibraltar by forcing the enemy out of the way all the way to Malaga, then they head north to Cordoba and join Alexander's 2nd t Army as we slog it all the way to Madrid in the heart of Spain.

"Of course we'll be landing north of Cadiz on Sword Beach on the Playa De Castilla. We fight our way inland and relieve the paratroops at the bridge over the River ..."

"Tinto", Duncan interrupted picked up the strategic list of targets for the 8th Army, "then the 8th Army joins up for us we move east to take Saville and hold it until relieved by forward units of the invasion. John stood in front of Sergeant-Major Lincoln and returned his smart salute palm outward. "Men, perhaps you are wondering what's inside these boxes here?" John turned and

13

pointed at the wooden crates that stood in front of them. One was marked 'Large', the other 'Medium' and the last 'Small'. Each was marked in stencilled black paint 'MADE IN MONTREAL, CANADA.'

"These boxes," the red-haired Canadian patted the closest wooden crate, "have been following us from Tunisia and have finally caught up with us. Just in time for us to wear as we go into action in Europe. We are finally being issued with green berets, the unique headgear of the Commandos. They've separated them into different sizes so those with big heads, like you Private Faulkner, can line up over here in front of me, medium size over there with Captain MacLeod." Faulkner at 6 feet three inches and two hundred pounds was a popular soldier, known to the whole troop so laughs and jeers erupted from the two hundred men on parade. "Medium head-size Commandos can line up in front of me and the small head-size Commandos, but no less tough, can line up on the other side where Sub-Lieutenant MacLeod is. All right, fall out and form lines in front of your size crate."

Once they had been fitted with the berets the soldiers smoothed them down on the right side to fold crisply and resumed their positions on parade standing at ease their hands held loosely together behind their backs, legs apart. "One for your Srn't Major," John said tossing a large size beret to the Nova Scotian who caught it deftly and put it on. "Now one for me, medium for you Aubrey and a small one for Duncan should go nicely with the strange garb you insist on wearing instead of the proper issue battledress. You in your MacLeod tartan kilt will really put the wind up the enemy.

Duncan proudly proclaimed proudly "For D-Day I shall not only wear the beret, the naval jacket and the kilt, but I shall play the pipes. Try and stop me Aubrey. 'Scotland the Brave' is coming."

"Jerry beware!" the older Australian declared, "you know mate I can't say I blame 'em if the Jerries run with a bloke coming at them in with knobbly knees, in a dress sounding like someone squeezing a dying cat."

14

"Thanks for the compliment Captain Hunter," Duncan replied with mock politeness. The two men were from totally different backgrounds, the self-educated Australian from a large, poor family in Perth, Western Australia and the younger private-schooled Scot born into an important Edinburgh family enjoyed teasing each other. In reality they respected each other's leadership and courage in battle. John knew they thrived on competing with each other to the benefit of the unit and did nothing to stop their bickering until it got on his nerves.

Sergeant-Major Francis Lincoln, known as 'President' Lincoln in honour of the American President who emancipated the American slaves in the 1860s bellowed out in his stentorian parade ground voice. "Parade. Parade A-tten-shun!" The two hundred men stood to attention standing straight crashing their right boots down onto the ground next to their left. *Heads up. Chest in.* "Right you lot, Weapons and full kit inspection at 1700 hours check your weapons, sharpen your bayonets and wear the green beret with pride. Now a word from Major Stafford."

Lincoln about face smartly and saluted briskly to the C.O. "A Troop ready for inspection, Sir."

John returned the salute. "Men, stand at ease, Stand easy. In five days we land in Spain, along with tens of thousands of other allied troops. We have trained with landing craft storming similar beaches to our target Juno Beach. We know we can do it in any weather, any time of the day or night. Tonight we will move by lorry convoy twenty miles to Tangier and await embarkation on the ship which will carry us to the coast where we board our landing craft.

"All across North Africa, the Azores, Medeira and the Canary Islands vast preparations are underway for the largest amphibious landing in history. We are just one small part of D-Day, but every part is crucial, each one of you is important. Each unit has a job to do. Once we arrive at Tangier we will spend three days going over every detail once again of our part in Operation Overlord our final rehearsal. Then we board the ship and get to

15

sea. Let's get it perfect and we shall reach our objective. I know you feel the excitement like I do. Get some rest before the inspection. Over to you S'rnt Major," John turned to 'President' Lincoln his blue eyes twinkling as if to say 'I would like to say over to you 'Mr. President' but I had better follow proper procedure and all that'.

Lincoln saluted his right palm outward snapping up to the Royal Marine badge on his new beret and John returned it "Parade! Wait for it, P-arade by the right, dismissed." The two platoons each smartly turned to the right and walked off the red soil of the Moroccan parade ground. Some ribald comments were thrown Corporal Williams' way for his eagerness to get off-parade causing the comment from their Sergeant-Major who showed a tough exterior concealing a soft centre. He was hard on his men but would go to hell and back for them. In return he was respected and liked.

Williams shot back, "Got a lot to do with my kit and the Major's, haven't I? After all I am his batman, he's entrusted me with getting his sword sharpened so he has," the Welshman boasted to his mates with a sense of pride. John's batman was responsible for the C.O.'s kit and uniform. Williams was also one of several designated snipers of the unit but also had the reputation for being lazy. He did not tell anyone that his real concern was making it to a meeting of NCOs to discuss the latest round of bets on the weather on D-Day, four to one on cancellation due to storms. Williams was placing five pounds on going no matter what, he felt reckless. "You can't take it with you. Besides, the Spanish don't use our money, so as long as we get ciggies, wine from the Spanish Reds and grub what else do we need? A Jerry bullet reduces all debts and winnings to nothing, so what the hell I say."

CHAPTER TWO   MOROCCAN TYPHOONS

*"Operation Overlord is set for May 1st, 1944. The port of Cadiz,
Spain will be taken by the
American 2nd Army at Omaha Beach and the British 2nd Army at
Juno Beach. The American 6th Army and elements of the British 8th
Army will reinforce our forces on D-Day plus 4. The Canadian 1st
Army will take Lisbon on Gold Beach. A coup by pro-allied
generals and politicians in Lisbon
will take place two days before D-Day.
Detailed planning will now be our priority."*

*General Omar Bradley, to his army commanders, Americans
Hammond and Bakker, Britons Alexander and Montgomery and
the Canadian Crerar.*

Casablanca, Morocco, 3 November, 1943

After the parade was dismissed John conferred with Aubrey
and Duncan. "I'm going to visit 'Brock' Badger, he wanted some
of us to come and see his Typhoon plane this afternoon we could
have a beer or two with him at his squadron's mess. I asked Mr.
President if he wants to join us he's been a bit quiet lately working
too hard, this will do him good. He said sure."

"Sounds good, we squeeze into a jeep but I'm only coming
as long as Aubrey promises not to start some kind of saloon
brawl," Duncan joked.

"Just for that Dunc, I'm going to bring my didgeridoo.
There are a few true-blue Aussies in Brock's squadron I've heard
and it will be a little taste of down-under for them."

"I can't wait," Duncan quipped sarcastically.

"Don't worry Duncan, maybe he'll take you up in a Mosquito while I perform. That's a two-man plane, room for a Scot if you tuck up your kilt and sporran." Aubrey shot back. With a flourish he took off his Aussie hat. It was the standard light brown stiff bush hat, the brim folded up on the left side of the crown. It was held in place by a brass badge of wooden wheeled cannon beneath a St. Edward's Crown with the inscription 'Royal Australian Artillery'. He vigorously scratched his mop of fair hair. I think I'll wear my green beret when it gets cooler, when we get further north.

Duncan was a veteran of a Royal Navy destroyer Mosquitoes are fast but the airframe is an all-wooden construction hence the name the 'wooden wonder'. I'm looking forward to seeing one up close."

"Good, everyone's happy," John said, "I've got a jeep ready for 1400 hours, see you then.''

John drove their jeep the six miles to the entrance of the largest airfield of the 2nd Tactical Air Force. An American white-helmeted military policeman packing an automatic pistol in his holster asked for his papers. The five Red Dragons admired the impressive display of American 3" M and 40 mm M1 automatic anti-aircraft guns in sandbagged positions defending the airfield.

"Lots of anti-aircraft weaponry here. Expecting Jerries?" Aubrey asked.

"No we just have them out for fun, sir." The Sergeant said laconically, "We just ran them out of Africa but we've found you can't trust them, those krauts and wops might sneak back." Attempting more humour the Sergeant added, "I hear you Limeys are thinking of joining us in invading Europe."

John bristled, "Loose lips sink ships, Sergeant. Two of us are Canadians, one is an Aussie and if I don't get him out of here he may forget the rule about officers not striking lower ranks. The only Brit here is wearing the kilt and the word Limey is actually respectful because it recognises that the Royal Navy cared enough about their men to ensure they received fruit to prevent scurvy. Men like Sir Frances Drake and Captain Cook taught the world what had been discovered by De Gama and forgotten about nutrition at sea. Now Sergeant we're visiting a friend in 33 Squadron RAF, where do we find him?"

"The ... RAF guys are a mile that-a-way," he pointed down the dirt road, "look for the sign." He added "Sir" as an afterthought, handed back their passes and saluted reluctantly. John returned the salute, thanked him, determined to be polite with the Yanks put the jeep into gear and shot off in a cloud of dust. Aubrey clutched his Aussie bush hat to his head as a gust of wind threatened to whip it off. A pebble shot back and hit the MP's white helmet leaving a dent. The army cop shook his head as he inspected the damage wondering at the strange garb of his British cousins, with their odd green berets and exotic red dragon patches on their right shoulders underneath a shoulder flash declaring ROYAL MARINE COMANDOS. *One had a Limey navy jacket and a plaid kilt with a leather pouch. Another, obviously an Australian, clutched a strange object that looked like a wooden bazooka with painted designs.* He wondered about the black fellow in the Sergeant-Major's uniform with the knife-edge creases in his uniform. *A black man in the same jeep with white officers and he's not even the driver!* His mind goggled, *"What the hell is the world coming too?* Something in the way the Sergeant-Major had looked at him made the words of thinly veiled criticism die in the thick-necked throat of the GI. He shuddered at the idea of meeting the black on the battlefield or anywhere in hand-to-hand combat, his build and quiet confidence reminded him of Joe Lewis who he had met walking inside Madison Square Gardens. What a fighter, what a fight, what a leave that had been for an Idaho boy on the loose for the first time with a wallet full of greenbacks. "Negro boy or not I'm glad he's on our side."

He found out that the Red Dragon had fought as guerrilla fighters in Wales then with the Desert Rats from Africa from Egypt to Tunisia making a name for themselves attacking a German rocket base in Libya. Thereafter he looked at the nick in

19

his helmet from the rock they kicked up as more of talisman than an affront to his pride.

As John drove up to the sign indicating the RAF airfield a squadron of Hawker Typhoon 1B fighter-bombers were revving up their 2,200 horsepower Napier Sabre inline engines. The ground shook and the air buzzed with power. Each of the sixteen fighter-bombers laden with eight rocket projectiles or two 500 pound bombs rose into the air with a roar.

Taking off in waves of four they gained height quickly over fields of onions and melons and headed for targets in Spain or enemy ships. The softening up of German and Spanish defences was becoming an ongoing process as sortie after sortie of aircraft were sent. John, Aubrey and Duncan watched fascinated as the dots in the sky disappeared and new dots appeared flying but their rocket racks were empty in almost at ground level from the Mediterranean. These were also Typhoons but their rocket racks were empty. They came towards them at four hundred miles-an-hour slowing down as they lowered their flaps and undercarriages to land. John noticed twigs and small branches caught in their wings signifying they had been doing some hair-raising low flying to shoot rockets into gun emplacements or at trains with pinpoint accuracy.

The planes taxied towards them, the Commandos squinted as the propellers whipped up the red sand into their eyes. John recognised Brock's plane which had a badger painted on the side of the cockpit alongside several black crosses indicating enemy planes shot down. 'Brock' Badger's plane's fuselage had the call letter J before the RAF roundel and OE after it. The starboard wing was riddled with holes from enemy fire and one of its four Hispano 20 mm cannons was no longer protruding from the wing but had been sliced off. Brock feathered his engine and turned off the ignition. The powerful three-bladed propeller came to a gradual stop. He slid back the cockpit and climbed out onto the wing. The pilot took off the brown leather flying helmet with sewn in radio headphones by each ear, his goggles were loose around his neck.

He ran his hand through his dark hair shot through with white stripes like a badger, hence his nickname. He had been teased unmercifully at school for having hair like a badger and a surname that said he was a Badger. Now he laughed at it, it was an apt nickname and he had heard worse. He took off the bright yellow 'Mae West' lifebelt in case he ditched into the sea revealing a light blue open-neck cotton shirt. Around his neck he had a white silk scarf dotted with black dots. Harold Badger, DFC, recently promoted to Flying Officer from his long held rank of Flying Sergeant, squatted down on the thick wing of his aircraft in his faded shorts. Incongruous yellow socks were rolled down around his ankles and crepe-soled, suede blue desert boots.

John called out "Hi Brock, what a horrible pair of knees. You'll frighten any WAAFS away with those shorts." They had shared several adventures the last involving the mad flight from New Britain to Gibraltar in a commandeered Italian bomber.

"Quite the opposite, John. Here they come now." Brock told him as the thirty-three year-old jumped down five feet from the wing onto the coastal sand.

A flock of dark blue overalled WAAFs, Women's Auxiliary Air Force personnel, ran over to Brock's plane. One with a clipboard took notes of the damage, another drove up a fuel bowser and connected the fuel hose to the fuel tank nozzle in the wing, another removed the base of the damaged cannon and went off to fetch a new one   The Sergeant in charge of the squad announced, "Welcome back, Sir. We'll check it out and have a new cannon installed and get some of those holes patched up-should take three hours you'll be ready for your afternoon sortie."

"Thanks, Sergeant," Brock grinned, "I shall leave my kite in your capable hands. Aren't they wonderful?" Brock said waving at the girls as he strutted up to his friends. "Well aren't you in action yet, leaving it to the RAF for now, eh?" John slapped his friend on the back.

"Remember when we stole that German helicopter right under their noses in Merthyr Tidfil?"

"You're getting cocky again, pride comes before a fall."

"I can't help if the girls hold me in high esteem." He exchanged greetings with the others. He had met them when assigned to their Welsh mountain hideout in order to steal a *Liebel* helicopter. "How's Bertha 'Mr. President'?" he asked Francis Lincoln.

Lincoln's eyes glinted with pleasure that the pilot had remembered. "Bertha the Bren gun is doing well. She's seen me through some tight spots. And at least Bertha is a good sailor I am not looking forward to crossing over to in a landing craft but I can't let on, I have to set an example."

An image came of breakfast filling up the deck of the Landing craft but Duncan wisely did not give it voice. Instead he asked, "Can I sit in the cockpit?"

"Sure," Brock agreed, "the 'erks' have checked the instruments."

Badger pointed out a small step in the fuselage and hoisted him up. As Duncan sat in the cockpit, 'Brock' stood on the wing and pointed out the different gauges. "It's a pretty small joystick isn't it, just a ring on a stick with two buttons on the wheel?" the Scottish sub-lieutenant observed.

"Yes, the top button is the gun button and the one below is for the camera. I took some film of my 'rhubarb' attack on a tank train. The rockets shooting off in a stream of smoke make for gripping viewing, all the rps shot off hence the empty racks," he gestured to the underside of his plane's wings. "The train was near Malaga. The Jerries and Spanish are having a terrible time preparing an invasion force capable of taking Gibraltar thanks to the 2nd Tactical Air Force.

"Now we turn our attention to their defences on the coast near Cadiz where you're landing. The heavy bombers start soon.

We could have a look at the film in the projection room before you go."

"Great idea," John agreed, everyone nodded, "but I would like to try out the cockpit first."

"No problem. Just fold yourself inside the cockpit John."

Over lunch of sausages, peas and mash washed down with tea 'Brock' regaled them with the details of his recent raid on the Spanish port of Algericas, the staging port for the German and Spanish invasion force bound for Gibraltar when mastery of the skies is wrenched from the allies. John had to press him for all the details on the awarding of his Distinguished Flying Cross. "Well my pilot in a night-fighting Beaufighter got one as well but posthumous I'm afraid. Darjit Bannerjee was the bravest man I ever knew. We had just shot down the incredible score of four bandits in one sortie. I was his radar operator they were short of them so I volunteered. Since I was given intensive training in Canada before being sent to Wales and I wanted to make myself useful in Gib after we took that Italian bomber from Cornwall.

We made a good team, shooting down thirteen bombers in twenty-nine scrambles. It was during an early morning raid on Gibraltar in January. Low on ammunition we were heading home when an Owl, a Heinkel He 219 *Uhu*, night-fighter shot us up. We were on-fire and in a shallow dive, the controls were not responding. Dipak ordered me to bail out, he said he had taken a cannon shell to his chest and couldn't jump. My chute caught on fire so I said I would stay with him and crash-land the kite. Despite his wound he struggled to take off his chute and give it to me. I told him to 'shut-up save your strength.' I pulled him out of his chair and prepared to push him out the cockpit hoping he could stay conscious long enough to pull his ripcord and open his parachute. Then he passed out.

"I don't how I did it but in seconds I took off his chute strapped it on myself and clutching him tight jumped out at what must have been two thousand feet. By luck since I am so thin the

23

chute held us both and we landed right on top of the Barbary apes but he was dead when we landed.

"He was a Sikh pilot from the Indian Air Force. Darjit always flew with his turban on and he told me that if anything happened I was to take his wrist bangle and kirpan he wore in his hair beneath his white turban, to his wife after the war so that is what I shall do. He got a DFC as well as me for shooting down the four Jerries in one night but it won't bring him back." They were all silent then 'Brock' brightened. "He would want us to go on living. How about a beer then go up in a Mossie have a look at the 'Med'? I notice you have brought your noise-maker, Aubrey, you must have heard we had some Aussies in our squadron. They're usually here this time of day when there's no mission on."

At the bar Aubrey took a swig of beer then proceeded to warm up the four-foot long didgeridoo made from a hollowed out eucalyptus branch decorated with red kangaroos and yellow snakes, circles and diamonds. By an open window a Czech Flight Leader from Prague clutching a mug of beer climbed onto a chair and announced that everyone was invited to sing the Czechoslovakian national anthem he passed around copies of the words which he had copied down in the British Library Reading Room when on leave in London before the battle for the city began. He read out the words and had the mess repeat them, with a nod to the pianist to begin he began singing, waving his arms with gusto as he conducted. The pianist was an Argentinian pilot whose jacket hanging on the chair sported the blue and white ribbon of the Distinguished Flying Cross. John noticed that since the Royal Auxiliary Squadron had fought from the Battle of Britain, over Iceland then in the Desert Air Force, half of the sixteen pilots sported DFC or DSO ribbons. Brock himself had been awarded one. Aubrey joined in providing an exotically stunning bass line while a Malayan flying officer displayed percussive talent with his hands on top of the piano and for variety banging two copper ash-tray. As the anthem reached a final crescendo the 'concert' was met with cheers. Aubrey grinned as the Aussie pilots lifted him onto the bar. They bought him pints of beer and tried miserably to

24

imitate the sounds he made on the Aboriginal instrument. The other pilots ambled over to the bar served by a steward wearing a starched white jacket. "I can safely say that was the first time the Czechoslovak national anthem was accompanied by a didgeridoo," Aubrey declared.

Squadron Leader Jack 'Jacko' Jackson said to John in an Australian accent softened by schooldays in an English boarding school, "Ah, a bit of home. Funny, I never liked the sound until now. Bit of a city bloke me – Melbourne. Where's he from?" he inquired of Aubrey.

"He tells us Perth, Western Australia but we think he's making it up it, could be another planet," John quipped.

"No, no there is such a place, though Australia is in many ways an alien place to outsiders. Where else do you find black swans and a mammal called a platypus with webbed feet that lays eggs? The black swans come from Western Australia where Perth is, hence Black Swan beer which you're drinking. I wangled some crates from a shipment sent to the 3rd Australian Division."

"He does have his moments, particularly bowling grenades at the enemy, he is a great cricketer."

Meanwhile Aubrey was holding forth with his audience, "I'll teach you but it's thirsty work I warn you. First let me tell you about my Aborigine blood-brother Nelson Pilgrim who taught me how to live in the outback and make and decorate this didgeridoo."

John finished his beer, "Oh no, I see it coming, the story of how you killed a snake for the tribe to eat. It's time to go for a ride in the Mosquito," he appealed to Brock.

Brock led John, Duncan and 'Mr. President', to a corner of the airfield where five, two-engined Mosquito fighter-bombers were parked. Brock signed out one from the Sergeant in charge of the hanger. "Just a test run."

"She's all fuelled up and ammo in place."

"I'll take up Duncan and Mr. President first."

Twenty minutes later the two-engined de Havilland Mosquito landed and the Nova-Scotian descendant of African slaves shipped to America in appalling conditions took Duncan's place sitting behind the pilot in the navigator's 'office'. "Wow what a ride. The Med was an azure jewel," Francis Lincoln waxed lyrical as he stepped down the small metal ladder at the end of his trip. "Thanks Brock."

Brock started the engines once again and the fighter-bomber ran down the runway picking up speed to over one hundred and fifty mph the in-line Rolls-Royce engines purred as they revved up. John was amazed at the immensity of the air base as they flew over it and over the coast.

"Big isn't it? No wonder we control the skies. About ten miles out from here last night a Wellington bomber used its radar and mounted searchlight and caught one of the *schnorkel* U-boats on the surface. They have an extendable breathing tube allowing them to replenish the air made foul by their diesel engines but eventually they surface to replenish their batteries by running their engines on the surface and get a complete airing. A couple of 600 pound bombs put paid to it. Their *Wanze* radar meant they knew our plane was near and their deck-gun and the machine-gun on the conning tower were manned but the front gunner handling two .50 Browning guns on the 'Wellie' got 'em." John marvelled at the crystal clear scene below as they flew over the pristine sandy Moroccan beaches as they headed out over the sea. He could see several Allied naval vessels and some fishing boats leaving white wash behind them as they made their way over a smooth sparkling sea. Above them was a sharp blue African sky and crisp cumulus clouds. "This is really something."

"Yeah, I know," Brock replied as he took the Mosquito down to just feet above the waves. Badger spoke into the mike in his oxygen mask since the whine of the engines made easy speech difficult. "Let's see how fast she can go-should be around four hundred miles an hour."

John was impressed as he was shoved back into his seat as they accelerated, "Whew, this is one fast plane Brock" he said pressing the intercom switch in his oxygen mask which was not clipped up on one side since it was not needed. "I intend to come back with Felicity and enjoy the beaches when the war is over."

"A good idea but to get back to 1944; do you think the Jerries and Spanish know we're coming?"

"Yes, but they don't know when or where. We do and we are more than ready. The brass hats say we have the largest invasion force assembled in modern history. The enemy have had only a few months to extend the Atlantic Wall of defence, *Festung Europa,* in Spain since Franco joined in the war against us but the Spanish coast is long. They don't know where we are going to strike. I've been reading about how Wellington fortified the *Torres Vedras,* Portugal's natural border with Spain during the Peninsular War. From those heights he struck at the French armies occupying Spain in 1809 and withdrew to them in winter since he was vastly outnumbered. When the French armies had been whittled down by disease and casualties from his attacks and their supply lines damaged by partisans he destroyed them and marched to Madrid then France. In the faster war of today I believe the top brass would like to see the Canadians head east to Madrid while I see Monty's 8th Army and Bradley's Army landing on either side of Cadiz take the port so they can re-supplied and push North to Madrid and Barcelona crushing the Germans and Spanish.

"For all they know it is Toulouse or Malaga or leapfrogging from Gibraltar or even an attack on force on Spain with the big landing somewhere else, like Sicily. Likely landing sites are being pounded. We have a huge invasion fleet even as we speak assembling secretly. The enemy do not know that invasion was imminent it's D-Day minus 3 days."

As he talked John unconsiously felt inside the neck of his short-sleeve khaki shirt. Yes, there it was fastened to a thin silver chain, his guardian angel, a coin from the reign of Charles I called an Angel because it depicted one fighting a dragon, on the obverse was the head of the King Charles I who had his own head struck off in 1649 after being found guilty of 'treachery' against his people by Cromwell's hand-picked judges. John and Alan each had one from a bag of coins their father had shown them when they were children. "These Stuart coins were passed down to us from our ancestor, Captain Richard Stafford. He was a Cavalier fighting under Prince Rupert for Charles I throughout the war. He was mortally wounded at Naseby in 1645. He made it home to Burton-on-Trent to die in his manor house and gave this bag of money including these coins to his twelve year old heir Charles to treasure. Charles lived to see Charles II restored to the throne in 1660. He became an officer under John Churchill later famous as the Duke of Marlborough. Ever since we have had a soldier in every generation. Every one of them took one of these coins for luck. Now we have two. So take one each," he had said when they both joined up at the Armouries in the Royal Hamilton Rifles. "I have had them put on a silver chain to go around the neck."

As they turned back John told Brock about his leave in Fez wandering through the maze of centuries old medieval shops in the old city. "It's another world. The senses are overpowered in the Medina by the pungent odour of coffee, dates, marzipan, roasting lamb, the buzz of flies, the stench of dirt and donkeys carrying wood to the miniature hells of the metal workers working in tiny stone rooms with ancient forges sweat pouring from their foreheads. No-one knows how many live in the medina. I was advised to hire a guide and I'm glad I did, you could go in and never come out without a ball of wool. It's worse than the Hampton Court maze.

"Best of all was seeing where the 'Med' meets the Atlantic at Cape Spartel. That's right up there with riding a camel along the beach in Casablanca. The funniest thing was the guide in Marrakesh who wanted my copy of Churchill's biography of the first Duke of Marlborough I was holding because he was very interested in 18th century history. I mailed it to him yesterday when I finished it."

In Ottawa the Prime-Minister in exile of Great Britain, Clement Attlee sitting in his Langevin spoke in his usual terse manner to President Roosevelt on the scrambler phone line in a conference Block office in the Houses of Parliament on the hill on one of their regular calls. If there were six words to describe the Labour Party leader and now Prime Minister of the coalition British government in exile they would be: social worker pipe smoker monosyllabelic delegator.

The short balding, moustached Englishman shared a few points with his American equivalent the more powerful, voluble, outgoing American aristocrat with a heart, FDR. The official British-Canadian telephone censor Ruth Ive listened in ready to cut the call if either of them spoke in too much detail just in case the enemy had tapped into the line. They had continued the pattern set by Roosevelt and Churchill in 1940 in London to Washington by outlining the points upon which they would talk ahead by telex. The early calls were by trans-Atlantic radio telephone line via a secret radio exchange in the basement of Selfridge's department shop in Oxford Street. Now the radio telephone exchange was located in rooms in Rideau Hall, the Governor-General's residence on the east side of the canal cutting Ottawa in two. "Franklin, it is Clement. I hope you are well and you have your discussion itinerary in front of you.

The six foot three inch tall President sat tall in his chair in the Oval office. His regular exercises meant his upper body was muscular but his legs were thin and could no longer support him. He had long ago suppressed the anger that hit him after catching polio aged 39 in 1921 but visits to the healing spa at Warm Springs, Georgia and the care of his wife had done wonders. He pulled out the cigarette holder he habitually had between his teeth. "I'm well Clement we are making progress here in America. The tide is turning I feel it. On point one I concur with you and Mackenzie-King. The 'Lebanons' must be used to the maximum of their capacity even at the risk of losing them to enemy action.

On point two I am assured we shall have the Mulberry project and Operation Pluto ready for transport from the location we agreed from and being ready for assembly. On Point three our people are making progress on solving the problem and we are testing it now. It will be a great relief to find a solution. On point four."

Clement interrupted. "I think we must meet to talk about Point Four Franklin."

"We are meeting next month. We can talk then about Operation Wyoming. Also we will have reports on items A, B and C we requested from our chiefs of staff and advisors."

"Point five Franklin", the British PM asked, "Mackenzie-King and I want to reconsider our strategy (this was regarding long range bombing of purely civilian targets the combined British-Canadian war cabinet in Ottawa believed the Allies should concentrate their bombing of docks, railways, airfields, munition factories not cities per se since it does not lower morale and costs a great number of losses in personnel and aircraft) I am with King on this point and will speak for himself when we meet. "Fair point Clement I will reconsider my position."

"If I am advised that your proposal achieves our strategic aims and conserves our air-crew from unwarranted loss then I will reconsider" FDR continued. "Point seven. Operation Overlord is proceeding according to plan."

"Glad to hear it. That's it. We still have patches of snow but birds are singing. Well Franklin my wife and I wish you and Eleanor and family a blessed Easter."

"All the best to you and Violet. Spring is here and I am optimistic. Goodbye."

"Goodbye Franklin." Attlee rang off and rummaged in his tweed jacket pocket for his pipe. He was a socialist, educated as a barrister at Oxford, a Major in the British army at in W.W. I he was wounded at Gallipoli. He joined the Labour Party and became Mayor of Stepney then an MP in London. Rising through the ranks he became party leader and joined Churchill's coalition war cabinet as his quiet deputy Prime Minister to the Conservative 'bulldog' who rallied the nation. He took Churchill's place as Prime-Minister in-exile in Ottawa after his friend and colleague died of a heart attack in Australia in 1941 hours after hearing the USA had entered the war alongside Britain when Hitler invaded Ireland.

*

D-Day Minus1. Major Stafford waited in the meeting hall as the men of A troop took their seats in front of him. "You can smoke during the questions; as you know we are going into action on 1st May. General Bradley will be giving us the final green light but weather permitting we board at 1900 hours tonight.

There was an excited buzz of interest and muttered exclamations. "Right men, settle down. We are ready into Europe and take it back from Hitler. This is the beginning of the end of Adolf's 1,000 year empire and we have the honour of being at the right time and place to stop him and his pals Mussolini and Franco. We are the best trained and equipped army in modern times. As you know we are first on our section of Juno Beach just north of the important Spanish port of Cadiz. We shall go over the plan again step-by-step." After the lecture John took advantage of the hours before they boarded their ship in the harbour to put his booted feet up and read what he always read before he went into action, *The Iliad*. He opened his dog-eared Loeb edition in English and Greek. He had carried the book through the brief Norwegian campaign, the Battle of Britain, the Welsh mountains and through Egypt, Cyranecea, Tunisia and Morocco. It had even entered the Tower of London in the pocket of his black *Kreigsmarine* jacket when he succeeded against the odds in snatching Edward VIII out of his unreal existence as King of New Britain and enabled him to be sent to his ranch in Alberta, minus his wife, Queen Wallis. Dipping into Book Two John stopped after reading "since now thou might take the broad-wayed city of the Trojans" to think about the landing by the Greeks at Troy in 1,250 BC written down by Homer five hundred years later. *Now it is 1944, over three millennia later, and I am leading men in another momentous invasion at the other end of the Mediterranean from ancient Troy in what was now Turkey. This is one of the great moments in history and I am here* John told himself. *It doesn't feel real yet but it will very soon.*

*

In Rejavik, Iceland a British General, incongruously wore a black tank beret bearing two badges, the Royal Armoured Corps lozenge shaped Great War tank and the General's insignia of crossed batons within a laurel wreath topped by St. Edward's Crown. The jaunty figure was visiting a British and Canadian army base. standing on the bonnet of an olive painted Jeep parked in front of ten thousand soldiers in ranks. As expected he waved them towards the jeep to make a circle around him. Excitedly they rushed forward keeping a respectful five feet away from the jeep in a battle-dressed khaki mass. This was their idol, the general who had won the great victory at El Alamein, the short, irascible, brilliant man who turned the tide of war in 1943.

Like the great commanders who preceded him, Malborough, Nelson and Wellington, Montgomery always conserved as many men as possible and only attacked when reasonably sure of victory. The blue-eyed, middle-aged General wore a short moustache. He exhorted the troops to fight like lions in the campaigns ahead to free Europe he spoke with his customary lisp, a sign of his time in the Indian cavalwy, as he put it. The men responded with cheers and laughter at his jokes. 'Good old Monty' they called and gave three cheers when he sat down and his driver drove him slowly through the melee so the men could touch him or shake his hand.

Icelandic civilians working at the base looked on with interest but some of the eyes were unfriendly. When the owners of those trained eyes returned to their homes and turned on their radio sets to talk to their *Abwher* masters in Scotland or Norway they reported that General Bernard Law Montgomery was on the island visiting troops.

Back in Rejavik at Air Marshal Dowding's HQ, the commander of the island whose rule was approved by the Danish government in exile, poured a whiskey and soda for Monty sitting in his study. The servant left the room as the Air-Marshal hoisted his whisky tumbler. "Chin-Chin," Dowding toasted raising his glass. "May I?" the General asked pointing at an open cigarette case.

"Certainly, but I thought you were a stern non-smoker, a bit of a tyrant if truth be known."

"Air-Marshal, what if I told you that this little finger on my hand here," he held out his hand, "is porcelain. I lost my own in the last war but Monty did not. I am authorised to tell you that I am not actually Montgomery. I am a decoy to fool the Germans. My real name is, well it doesn't matter. But I am the spitting image of the great man, I am just an actor and it is very satisfying to know I am pulling it off. The real Montgomery is in Morocco commanding the British and Canadian forces, working hand-in-glove with the overall commander o General Bradley. We want the Jerries to think he is here as a prelude to an invasion of northern Europe. Hence all the activity, large convoys, fake landing craft by the score, dummy airfields, ammunition dumps, parks loaded with fake tanks and trucks."

Dowding placed his drink down and placed his hands together in amazement. "My God if you had us fooled then how on earth is Jerry going to tumble this wheeze?"

"Precisely, so far our luck is holding. Tomorrow I continue my tour of army camps. It raises their morale to think I am Monty."

"Here let me pour you another drink .... er, Monty. Ha, I wonder what your namesake is up to right now?"

*

The real General Montgomery, Viscount of the Pyramids, was in a heated discussion with the overall commander of D-Day, General Omar Bradley his deputy British General Alexander and

Monty's own subordinate, General Harry Crerar the leader of the first Canadian army. Napoleon IV leader of the Free French Division to land with the British was sitting observing Monty in action. "It is late in the day but I advise caution. I am gwateful to lead my new command, the 2nd British army with some units of 8th Army Desert Rats into Spain," he said with his customary lisp, "and fight alongside our American allies to take Cadiz and move to Madrid or to France as the situation develops. However, I am sorry I was overwuled regarding the feasibility of the Canadians landing in Portugal.

"I am still concerned about the splitting of our strength into two widely separated strikes-2nd Army north of Cadiz in concert with 1st American south of Cadiz but then the Canadian army hundreds of miles up the coast of the Iberian Peninsula at Lisbon.

"We should concentrate our efforts. I know that if you General Bradley as commander-in-chief insist then the Canadian army under Hawwy is more than capable of taking Lisbon and pushing into Spain but due to the effort needed to take Cadiz and break out from that bridgehead on the third day into Spain splitting our forces with a Portuguese venture with longer ocean supply lines than ours in the same week is a vewy wisky strategy.

"The Germans could move their *panzer* reserves very quickly and meet you on your way into Spain in four days of course then strike south at the main threat which are the two armies breaking out from Cadiz. They will have to decide how to divide reinforcing their front in Portugal and contain our beach-heads on the Andalusian coast on the South West of Spain. They should see the attacks on Cadiz as the greater threat and turn their forces in southern Spain ready to invade Gibraltar and their *panzer* reserves in central Spain against us in Cadiz. Then they will probably bring an army from Brittany across the Pyranees and attack the Canadians in Portugal from the north hoping to cut them their supply line from Lisbon but that is not guaranteed. The Germans may decide on a risky strategy themselves to wipe out the Canadian Army first then deal with us, if that is their decision we cannot reach you in Badajoz Harry until D-Day plus 5 you will be out of reach until then.''

"What's your opinion Harry?" Omar Bradley the tough but kind 'soldier's general'turned to the portly, staid but astute Canadian general from Hamilton, Ontario who commanded the men of the 1st Canadian Army and Free French Divisions. He was younger than Montgomery his short brown moustache was not speckled with white hairs as his commander's.

"We learned a lot in September when the largely Canadian attack in force on Sicily tested our landing ships, tank control on beaches, assault tactics and overall amphibious landing strategy. Saturation bombing of the morning of the assault and naval bombardment just as the LCs are hitting the beaches is crucial along with naval bombardment at the same time is crucial. We took 9% losses but I volunteered our army and we learned valuable lessons from mistakes which will not be repeated this time: poor shore to ship communications, lack of 'funny' armoured vehicles to cover tank ditches and blast anti-tank defences and a lack of air and naval support. I believe we can expect 5-8% losses given our control of the air over the beach-heads and the work that has been done to prepare.

"If the coup planned by anti-Nazi generals in Lisbon succeeds in ousting the dictator Salazar we may only get token resistance from units loyal to Salazar but are ready for anything. If *panzers* from France or Spain come to meet us we shall overcome them. We shall get to Badajoz and hold out until we link up."

General Bradley leaned over to listen to a murmured message from his aide, a Brigadier-General. "Thanks." He looked at Montgomery and Bradley and grinned. "Gentleman, we have just received word that the leaders of the Portuguese forces headed by Admiral De Silva have successfully taken over the reins of government in Lisbon. There was some fighting in Porto between the pro-junta troops and Salazar's army but they have been arrested. The rest of the country is coming out against Salazar and his recent promise of making a defence treaty with Hitler and Franco."

General Crerar spoke, "Thank God. It will allow us more time to get over the mountains into Spain"

Our advance people are being flown into Lisbon to meet with the Admiral and see the situation for themselves and reporting to me."

Monty drew a large starched, white handkerchief from a pocket in his baggy khaki cotton trousers and blew his nose noisily. "Good but you may find the Portuguese on your side more trouble than they are worth, Wellington found that. So you still think you can secure Badajoz on the Spanish side of the Torres Verdes mountains in six days? It is crucial we stick to the schedule. It would be better for you to land in Andalusia like us if it would mean you can move more quickly."

"My troops can do it Monty we just need fuel, ammo and food for my troops. By D-Day plus nine I am to take Saville and push north-east to link with you as you head east. Meanwhile the Americans take Cadiz and Malaga it all has to go like clockwork as you say."

Monty continued that thought, "Then General Bradley's army punches north to Madrid as we, Canadian and British, head north to the Pyranees and into France."

Napoleon IV spoke for the first time his hand ceased stroking his Van Dyke beard. "Excuse me gentlemen, I zink General Crerar is right 'is army including the Free French Brigade, will fight zaire way to Saville on-time and take it. I am glad zat it looks as if zere will be help from Portugal England's oldest ally. Eet was very wise to let the Portuguese Generals aware with ze disgusting evidence we 'ave of the German death camps. Zey are Roman Catholic conservatives in Portugal but zey are Christians first and are suspicious of Salazar getting too friendly with Franco, a Spaniard, and Hitler a German. I believe zat many Spaniards 'ave been waiting to rise up against Franco. They will come to our aid as they did when Wellington took on my ancestor France in Spain in 1809."

Bradley had the Meteorological officer report on the weather for the next week. "It looks good," the RAF commodore explained in his clipped Oxbridge accent. There is a storm building up probably reaching Cadiz on D-Day plus 1 but for the day before D-Day with the ships at sea there will be moderate winds with a bit of chop-in other words-seasick troops. However D-Day promises to be calm and sunny."

"Good," Bradley said. "Let us recapitulate, the Canadian Army lands near Lisbon at Sesimbra codenamed Gold Beach. The 2nd US army lands south of Cadiz at the bottom of the peninsula at San Fernando Beach codenamed Omaha Beach. They establish the beach-head and move up the peninsula to seize Cadiz harbour. 2nd Army lands at Rota on the mainland facing the harbour, codenamed Sword Beach. It will establish itself and move south to protect the eastern flank of the American 1st Army. Then the American army moves east to Malaga and Granada then north to Madrid. The British army moves north-east to Savilla and Cordoba and move north to link up with the Canadian Army which will have struck through Portugal into Spain to take Badajoz. If the strategic situation is favourable the American army will take Madrid while the Brit-Can army will move north as fast as possible into France.

"Convoys of troops and equipment are on their way from Casablanca, the Azores and the Canary islands. The US Navy, Royal and Royal Canadian Navies with the help of Free French, Norwegian and Dutch vessels includes five battleships, four aircraft carriers, two bergships, ten cruisers, forty destroyers, twenty frigates, twenty five submarines and eight hundred landing craft and fifty troopships. The 1st allied tactical air force flying from Morocco consists of eighty squadrons of heavy, medium and ground attack bombers and fighter planes from the USAAF, RAF, RCAF, Free French, Polish, Hungarian Czech and Romanian air forces.

"Our deception plans involved a body washed up on the coast of Scotland with fake plans for an invasion of an imminent invasion of Norway, the presence of Monty's look-alike visiting garrisons on Iceland, the arrival of large convoys to Iceland of what looks like armaments and troops and landing craft and artillery. We also have an invisible radio war increasing our air and naval signals in the north Atlantic area to match a possible invasion. We are also jamming enemy radio and radar systems in Scotland and the Faroes and increasing air attacks.

"On the night before D-Day we begin radio and radar jamming around the Iberian Peninsula and heavy air bombardments of enemy positions along the coast with naval bombardments and air raids on coastal and inland targets such as ammunition dumps, railways, airfields, enemy HQs. The Spanish resistance, essentially the Spanish Communist Party, will be blowing up rail-lines, telephone lines, bridges and providing information on troop movements."

*

General Francisco Franco dictator of Spain and the leader of the far-right *Falange* party which won the recent bloody civil war in 1938, contemplated the shrivelled hand in glass that reposed on a small table in his bedroom. A silver crucifix with a bleeding Christ hung on the wall. *"Did I do the right thing joining the war alongside the Axis?"* he asked softly as he as sat down on his bed.

He lay down in his uniform and fell asleep. He dreamt he was in the Escorial Palace and zooming along the corridors and beneath the splendid works of art by Valesquez and El Greco all the while held in the upturned shrivelled hands of St. Teresa of Avilla. She was renowned for levitating in her spiritual encounters with God. Now, he too was rising up to the ceiling thanks to her. At the golden altar of the chapel stood Adolf Hitler dressed in a white tuxedo and Mussolini in a straw hat and a fisherman's rough clothes. The Emperor of Japan came through the wall stood beside him, touched him with a hot hand and then went back the way he came.

Now he was hovering over a rock in the wooden floor. It was surrounded by water. His ships and troops were heading towards it, they were miniscule. He stooped down to help them but he was clumsy and splashed, boats tipped over, minute Spanish planes flew into him. Then he noticed pin-pricks from shells fired by the British on the Rock of Gibraltar. Franco woke up perspiring. *It's too late. I am committed to Hitler. But he will help me. He is strong. We will take Gibraltar. He must give the order soon.* But in his heart there was a nagging ache that meant he was not so sure.

*

In Ottawa in a private meeting in the Mackenzie-King's office in the Canadian House of Parliament, Attlee and Mackenzie-King were in full agreement. King spoke, "Clement, all reports are that the Portuguese generals are as one in opposing the pro-Nazi leanings of Salazar and are eager to show that Portugal is indeed England's oldest ally and will help their cousins the Spanish be liberated from Franco's rule. The Portuguese coup plotters are disgusted with stories of Nazi death camps across Europe and the use of germ warfare against America, they are Roman Catholic conservatives yes but they are Christians first and they are worried Salazar will take Portugal into the war on the Axis side as Franco did with Spain. Franco will now pay the price for that. The resistance movement in Spain thanks to the SOE is ready to help us. General Crerar is my approved commander of the Canadian army to land in Lisbon but we are promised that the navy and army in Portugal will follow the orders of the Admiral and general who will lead the coup two nights before D-Day. The Air force we are not so sure of but you will have the squadrons of the bergship HMCS Iroquois providing air cover.

"The closest German units are in Malaga, the Spanish army has only third-rate troops along the Portuguese border so sure are they about Portuguese. But it is part of the plan of Operation Buster to force the enemy draw first-rate Spanish troops and Germans ready to take Gibraltar. We know that the Germans are sending a Panzer Division and an infantry division by train from southern France to Malaga for their attack upon the rock of Gibraltar. We will meet them and destroy them. Hitler and Franco will not invade Gibraltar once we have landed and threatened to zip up the Iberian Peninsula and into France."

"Willie, I think our joint war-cabinet and FACE have prepared everything possible for the invasion. Now we need good weather and luck, pray for it."

"I will Clement, I will."

CHAPTER THREE *REICH KANCELLORY*

In his *Reich Kancellory* in Berlin Adolf Hitler worked at the large marble map table in his spacious office. He revelled in the building remodelled by two shifts of 7,000 labourers working around the clock in nine months in 1935 under the expert direction of the Nazi leader's favourite architect, Albert Speer. At that time he assured Speer that money was no object in planning a modern Berlin of massive monumental domes and buildings to be filled with the world's looted art and honouring the *Wehrmacht* with overpowering displays of tanks, aircraft and artillery upon pillars. The building was designed to impress visitors and its staff and this it did admirably. The entrance displayed two imposing if ungainly naked statues of men; 'The Party' and 'The Army.' The former bore a flaming torch and the other a sword, since they were eight times the height of a man they were both impressive. When work began on his seat of government Hitler had been complete political master of Germany for two years after being sworn in as Chancellor. He won election through successful bullying tactics coupled with a naive estimation of Hitler's intentions by the establishment. In the early days of 1933, after gaining political power, his Nazi party destroyed the Weimar Republic's democratic constitution and established the National Socialist police state.

Everyone underestimated me. They thought I was a minor, ranting politician from a splinter workers' party. The weaklings in pay of the Communists and the Jews threw me in jail and laughed at me. Well now, in 1944, I am the master of Europe. We, the Axis powers, the Reich, Japan, Italy and Spain, are on the verge of conquering the globe. True, I have suffered a reverse in North Africa with the loss of the Afrika Korps but under my leadership the Reich has the resources and the will to keep up the pressure against American and British forces and strike out in a new direction.

Victory over the corrupt, weak democracies and Stalin's Communist Russia is our destiny, timing, strict discipline and resolve are what is needed, attributes I hold in spades. The 1938 peace treaty with the Soviet Union was a temporary expedient to save our forces for other campaigns until we are ready to attack and obliterate them. I seized power through exploiting people's fears and hatreds; utilizing Goebbel's brilliant propaganda and utilising our street fighters, the hundreds of thousands of fanatic Brownshirts to crush our rivals and opposition. Oh, how they misread me. Those lickspittles thought I was a crackpot but I showed them. He smiled as he thought of the tens of thousands of political opponents who had paid the price of crossing him and spent their last days in a concentration camp.

The *Reichkanzler* stood poring over his designs and maps of Gibraltar and the United States upon which his aides had placed a plastic sheet in red and blue grease pencil markers with the strength of German and enemy forces. Sunlight flooded in the window illuminating the design of the super tank he had promoted with the Mercedes designers. He was keeping his top generals waiting but he did not care. As he glanced down, his short sweep of black hair fell over his brow. In front of him were spread large scale technical drawings of the Mammoth he was promoting to spearhead his future invasion of the Soviet Union. The four-engined steel monster armed with two 105 mm howitzers able to lob a 32 pound shell 11,000 yards was an idea born in the trenches of the western front in 1918. He saw the first lozenge-shaped British tanks battling with German ones emblazoned with the Hun Cross. *If I was in charge*, he had told himself, *I would have super tanks built by superior German engineers they would be unstoppable.* He harboured and nurtured it while recovering in hospital from a gas attack. *From obscure corporal to master of Europe in just over twenty years!* Adolf Hitler, the son of an Austrian customs officer guarding a middle European backwater, rubbed his hands with excitement.

Two piles of books kept the left corners of the unrolled tank plans fastened while the other ends were anchored by a metal model of the newest aircraft carrier Hamburg and his glass of water. *Hmm, keeping the four large diesel engines cool will be a problem in the excessive heat of the Caucasus in the summer, let alone in Iraq as we seize the oil field at Mosul and move into Afghanistan then India. Krupp's designers are quite correct, lightweight but effective refrigerators must be designed and tested. We must have liquid cooled engines, with water cooled by battery operated freon units, like refrigerators.*

Three admirals, his top army generals and the head of the *Lufwaffe* Germany's massive air force and his deputy commander waited impatiently outside his massive office wooden doors.

Helmeted, long black-coated, white-gloved *Liebstandart* SS bodyguards stood guard outside the building, along the hall and outside the Fuhrer's office. Each carried a polished *Mauser* rifle affixed with a brilliantly shining bayonet. The military leaders had walked down the marble gallery to the Fuhrer's office, more than two times as long as the French Palace of Versaille's Hall of Mirrors, the site of the 1919 Peace Conference which Hitler viewed as the shameful revenge of the world against the Second Reich whose only fault had been losing the 1914-1918 war due to betrayal by capitalists selling out to Jews and Bolsheviks. He conveniently denied that the Kaiser Wilhelm II and his generals had long planned a massive attack upon France through neutral Belgium as part of a design to control as much of the world as they could in 1914.

The ceiling of the hall was thirty-three feet high, the monumentalism of the Chancellory reinforced that in the Third *Reich*, the individual was dwarfed by the power and might of the totalitarian police-state led by the great leader, chairman of the Nazi party, *Reichkanzler* Hitler. There were chairs precisely positioned every twenty feet but they stood in a group, as if clustering together to shield themselves from the yawning space of the enclosed void threatening to swallow them. Kept waiting they glared at the German eagle wings outstretched clutching a swastika-emblazoned wreath in its talons that soared over the top of the gargantuan door to the Fuhrer's office. It glared back. Behind the doors the *Fuhrer* stood at his desk his arms straight, his knuckles resting on the plans, lost in calculation. He wore a white shirt, black tie and his double-breasted grey Fuhrer jacket decorated only with the white *Reich* eagle on his left sleeve and Iron Cross medal won for bravery during the First World War as an infantryman in the Bavarian Regiment serving on the Western Front. He decided when he began the Second World War that he would wear only that style of clothing until victory. He preferred a simple life, a plate of strudel, holidays in the Alps or at Dumbleton Hall his English retreat in Worcestershire where he persevered in his struggle to become an English gentleman. This year he would master grouse shooting he vowed, *but first I have to deal with the war, so much to do, to destroy, to seize.*

He remembered the improved tanks unleashed by the British in 1917 against the German trenches and how impressed he had been about this new weapon which eventually changed the static warfare of muddy trenches in layers underground, thousands of troops dying in just hours trying to take fifty yards of territory ravaged by machine guns, rifle fire and artillery fire into a more mobile conflict. He looked at the designs the Krupp works sent him of the prototype on the highly polished desktop. An aide knocked and opened one of the doors to his office. "*Riechskanzler*, your commanders asked me to remind you of your appointment with them this morning. They are waiting."

Hitler looked up. "*Yawohl*, always meetings. Show them in." The aide ushered in *General* Adolf Galland, veteran of the Battles of France and Britain wearing a blue-grey uniform. He was followed by *Feld Marschell* Gerd von Runstedt in *Wehrmacht* grey, and *Gross Admiral* Doenitz head of the *Kreigsmarine* wearing a black-blue naval officer's uniform, double breasted jacket and trousers. Last was a sinister black clad, slight man who wore wire framed spectacles that seemed too small for him, and closely cropped hair. It was *Reichsfuhrer* Heinrich Himmler commander of Hitler's elite shock-troops. The only relief from black was the silver piping and decorations on his sleeve and lapels and the gleaming skull and crossbones of the SS adorning his black officer's cap. The cream of Germany's armed forces and their staff officers stood before the diminutive man with hypnotic eyes who moved to his smaller desk to sign some state documents placed in front of him by his smartly uniformed adjutant. Then the *Fuhrer* looked up and languidly lifted his right arm in salute his right palm outward as his top military leaders snapped their right arms out straight and said in unison, "*Heil Hitler!*" Hitler gestured towards some chairs and sat down with them.

"Well? Has Roosevelt come to his senses and surrendered yet?"

There was a tense silence. "Just a joke, he will, he will. The plague attacks are really pushing the Americans up against the wall. The spraying must continue. We must reinforce success. We have the men and equipment to not only wipe the Americans out but this year we will destroy our greatest enemy, the Soviet Union. We will do it before they ally themselves with the so-called Earth Government and attack us. I call this Operation *Angriff.* It is time to rid the world of this poisonous empire that, with its Jewish supporters, infects the world."

Admiral Doenitz spoke first. "*Mein Fuhrer.* We believe that the enemy is poised to strike a blow against us. Intelligence reports from naval and air patrols and our agents reveal that the Allies are planning something very big. It has been months since they succeeded in ... in forcing Rommel out of Africa ... for the time being." He proceeded carefully so as not to antagonise the *Fuhrer* and create one of his screaming fits.

Himmler interrupted, "*Abwher* agents, though I am loath to give them credit since the SD, our own SS secret police, is close to my heart, report that Montgomery is in Iceland. Experienced agents report that there is a very large increase of convoys and flights to Iceland, a tremendous build up of troops, aircraft, vehicles, tanks and artillery as well as naval vessels and landing craft in the ports."

Hitler turned to Galland. "Do *Kondor* air patrols confirm this?"

"*Ja*, as well as our new reconnaissance Me 262 jets taking photos. There is no doubt that the enemy are ready to strike a blow against northern Europe. But of course there is also a large Allied force in Morocco and there has been a constant stream of convoys and air flights from North America."

"*Nein, nein.* Their armies are exhausted after fighting our *Afrika Korps.* They will attack Norway because they know that invading Scotland is exactly what we would expect them to do to relieve their own people and seek revenge."

The German naval commander countered, "It could be a double bluff. How can you be sure they will not invade Scotland?" Doenitz asked. "Scotland is closer to Iceland than either Norway or Ireland. Their supply lines would be shorter. They could also invade southern Europe in Spain or Sicily from North Africa the supply lines are much shorter than to Norway from Iceland, perhaps attempt two invasions."

"Tell them what the *Gestapo* found in Scotland this week *Reichsfuhrer*," Hitler asked.

Himmler, Hitler's greatest ally along with propaganda minister Josef Goebbels, dew himself up to his full height, five feet six, in his gleaming jackboots, "Three days ago a body was washed up on the shores of Scotland, it was that of an American naval officer carrying maps and notes regarding an invasion of Norway on the 28th May this year. His ship was sunk by a fascist Royal Navy submarine off Iceland ten days before."

Feld Marschall von Runstedt turned on Himmler, "We need more reconnaissance flights over North Africa and Iceland. We can reinforce the defences in Norway and Scotland but we should consider an Allied landing in Spain or Sicily. The OKW believe we should be the ones on the offensive from Europe. We should be planning attacks on Iceland and Morocco before they attack us."

The *Luftwaffe* commander jumped in, "The allied superiority in the air in the Mediterranean and Atlantic theatres is a problem. Our *Focke-Wulf 190s, Heinkel* 112s and *Junker* 188s are no longer faster than the enemy fighters. We need jet-fighter planes in the European theatre, the first *Staffel* of ME 262 *Stormvogels* are being sent to America but the factories are being encouraged to produce produce more piston engine aircraft and not re-tool to make large numbers of jet fighters and bombers," Galland pleaded. He was a veteran of the Battle of Britain who had first-hand knowledge of modern air warfare unlike the First War air force veteran Goering whom he replaced after he was killed by a sniper at the coronation of Edward VIII and Queen Wallis.

"Enough!" Hitler slapped his black-trousered legs and stood. He strutted towards the globe in the corner of his office his *Wehrmacht* leaders followed him. "It is obvious that the enemy is massing *ein Anfall* in Norway.

"We have time to reinforce Norway and strengthen the sea defences, this will begin at once but nothing will deter us from the most important development in the war the invasion of Russia! It will start with the complete destruction of Moscow by a secret weapon, *die Atombombe*. We shall destroy Stalin's Russia before he turns on us. I have ordered Speer to have the aircraft factories concentrate on producing as many fighters and bombers as possible and gradually have them create jet squadrons."

The *Wehrmacht* chiefs looked at each other stunned into silence but Hitler was in full flow. "This will be followed by the strike by an *Asia Korps* under the command of Rommel to the oil rich South-West industrial area of Russia, Persia then through the waste of Afghanistan to India where our victorious army will link up with our Japanese allies striking through Burma. Then our combined armies will crush British rule in India. After that we complete our occupation of North America. We will then turn our might against the allies in Africa and wipe them out.

"Heinrich Himmler and I have been planning an uprising of Muslims living under British rule in India and serving in the British army around the world. The Third *Reich* will incite a holy war, a *Jihad* against *die Briten*. To accomplish this we will obtain Zulfigar, the greatest symbol in the Muslim world. The sword is reputed to have magic powers that allow its owner to achieve dazzling victories and feats of strength. Often it is depicted as having two blades to emphasize it can be so swift it can strike in two locations at once.

"According to legend whoever finds it can wield immense power over the Muslim peoples in India, Central Asia and Egypt. If we have it Berlin and it is authenticated by the Grand Mufti of Jerusalem who is already a friend to us we can rally millions onto our side in a holy war against the British in India, Asia and Egypt. Zulfigar was given by the Prophet Mahommet to his son-in-law a warrior called Ali. An archeaological team of SS experts is being assembled to locate it and bring it to Berlin. Holding it in full view of the world's press photographers and newsreel cameramen the Grand Mufti will declare a Jihad against the British to coincide with our thrust through southern Russia, the Caucausus, Iraq, Iran and Afghanistan to India's Hindu Kush. Finding Mahommet's legendary sword before they do would be a master-stroke that will paralyse British resistance. Their imperial armies will collapse like wet card-board.

"Next week the greatest weapon in our arsenal is to be fully-tested in Paraguay. If successful, within three months we shall have two or three A-bombs to use against the Soviet Union and knock it back into the stone-age. At the same time we will wage an unprecedentedly powerful *Blitzkrieg* to take their oil fields and industrial areas to the south. We will not repeat Napoleon's mistake in trying to take Moscow and failing, it is too far and the Russian winter is cruel. I am only interested in wiping out the Communist control centres in Kiev and Moscow. Each *atombombe* will wipe out government. Our invasion will be to the south-east through the Caucasus. Now you see why I have put Operation Felix, the taking of Gibraltar on hold."

Hitler's top military leaders drew in their breath at the audacity of the Fuhrer's plans. They looked at each other in consternation. They felt Germany had taken on too much invading North America and should prepare for an assault upon *Festung Europa* by taking Gibraltar quickly but wisely kept silent they knew that the *Fuhrer* did not take kindly to anyone daring to question his strategy which was based on his luck and intuition.

"I realise that apart from our esteemed head of the *Luftwaffe* General Galland, you did not know that our weapon research had reached such heights. Tests of *Sieg* or Victory-3 Thor's Hammer rockets are being undertaken at Peenemunde and the Isle of Wight. By the end of this year they will deliver high-explosive or germ warheads across the oceans. Targets will be New York from Ireland and Iceland from Scotland. *Gross Admiral* Doenitz and I are looking ahead at Neptune submarine launched missiles within five years. Admiral Doenitz, how are plans for U-Boat rocket launching progressing?"

"*Mein Fuhrer,*" the pinched, thin-faced Admiral Doenitz replied, "Early trials in the North Sea and German Channel are coming along slowly. The sealing of the rocket silos in the test U-boats is tricky. We also need to design, test and produce very large rocket carrying *Unterseeboots* within two or three years but our naval architects and shipyards are utterly overwhelmed. Realistically it will take seven years as if we are lucky."

"Just get it done. I want to reach everywhere in the world by 1950. Launching them from submarines in the Atlantic, Pacific, Indian or Arctic oceans means no target will be unreachable, even Ottawa, the home of that British viper Clement Attlee.

The Air Force commander interjected, "Regarding the *atombombe*. Our store of uranium is limited as you know *Mein Fuhrer*. Good quality uranium is available to us only from Japanese controlled northern Australia since the enemy control the Belgian Congo and Canada. There are possibilities of it in Iran. We have enough for two or three bombs this year, if our allies the Japanese are able to maintain control of northern Australia. we should have six bombs within two years."

"If. If? There must be no question of if. I demand bombs for our attack on Russia, and more for our final assault upon America and Canada!" Hitler demanded raising his voice. "I will not listen to defeatist talk!" he sputtered then regained control. Taking a pill from a box in his desk drawer he swallowed it with a gulp of water. "Now let us discuss the details about our defence of Norway."

*

Hitler's hopes would have been dashed if he had any idea that the 'Montgomery' seen in Iceland was an actor, and the body bearing the 'Norwegian invasion plans' and most of the troops, landing craft and equipment ready for the Scandinavian invasion part of a masterful campaign of deception. The American Commander was a high ranking American sailor but had died of liver failure not enemy action and his body had been purloined from a mortuary in Kevlavik, the lungs filled with sea water. If he could have known that his top soldier, von Rundstedt was correct, that the Allies were indeed ready to land on the Iberian Peninsula, it would have given him an apoplectic fit.

*

In Tangier the leader of the Free French forces, Napoleon IV climbed into the jeep driven by his favourite American, Evelyn Carr. She was his personal driver seconded to him at his request from General Bradley's staff. She recollected how she had first met him the year before in Cairo when he was fresh from his victorious coup in French Indo-China against the treacherous Vichy Government in league with the Japanese. He had masterminded a brilliant guerrilla war in the jungles of south-east Asia then come to the Casablanca Conference to meet Roosevelt, Attlee, Mackenzie-King and Chang Kai-shek. On the way he had wangled his way into a mission with Brigadier Orde Wingate by impersonating junior French soldiers assigned to a Long Range Desert Patrol mission. .

50

Evelyn Carr shut the door of the olive green Oldsmobile sedan as the short soldier with the thick accent and a *Kepi*, its brim encrusted with gold, leaned back and lit a cigarette. She climbed into the driver's seat. Evelyn no longer noticed his shrivelled left ear such was the charm of the descendant of Napoleon I who had led a successful revolt in French Indo-China against the pro-fascist Vichy government. He still tried occasionally and unsuccessfully to seduce her but she was two steps ahead of him allowing him to have dalliances elsewhere while letting him wine and dine her, but no more, when it suited her. She wasn't sure if she loved him or not or whether anything formally romantic was possible between the potential leader of post-war France and a Yankee girl with no pretensions. "You want to know what eet iz I like about you Eveleen?"

"My driving."

Napoleon chuckled, "Your wit is exquiseet. I do not know what I will do without you when I jump into Spain in a few days?"

"You will be too busy to think about me, sir."

"Zere you go with the 'sir' again. Charles is fine."

"I like to be professional; while I'm driving now you want to go the British hospital to see that nurse, Susan isn't it?

"Yes, Nurse Day. I wanted to give her some flowers and wish her luck she and her sisters will be running once D-Day begins. She nursed me to health in Alexandria and I shall never forget it."

While Evelyn waited in the car looking at the fishing boats coming and going from the harbour the French leader entered the hospital and went to the main desk. "*Excusez moi*, I understand zat ze Flyeeng Nighteengales are in Tangier attached to zis hospital."

"Yes Sir, you mean the Queen Alexandra's Royal Army Medical Corps, QARAMC."

"*Mais Oui, certainment.* Zere is a nursing sister Susan Day she looked after me."

"Well you are in luck General. I know her. She is in the dispensary picking up some supplies. On the third floor, Room G5."

Napoleon bounded up the stairs as fast as his platform shoes allowed him, his vanity had no limits but he had a kind soul. Susan noticed the bouquet of roses waving at her from the doorway and curiosity drew her from her kneeling position packing boxes with morphine and hypodermic needles. ""What? Napoleon? What a surprise!"

"*Pour vous*, Sister Susan."

"You shouldn't you know," she smiled.

The Free French leader bowed. "From one friend to another I know you 'ave your *Alain* and repect zees. I will congratulate your *Capitain* on your selection of 'ím. Zees ees *un autre merci* for looking after me."

Susan took them from him, "Then I accept them. I have to get these boxes to our aircraft I don't suppose you are heading out of the city."

"My American driver friend and I shall drop you off on the way to my HQ. Let me 'elp you pack I inseest."

Susan always loved to relate how just before D-Day Napoleon IV gave her flowers and helped her pack medicine for her 'Flying Nightingale' work in Spain and always smiled fondly when she told it.

*

In an office of the second floor of the Reich Chancellory Heinz Gerhard studied the documents Hitler's secretary had given to him, a trusted member of the *Fuhrer's* staff asking the Spanish dictator to contribute 10,000 troops to an army being assembled to rid the world of Communism to translate. One was a letter to General Francisco Franco from Hitler outlining his plan to seize the industrial and oil production centres of Russia and move east to link up with a Japanese army in India. It was noted that Spanish aircraft were not needed for the campaign since bombs of a new type and great magnitude would be used to erase several Soviet centres and destroy the Soviet ability to react. Heinz read it three times committing it to memory and began typing up Spanish copies as directed. He made sure to make carbon copies on his typewriter. One of them would be kept for his own use.

Next he read through a brief report on an SS Archaelogical project to be translated into Arabic, Parsi and Turkish for distribution to selected Pro-Nazi Muslim leaders and academics in the Middle East, Turkey and Iraq. The report described an ancient sword known as Zulfigar that an SS team was preparing to locate in the Middle East or Central Asia, it asked for any information on its whereabouts to be given to the closest German ambassador or representative. It stated that the *Fuhrer* himself put credence in the existence of the sword given by Mahommet to his son-in law and used in battle by him and wished Germany to locate it and protect it for the Muslim peoples, proof that despite fighting in a terrible struggle the *Reich* looked to its Muslim friends and the future when victory had been secured and the Arab nations were given higher status in the new world order, meaning in Nazi terms that they would become a source of cheap labour and take second place to Aryan needs. Hans scoffed at the cynicism and opportunism hidden by honeyed words. Hitler cared only for allies in his struggle once victory had been achieved they could be jettisoned when suitable.

The translator, who was adept at most major languages worked for an hour carefully putting the report into Arabic. Hans typed up a German copy with carbon copies for two of his staff who could translate the document into Parsi and Iraqi. Again he put aside a copy for himself then called in one of his staff who could translate requested languages. They were two very interesting items, the first of terrific import to the war effort, the second of secondary importance it would seem but could be useful. He knew someone who would be able to get the information to people who would be able to put it all together with all the other bits of information they gathered from around the world. *But I,*

Heinz considered, *am as far as I know, the only man the allies have in the heart of Hitler's world. I can feed them information vital to the prosecution of their war effort. Some would consider me a traitor but I see myself as a true German patriot. Hitler is an upstart and the Generals who serve him weaklings willing to let him drag down our great nation. I want to leave my child a Germany that is free of evil, worthy of being welcomed back into the circle of civilized countries.*

He thought longingly about his wife Ingrid and their baby in Stockholm. He was due some leave but work was piling up, the *Fuhrer* was ferociously busy and he had to arrange a meeting with the American agent he was assigned in Berlin to whom to pass on these momentous secrets. Sometimes the man, a rare book dealer was not available since he attended auctions in Paris, Switzerland and Sweden. Seeing him was more important than his selfish desire for a holiday.

*

In the Yorkshire Dales a pair of jet black ravens known as Jeremiah and Croakey were in a barn helping an old soldier with neat white hair and a short cropped grey beard by carefully dragging rats by the tails with their long cruel yellow beaks which had whiskers springing out at their bases. What made this scene even more extraordinary was the plastic explosive stuffed into the body of each disembowelled rat. The birds hopped along and dropped their rats into a pile at the end of a bench. There Charlie Gates carefully applied detonators and sewed up the stomach of each rodent. He placed them into a wooden crate marked tractor parts. Charlie, the last Yeoman Warder and Keeper of the Ravens at the Tower of London, talked to the birds as he did when the ravens strutted around the Tower of London before he spirited them away in a basket during the raid. He had great faith in 'his birds' the last two ravens at the Tower of London. He had escaped with them in a wicker hamper standing on turf from Tower Green.

"By gum Croakey and Jeremiah you're a great help. Our little friends will be tossed into open coal carriages of trains heading for munitions factories from railway bridges to explode when they are placed into the factory boilers." Charlie lowered his voice to a whisper and the birds came close to him looking up with black eyes their heads tilting towards him. He was well aware of the old legend that if the ravens ever left the Tower Britain would fall. "While you are alive and we have a bit of the grass from the Tower you haven't really left it. There's nowt to stop us."

CHAPTER FOUR   THE EMPEROR

His Imperial Majesty, Hirohito, 124th Emperor of Nippon finished breakfast with his wife, Empress Nagako in his Tokyo palace. He had one hour with which to play with his son in the gardens, then his Prime Minister. General Tojo Hidecki would be coming to report upon the war's progress. His previous Prime Minister, Prince Konoye, had recommended that he establish an Imperial Headquarters during the war with China in the *Akasaha* Palace and the Emperor had done so. It certainly helped him exercise his role as commander-in-chief and foster inter-service co-operation between the rival forces the navy and the army who each operated their own air force. It also allowed him to closely observe his admirals and generals.

Tojo had his feared secret police but the Emperor had his own ways of gathering information, the royal family was large and its members and loyal friends were scattered in the top levels of the civil service and in the services. The Premier would have been surprised at just how much Hirohito knew and the secret plans the Emperor had if the war began to go badly wrong. The Emperor usually visited the Imperial headquarters every morning but today he was happy to have Tojo visit him in a reception room. Today was a day for contemplation.

Tomorrow he would be taking a train to the navy base at Osaka to inspect the heavy battleship Yamato, named after the first Emperor from 660 B.C. It had just been fitted with the latest radar, radio and analogue computer-assisted gun systems using the miniature trans-conductors that were revolutionising the weapons of the Imperial Japanese armed forces. The Yamato at 72,800 tonnes was the undisputed steel leviathan of world navies, since the sinking of the Bismark and Tirpitz. Each of its nine 18.1 inch guns in three turrets could fire a shell 25 miles. Each turret weighed 3,000 tons, as heavy as an American destroyer. The ship could reach a rate of 27 knots at top speed, 50 kilometres an hour. Hirohito was most pleased with the gold *Kikusi* crest at the prow of the vessel, with a six foot diameter it displayed to the world that the Japanese navy recognised the behemoth and its 2,700 crewmen as an important ship in the service of Imperial Japan since it was only displayed by capital ships. As yet the Emperor did not know that the Canadian bergships were of even more immense size but even if he had, he would have dismissed them of being chimeras, made of frozen water mixed with wood pulp. A mad western idea.

Hirohito even as a boy always loved animals, birds and fish. He was happy to take his eleven-year-old son Akihito into the palace gardens with a bag of food to feed his golden carp and chase butterflies with small plastic nets on the end of wooden handles. His son bowed as his father approached. He was wearing his white admiral's uniform so the son knew that he would be meeting with his Prime Minister. The son was old enough to detect that his father became inscrutable when in the presence of General Tojo the man who governed Japan in the name of the Emperor with his parliament, the Diet. But when he and his father were alone in the garden, playing with an electric train set, or watching educational programs broadcast from the new Tokyo broadcasting centre on the *Telefunken* television set given to the palace by the German ambassador they were happy, his father relaxed and unworried.

"Your Majesty, has Singapore been taken yet?" the little boy asked. This was his daily question.

"Not today my son any day now."

"Do we still have Hawaii and some of the USA?" The boy stabbed his pudgy fingers at the map pinned to the wall of the nursery.

"Yes we still have them and best of all I have time to take you into the garden. I have food for our favourite fish and some nets, today I think we shall try and catch some butterflies. They have the most beautiful black and pink hue. They are Byasa Alcinous, their nickname is swallowtails. I spotted them as your mother and I had breakfast outside. One of them landed on my plate and ate some honey." The boy laughed at the thought of a butterfly landing on the imperial china and taking the Emperor's honey.

They walked out into a sunlit garden of well ordered trees, raked gravel, flowers and small wooden bridges, stone lanterns and grottoes, swell-stocked ponds of carp beckoned them. Akihito ran ahead waving his father on. Together they threw bread into the pond and watched the golden fish jump up and snap at the crumbs, almost jumping out of the water in their excitement. *If only I could do this all the time instead of presiding over this never-ceasing war* Hirohito thought. *Enough. I must enjoy this precious time with my son the next Emperor. It is my job to keep Japan strong and prosperous for him and his people, it is what I am trained to do and I shall do it, now to clear my mind of worries and live in this moment of sunlit bliss.*

The bespectacled Emperor bent over and smiled at his son and patted him on the head. "Come on let us see who is first to catch a butterfly."

Later the Crown Prince began his lessons with his tutor Hirohito went to his Shinto Shrine inside the palace and knelt in prayer. Then he went to a reception room and waited.

"Prime Minister Tojo, your Highness," the Emperor's Chamberlain announced. A man in brown army uniform, brown leather jackboots and a peaked cap emblazoned with a red star bowed deeply from the waist, his samurai sword in its scabbard stuck out behind him as if he was a male bird with a red decoration on his head, brown feet and a tail that jerked up. Hirohito sat straight with his hands resting palms down on the long conference table. As the Emperor indicated he should sit, General Tojo waited for the chamberlain to pull out his chair and sat.

"General, what do you have to tell me today?"

"Your Imperial Majesty, it is my honour to report that a convoy of 80,000 troops are on their way from Hawaii to California. The American General Mack Clarke's army is a

58

worthy opponent but their ranks are ravaged with sickness from the germ warfare we have been prosecuting. They have no antidote to the artificially enhanced Spanish flu bacillus our scientists created in the army research laboratory in China." Tojo opened his mouth to continue but Hirohito interrupted, this was unusual but the cunning and highly intelligent General who had been first in his class at military college expressed no emotion. He closed his mouth.

"These germs we are releasing are deadly to all humans are they not? What would happen if they made their way to our Japanese home islands?" Hirohito asked.

Tojo did not reveal that he had last week ordered the senior biochemist at the University of Osaka to bring back a vial of mutated flu germs from China so he could work on an antidote with his research team using one of the few electronic microscopes available in the world. The equipment was too delicate to take to China. The premier did not wish to unnecessarily alarm his Emperor who looked pale. The worried look that only occasionally flashed over his face was becoming a fixture. Upsetting the Emperor would only lead to more bothersome, difficult questions.

The man-God sitting upon the Chrysanthemum Throne was a dilettante who thinks he knows about military affairs, in the normal scheme of things he would not rise above a junior officer Tojo thought but the Emperor was not normal. He was *Nippon* in the flesh to those who practiced the Shinto religion. Over the years of his reign since 1926, named at the outset as the era of heavenly peace, the worship of their ancestral religion had become strictly enforced throughout Japan as militerisation and fascism became the norm, the bulwark against what was perceived as a weakening in traditional beliefs and a growth in far-left revolutionary opposition to the Emperor due to the Depression, social unrest and liberal criticism of Japan's expansion in China. Gradually in the 1930s the feudal, ultra-conservative Samurai warrior mentality supplanted western idealogy in all military circles and, since the

59

military increasingly took over government positions, in day-to-day life in Japan. The Land of the Rising Sun was a police state since Tojo ran the secret police and the government.

The conservative Hirohito had never spoken on the radio to his people and was known to most of them only by reputation or glimpsed by several million citizens over the years in carefully orchestrated visits to different cities. The average Japanese knew he was their Emperor and would have recognised him from newspaper photos, newsreels or postcards of him positioned in a place of honour in humble homes, a deity to be worshipped.

Hirohito wanted to conserve the traditions of respect and order in modern Japan and ensure it was safe from encroachment by the United States into Asia and the Pacific. A powerful army and navy protected the all-important trade which his kingdom of islands depended since they lacked natural resources such as coal, iron, rubber and enough food to feed its people. The islands relied on trade, it was their lifeblood. The Emperor blinked as Tojo gave him an evasive answer. He was beginning to lose patience and respect for this prime minister who he had asked to lead his government. *I chose a gasconade to be my premier, he thinks less and less of humility and restraint.*

"It is now 1944, we have been at war for eight years since our actions in China began. I am prepared to lead my people in war but it is taking a very long time to achieve victory. I am told some of the populace are beginning to ask questions and resent sending their sons off to war and having them return blind, or without limbs or not come back at all. Most die as heroes with my name on their lips, *Banzai*. But remember I proclaimed my reign to be known forever as 'Heavenly Peace'. I want to live up to that name. I want Japan strong and unassailable with a promising future as a world class industrial power trading our products around globally, not a weak and defeated wraith, a wreck of a country. You keep saying America is on the ropes like an exhausted boxer but it would appear he keeps getting up from the canvas floor.

"I think we should offer them tempting peace terms. I want you to open secret negotiations with the Americans through our ambassador to Switzerland, there must be a way to end this conflict.   You and the general staff are playing for very high stakes, we are in a strong position to negotiate."

"Imperial Highness, forgive me for not explaining how well we are doing." Tojo was respectful but adamant, "We and our allies are on the verge of winning the world, we will be on par with the Europeans for the first time, we will be paramount in Asia and a partner with Germany ruling North America, Southern and eastern Asia and the Pacific will be Japan's for centuries. Besides, Roosevelt and Attlee have said they will destroy us for what we have done to them."

"If Hitler attacks Russia in a few years or after the war is over do you believe Hitler can win against Russia?"

"Yes, we beat Russia in the 1904-1905 Russo-Japanese War, the Finns gave Stalin a drubbing in 1940 so can Hitler. Hitler's liason officers have spoken to us about invading India and linking up with a German Asia Korps later this year, as you know."

Hirohito countered, "Stalin has a very strong army and is without scruple, he would be a tough opponent. Our agents report that Stalin has moved many factories east of the Urals far away from Germany. It is too large for Hitler to take on at the same time as the USA. It is not too far from Russia to Japan but it is a very long way from Berlin to India. Do you see my point prime minister? The Allies will find a way to cut Hitler's supply lines from Europe to India and they will destroy him. If Hitler is at war with the Soviet Union then Stalin will declare war against us his ally. Japan is not destined to rule half the world in my lifetime we do not have the resources to control such a large amount of land and keep it secure from internal insurrection. We would inherit the problems the British have with independence movements if we take India and Burma.

"I admire the British who built their empire slowly, almost by accident.   It began by skilful use of their Elizabethan navy and intrepid exploration. We have achieved much, we should absorb it. To succeed too quickly is to leave us open to the anger of the Gods, it is what the Ancient Greeks called hubris you are aware of this. We should not lose what we have by attempting too much. We must learn from history. I reveal my inner thoughts to you because you are my prime minister."

With a blank look Tojo looked across the table at his monarch his intelligent eyes did not reveal the impatience he felt in his heart. *Fool, weakling, we are in a position to win total victory and place Japan in the position of ruler of the eastern hemisphere from the Indian Ocean to the Rocky Mountains.   Now he is lecturing me.*

The lecture continued.   "Russia – the Soviet Union is no friend to us.   Remember I supported north faction Hokushin-pa, before I agreed that we should strike south to ensure the oil supply from Java. I do not trust *Herr Hitler*, he has broken his word many times as a politician. We are his allies only as long as it suits him. His peace pact with Stalin means nothing now. Military attaches bring us plans for us to invade India while he invades Russia. We have committed ourselves to 'Strike South' I was advised against attacking the Soviet Union when we had the chance in 1936. I acquiesced to expanding our interest into South East Asia for the security of markets and resources. Now our ally wants us to take India so the Third Reich can take the industrial areas of the Soviet Union and the oilfields in southern Russia and in Iraq. I think it is unwise. Invading India when we are under attack from a resurgent nationalist army in China and are on the defensive in Australia is a bad strategy.   Our forces are being stretched to the point of inefficiency by operating in North and Central America. America is still fighting back fiercely, I admire their courage."

"If we do not invade India we break the Axis alliance it is possible that Hitler will be our enemy," Tojo countered.

"Even if we win the world together eventually he may become our enemy anyway. He is a megalomaniac. I am not." The Emperor angrily struck the table with an open hand and stood up. "It may be we have to invade India since we are in an alliance with Hitler but we can make it a token invasion. I want us to achieve victory where we need it most – Singapore, Australia then America. Not India. We shall discuss this at the next meeting of the Services Council the day after tomorrow" Hirohito stood up. The interview was at an end. Tojo stood and bowed and the Emperor returned the bow. Only after Tojo left, walking backwards still bowing, did Hirohito reflect upon his secret cabal the 'Grey Foxes'. He knew he could call on them at any time to seize control of the army and navy from Tojo and the current generals and admirals. But it had to be only as a last resort and at the right moment to succeed.

He suspected Tojo was like Cassius in the Shakespeare's play Julius Caesar, 'an ambitious man'. It was not inconceivable that he might be planning to replace him as emperor with his son who would be a puppet with he prime minister as an all-powerful regent eager to rule the world alongside Adolf Hitler. Assassinations and intrigue have been common enough in our history the forty-three year old monarch considered as he walked out into the garden to find peace in the solitude of the *Kahikodokoro*, 'the place of awe', which were the three Palace Shrines to the Sun Goddess containing replicas of the three famous objects sacred to Nippon: the mirror of the Goddess of the Sun, the necklace of agriculture and the sword. At each shrine he prayed to his ancestors and sought the answers to his questions: Would they win the war? What did the future hold? What could be done if they lost? Could the Germans be trusted? He repeated the famous tanka by Emperor Meiji, the first modern Emperor who presided over Japan ending its self-imposed isolation from the influence of Europe and America through its industrialization and victory against the Russians.

"Across the four seas all are brothers

In such a world why do the seas rage, the winds roar?''

A butterfly flew over the shrine of the sword, but Hirohito's eyes were closed behind his round spectacles. He heard the beat of its wings as it hovered over his head and flew in a circle around him. *Thank you. I shall be as delicate as a butterfly. My enemies will not see me. They will hear me only when I want them to.*

CHAPTER FIVE   LORD ROBERT'S DISPATCH

In October 1879 Major-General Frederick Sleigh Roberts led the Kabul-Kandahar Field Force through the mountain paths of the Hindu Kush, the North-West frontier of the British Raj-India. As the seven thousand Indian and almost three thousand British troops with two thousand cavalry horses, eight thousand donkeys, mules, camels and ponies carrying supplies and small mountain-guns descended into the rugged land of the Afghans. They broiled in their red woollen uniforms in the 110 degrees Fahrenheit daylight temperatures. At night they wrapped up as best they could to warm up trying not to imagine what it would be like in the winter if stuck in the mountains. Behind any ridge or rock could be a tough crack-shot Afghan warrior bent on killing the British invader. Robert's force was dispatched from India to Kandahar in the Second Afghan War to ensure the previously co-operative Emir did not allow Afghanistan to fall under Russian suzerainty.

On his mind and that of his officers was the knowledge that British consul and his guards in Kabul had been killed in an uprising against the rule of Emir Mahommed Yaqub Khan the month before. This echoed the First Afghan War of 1842 which resulted in the disastrous retreat of the British army from Kabul. The British garrison commander was murdered after neglecting the warning signs of rebellion. His troops and their wives and children in the cantonment in the Afghan Emir's capital had been surprised by an insurrection in the capital city and eventually allowed to leave for India. However, Ghilzai tribesmen massacred all 690 British soldiers, 2,840 Indian soldiers and 12,000 camp followers including women and children except for one man. He was allowed to escape and take the news back to the British Raj at Jellalabad his name was Dr. Bryden of the Somerset Light Infantry. It was a story familiar to John and Alan Stafford and every member of the Royal Hamilton Rifles a sister regiment to the Somerset Light Infantry.

Now his work was done, he had destroyed two Afghan armies; one at Char Asiab after which he had taken Kabul then Roberts had force-marched his 10,000 strong army the three hundred miles to Kandahar relieving the British survivors of the defeat at Maiwand under siege by the Governor of Harat, Ayub Khan. After marching for days in horrific daytime temperatures and sleeping exhausted for six hours in the cold nights Bobs' men routed Khan's army at the Battle of Kandahar in 1882.

Abdur Rahman, a strong leader, was established as king with Roberts's backing and signed the peace treaty accepting British control of the N.W. Frontier passes of Khyber and Michni. It ensured King Abdur did not allow Russian infiltration into Afghanistan. Afghanistan was now a pro-British buffer state between Russia and British India, an important player in the 'Great Game' between the Tsar and Queen Victoria's diplomats, a game later immortalised in Kipling's story *Kim*. In return the British army was to return to India. The new king sent messages to the chieftains of the Afghans telling them the British were no longer enemies but to be treated as guests.

It was dark just outside Kandahar where 'Bobs' victorious army was encamped. The city had once been known as Alexandria, after Alexander the Great whose Macedonian empire at its greatest extent in 330 B.C. stretched through Greece, Persia and Afghanistan to India, through the strategic gateway of the Khyber Pass. Alexander the Great was known as Iskandar to the Afghans and that accounted for its modern name. It was raining hard, though often Afghanistan was a place of arid desert, row upon row of brown mountains with treacherous paths and a maze of peaks and huge swathes of flat arid scrubland and fields of huge poppies source of the opium to be sold in China by British traders. A thunderous battle was taking place over-head. The heat of the day was replaced by a beneficent sweet coolness, the troops relaxed despite being wet. Their fires were dampened down but they had eaten and had cha from their Indian *cha-wallahs* to drink. To celebrate the peace that had broken out, Roberts, known affectionately as 'Bobs' the soldier's soldier, had allowed them a ration of rum to toast Queen Victoria. Every night before sleep 'Bobs' pored over his maps and had a whiskey and soda with his senior staff.

All day he had been in discussion with local tribal chieftains of Harat. Roberts assured scores of headmen they should support their King and that his army would leave for India once he received orders from Delhi but if the Russians intruded upon Afghan soil the British army would return with the support of the king to help him fight against the intruders.

A tall Afghan warrior wearing a pukul, a round, flat woollen cap, and a white shalwar kameez, a long shirt over loose trousers, rode his horse alone to the British army's encampment. He had a long-barrelled rifled musket, a Jazail, strapped to his back. The Pathan tribal leader, Saya Agha uttered the only English name he knew "Rob-erts" to the Sepoy sentries on piquet duty. Their British officer escorted him to the General's tent arranged for his horse to be fed and watered and temporarily relieved him of his intricately engraved rifle which he inspected with interest.

Agha looked forward to meeting the Briton who had fought bravely and commanded his men with great skill. True, he was an infidel but he was a brave, just soldier and that was even more important to him. He and the other chieftains would make obeisance to the defeated king in Kabul but carry on with regular lives of feuds and hunting made better by captured British rifles and ammunition.

General Roberts' translator who spoke Pashtun, Brigadier Danger, entered the tent saluted and announced, "Sir, Saya Agha, one more Pathan chieftain, is outside waiting for an audience with you. He wishes 'Ro-berts' long-life and God's blessings." 'Bobs' looked thoughtful and a pang squeezed his heart, yes his family was far away, but the family that meant most to him right now, was here, the rough men from the villages of Ireland, Somerset, Northumbria, Scotland, Wales and slums of London sporting red woollen jackets, white pith helmets, tough bronzed skin and side-whiskers. The hero of the Indian Mutiny had ridden his horse at the head of a marching army out for revenge for the debacle of the First Afghan War which saw hundreds of British women and children slaughtered. He had achieved it by defeating the enemy and hanging the men responsible for the insurrection in Kabul and bringing law to the city in revolt, no more no less. British justice must be seen to be fair and impartial. His orders were to stop the Afghan monarch from siding with the Russians and he had succeeded; the peace treaty was signed and an Afghan ally capable of keeping the unruly tribes subservient was secure on his throne.

Captain Hartley the general's secretary entered the tent sat at the portable oak desk carried by a donkey over the mountains to the plains of Afghanistan and dipped his wooden pen's nib into the glass well of ink to make a record of the interview

"Show our native friend in," Roberts asked as he sat in a camp chair and allowed his Sikh servant to squirt some soda water from a siphon into his tumbler of whiskey. He took a sip as the visitor stepped into the canvas tent and made the salutations of greeting with his left hand. The General bowed in return and admired the magnificent sword his aide-de-camp, Lieutenant John Sherston of the Rifle Brigade, received from the tribal leader. The General waved his hand to indicate that the sword should be returned.

"Excellency, I bring you greetings and long life. I have something important to tell you but first I must tell you how impressed we were by the bravery of the British soldiers we defeated at Maiwand in July before you came and defeated us at the gates of Kandahar. Our 12,000 men fought 2,500 of your British and Indian troops. At the last we had one unit down to two officers and eleven men in the village of Khig behind a walled garden. The officers led the men into a charge against us firing their rifles. So astonished were we at their valour that not one of our army could advance until the last man fell although we were many thousands. You have been worthy opponents and I am glad that we now are friends."

Roberts replied, "I thank you for your commendation. I too am happy that peace now exists between our two peoples. Those men of the 66th Berkshire Regiment of Foot were brave men as you say. What is it you wish to tell me?"

"Since the battle I have had wonderful dreams that have both excited and puzzled me. They are gifts from Allah, showing me what could be in the days of our descendants. I have been commanded to share them with you. On the way here I had thoughts of not telling you my dreams since you are an infidel, then the Prophet stood in front of me and commanded me to meet you and share the dreams he sent to me. Allah has shown to me that you may be a heathen but you are a man who can be trusted with what I must tell you."

'Bobs' smiled grimly, this was not what he was expecting, not the usual recital of tribal hatreds and old scores over this village and that well. *If only the man knew just how few the soldiers of the Queen actually were. The British Empire was protected by a thin red line of soldiers scattered around the globe ferried and supplied by a large navy. Technical superiority, thanks to the industrial revolution producing good quality weapons, winning tactics, brave troops and good leadership, in most cases, had meant it usually prevailed. Yes, the Afghans are formidable, tough as old boots. Their lovingly hand-made antique rifles, jazeils, had a longer range than the British army issue Martini-Henry rifles, two miles as opposed to 1,500 yards, just under a mile. But the Martini-Henry rifles issued to British and Indian soldiers could shoot twelve rounds a minute a fusillade from experienced soldiers was a devastating, usually unbeatable combination.*

"Sullivan, have your pen and ink ready; when I am put out to pasture I can add this to my memoirs, local colour and all that."

To his guest Bobs replied carefully, "I thank you for your kind words, and in the name of our Queen Victoria, Empress of India wish you and your people peace and prosperity." Danger faithfully translated the welcome.

The Pathan leader digested this and replied, "We have had a meeting of our tribe leaders to discuss the new situation. We are loyal to Ayub Khan and since he has signed a peace treaty with you, you are guests in our land. You shall have no fight with our people as long as the King is at peace with you," he said with a twinkle in his eye. "The British I have met I like for the most part, not the Russians, they are not so subtle. You are just you only hanged those that led the revolt against the British and have let the others go. You are merciful and many fathers, mothers, brothers, sisters and sons praise you."

"Please sit. I am forgetting my manners, let me order some food and drink for you." Roberts instructed his servant who returned later with some cold meat, chuynry, jipatis and tea. The man ate and drank with relish and then asked permission to tell them about his dreams. "Zulfiqar the prophet's sword perhaps you have heard of it? It has been missing for hundreds of years some say it is in Mecca others say it is in Antioch or Damascus, broken, hidden or maybe lost forever.

"The Prophet, has shown me in a dream where it is, Allah the Merciful has told me I must share its location with you. The dream revealed that many years from now when our children's children are dead and our great-grand-children old there will be a great war and here in our land British soldiers will come again but they will not wear the red coat. Some of these soldiers wear red hats and drop like the angels of heaven from the sky but whether on the ground or from heaven they all wear brown clothes like the rocks of Afghanistan. Some fly in great winged beasts. These future soldiers will fight a European people like yourselves."

"Russians by God," Danger exclaimed. He did not put much faith in flying mammals but he did believe in Russians, after all they had been the enemy in '52-'54 in the Crimea. "Were they Russians sent by the Tsar?" Danger asked the chieftain. *Perhaps*, Danger thought, *this headman had seen Russians recently, probing to gain advantage in Afghanistan.* Roberts listened attentively, since 1825 when Nicholas I came to the throne, Russia had seriously continued the age-old search for a warm water port in the Mediterranean begun by Peter the Great in the seventeenth century, continued by Catherine the Great and Alexander. Now Nicholas I looked to Central Asia, far from strong French and British influence, as a route first to the Black Sea then to the Indian Ocean. Controlling Afghanistan was the key to India. With India under its control the Indian Sea could be renamed the Russian Sea. By making one vast kingdom after another a vassal state, Russia could be in an unassailable position in fifty to one hundred years. Russians in the form of soldiers, spies and merchants sometimes fulfilling all three roles had been criss-crossing Turkestan, Afghanistan and Central Asia for many years building up alliances with Kings, Emirs and tribal leaders against the British.

"No, not like the Russians," Saya Aga replied. "I know what they look and sound like. I met some years ago. Some spoke our language. The army in my dream come from the far west but spoke in a strange speech, one I have never heard. They will arrive in metal chariots using not horses or camels to give them power but unseen magic. Each chariot was mounted with cannon or several cannons I could see them shooting at our people who fought against them with rifles. They will not care for the Afghanistan people we are just a bridge to India, they will kill all who stand in their way and imprison our king. Our people will fight with you against them.

"In the name of their cruel leader his men will torture and kill and he will try to find where Zulfiqar lies because if their King holds it above his head he will control all the Muslims in the middle east and Asia and in India where you have such men in your large India army and turn them against you. Their king who sets himself up as a god is Hitter. But he would use the sword not to further Islam the holy religion or the Prophet, Blessed be His Name, but to further his own empire. He is evil, without belief in God or even gods of any kind, unlike us Mohammedans, you Christians or the Hindoos in India. He will have the power to rule over many tribes all over the world and make them slaves but we shall fight him. Afghans will never be slaves."

71

Danger translated and Roberts replied, "We British have a song about our sailors who rule the oceans. 'Rule Britannia, Britannia Rules the Waves, Britons never never shall be slaves.'" Roberts recited the words while the Afghan stroked his greying beard.

"Will you sing it for me, Excellency?" The translation took a few moments.

Robert's eyes flicked to the Brigadier's. "Ahem, my voice is not a good one ... "

The Captain piped up, "Excuse me, sir, I'm a tenor. I can sing it if you wish to impress this warrior fellow. I sang it recently at a party with naval officers in Bombay so I should be on key."

"Please entertain us," General Roberts said his eyes amused. He looked forward to the normally reserved Captain pushing himself forward. He sang clearly with a melodious talent. 'Bobs' closed his eyes and listened to the song. The Pushtun chieftain did not understand the words but clearly relished the martial style of the music. Such was the power of the song that even a mountain tribesman in a landlocked country quite recently an enemy of Great Britain, found his body sway mystically as if he was in a trance.

Brigadier Danger waited until the callow officer's dulcet tones flew away into the mountain air, then translated the words as best he could. The warrior listened gravely, asking Danger to translate the words again. After a few moments ruminating while he sipped his tea he pronounced judgement, "A good song. You rule the seas, we rule the mountains and we both never never shall be slaves. I love this repetition." He laughed and 'Bobs' found himself laughing loudly with him.

Roberts looked the Afghan in the eyes, "Now this er, Zulfiqar, tell me where you believe it to be?"

The elder stroked his beard and squinted in deep thought. "Perhaps you think I am the one to find it and give it to my king or a mullah. Allah has told me now is not the time for it to be found.

It will be in the times of our grand-children and great-great grandchildren. It will take place when Hitter will want to kill all the Jewish traders in Asia and control Muslims for his own ends. It will be a bad time because the Russians to the north will be led by another cruel king, a man who has a name like Satin and he also would like to be Lord of the Pathans. But Allah tells me he will lose his power and become a wanderer.

"Hitter will stay evil as long as he lives. He must not find it the sword. It should to Mecca or Medina or at least remain hidden from those who will not protect it. Many think it is a children's story a fable, or that the sword with its special powers never existed or was lost or destroyed many years ago. But I know it exists and is waiting to found and cared for by someone who has no evil intent." He stopped meaningfully in his narrative, "If it falls into the wrong hands it could cause great trouble the Prophet warned me. It could mean the end of belief in the God of mercy, peace and kindness by the Muslim people. They could be led from their belief to follow this Hitter as the new prophet by virtue of the sword he could steal and claim as his own.

"Allah the merciful has revealed to me future days and the location of this sword. He has told me to come to you even though you are an infidel and that all will resolve itself into peace and from paradise we shall both see things unfold from these times that see us enemies to the time we shall be friends."

As he left the tent he bowed to General Roberts and as the chieftain walked to his own tent they could hear the Afghan, first humming the tune of 'Rule Britannia' and then singing roughly but with passionately adding his own words lauding the beauty of his land and the courage of its people in a unique Afghan version of the patriotic song.

"It's a bit fanciful, Sir," Danger stated.

"Yes," Lord Roberts said, "But so is the Bible, remember Psalm 22 in the Old Testament? It clearly predicts that the son of God will be treated as an outlaw and dice thrown to divide his cloak when he is executed. It was written many years before our Saviour was born. God moves mysteriously, I think Ayub Khan's prophet, who recognised Christ as a prophet also, may well have spoken to him. I want it written up and sent in tomorrow's dispatches to the Viceroy in Delhi."

The Afghan's prophecy was sent by messenger on horseback with a small escort but they were attacked and killed by a group of Russian spies masquerading as Turkomen traders. The dispatch pouch was taken from the dead messenger. The Russians in their turn were killed by Pathan warriors for their horses. They took the leather bag to their lair in the mountains of Arghandab but since they could not read it the envelope of dispatches in the blood-stained satchel was forgotten. In 1926 a British archaeologist on an expedition from Kandahar looking for Mongol artefacts found the forgotten dispatch while taking shelter from a storm in a cave and took it back to the British Museum.

Eleven years later a curator in the museum explored a dusty room full of wooden boxes marked 'Afghan Documents' intent upon sorting and cataloguing the neglected acquisitions. Screwing his monocle tight into his right eye socket as he bent over, the historian noticed a leather strap sticking out of the opening of one opened box and he pulled out a stained and worn leather pouch, like a schoolboy's satchel. He opened it and drew out the good quality paper still intact and clearly signed by General Roberts. Scratching the tufts of white hair that grew in his ears in nervous excitement, he sat cross-legged on the floor for an hour reading and re-reading the tight Victorian script written by Captain Hartley over sixty years before. Something told him not to publish any information about this find until he had discovered the sword for himself but then the pressures of work and the oncoming war put it in the back of a mind which was taken up by first ensuring the safety of the Rosetta Stone and other priceless items and then of an even more immense task which became more pressing as invasion loomed and became a terrible reality.

*

It was raining cats and dogs in London on Saturday 10 March, 1944 when a balding man sporting large bristling eyebrows and a grey fedora splattered with raindrops pulled down over his right eye, tugged on his Macintosh. He splashed down the steps of the British Museum in Russell Square and hailed a passing black taxi cab. "Fortnum and Mason's, Piccadilly," the man said as he got in the back of the cab. He sank back into the soft black leather seat amused by British fascist army officers in grey-green uniforms running to get out of the rain. One of them held his arm out to open the door of the taxi as it paused in traffic.

"Get away from those idiots. Put your foot down!" the man growled to the cabbie. The taxi driver who also had no use for fascists squealed his tyres as he deftly manouvered the cab out of the jam into a puddle splashing the jackbooted officers and sailing out of the way of an oncoming double-decker bus throuh a u-turn. There was a blast of horns and the passenger congratulated the driver. The driver would have been surprised if he had known that his fare was C in charge of the secret resistance group, Free London. C was really Anthony Smythe Armstrong a curator at the London Museum. C was the head of ten thousand men and women working underground as full-time SOE operatives or, more often, as secret part-time gatherers of information ready to swing into action in the course of their jobs when necessary, in a bank, a shop, a railway station, factory, airfield, or Whitehall office. He was on his way to meet a history researcher, Professor Peel from Oxford University, an expert on Asian history who had phoned and requested a meeting. Peel used a meeting code-word for out of town operatives coming to London.

"Ah, Professor Peel I think," C announced as Peel was led to his table by the maitre'd. A middle-aged man with fair hair neatly parted and a charcoal double-breasted suit from Savile Row stood up leaving his Dunhill cigarette burning in an expensive glass ashtray. "Pleased to meet you, I am Anthony Armstrong, Chief Curator Asian Antiquities, British Museum. Thank you for coming. It is for a good cause as you know."

The professor shook the proffered hand, "I will help as much as I can. I have several hours before I catch the train."

"Let me begin by saying I was up at Oxford two years after you but your reputation as a scholar was held up to me by my Classics Professor as a great example. I enjoyed your paper criticizing the cleansing of the Elgin Marbles before the war and considering their return at some time in the future, although I cannot imagine Greece ever being in a position to house the originals, that area of the world would seem to be always in a state of chaos. Then again our part of the world seems in turmoil just now. Shall we sit down?"

Armstrong spoke in low tones, "I have a request which is of the utmost importance to friends overseas. It's about an ancient sword Zulfiqar. It means 'spine cleaver' and was supposedly given by the Prophet Mahommet to his son-in-law, Muhammed Ali. It may or may not have existed and if it did it seems to have been destroyed or lost in the mist of time." He stopped as the waiter arrived with a bottle of wine and tested the claret as the waiter poured a small sample. Armstrong nodded and went on in a more enthusiastic tone, "Have a look at this, particularly page 54. It concerns archaeological research on the Alhambra Palace in Toledo, Spain. A team of fascist archaeologists I led recently found some interesting artefacts. I need your opinion and a few notes. If you wish to write them in ancient Greek down on the back of the draught of my paper that would be good, I wish sometimes we could converse in it all day."

"By all means," Peel agreed reached over and took the document. He removed his monocle from his left eye-socket and delicately cleaned it with the Etonian tie that he deftly pulled out from behind his flowered waistcoat and popped back into place with a flourish. He read swiftly through the thesis's précis and quickly reached the designated page containing the secret information. Between the lines in English about the Moorish Palace of Alhambra were questions in ancient Greek - the lingua franca of scholars like Peel and Armstrong. Does Zulfigar the legendary sword exist? If so where might it be? Do these locations sound possible to you? Following the question were a list of possibilities. The professor read and pursed his lips.

"Possible, possible," he said quietly.

C nodded curtly and smiled inwardly. Warming to the idea of deception Peel began to criticize Armstrong's thesis on the Alhambra even though that was not the reason for them to meet. "I don't agree about the size of the palace gardens on the hillside. They were not as large as you claim but perhaps you can tell me why you challenge the accepted size of the orange groves and terraces! Here, I'll jot down some queries you will have to answer before you publish." Peel wrote with his fountain pen in Greek of everything he had ever heard or read about the sword.

This is unbelievable, C thought, *that I should stumble across that Pashtun chief's revelation given to Lord Roberts, eight years ago on a sultry August day and then in the middle of World War Two be asked about it and be able to answer. If I wasn't an atheist I would say there are strange co-incidences at work. I should have done something about it but by the time I was ready to organise a team to look for it the war was imminent and I was asked to become C and control Free London in 1940, so it was too late.* The waitress came and took their lunch orders. Peel began to write upon the sheets with enthusiasm. Over brandy and coffee the Professor passed over the notes to C to digest. C's bristling eyebrows raised ever so slightly but apart from that subtle show of emotion and interest his face was impassive. *Hmm,* he thought, *this is very interesting. I am sure I have come across that term "In the mouth of the earth" related to the sword in a book somewhere, was it in Teheran or Berlin? This gives us something to add to what I have which should help track it down.*

Professor Peel put down his extinguished cigar. "A lovely luncheon, but alas I must return to Oxford." After saying their farewells C returned to his office at the V&A made a copy of the notes, put them under lock and key, then took the originals to an SOE courier who carried them onto a ferry from Liverpool to

Northern Ireland and took passage on a sub off the Ulster coast. Within seven days British and Canadian intelligence officers in Ottawa were in receipt of the important message. A group of high-ranking officers gathered in the Ministry of Defence building on Sparks Street. Colonel Henri Le Meseurier a French-Canadian with a good command of English, albeit with a *Quebequois* accent, was chairing the meeting as head of Canadian Military Intelligence. He was a good friend of John Stafford's father since they served together on the Western Front in W.W.I. Henri was the father of SOE agent Felicity placed in occupied London as a fashion designer. When his friend's son John married Felicity in New Britain in 1941 despite the war, after working together in Operation Lion-Heart, he became John's father-in-law.

Le Meseurier called the meeting to order. "Gentlemen, just to recapitulate for the benefit of CIGS, Field Marshal Brooke who just joined us; Prime Minister Attlee has authorised us to contact agent Sphinx in Jerusalem. His orders are to find the legendary sword Zulfiqar before the Nazis get their hands on it. Muslims believe it has magic powers. It was given to Mahommet's son-in-law and used in battle making its user invincible. Thanks to an agent in Berlin we know the Jerries are after it to use to gather support in the Arab world, eet's value as a propaganda weapon is immense.

"Experts 'ere and in Great Britain agree it may indeed exist and C in London knows where it may be thanks to a dispatch from Lord Roberts he found in the British Museum."

"Well, are you going to tell us where it is or leave us in suspense?" the head of British Military Intelligence asked impatiently." Henri put him out of his misery, discussion ensued and a plan of action decided upon. Le Meseurier made the wishes of the committee clear. "We shall send a message to our man in Jerusalem, Sphinx. He will arrange for one of our agents to find the sword and bring it to Cairo."

Field Marshal Brooke said, "Very well, but this Sphinx can you tell us something about him? I have seen his codename in several reports."

Henri Le Meseurier responded jocularly, "Since you happen to be the man commanding British and Imperial armies around the globe I can tell you that in 1935 an Aircraftsman Ross died in a mysterious accident riding his Brough motorbike on a lonely road in Dorset, England near his home in Clouds Hill. His real name was Colonel T.E. Lawrence, world famous as 'Lawrence of Arabia' leader of the Arab revolt against Turkish rule. As far as the world was concerned he died and was buried. But long live Captain McDougall an innocuous, even boring military man, with archaeological training and a love of the Middle East who decided to spend his days in Palestine with a variety of friends and acquaintances visiting him and inviting him away to 'various archaeological digs near and far.' Advanced surgery and a new identity created a new man with old knowledge to be used by British intelligence, a brilliant scheme envisioned by Churchill and put in place by Prime Minister Baldwin one of the few times Baldwin agreed with the great old man."

Field Marshal Brooke pursed his lips and stroked his dark moustache his eyes behind his brown horn-rim glasses his eyes were round with surprise. "Amazing. Winnie never told me about that, crafty devil. What an amazing turn-around. Last I heard Aircraftsman Shaw wanted the anonymity of testing speedboats on the south coast to pick up ditched airmen."

Le Meseurier summed up, "He still has anonymity. Churchill met him and told him about what Hitler planned and what was looming within five to ten years. It convinced him to 'die' and emerge with a new identity as Captain McDougall our man in the Middle East. His knowledge of the Arabs is indispensable. He has agents from Egypt, through Trans-Jordan, Saudi Arabia, Palestine, Syria, Iraq and beyond."

CHAPTER SIX   THE CAT PEOPLE

The Isle of Wight, just a short ferry ride from Portsmouth or Southampton on the south coast of England, was known as Vectis to the ancient Romans. It was a scenic tourist destination before the war's beginning in September 1939. Charles I had been imprisoned there during the Civil War in the 1640s and Queen Victoria put it back on the map in the1840s when she and Prince Albert had Osborne Palace built and often they visited with their growing family. The cliffs, fields and sea views were still upliftingly beautiful despite the barbed wire, flak and coastal guns and a garrison of fascist troops. However, its secrets were far from inspiring: a concentration camp near Ventnor, an underground rocket factory and a rocket launching and test-firing range. In 1944 the tourists were not English but Germans or Italians enjoying the sea or yachting at Cowes well away from Kz1 and weapon test flights. The weather of the island and its surrounding waters ranged from idyllic in the summer to foggy and unpredictable in the tempestuous days from autumn to spring as it had been in 1588 when the Spanish Armada had been battered, destroyed and dispersed by a gale force storm as well as the cannons and fire-ships of Drake, Raleigh and Hawkins's royal fleet of galleons in the service of the Virgin Queen, Elizabeth I.

Many of the occupants of the twenty-mile long island had been resettled on the mainland, while several hundred had been killed fighting the Germans when they invaded. But there were still thousands of islanders living on the island, farming or fishing. Hundreds were members of the Iron Duke Commando which led the fight for freedom in southern England, including Marcus Jeffries and Charlotte Lawrence.

Seventeen-year-old Marcus was a scarecrow figure rarely seen out of his navy blue raincoat which he had outgrown and which had seen better days. He rescued Charlotte in 1941 from the night-train delivering prisoners to the concentration camp Kz1 just ten miles from their home on the south coast of the Isle of Wight.

He took her in at his cottage and passed Charlotte off as a cousin who had been orphaned during the Battle of Britain and had nowhere else to go. His story had been accepted by the villagers of Brighstone who had taken to the pretty, outgoing Charlotte Lawrence. Marcus was the perfect gentleman and perhaps because of this Charlotte fell in love with him. They seized the opportunity to fully express their love for each other, knowing the enemy could come crashing through the door at any hour since they were both active in the resistance. Their romantic relationship evolved into Marcus taking birth-control precautions using 'French letters'. Then Charlotte had talked about having children in the summer of 1943 then she confided to him that she was two months pregnant, "having our baby – boy – girl -doesn't matter which".

Marcus was at first bewildered, it did not seem possible that he, an orphan at six years of age when his missionary parents in India died of smallpox, could find himself a father just eleven years later. Yet what a lot had already occurred in just over a decade. A kindly Indian friend of his parents had looked after him and taught him to be a cobbler. With his skin burnt by the sun, covered in dirt with unkempt hair he had worked in the market of Lucknow in Utter Pradesh by himself after his protector died. He was discovered by a couple from the Isle of Wight touring India on the one great holiday. They were amazed that the scruffy lad they literally bumped into spoke excellent English. They brought him back to the island but they paid the price of defiance of the new masters in October 1940 when they were shoved up against the wall and shot by German soldiers for talking against the new regime.

He saw Charlotte and this coming child as gifts from God, as were his own parents, his 'Uncle' and his liberal-minded adopted parents who insisted on him calling them Ron and Phoebe when no-one else was around. He was elated to realise Charlotte was happy to have the child. He fussed over her but worried about how he would have to spin a tale to the locals of his cousin 'getting in the family way' with someone who took advantage of her when she stayed over in Carisbrooke. "After the war we shall move to another part of the island and have lots more children. I cannot believe I am going to be a father. Your parents will be angry with us, me particularly. I suppose we had better think of getting married; after all your father is the Bishop of St. Albans."

"Don't worry Marcus, my father and mother will understand. I will write to them and explain. You saved me from the camp and we helped them after they escaped from the camp. They and I will never forget that. As long as we marry," Charlotte had told him.

"There is no-one else I could imagine living with for the rest of my life - marry me Charlotte now, this minute," had been his reply.

All this ran through his mind as he rode the butcher's bike with its large wicker basket attached to the handlebars. It was four miles ride from the Butcher's where he worked doing deliveries of rationed sausages, bacon, pork and lamb chops and mincemeat. Often hidden inside a wax paper wrapped order or in the hollow of the handlebars was an Iron Duke message. He savoured the late spring, after a long frosty winter with meagrely rationed food, looking out over the fields of wheat and yellow mustard, the flowers growing in the hedgerows alongside the dirty road that led to their cottage. He whistled 'One man went to mow' but soon found he didn't have enough breath to finish since he was pedalling uphill so he shifted to recollecting conversations with Charlotte who was waiting at home. She would have his tea ready.

"I'm home Charlotte," Marcus called as he closed the front door of their isolated cottage behind him.

"I'm in bed," she called out. He walked into her bedroom, "I'm getting birth pains, it's too early ... Marcus. I'm frightened things don't feel right ... fetch the doctor," her exhausted voice pleaded. He sat on her bed, took her hand and squeezed it looking concerned, gently touching her long fair hair and her smooth, pale, perfectly clear sixteen-year-old face, which was unnaturally flushed and covered with perspiration. She was still unbearably beautiful despite the pain revealed in her eyes and the tense gritting of her teeth.

I love you her so much it hurts. God, please help her and the baby.

"I'll bike up to the telephone box and phone him. Be right back," he called as he dashed out through the door.

The young man ran back to the barn and pulled out his bike. He was watched by the glowing green eyes of a large cat which peered at him in the gloom. The black feline creature rippled with muscles as he padded out of the barn to check on his master. "Aztec, climb into the cottage over the half door at the back. It's open. Look after Charlotte. I'll be right back."

The jaguar looked disconsolate and his tail zigged and zagged in impatience. He rubbed his taught black body against Marcus's legs then sprang powerfully towards the rear of the cottage as instructed. Marcus quickly registered that the bullet wound Aztec received last year from the German SD officer hunting the 'monstrous wildcat' terrorising the fascists on the island had completely healed. Aztec relished running across the fields of the island with Marcus, the human who had found him the runt of the litter left for dead when the circus fled the island just before the invasion. Marcus had told him to look after Charlotte who he also loved. Time to roam with Marcus later as they often did at night.

Marcus rode like a bat out of hell his raincoat flapped into wings as his legs pumped up and down athletically jerking the bike speedily along the lane to the telephone box at the road he remembered: "Marcus, I am thinking of joining the New Land Army, you know women farming. The phony prime minister is crowing about his great accomplishment, getting permission from the Jerries to have food grown by our Land Girls over a certain amount that is sent to Europe to be kept here. It would seem to be the only way to feed the men, women and children of our country until liberation."

Marcus recollected his reply. "You believe him?" *God don't let the baby or Charlotte die, or come to harm. Please let the doctor come quickly ... say it is something quite simple to fix.* As he glided downhill at bone-shaking speed his thoughts came quickly and unasked into his consciousness. His mind could not settle upon any one thing; it flipped back and forth pivoting upon the conversation they had about her desire to join the New Land Army. "You believe him-Lord Eastbourne?" he had asked.

"Not normally but I think he means this. If someone comes to cart off our produce and send it to Europe he'll get a bullet between the eyes from some resistance crack-shot."

"Yeah me, I'm a good shot with a pistol. I'm getting better with the rifle I have hidden. You know at night on my walks with Aztec or on resistance work I have my *Luger* tucked into the back of my trousers with my belt done up tight".

"I wish you wouldn't take it. You are going to get picked up by the Gendarmes one of these nights when you go rambling with Aztec after curfew. They'll arrest you and I'll never see you again."

"They'll have to catch me first. You know I'm the rain-coated rover of the Isle of Wight, famous in this cottage. It's Aztec who's famous throughout Great Britain as the nocturnal phantom, the giant wild-cat on the island. You know his species, the jaguar, means 'killer that takes his prey in a single bound'. By the way I have two points against you joining the land army. It's tough work and it could mean you moving away," he firmly stated showed he was frightened by the thought of her leaving.

"I've always wanted to work on a farm, my whole family picked hops in Kent every summer. I grew up with it. Silly, I can still stay here. A lorry can pick me up early every morning. it would be a local farm I work at. Besides it wouldn't be for too long. You see, I am expecting a baby."

"What? Marcus said in shock, "A baby. A baby is that what you said?"

"Yes, I am not expecting anything else. We did talk about it, we agreed. You haven't been using rubber johnnies for ages."

"I just thought it took a long time or that there was something about me ... that I couldn't ... that I was too young. It's different talking about it then hearing that you are going to have a baby." He sat down with a grin on his face, "I'm going to be a father." He said wondrously.

"With the baby we need more money coming in. I'll work until the doctor says I should stop then nurse the child. I'll go back to work after nine months. Mrs. McGarrity down the lane is good with children she has agreed to look after it."

"I love you Charlotte I will care of you and our baby," he kissed her tenderly and held her close. "And if you want to work if the doctor says it is alright, go ahead."

"Aztec will be jealous when there are four of us," she joked.

"He'll be fine. I'll still be getting him meat from the butchers and taking him hunting hares and deer. I can't believe it. I'll go and tell Aztec."

"Can't it wait just a bit?" Charlotte asked and kissed Marcus. That was months ago. Everything was going well until today and now she might lose the baby or die herself.

He made the phone call in the red telephone box marked 'George VI' since it was erected in 1938, before the King was killed in a Blitz attack on Buckingham Palace. Marcus put his pennies into the B slot dialled and pushed the metal button when he was connected and pushed the A button. It rang brrrr brrrr and was immediately picked up, "Fairview 55 Dr. Jeffries." Breathlessly Marcus blurted out, "Doctor, Marcus Jeffries. It's Charlotte the baby is coming early."

"Right Marcus, I'll be there in my car directly. You get back to her and try to keep her calm."

"Right Doctor. Bye."

*

The doctor closed the bedroom door to behind him. He knew and liked Charlotte and Marcus, he did not condone their relationship which had become obvious when she came to him with symptons of pregnancy but he respected them. He also was a member of the resistance and treated her father after the break-out from the concentration camp. He even knew about Aztec and was content to leave the four foot long beast lying on the wooden floor at the foot of the bed keeping guard over the sleeping young woman and the bundle she cradled. Dr. Thatcher woke up Marcus who had fallen asleep. His head slumped over the wooden kitchen table exhausted by worry.

"Marcus, Charlotte is sleeping, she is well but the baby did not survive. It was too small. I am very sorry."

Marcus registered shock and grabbed the doctor's arms. His mouth opened but nothing came out. "I tried everything even breathing gently into his small mouth."

"His mouth?"

"Yes. It was a boy. Marcus get a grip, you are both very young. You can have more children if Charlotte takes care of herself in her next pregnancy."

Aztec pushed open the door and padded upon the flagstone floored kitchen and rubbed his black muscular bulk against Marcus's leg as if consoling him, then pawed at the green door adding more scratches to the wood that he had marked since he was small enough to be held in Marcus's open hands. He was one hundred and eighty pounds of sleek muscle and tendon, sharp white teeth all held in a dark soft coat in a subtle roseate pattern discernable only close up and in good light.

86

"Now I want you to come and hold your son with Charlotte and spend a few minutes together. I'll make some tea. Leaving Charlotte clutching their baby Marcus joined Doctor Thatcher in the kitchen. He told Marcus that the baby must be buried soon. "I will phone Reverend Shepherd at All Saints and ask him to come by as soon as he can. I'll warn him about Aztec. Marcus, he may not be able to bury your son in the church graveyard, you are not married?"

"No."

"You love Charlotte and she will need you. Her grief will be strong for months. She's weak but I don't think she has to go to hospital. I'll be checking up on her daily. I've given her something to help her sleep. There is nothing wrong that time cannot heal. When the time is right and you are married you can try again for children.

"I'll be here for her."

"Good man. I know you are both young but you are both more adult than most of my patients twice your age. You know you have a friend in me. If you ever need anything my I will help and I am not the only one."

*

"Marcus Jeffries isn't it?" The vicar with brown hair falling over his forehead and a few youthful pimples fading on his face had an innocently taking in his dog collar and black clerical shirt enthusiastic manner which instantly endeared him to Marcus. Marcus looked him up and down taking in his dog collar and wrinkled black clerical shirt and scuffed shoes. It was the first time their vicar had entered their humble dwelling. "Yes, thank you for coming vicar, come in. At least your black shirt does not indicate you are a fascist blackshirt."

"I should hope not Marcus. How are you?" Prescot asked with sincerely.

87

Marcus replied "I'm numb, like I am acting in a play, nothing seems real. Can you bury a baby born out of wedlock in consecrated ground? I mean we aren't married but the baby … is innocent." Marcus glanced at the shoe box on the table and the priest's eyes followed the glance and understood that what was inside.

"Yes Marcus I can see that. My opinion about many things I used to think of as crucially important have changed since the occupation. The war has forced many of us in the Anglican Church to ask deep questions like what does God intend for us? What is important to his son Christ and to us? Number one is not following the phony Archbishop of Canterbury and his Nazi directives. Luckily he enjoys theological conferences and hijacking them so he hasn't changed things at the sharp end in the small parishes. We can still get away with being Christians. It has not come yet to swearing allegiance to the church of Adolf Hitler but it will be inevitable if we don't win the war. I have even heard that there is talk in Lambeth Palace and Whitehall about building new churches in the shape of swastikas as a millennium 2000 project, talk about long-range planning.

"I am more open to God speaking in my heart and my Bishop feels the same way. Consecrated ground, isn't it all of the British Isles consecrated now since our lads' blood has been poured into trying to stop the barbarian hordes?" he mused. "Isn't the whole planet Earth consecrated because it was created by God the father and given to us as stewards. And what a bloody terrible job we have been doing looking after it."

Marcus looked questioningly at the earnest young vicar. This did not sound like the previous priest at All Saints when he attended Sunday school.

"Yes, your baby will be buried in the churchyard. However in return I want you and Charlotte to marry let's say in two weeks as long as she's strong enough. We can talk about a headstone tomorrow the parish has a little money set aside for emergencies."

"I have some money from my parents I can pay for it and I will ask her to marry me, we ... we were going to wait until the end of the war but now ...." Marcus felt a lump coming up in his throat and swallowed. There was a friendly silence between them for a few moments. Marcus asked, "What about the banns you have to read them three times don't you?"

Reverend Prescot pursed his lips then brightened, "I shall read them but at special services for the elderly who are deaf and probably do not know you anyway or I could just mutter your names under my breath during the announcements. Or if you wish I could personally speak to everyone in my parish who thinks Charlotte is your cousin and explain the truth to them that there has been a tragedy but there is something we can as Christians do to help you both, to allow you to marry and have children in the future if that happens. You would not have to move away. *I will present it in such a way that there will be no objections. Being a vicar in a small community has its compensations, I know all their weaknesses and sins and I can use that knowledge to do God's work.*

Marcus grasped the rector's hand and shook it. "If Charlotte agrees I will do it Vicar." Marcus knocked on the wooden bedroom door at the end of the cottage hall and put his head round. "Charlotte, it's Reverend Prescott, Charlotte. He's come to see how you are." Marcus paced back and forth in the living room he could barely hear a murmur in the bedroom as the vicar and Charlotte spoke softly.

At least she wasn't crying, that had filled all yesterday and when she finally slept he had gone for a walk with Aztec, shedding a few tears kneeling by the cliffs looking out to sea. He had noticed bright lights on the horizon between him and the Needles at the west end of the island he estimated them about three miles away. There was a great roaring sound and a shooting star shot heading into the heavens, with two streaks of yellow and orange light pulsing behind it. Marcus was fascinated by aviation and in particular rocket experiments by the Germans and Russians before the war and was aware that inventors like the pioneering Godard and latterly Wernher von Braun had grandiose plans for rocketry. He took out a notebook and made a note 'New German rocket with two engines flying vertically upwards until it disappeared out of sight of the time. The engines burnt with pulsing yellow and orange light.' He added the probable location of the launch area. He knew that von Braun was involved with the rocket factory at KZ1 six miles away to east just inland from St. Catherine's Head. It would seem the Jerries were testing a new type of rocket. The young man had reported on S-1 and S-2 test flights before but this rocket was much more powerful.

German rocket test at night 2 am Friday? 29 April two engines with yellow and orange flame emissions pulsing for two minutes until it rose out of sight vertically into the sky. Estimated launch site three miles west of Brighstone, Isle of Wight, near or at the coast.

Possibly Freshwater Bay.

"Iron Duke should know of this, dead baby or not," he murmured to Aztec. He felt good that for a moment he was not thinking of the loss. Then the emptiness flooded back and threatened to engulf him and sweep him out to sea. He gripped Aztec as reassurance he was quite safe. The jaguar stood looking up at his master with green luminescent eyes reflecting the image of the full moon in each highly reflective eye, a sign Marcus had read indicative of the beast's ability to divine the future according to the natives of South America. Then Aztec lowered his head and lapped up some water from a puddle with an orange tongue.

While the vicar did all he could to reassure Charlotte, Marcus, back home, picked up the shoe box containing the body of their baby on the kitchen table. It felt lighter than a pair of shoes. He opened it and saw their son, William Winston, wrapped in a new linen tea-towel, his eyes were as if he were merely asleep, his little face serene in death. *Such delicate eyelashes and perfect fingers.* He replaced the top and held the wooden chair tightly.

The clock ticked loudly. After what seemed two, but was really fifteen minutes, the door to the bedroom opened and the priest walked into the living room. "Please go to Charlotte. She says if it is alright with you I will take the child and have it prepared for burial tomorrow at 2 pm at All Saints. She will come to the ceremony and I will ask some of your old school friends in the congregation to come. I will explain the need for discretion. How about I come and pick you up in my car at 11 am and take you home? My wife Judith and I will be pleased to have you come for lunch before the ceremony. But leave the jaguar at home, eh. He is the most amazing animal I have ever seen, I think he is behind all the folk lore about a big black cat on the island."

He winked at Marcus, "Don't worry I'm not going to tell the authorities, many of us are doing our humble bit to free Britain. Just don't bring him to the funeral."

"I don't know how to thank you enough," Marcus confessed.

When Marcus went into Charlotte's bedroom she was sitting up, her pillows plumped, looking out the window at the pine tree woods behind their cottage. She was pale but smiled at Marcus. Aztec was sitting on the floor his large paws resting on the quilt on the bed, looking like some strangely large and strong domestic cat. His large black head with long whiskers was resting on his paws. *It's hard to believe*, Marcus thought, *that this peaceful animal has knocked off more of the enemy than most seasoned soldiers. Appearances can be deceptive, after all I killed that German soldier on the cliff-edge with a rock and took his pistol in revenge for the death of my parents and I don't think I look like a madman.*

"Marcus, talking to Reverend Prescott was just what I needed. I'll get up shortly. I'll write a letter to my parents then we can walk to the pillar-box in the lane. But first I want to talk to you about the funeral tomorrow we must wear our best clothes."

91

Marcus bent down and kissed her cheek. Charlotte smiled. "When you're ready I want to talk to you about getting married," said Marcus, "doing things properly as soon as we can. Will you marry me as soon as you ... feel up to it? The vicar is going to square everything with the villagers we won't have to live a life of deception, except for our resistance work of course. We can wait as long as you like."

"I would be a fool to say no. I still want to work in the land Army and if I am married I can ward off the advances of any randy farmer by showing my wedding ring. Thank you Marcus- for loving me."

CHAPTER SEVEN   7MM WALTHER

New Scotland Yard once the envy of police forces around the world home of famous real and fictional detectives was now also the headquarters of the *Sicherheitdeinst* known for convenience as the SD, these were the SS Secret Police who had an even more ruthless reputation than that of the *Gestapo*. The SD had the top floors, the *Gestapo* had the first floor. They shared the bloody-walled cells in the basement; any prisoner sent there often wished he or she was dead. The pre-war police inspectors had been replaced by detectives with fascist credentials who had no sentimental attachment to habeus corpus or to any notion of suspects being innocent until proven guilty by a jury of twelve honest men or women.

Otto von Darmstadt leaned back in his chair stretched out his jack-booted legs and crossed them upon his desk. The *Hauptsturmfuhrer* was being watched by the bulging eyes of a pickled 'dragon' in a sealed glass jar. A strange dead creature, its claws sprouted pointed miniature daggers. The creature's lair on the desk was next to the silver-framed photo of his uncle, Count Manfred von Darmstadt in happier days as the first German governor of London before he was made wheelchair-bound by a Commando raid on the Tower. Otto von Darmstadt adjusted the magazine catch at the heel of the butt of his *Walther Pistole 38,* took out the magazine of eight 9 mm bullets and pulled back the slide to eject any round in the chamber. Following correct procedure he checked the chamber by looking inside the ejection port then he released the safety catch on the left side and pulled the trigger.

There was a soft click. Satisfied he pushed the magazine back into place and looked at a bust of Sherlock Holmes on a bookshelf on the wall which was missing his pipe, most of his deer-stalker hat, his nose, ears and eyes. He had blasted them all off as target practice. Von Darmstadt aimed his pistol at a colour photograph of a jaguar pinned to the wall in the adjoining room and fired. A hole appeared in the body of the black cat. *Good that's what I want to do to that big cat that almost killed me on the Isle of Wight. I can't say whether I would prefer to kill that cat first or one of the Stafford brothers or all three at once.*

His English driver and batman *Rottenfuhrer* Philip Grey called out from the next room. "Safe to come in *Hauptbanfuhrer?*"

"Yes, quite all right Grey." The German spoke excellent English he studied at Oxford before joining the SS like his favourite uncle. In 1937 a white-haired warder called Charlie Gates had given him, his uncle and Lord Eastbourne a fascinating tour of the Tower of London. Manfred was a protégé of the head of the SS, Heinrich Himmler and was a hero of the *Blitzkrieg* on Belgium. He almost succeeded in kidnapping princesses Elizabeth and Margaret but made off with some of the crown jewels instead. Later he succeeded in his mission to snatch the Duke and Duchess of Windsor from the Bahamas so Hitler could place them on the throne to do his bidding as Edward VIII and Queen Wallis. Grey entered thinking of how he hated von Darmstadt and all he stood for but his job as a member of the resistance was to learn what he could from the SD and funnel it back to Free London. The information he had passed on had allowed scores of resistance men and women to escape the clutches of the fascists in SD raids. "I think you need another bust of Sherlock Holmes, sir. I'll look out for one in the antique shops in Chelsea and Knightsbridge.''

As usual his superior did not listen but continued following his own train of thought. *To kill either Stafford, or both will be a real pleasure. First I shall shoot each in the ankles, then the knees then between the eyes.* Von Darmstadt looked at his pickled 'pet', 'Siegfried'. It had been presented to London's Natural History Museum in Kensington by the German embassy in the 1890s but the curators despite studying it and finding it flawless did not believe it was anything but a sample of clever German 'scientific' trickery. The SS man was realistic enough to know that most certainly it was a fake but a damned ingenious one. *Not a seam.* Realising Grey was standing in front of him, Otto von Darmstadt proclaimed, "SS men are mechanized fighting Teutonic dragons for the Third *Reich*, more noble and Aryan than John Stafford with those damned bedraggled Red Dragons fighting us in the wretched valleys and mountains of that God-forsaken dump of sheep faeces and rain, Wales." The SD officer thumped his fist fiercely on his desk making his small dragon jump in its formaldehyde solution then sink back into his normal rampant position standing on the base of the jar.

Grey winced inwardly at the Teutonic pomposity but kept his face emotionless. It was the best way to deal with von Darmstadt. Since his commanding officer had almost died on the Isle of Wight the year before trying to kill that big cat he was even crueller and more foul-tempered than before. Grey wore the British SS uniform of a Sergeant and was Otto von Darmstadt's assistant and driver. What the Storm Band Leader did not know or even remotely imagine was that Philip Grey, supposedly a loyal British Blackshirt from Leeds, was a member of the resistance who had infiltrated the SD HQ in New Scotland Yard.

"I'm going to the Tower, meeting with the governor and Heinrich Himmler then I shall visit my uncle at the Lord Mosley Hospital. Once you've finished typing those letters just put them on my desk for me to sign, then pull the file on suspected resistance fighters at the E. India docks, have my official Bentley's oil checked and clean it, then take some time for lunch. I'll drive my own car to my appointments."

Grey clicked his jackboots. "Yes, sir." He hid the disappointment endured whenever he heard the new name of the once proud King Edward VII hospital for Officers St. Agnes renamed in honour of the National Socialist Party's moustached founder, Lord Oswald Mosley who so admired Mussolini and Hitler. He was a British veteran of the Great War who had, in the 1920s and 1930s, become disenchanted with the slowness of the democratic government to respond to the social ills of Great Britain, the economic depression of 1929 and its refusal, in the British tradition of fair play and common sense, to blame the Jews and socialists as his fascist party did.   That the Jews and Communist intellectuals were to blame for all the problems of Great Britain was patent nonsense, believed only by a few of a population of thirty million.   With the occupation, Mosley's Blackshirts were instantly given power beyond their wildest dreams including those of Lord Eastbourne who became Prime Minister of Great Britain.

The officer stood up, placed his pistol in its black leather holster, put on his black SS cap at a jaunty angle and saluted as he left, "*Heil Hitler!*" Grey returned the salute and went off to his duties to which he added microfilming the Docks file. He could drop the film off to his contact at the Scotland Yard garage when he picked up the car.

Hauptsturmführer von Darmstadt zipped in and out of the London traffic along the Victoria Embankment comfortably sitting on the dark brown leather upholstery of his Alpine white sports car. He pressed the fuel pedal of the 1938 BMW 328 down hard. It responded with a surge of power and leapt towards his destination the Tower of London in the east end of London.

Showing his pass to the SS guards the feared officer screeched into the Tower and spitting gravel parked by the Tower Green, site of the execution of many famous prisoners such as Anne Boleyn and modern ones like Charlie Chaplin whose head had rolled, his blood staining the grass as the German axe-man slung the body onto a cart and wheeled it away. Chaplin left Hollywood and came back to Britain in 1940 to help orphans in London get out on the last trains to leave the capital. Then like the 'little tramp' character he made world famous in his films, he set out for the western ports and potential freedom hitching rides. Unfortunately he was recognised by a fascist who promptly handed him over to Mosley's men manning a roadblock in Salisbury. There was no trial, it was enough that he was on the blacklist of Jews and enemies of the *Reich* who were marked down for execution. He spent a week in the Tower then his head was struck off and stuck upon a spike on Tower Bridge until it rotted and fell off into the Thames.

A uniformed official greeted von Darmstadt's arrival at the governor's office in the White Tower. "*Reichsfuhrer* Himmler and London Governor Schmidt are waiting for you *Hauptsturmfuhrer*." After salutes the twenty-five-year-old SS officer was offered a seat by the governor. The head of the SS took off his gloves and sat down crossing his legs addressing his very junior officer in the *Reich's* elite fighting force. "You are needed to go on an archaeological trek into Asia and find a sword revered by the Muslims called Zulfiqar. The *Fuhrer* believes it has magic powers as well as being a powerful symbol. If it is in his possession it will increase his status in the eyes of the Muslim Arabs and Asians. They will rally to him and his friend the Grand Mufti of Jerusalem will declare a *Jihad* against the Allies. You have experience in investigating ancient ruins?"

"*Jawohl, Herr Reichsfuhrer*, I trained at Oxford then the University of Berlin reading archaeaology. I was on expeditions to Turkey and Mesopotamia in 1938 and 1939. I would be honoured to go."

"*Sehr gut*, the *Fuhrer* will be pleased you have agreed to lead the expedition. He is already impressed with the planning of the underground New Berlin in a secret location in Europe being undertaken by your uncle. Your SS archaeological squad have been hand-picked by me and will be in Berlin by the end of next week. They include three men who went with Ernest Schafer to Tibet in 1938 to find proof of the first Aryans, our Nordic ancestors, released from imprisonment in mountains by thunderbolts at the dawn of history."

Governor Schmidt, a Viennese who constantly munched on sweet pastries washed down by constant cups of strong coffee, held a plate, empty save for some crumbs and a fork. He turned his head interrupting his gaze upon the view outside his White Tower office and interjected, "*Herr Reichsfuhrer* I am fascinated by the World Ice theory that all life began from frozen water in space and on earth. The first Aryans, the super-race of which we are living guardians, were created and covered in ice in the mountains of Asia and released by thunderbolt energy. Our direct ancestors, pure, intelligent and strong, scattered and settled in northern Europe and India overcoming all attempts to defeat them. Most interesting!"

"Good to see you keeping up with the latest developments in German science, governor," Himmler took a sip from his gold painted porcelain coffee cup then continued. "Schafer is currently carrying out further measurements of craniums of Danes to map the spread of the Aryans to Europe in the mists of time. Darmstadt, your mission is of more immediate importance to the war effort. You will head a team to locate Zulfiqar and bring it to Berlin. We believe the sword is in Central Asia. Historians and operatives in the field have already been researching and making inquiries in Mecca, Jerusalem, Cairo, Syria and Istanbul. Ancient histories and legends tell us the sword was taken from Damascus far to the east along the Silk Trade route to China for safekeeping during the Crusades. Then it was lost in one of the bloody struggles for power with the Mongols in Afghanistan. Here is a report which will help you."

Schmidt finally ceased admiring the view of the green. He was proud to be in a fortress built by the bastard duke of Normandy known to history as William the Conqueror, a descendant of Vikings who had settled in Normandy across the German channel. William's massive fortress was completed in 1100 to consolidate his ruthless control of London and the kingdom after his narrowly won victory over his cousin, King Harold and his Saxon army at Hastings in 1066. Norman masons supervised by Gundluf, the Norman Bishop of Rochester used Saxon labourers to build upon the old south-east Roman wall of Londinium in the 1070s. Now the Germans were the new conquerors. "Here in the heart of London within the eleven-foot-thick stone walls of the Tower we must drink a toast to the success of your mission." He poured each of them a glass of Courvasier cognac and the three SS men lifted their glasses to the portrait of

Adolf Hitler on the wall of the governor's office from where he controlled the fascist 'above-ground' London, although sometimes he had a sinking feeling that the 'underground' movement' could never be eradicated completely. It always seemed to pop back no matter how many he shot. *Bury those thoughts they are not suitable for an Aryan destined to rule the world.*

"To bringing back the sword," Otto von Darmstadt toasted. "I have always been a hunter, now my prey is waiting. I shall just follow the spoor to its lair."

Exultant with his new assignment Otto gleefully listened to the New BBC Radio 2 channel of light music and quiz shows on his car radio. Contestants were answering questions about British history and hesitating on one question. "The War of the Roses 1455 to 1485. Come on that's easy," he called out at the top of his voice. He drove west along Piccadilly towards Belgravia past Hatchard's bookshop 'By appointment to His Majesty King Frederick' to his right on the south side, the Royal Academy with its marvellous courtyard passed by on his left and he passed Fortnum and Mason's and the Ritz Hotel just before Green Park. At the end of Piccadilly at Hyde Park he followed the road outside Apsley House, the Duke of Wellington's home and zoomed under the Wellington Arch which contained a small police office. A blue-uniformed constable stepped outside adjusting his helmet as the BMW sports car narrowly missed him. The PC swore it purposely tried to hit him. Looking at the German car he took down the licence number then cursed under his breath. "Arrogant bastard." He knew some people in Free London that could arrange something to happen to that car preferably while the driver was in it. There was no point following normal procedure, Germans were granted official 'diplomatic immunity' for any act.

Darmstadt chuckled at the look on the policeman's face as he glanced back in the rear-view mirror then drove right onto Grosvenor Crescent near Hyde Park in Belgravia. He had no time for the regular police; they represented the old Great Britain, not the SS - dominated new regime. He contemplated the history he had read of the hospital where his uncle was convalescing. It was founded in 1899 by two sisters who gave their home as a hospital for wounded officers returning to Britain from the Boer War. It was called the Edward VII Hospital for Officers Sister Agnes, after the Agnes referring to one of the sisters, the King who was the first patient. Now it had the same name as the man who led the one-party House of Lords. He saw the new metal letters LORD MOSLEY underneath the New British flag, a Union Jack with a circle in the centre showing the crooked cross, the Nazi swastika. He parked and left his car under the watchful eyes of four machine-gun toting gendarmes, burly British fascist policemen in black shirts, high-necked jackets, trousers, hats and jackboots. They saluted him with gusto throwing out their right arms, their armbands showing the New British flag, in the Nazi salute. *That is the face of New Britain*, thought von Darmstadt *and I love it*. He languidly returned their salute and made his way to his uncle's private room. The duty nurse told him that the patient was wheeling himself around the courtyard garden since it was such a lovely spring day.

"Ah, uncle Manfred I have news to tell you!"

Count von Darmstadt, SS *Gruppenfuhrer*, Iron Cross with oak leaf cluster, spun the thin, hard racing bicycle wheels of his specially designed aluminium wheelchair past a magnificent display of purple irises. "Nephew, I have news for you as well but yours first." Otto explained his assignment in Asia. "Very exciting! I know you shall succeed, that is why Germany is winning the war our intellect is superior. My news is two-fold; my surgeon Mr. Crusoe says I am well enough to go to Norway with a nurse and this wheelchair and," Manfred twisted himself around with an effort ensuring no-one was close enough to eavesdrop, "to supervise the building of my dream - the underground fortress redoubt of Aryan supermen and women, Valhalla."

"It has been approved?"

"*Jawohl*, Himmler himself came to tell me. Hitler signed the order beginning the secret construction of Valhalla using caverns carved out by tests of a new weapon. Manfred Von Darmstadt rolled his wheelchair to his nephew and excitedly shared his plans for a Nazi underground city which would preserve the Nazi civilization just in case the Allies were able to surmount the odds against them and subjugate Germany or even obliterate it with some, as yet unknown, super weapon.

"It will be in Norway under the ice. Only you and those in the highest authority will know of it, at the moment only Himmler, Doenitz and Hitler know of it. Not Goebbels, he may not be able to keep it secret while he sleeps with all those women, I feel for his poor beautiful wife. The underground city, a Nazi redoubt unknown to the allies allowing us to continue the war for centuries. It will be called Valhalla."

Otto remembered von Braun's ideas, including Nazi cities floating islands circling the globe like something from Gulliver's Travels then his uncle launched forth. "Asgard, the top of the tree of Nordic creation, Yggdrasil. Asgard was the home of two races of gods, the Aesi and Vanir. Each god had his own hall, the greatest of which is Valhalla the hall of slain Nordic heroes. I shall build it underground, safe from prying eyes. It shall be a last stronghold in case we lose the war, which I do not believe possible, but Hitler wants me it ready."

"Hmm," Otto said dismissively, we cannot be defeated, we are the master race. I will go to Asia soon and return bearing the sword once owned by Mahommet and use it to rouse the millions of Muslims under British rule from Cairo to Calcutta to rise up in revolt. It shall break up the creaking British Empire that is on its last legs."

"Nephew, tonight, since I cannot sleep for excitement, I shall design a wheelchair with an electric motor which I shall have built. Wheeling this is tiring and I want to conserve my energy for my work. It will be a good design for wounded German soldiers as they go back into civilian life." Manfred von Darmstadt felt a pain in his stomach reminding him of the wound that reduced him in one minute from an active SS officer with the world at his feet, to a bleeding wreck close to death, all hopes of continuing a glorious military career *kaput*.

"No word on the whereabouts of John Stafford yet? It would be a coincidence if you came across one of the brothers in your travels. He is out there somewhere."

"The Red Dragons are said to be in North Africa at least they were before the *Afrika Korps* withdrew.

There is also his brother who I almost killed at Kz1, I wonder where he is?" Otto knew that John Stafford was the Commando who left his uncle for dead in his attack on the Tower to free Edward VIII and Queen Wallis. *Wouldn't he be surprised to know that the Count survived the Canadian's sword thrust into his stomach and the hail of bullets that killed every other SS soldier they attacked. Manfred von Darmstadt would never walk again and would need a colostomy bag until the end of his days but he lived and was even more of a dedicated Nazi who had turned to big ideas rather than military missions to satisfy his ambitions.*

Back in his office Grey was quick to notice the good mood in which his commanding officer returned. "Hope you like the bust, sir. I think it is rather good."

"It is excellent and I shall save you future expeditions by refraining from shooting at it. I only do that when bored and I am certainly not now. I am off to Asia and I was wondering if you wanted to come with me."

"Thank you, sir. But I have to stay here, my mother in Leeds you see, she's very elderly and I must see her at least once a fortnight, that's where I go on my leave, sir."

"Very commendable, Grey. I'll let you off, this time."

*

Charlotte was rotating her new wedding ring upon her finger in frustration as they walked in the lane. "It's a mad scheme Marcus, absolutely bloody mad – oh you make me angry sometimes! I mean I am feeling better thanks to your loving care and you are letting me join the Land Army. I'm looking forward to starting tomorrow. I get a lift at 5 am. But really this plan of yours is crazy!"

"It's a bold plan Charlotte," Marcus defended his idea, "We get our SD chum von Darmstadt to worry about the big cat loose in London and stop him coming down to the island taking pot-shots at Aztec and disturbing our lives here. Free London needs us. Besides Aztec will like a visit to the mainland, tame stuff for him. You are feeling a lot better, we got married last week and we have had the best honeymoon of them all, here by ourselves happy. You start work tomorrow in the land army so it will be alright if I go for a few days."

"One of the biggest cities in the world crawling with Nazis, even the Londoners would be frightened of Aztec. I am now Mrs. Jeffries and I don't want you to go." She frowned but could not help laughing as Marcus grabbed her and began to tickle her.

"Well, Mrs. Jeffries that's true and I am very happy. It wasn't my idea, the Iron Duke people suggested it. It's my duty. I am taking him to Kew Gardens, it's a big park we'll be safe. I was there once with my parents. He'll love it. Free London is helping me once Iron Duke get me there."

"Kew Gardens?"

"Free London want to do some work in King George III's old palace at Kew and Queen Charlotte's cottage which are derelict at the moment. Under the guise of turning them into museums they are preparing them as resistance headquarters when the liberation comes. If there are sightings of a big cat it will put the fear of God into the Gendarmerie, and German patrols across London. It's all figured out, Charlotte," Marcus said, kissing her. "Droppings from the jaguars in the London Zoo will be scattered strategically every so often in Hyde Park or Regent's Park or Epping Forest coupled with rumours of sightings that will draw attention from Kew once we are long gone."

"Delightful, it sounds like mucking out the cow barn."

"Captain Bartlett has ordered up a moving van to come by with a crate for him. I go along as an assistant to the driver. Our cover is moving furniture from a house to London, we really do have furniture. We leave tomorrow morning early, I told the butcher I had to help my uncle moving some furniture. We have travel permits. He gave me some extra sausages to supplement our rations. I thought you would like them to keep up your strength."

Next morning the Bedford moving van marked 'Paddock's Furniture Removals' in orange script on the green paint of its panelled sides drove into the Kew Gardens' main gate in the south-west part of London. In the cab were Marcus and to his right the driver a member of Iron Duke who took over from Captain Bartlett at the ferry terminal on the island.

The aged watchman in his hut creaked to his feet like some 'Charlie', the name applied to overweight, drunken watchmen hired to protect fashionable squares of residences in west London from the mob in the 1700s when footpads and toughs with crazed hair called Mohawks stole and killed in the dark streets. One of the ancestors of the modern guard was a real 'Charlie' on watch in 1724 when he was enticed from his wooden hut and carried by a gang to the Thames, tipped in and almost drowning survived only to die of pneumonia a week later. This distant offspring left the warmth of his wooden shelter to speak to the driver.

"You delivering the items for the palace?"

"That's right mate, just come from Hampton Court with some furniture."

The watchman grumbled, "Just sign here, have to be so ruddy particular these days." He shoved the clipboard under the driver's nose. The gnarled watchman with a twisted nose, who reminded Marcus of the strange character who perched on a gravestone and frightened the life of the sexton in Mr. Pickwick, grunted as the driver returned the clipboard to his clutches. With a pang he realised he was missing their evening reading to Charlotte. They had started Boswell's Life of Johnson after finish Tolstoy's War and Peace. He regretted leaving her but she knew he had to help win the war.

"Bit late aren't you?" For a watchman who was supposed to have been 'squared' by Free London he seemed cantankerous. The driver decided he was one of them and put his lack of co-operation to deafness, crankiness and general old-age.

"We were loaded up at four p.m. but it took ages to get permission from some curator chap, didn't get away until six."

"You know where the palace is?" he snarled, it was a more of a statement than a question.

"Yeah, I've been bringing deliveries of furniture all week haven't I? Thanks anyway."

"Right," the old man said without looking back, eager to shut the door of his warm sanctuary from the world.

They drove into the large royal park known as Kew in the south-west of London on the south bank of the Thames. They drove down a narrow road, originally built for horses pulling carriages, about a quarter of a mile alongside what looked like a scenic man-made lake on their right and massive glass greenhouses on their left and parked the lorry in front of a large dark brick building in the Dutch style. It was built in 1631 by a Flemish merchant, Samuel Fortrey. George II's wife Queen Caroline chose it as the home for her three daughters in the 1700s.

The men in the lorry and the driver busied themselves helping the Free London worker unload the delivery of steel reinforcements to make the palace impervious to artillery fire and bombing so it could become one of several London HQs for the planned uprising. "The watchman will be kept quiet with lots of beer and brandy never fear", Marcus was told by the resistance operative in the run-down palace. Marcus slipped Aztec off his

105

lead and led him to the pond for a drink of water before ranging with his jaguar through the expansive grounds looking for a target. Climbing over a stone wall they moved through the shadows of the dark night and coming across a Gendarme walking away from them on patrol Marcus let Aztec go with a whispered instruction. The cat reached the fascist in just three or four bounds and bit into his head. As the man fell Aztec placed his paws on his back and coughed his victory cry. "Come on Aztec. Good boy." They climbed back into Kew Gardens leaving the body to be found and examined. The Gestapo ascertained that "death had occurred due to an animal attack possibly a large cat escaped from a zoo."

Within days it was all over London. "Did you hear about the Gendarme killed by an animal?"

"No but I'm happy about that. What the hell was it? A lion?"

"No-one knows, sounds a bit like those killings on the Isle of Wight. Strange that."

"We're a long way from there. Must be from the zoo."

*

At the new *Luftwaffe* concrete airfield at Heathrow, a pair of Junkers transport planes took off heading for the continent. One was heading for Berlin, the other for Norway via Copenhagen. Inside the first was a man looking for a legend. Inside the other was a man in a wheelchair who wanted to be a legend - the Nazi who ensured the *Reich* would survive any setback by building an underground city for Aryan warriors, a breeding ground in a subterranean fortress. Uncle and nephew waved at each other across the tarmac before the planes made their way one after the other.

In Kew that night as Marcus explored the three hundred acres of the gardens, they roamed to the very edge and Aztec came across a Gendarme patrolling on the street on the other side of a low wall. "Get him Aztec!" The jaguar responded with his trademark cough like the roar of a lion or the growl of a dog. He

106

leapt upon the wall and sprung forward leaping into the air and bit into the head of his victim and another enemy of freedom lay dead. The next day the London legend was born as the word spread. Marcus was ready to establish his pet's reputation as the nocturnal fiend in the imagination, what there was of it, of London's Gendarmerie and German occupation troops.

CHAPTER EIGHT   FREE LONDON

"Television has a very great future after the war. Perhaps it will completely replace the cinema."
Josef Goebbels' diary entry

Felicity walked gracefully through the lobby of the Savoy Hotel where she lived in a suite on the third floor overlooking the Thames. Her high quality tailored clothes, beautifully coiffured shining brown hair put up in the popular Regency style and confident carriage made eyes turn. She was on her way to catch a taxi to Jonnie Hawker's haute couture shop House of Mayfair on New Bond Street where she worked as fashion designer.   Blue-overalled workmen were installing a large wooden box with a glass screen by the wall between some soft chairs and a couch.

"Roberts, what's that?" she asked the doorman.

"A television, Miss Felicity," he replied, "we had one here before the war but with Chamberlain's declaration of war the broadcasts from Alexandria Palace stopped. The 'loyal' BBC has started them up again, beaming across the British Isles. You're going to Ireland next week aren't you maybe they will even have it there?"

"What an amazing world we live in Roberts," she proclaimed conspiratorially in her soft voice her green eyes soft with amusement.

"Yes isn't it just? Perhaps," he lowered his voice to a whisper, "not quite as we would like but we're working on it," he tapped the side of his nose. He, Rogers the lift operator and the manager knew that Felicity was a member of Free London. They did not know however, how important she was in gathering and passing on information she gleaned in her elite seasonal circuit of fashion shows, horse races, gallery shows, operas, theatre opening nights, film premiers, cocktail parties and night clubs of the West end overrun with fascist politicos and military personnel with secrets to spill when they were drunk.

*

At the University of Toronto's baronial Hart House Lieutenant Colonel Henri Le Meseurier lit a cigarette from the fire raging in the medieval castle-size fireplace at the university's neo-Gothic student building built by the Hart family. He and his old friend Colonel Desmond Stafford stood amiably as old comrades. On the walls above them stood rows of wooden painted shields depicting the coats of arms of universities of the Allies in World War One: Russia, Britain, France and Italy. "It eez always good to see you my old comrade," Lt. Colonel Le Meseurier said as he lit Desmond Stafford's cigarette from his own. They both smoked in silence locked in memories of smoke and flames, the battles in the trenches through which they fought and led men. They had survived and had children but still felt that faint aura of guilt old soldiers of whatever rank always feel after combat even decades later, the guilt of surviving, of wanting to make the most of it in thankfulness and as a tip of the hat to those who could not be with them. Desmond looked up at the painted wooden shield depicting the red dragon of the University of Kazan and felt a pang in his heart as he thought of his eldest son John 'somewhere in Morocco' and of youngest son Alan on special duty in the Middle East.

*

Seventeen-year-old Patricia White stood blinking in the spring sun as she emerged from the Cannon Street tube station at 8:40 am. She had taken the eight o'clock train from Weybridge, Surrey where she lived with her parents to Waterloo Station where she caught the Piccadilly Line north to Charing Cross then switched to the eastbound Circle Line to Cannon Street in the heart of 'the City' the financial centre of London. She observed armed Gendarmarie on patrol, one of them waved her over and checked her cardboard identification card. "Better get to work sweetheart," he told her shoving the card back into her hand. "Don't want to be late do we?" *I can't get used to Gendarmes in jackboots sticking*

109

MP38 machine-guns up your nose while asking for tickets and i.d. cards whenever they feel like it. It makes my skin crawl,'' she thought, *even if I have been to London several times since the occupation for Christmas shopping and to see a concert with Mum and Dad at Wigmore Hall or a ballet at the Royal Albert Hall.*

She stood on the south pavement of Fleet Street several hundred yards east of St. Paul's Cathedral and west of the Tower of London looking up at the three floor Portland stone Art Deco building. She did not know Felicity and her spying antics in Mayfair or the fact that she had once been near to being thrown off the top of the cathedral by a *Gestapo* agent, having killed another in a hair-raising chase up the stairs to the top of the massive dome, if she had she would have expressed total admiration. An inscription on top of the building proclaimed it to be

THE LONDON CHAMBER OF COMMERCE.

She took a deep breath; in a few minutes she was to report for her first job interview as a typist. Crossing the road she noticed that against the blue sky marbled in the east by clouds the building was limestone grey, still boasting the sheen of new stone. The smoke from a million house coal-fires and factories had only just started to make a mark on it since it was built in 1937. There were a few light grey cement marks where pock-marks from bullets fired in the battle of London had been filled in. They straddled the brass numbers indicating 75 on Cannon Street to the left of the square doorway with two steps that led up to it from the busy pavement. The street was at one time the site of cannon foundries, hence the name.

The young woman looked up at the bronze torches with bird decorations bracketed high above the entrance. The metal birds' open wings flew up and supported the cup of each torch. Businessmen in bowler hats and wing collars and holding black leather briefcases walked by in earnest conversation about the state of the New British pound. A prosperous executive secretary from another building walked by, a fox fur complete with paws dangling and a plastic nose and eyes draped over the padded

110

shoulders of her coat. Pat was wearing a new Marks & Spencer's brown coat with a fashionable wide belt and pleats in the front and back. It had cost her all her saved up clothing rations but she wanted to look smart on her first day. The coat matched her light brown wavy hair which she managed to make less curly than it really was with the help of her friends and advice from her mother who had the same problem. She felt better seeing the birds, taking them as a good omen. She had studied a pocket dictionary in case there was a spelling test. Her mother had given it to her to read on the train from Weybridge, Surrey. She walked up the steps and pushed the door open.

"You look a bit thin for your age Patricia, Miss uhm," the interviewer glanced at her then down at her application form, which had been neatly filled out. "White. Must be the rations."

She ignored his comment. "My headmaster at Weybridge Grammar gave me this reference."

The supervisor read it and nodded. "Very good Miss White, you are 'intelligent, industrious, honest and punctual' and you 'can type seventy words a minute'. I think you will increase your speed with practice, you shall be working with us if you can start today that would be well. We have a lot of typing and our girls are having a hard time since we are so short, a lot of them were selected for the munition factories in the east end last month." He sighed.

Pat wondered, *does he hate the Germans, expressing it subtly with that sigh? Or is he just exasperated by the fascists taking his workforce without warning. 'Be cautious, girl', my father warned me. Not everyone is what they seem but thank God most are for the Queen and our good old England. But keep yourself to yourself until you get to know them,* wise words Pat decided. After all her father was in the resistance, but she knew that but no details, certainly not that he was one of the most important figures in Free London. She knew enough to fear for him though, for the future of Britain, for her own children if she ever had any. *I too will give my life if I have to,* she vowed.

Her boss showed her to her desk and introduced her to the floor manager. She took off her coat and hung it on the wooden coat hanger in the office. The secretaries sitting at their desks watched as the new girl walked to an empty desk at the left side of the room at the back.

She enjoyed her work typing up letters and taking phone messages and before she knew it was quitting time. She stepped out into the 'Çity' joining thousands of other men and women heading home. The pre-war square mile of the financial centre of Great Britain and the Empire, sharing with New York the stature of the world's foremost financial centre, had shrunk to being the financial centre only of New Britain subservient to the stock markets of Berlin and Frankfurt.

She brushed her brown, curly bangs off her forehead and straightened her Alice band in the window of a Boot's chemists as she walked to the nearby corner and crossed at the Belisha beacon controlled zebra crossing, so named for its white stripes on the black ashphalt of the road indicating a crossing for pedestrians. Drivers of taxis, buses, cars, motorbikes and lorries, going about their business in London were warned by the orange globes of the striped beacons that a zebra crossing was painted on the road and everything stopped. Except for a Gendarme armoured car which screeched around a corner and ran through the zebra crossing, almost bowling over the young lady. A German officer on the pavement cursed in German and English at the Gendarme commander who looked down superciliously at his victim, "Stupid *schweinhund*, you almost killed this young lady. You give the master race a bad name. No wonder the average Londoner hates us." He turned to Pat and held her arm gently, "Are you all right, Miss?" he asked while thinking this young lady was very much like his daughter back in Hamburg who had just joined the *Kreigsmarine* as a stenographer.

"Thank you," Pat said, surprised that a German officer could be so kind, but then it should not be such a surprise; "There are," her father maintained, "good and bad on both sides but one side has ruthless evil leadership totally committed to ruling the world and destroying all that is good, and they have a lot of people supporting them." *This man, Pat wondered, must be unusual in a world where all the children were being raised to worship Hitler and Nazism, he represents the old Germany. He must be from the old school.*

"I have a daughter back home your age. Let me walk you to your destination. I assure you I have only gentlemanly intentions."

"It is all right. I am just going home after my first day at work over there."

"Well let me wish you luck." He read the name on the building she pointed at, "London Chamber of Commerce, an excellent place to start a career in business. I will say *auf* ... I mean goodbye, perhaps we shall meet again I often walk this way." Pat said nothing but could not help being mollified despite her resolution to not fraternise with the enemy. *What a shame we have to fight the good ones as well as the bad,* she thought. Her father was a resistance leader in Free London and she was determined to get this job and do well, and keep her eyes and ears open to pass on any information about fascist banking or other details that might be useful. It was the duty of every true Briton to do what they could.

All seven hundred and twenty sirens positioned on rooftops across the sprawling metropolis of London went off for the first time at ten o'clock that April evening 1944 the night of a full moon, a bomber's moon. HMS Bulwark a berg ship using shadow radar equipment to fool enemy radar sailed off the coast of Ireland launched eleven squadrons of Lancaster and Halifax bombers hit the docks and munitions factories and military HQs with pinpoint bombing. The planes were joined by squadrons of B-29s and Lancaster bombers from Iceland. This was the first 500 plane raid on Britain using Logie-Baird's infra-red television equipped guided or 'clever bombs' allowing bomb aimers to see on a screen where the gliding bombs were going and guide them using radio signals to lead them to their target minimizing civilian casualties.

Bombing of anything but military or essentially strategic targets like aircraft and tank factories or oil refineries were discounted by Attlee and the war cabinet as a waste of aircrew and civilian lives. Baird's invention of Tele-control and Barnes Wallis's air-to-ground missiles enabled the commander of joint RAF-RCAF Bomber Command Air Marshal Harris to order 'spot-on' raids with precision weapons.

In their two floor semi-detached brick house in Weybridge that night Pat helped her brother pull down the blackout curtains and went to bed early with some books and her diary. When there was an air-raid she took her diary out to the shelter in the garden and wrote in it during the night and at breakfast the next morning. *'Air raid by Allies on London docks and aircraft factories by Lancaster and B-29 bomber planes. The sirens went off at eleven o'clock and we went into the Anderson shelter at the back of the garden, we are getting more air raids recently. Dick says the long-range bomber aircraft take off from Iceland drop bombs then fly on to Morocco where our boys are now with the Yanks and Canadians. There are safe airfields there and fighters escort them south.*

'We are all counting down the days to Monty coming back with a liberating army. Mum and dad say it may be a long time - years, Dick says anything could happen but until then 'I'm going to enjoy life as much as one can.' With his weak heart he is exempt from call-up which is good because he hates the fascists, it would kill him to wear one of their uniforms. He groans every time he reads about the fanciful exploits of the New Royal Air Force or New Royal Navy. He's a 'cub' photographer with the local newspaper, the Surrey Gleaner, and wants to own a newspaper one day after the war.

I made some notes about the people at work I have an idea for a short story. I'll think about it on the train tomorrow. ...

7 am the next day

The All-Clear sounded at 1 pm I was told but I slept through it. Toast and a tiny spot of butter and marmalade for breakfast with a cup of coffee and milk. No tea to be had anywhere since stocks ran out in 1941. Must go to catch the train."

That evening, the time of the largest ever air raid on the docks, tank and aircraft factories, in London Felicity selected a bolero to wear the next day at an engagement garden party at Buck House for King Frederick and Princess O-No. Outwardly it would show she was thinking of New Britain's new ally, Spain, in the fight against the allies. As the air raid sirens wailed and the lights on the streets were turned off she joined the rest of the guests in the air raid shelters in the cellar. She was rather impressed, despite herself, by the Japanese princess who had a reputation for licentious living in rebellion against the strict protocol and conservatism of her uncle Hirohito's court. Looking ageless, she enjoyed passing herself off as an immature thirty or mature nineteen-year old as the mood took her. Carrying herself as a giggly young lady O-No had visited the showrooms in New Bond Street, insisting her chauffer carry in a silver tray with champagne and two glasses and serve her and Felicity's boss about a designing a wedding dress with Japanese touches. Jonnie Hawker asked Felicity to come into his office and meet the important client who was accompanied by two Japanese secret policemen in pinstripe brown suits and trilby hats.

The short princess held out an elegant black-gloved hand, "Delighted to meet you Miss Felicity. I have admired your designs. Your Empire line gowns for the leading ladies in the latest Noel Coward play are ravishing." Her English was coming along very well but what she saw in the regal tub of lard known as King Frederick, a womanizing, German prince before being hoisted onto the throne of New Britain by Adolf Hitler and Lord Eastbourne, was beyond Felicity. He was a triple chinned, comical monarch of great girth, likeable if you forgot he was a stooge for

Eastbourne and his cronies. He seemed to exaggerate his own behaviour in a purposeful parody of the brandy swilling, food loving, saturnine figure personified by George IV in the Regency period. After all George IV was his Hanovarian ancestor hence Frederick's weak claim to the throne. As soon as George VI was killed in the blitz, Princess Elizabeth was the next monarch but Queen Elizabeth the widow decreed that her daughter deserved to live out most of her teenage years maturing as any other young adult and cope with growing up without her father and mother, then face the onerous task of becoming monarch. Victoria had become a very good Queen aged eighteen on the death of her uncle William IV. People forgot that she was once a fun loving young lady who fell head over heels for a dashing young Prince Albert. But those were more innocent days in many ways for civilisation. The outlaw Queen Elizabeth knew her daughter had the potential to be as great a sovereign as her Tudor namesake. It was what she prayed for every night.

*

At Killarney in the scenic Dingle Peninsula of Ireland the placid, if poverty-stricken days of horses pulling carts of locals had been replaced by the tanks and lorries of the mechanised National Socialist state of Ireland. Hostages were rounded up and driven to the country knocked unconscious then held up by strong-armed SS men against the barn doors of a farm. Japanese soldiers hammered one foot nails into their hands and feet. Japanese officers with smart brown caps and uniforms and brown jackboots directed that the men impaled upon the wooden planks be positioned in quads to make swastikas. Memento photographs were taken.

Two hundred miles away in London, the business of the day continued in the financial heart of fascist Britain. The great clock in St. Stephen's Tower in the Parliament buildings known as Big Ben, was once again working after crucial cogs, taken and hidden during the Battle of Britain were finally replaced by custom made replacements. The originals bided their time greased and lovingly wrapped, buried in metal containers in the large back

116

garden of the Lamb and Cauliflower pub in Surrey. Free Londoners ensured that sand was strategically sprinkled inside the clock gumming up its works so the hands stuck at eleven o'clock. As Radio Free Britain broadcast that night 'from somewhere in England'.

'Big Ben was allowed to work for one day so Londoners could once again enjoy its chimes, then was stopped at 11 o-clock am the time at which the 1918 armistice occurred ending the First World War and sealing the victory of Great Britain and the Allies on the eleventh hour of the eleventh day of the eleventh month 1918.

Last night a 500 plane raid on London and other targets was made by aircraft of the RAF and RCAF. All but seven aircraft made it safely back to Allied airfields. The targets included the London docks and factories making tanks and aircraft."

Felicity considered her past and her husband hundreds of miles away in goodness knows what situation. It was 1938 when John was a callow youth, visiting England and going to Germany for his studies as a spy for her father and Beaverbrook and in the background loomed the portly figure of Winston Churchill friend of Beaverbrook and Colonel Le Meseurier, moving heaven and earth in his wilderness years to prepare Great Britain for the inevitable fight that was brewing with *Herr Hitler* and the English-speaking world. In that summer of uneasy peace when Chamberlain falsely declared 'Peace in our time' John first declared his love for his childhood friend. From that moment it was understood they would marry one day.

They did marry at Hastings, Sussex on the south coast of England in 1941 but in circumstances that neither of them could possibly have imagined in 1938 when they fell in love. Then he was sixteen. She was one year older. Then war clouds gathered but who could have foretold the effective lightning strikes, the *Blitzkriegen* that forced France to sue for peace and saw a successful invasion of Great Britain. 1941 saw John and Felicity fighting for liberty in the resistance movement, she in London as a spy working as an haute couture designer and he as a Commando officer in, arranged to meet in Hastings and were married. The ceremony was held at the small church in Battle at the site of the Battle of Hastings where another invader, William the Conqueror defeated the Saxon King Harold.

Just yards from the River Thames by the Victoria Embankment in the Savoy Hotel, hard by the statue of the Boadicea, the ancient British Queen who rose up against the Roman invaders, Felicity Le Meseurier was leaving the hotel. She clutched an Arctic fox white fur around her shoulders, took one of the taxis lined up at the front door. The dove-grey uniformed doorman saluted by touching his finger to his top hat "Good evening Miss Felicity, off to the opera this evening are we?"

"You always guess correctly, Rogers." Rogers, and Robert the lift operator, were two of the staff who knew she worked for Free London because they themselves were part of it, up to their collars in the war against evil. She might pick up an interesting piece of unofficial gossip about a certain officer or politician that might lead to important revelations useful to SOE intelligence. She was part of the elite, the cocktail set of fascist wives, mistresses and New Royal Air Force, Army and Navy officers, politicians, civil officers and civil servants ensconced in the thousands of offices of the fascist civil and military service in the Portland stone buildings of Whitehall containing warrens of offices. London society based in the swanky west end area known as Mayfair knew her, as the New Times wrote; "that charming fashion designer who successfully captured the folk costume of the German empire in the season of 1942 and now was launching some dynamic new designs turning heads in the fashion shows in Paris and Berlin. Her latest cocktail dresses, original creations that despite being based on ancient Athenian sculptures and depictions of women on pottery had the air of a futurist space-cadet made famous by the stories of the darling of the new British intellectual classes, Jeremy Parker, who dreams of British Nazis landing on the moon and setting up a colony, fending off allied spaceship attacks for centuries. These costumes and stories have the air of promise about them, the bright future of the rest of the century and the 21st century that beckons the fascist states of the Axis alliance once the present struggle is won."

Felicity held her forehead which felt as if it was rising up fast like a balloon above the clouds and beyond to outer space where she felt one day men and women would fly and spin and cartwheel. She felt one of her daydream visions coming, imagined a million birds, empty streets and buildings, parks and cars of New York, an ocean filled with submarines, a space vessel with animals walking, padding, flying and slithering into it, Wales in great chunks with slices of ocean lifted as if by magic into the spaceship. She saw Russia, piles of fire half a mile high and a bearded baby, a future Tsar. The lake is black the silver-hilted sword Excalibur is lifted up through the surface in the sparkling sun by the Lady's hand which throws it into the hand of a young man on the shore. It is far into the future. *He speaks to me with his thoughts but I do not understand the language ... it sounds ...* she concentrated ... *no damn it, it's gone for now.*

The freely elected Parliament, presided over by Prime Minister Winston Churchill, had been replaced by a fascist House of Commons and House of Lords, packed with sycophantic Nazis and hangers-on. Double-decker buses and taxis took tourists from across *Gross Deutschland* and beyond to see the sights. Ironically during the nightmare of occupation London at night was once again lit up, ending the blackout, it was suggested by King Frederick to raise fascist morale and supported by the governor of London who saw it as a means of being better able to catch Free London fighters moving at night. The German-born King Frederick reigned from Buckingham Palace where King George VI was killed on the first day of the invasion wearing his admiral's uniform in a blitz attack on London. Queen Elizabeth although wounded in the eye was taken to hospital and broadcast to the nation later that day on BBC Radio vowing that Britain would not give up. She refused to leave in the evacuation but did send her children, the Princesses Elizabeth and Margaret to Canada. Now they lived in the Chateau Laurier Hotel in Ottawa with their grandmother, the dowager Queen Mary. As they grew older they were becoming more involved in royal duties, especially the eighteen year old heir apparent who every few months became Honorary Colonel, commander and patron to another regiment, squadron or organisation attending or attended more ceremonies and received politicians and diplomats and visiting dignitaries. Prime Ministers Attlee and Mackenzie-King talked with her about politics and constitutional monarchy and she was taught by experts on constitutional history, French, and world history. Princess Margaret fourteen years younger also attended important parades, christened ships, visited wounded servicemen in hospitals or gave out awards. Their mother the Queen Elizabeth became Regent until Elizabeth reached the age eighteen when she would be proclaimed Queen. The 'Outlaw' Queen Elizabeth, mother to the Princesses, was the legendary eye-patched, revolver toting leader of the resistance movement in Scotland. She flitted from farmhouse to castle, pub to church or fisherman's cottage, keeping one step ahead the enemy a price on her head of 10,000 New British pounds. Although she could not visit the regiments, naval and air force units with which she had strong links, such as the Irish Guards and the Black Watch, she was able to write to them. Queen's messengers carried her dispatches from Scotland to Canada.

The nation-wide rationing system saw to it that only the British fascist elite enjoyed a pre-war middle-class standard of luxury, while the majority of the population survived on barely sustainable levels as socialised industries sent materials to the continent arming the German war machine. Only members of the National Socialist Party of New Britain and registered supporters, possessed A level identity cards and the masses of soldiers and Gendarmes armed with machine-guns could stalk the famous streets like Piccadilly, Regent's Street and Berkley Square, the West End theatres and the nightclubs of Mayfair and Soho, after nine o'clock in the evening. London's governor, *SS Reichsfuhrer* Gerhard Schmitt, ensconced in the Tower often thrilled to the swooping of the Tower's eagle as it hurtled like a dive-bomber at any creature that dared to creep across the green where the executions took place. "I take care of the larger vermin my Eagle takes care of the smaller. It works well I think,' he confided to Princess Ono and King Frederick when they came for an eight course meal which included a rabbit caught by the eagle 'Hohernzolern' nicknamed '*Stuka*'.

In the foundations of the Great Fire of London Monument in Pudding Lane a few hundred yards east of St. Paul's and just north of the river Thames was the location of the telescope observatory built into the monumental column by Sir Christopher Wren. It was surmounted by a burning globe gilded in gold. It commemorated the 1666 fire which began in Pudding Lane at a bakery and spread throughout the city over two days. The narrow roads and closely built wooden houses of the old city ensured that the fire spread quickly until it was stopped by soldiers and citizens blowing up houses with gunpowder to create firewalls at the command of King Charles II. Over the next decade a new, better planned city grew with many of the old churches rebuilt by Wren. The telescope was gone but in its place was a VHF radio transmitter sending and receiving signals to and from Iceland and Gibraltar which could not be picked up by the Germans. This was the communications HQ for Free London. John Torrey and Joseph White leaned forward as C spoke to the assembled Free London executive.

"The day of the coronation the enemy will be expecting us to disrupt the service at Windsor Castle by some kind of attack. It worked last time when a sniper got Goering at King Frederick's coronation. This time we will do neither of these things we will instead begin the '1,000 days to Liberation campaign. It is designed to demoralise the home-grown fascists and remind the Jerries that they are unwanted guests who will eventually be ejected. I can tell you tonight that Attlee and Roosevelt will soon declare that within 1,000 days New Britain will once again be Great Britain. To co-incide with the landing of an allied army within three years we will begin stockpiling arms for the London uprising which is being planned so that we can take over control of the city and docks when the time is right and we are given the order. John and Joseph chortled with anticipation that they might live to see the day when freedom reigned once more. C began to explain how certain buildings had been selected and even now were being prepared, for use as headquarters. They listened fascinated, proud to be part of such an immensely important moment in history.

CHAPTER NINE   OWEN AND THE CHILDREN

The twelve children played happily upon the rocky shore, a buffer zone of sand and rocks between sea and land. The western promontory of Point Grey, an arm thrust from the British Columbia mainland of North America into the Pacific, protected the large port of Vancouver just a few miles to the east. Wreck Beach lay below the cliffs upon which had grown the buildings of the University of British Columbia during the first part of the twentieth century. Oblivious to the blustering wind the children hopped and slipped over weedy stones in the ragged but happy group children will form in the opposite way aircraft fall into squadrons and infantry into precise clockwork-like columns. The boys and girls were different sizes, but all were between eleven to sixteen-years-of-age. The youngest dawdled at the back, Nicholas Hind. He was an eleven-year-old from Port Stanley, Falkland Islands intrigued by a seal staring at him with large unblinking black eyes. It looked towards him, its head poking out of the waves like a soft submarine, and then dived down into the cold salt water. The group were slowly making their way toward a pillbox containing a five-inch gun manned by a squadron of bombardiers in the Royal Canadian Artillery. It looked out to sea at the bottom of the steep trail that led up the cliff to the university campus where they lived and studied.

The gun and its crew peered out over the rolling waves of the Pacific Ocean scouring the sky and the sea for any Japanese ships or aircraft. For this was March 1944 at the western frontier, along with Vancouver Island just twenty miles further west in the Pacific, of the Allied ground held against the fascists who controlled all Europe, except for Iceland, most of South and Central America and two chunks of the southern United States. In Mexico, two thousand miles to the south, General Patton's 6th Army fought like madmen. He was leading his victorious army through Mexico on its way south to Panama leaving blazing wreckage of columns of German and Japanese tanks, trucks and fascist troops in the tens of thousands behind him. Taking a seaport on the eastern coast of Mexico was a brilliant battle helped by the new four engine super bombers, Boeing B-29s which could carry heavy thermobaric bombs from airfields in the USA. The harbour had been full of Japanese and Latin troopships, freighters and warships when the 'big-birds' arrived in a 200 plane raid covered by Mustang and Thunderbolt fighter planes equipped with long range fuel tanks extending their range. Within ten minutes the attack on Pearl Harbour was avenged tenfold.

He was oblivious to any talk about bringing his army back to the USA to liberate the occupied states. His reply to commander of the army General George Marshal's order to halt his drive south and allow the United States to be secured from the invader was a harsh reply that included a fair number of swear words. "General, sir, I am afraid that the connection is not good I cannot hear you very well,'' Patton grunted chomping on a cigar "We are whipping the enemy and Goddam' it I am going to keep going until we have killed every one of them and then I shall come back and clean up any my colleagues have not dealt with. Better I keep myself from the plague bacilli, I give 'em a few days after they meet me and they will be dead! What did you say General? ... Lots of atmospheric interference, Sir, I have to go. Over and out.''

The wild figure leading the children, although hardly taller than the eldest of them, was a white haired man clutching a carved oaken walking stick. His long hair was whipped by the wind making him look like a Blakeian prophet in one of those Regency poet-artist's hand-painted prints. Beneath his coat and clothes a perceptive observer could pick out the muscles and tendons delineated in the red William Blake so loved, red from fires blazing from the combustion of imagination and prophetic intensity. But the children were not afraid, he had a friendly soft face, a restrained low voice and a heartfelt smile.

His name was Owen Gryffyd, a Welsh Druid. He had met their parents and sworn them to secrecy under the Official Secrets Act. Owen had assured them that the children would not be mistreated stating only in the vaguest terms what it was they would be doing. "Research has shown that children at the threshold of becoming young adults, entering puberty in other words, are at their most potentially powerful in a kinetic or clairvoyant sense. These particular children have been selected because they were known to have abnormally strong psychic powers, able to move objects, such as clock hands, cars or concrete blocks, cause time to slow down or even disappear from human sight.

"We, with your support and assistance, can work with these exceptional young people to harness these powers and use them in the war effort to defend what is most dear to us, our freedom, their future. This document you have all read and had a chance to think about before signing assures you that they will be looked after, well educated, provided good room and board and fairly supervised and disciplined by our team of teachers, house matrons, nurses, medical doctors and psychiatrists and you shall be allowed to see them on a regular basis. Having you live nearby will be a great support to them. The weekend will normally be free for everyone unless we are working on a special work. Sometimes we may have to travel with the children to safe areas of Canada or America you will be notified of this in advance and asked for your permission to have them travel with you. If circumstances are such that you are separated they will be encouraged to write to you but it will be censored, just like the mail and telephone calls of everyone involved in this project.

"You are asked to not tell anyone of their work, the cover story is that each child won a scholarship from a Canadian foundation, the Future Scholarship Trust associated with the University of British Columbia, to provide education in the environs of a university to help develop their intellectual powers, emphasising diplomatic skills and international co-operation to help rebuild the world after the war. I have shown you their classrooms and introduced you to the psychic and regular teaching staff who will be teaching and personally tutoring them. While we want them to help the world when they mature, their main and top secret work at the moment however will be helping us research the secret talents with which God has endowed them and, without harming them, study their psychic skills and develop their those gifts to help the Allied war effort. They will not be put in situations of danger other than that of living like the rest of us in a country at war. In fact, we shall give them extra protection because we believe they are very special. Of course we shall ensure that they do not have more than a healthy pride in their studies and work, we do not want to create a spoilt, arrogant elite. We'll leave that to the Nazis."

The forty-three-year old was the leader of the White Eagle Lodge of witches, spiritualists and psychics summoned by Churchill to fight Nazis in 1940. In October that fateful year, Owen Gryffyd was ordered to take as many of the secret weapon as he could to Canada and continue the psychic war from there. For over three years now he had led a band of American, Canadian and British psychics based in Canada. He had, with his eloquence and tenacity, united a disparate group of native shamans, witches and clairvoyants into an effective force secretly operating in what would have been considered a laughable type of warfare by the uninitiated. During the Battle of Britain Churchill left no stone unturned in his bid to wage total war. He asked Tudor Pole to help organise well known spiritualists and witches recruited into the lodge. Roosevelt, Clement Attlee and Mackenzie-King eventually also became convinced of the value of this strange group of men and women. Consequently, after Churchill's death from a heart attack in Australia at an Imperial War Conference in 1941 all that he had set in motion, continued. Lodge members had created a North American 'go away powder' and, perhaps co-incidentally, where most of it had been used, Allied forces had managed to at least hold back enemy advances far longer than could normally be expected, but it had not prevented an unexpected series of invasions of California, New Mexico, Louisiana, Texas and Florida by German-Japanese and Latin forces.

Their first group activity had been in Newfoundland directing their unified energy forces to send a storm towards the *Tirpitz* in the Caribbean in 1942. They successfully controlled a cyclone which slowed down the huge *Kriegsmarine* battleship long enough to sink him. Some diviners were working in California, British Columbian and St. Lawrence waters tracking submarines and mines, others were experimenting with mind-control of enemy soldiers, jamming radio waves by thought alone, expanding effectiveness of chemical bonds to eke extra gallons of fuel 'magically' from one gallon. 'Water into oil at the Wedding at Canaan' Owen had joked alluding to Christ's first miracle changing water into wine. Several White Lodge members stayed in occupied London, Dixon-Fairley being one. Continuing his pre-war career as psychic counsellor for the Mayfair-based social elite described so well in the satires of Waugh and Wodehouse, he was able to gather valuable information from important members of the New British regime including the Quisling fascist Prime Minister. Lord Eastbourne came for help in negotiating the slippery swamp of Nazi politics and his own paranoia of being discovered as being the progeny of the Duke of Eastbourne and a Jewish parlour maid which he never directly talked about but of which Dixon-Fairley was very well aware. He sent reports on Eastbourne's plans to the capital's highly organised resistance movement, Free London, which was itself part of a complex network of underground informants and resistance fighters throughout the British Isles, from Cork to Cardiff, Dumfries to Dover. Eastbourne did not suspect his thoughts were an open book to the gifted society clairvoyant.

On the other side of the world, clutching the tall oaken staff he had carved as a young man being instructed by his father in the ways of Druidism, Owen was a piece of Wales transmuted into the Pacific rim. The war, he mused, turned a lot of lives upside down, just like the Great War of 1914-18, its predecessor, breaking up my Druid apprenticeship. His hooded eyes looked at the children. It was not only a material war of bullets, ships and shells against Hitler, Mussolini, Franco and Tojo; it was a spiritual war, part of the total war in every meaning of the word between the Allies who made up FAN, the Free Alliance of Nations, directed at the top by FACE the Free Alliance Control Executive based in Washington,

D.C. But the day of liberation was coming closer if one hard-won step at a time. In 1940 the situation had looked desperate but after the victory at El Alamein in Egypt in October 1943 the sky had seemed less dark and hope suddenly grew in the hearts of free men everywhere that now was the beginning of the end. At stake was the survival of western civilization and what was one or ten or even a hundred years if at the end it survived and the forces of darkness, tyranny and evil were vanquished and exorcised from the world.

He pondered that it was 1944, the fifth year of war for Great Britain, Canada and the rest of the dominions and empire. The United States, just as in World War One joined late, but this time it had taken only ten months for them to get stuck in, after Hitler invaded the Eire, Republic of Ireland in June 1940. *Here we are exiles in Canada, a great, in several senses of the word, and broad land, which received us and provides the springboard for us to get back home and liberate what we hold dear. I cannot bear to use that horrible appellation the fascists now use to refer to as Great Britain, it would be like swearing like a drunken sailor in front of a bishop, or worse, my grandmother. Our White Lodge has succeeded in several projects, conjuring up a storm that slowed down the Tirpitz so it could be destroyed and divining the location of submarine-launched mines littering the harbours of Boston, New York, San Francisco, Vancouver, Halifax and along the St. Lawrence. Spiritual warriors, men and women gifted with psychic skills served on mine-sweepers or concentrated their energy upon prophesying fascist intentions in southern California, Mississippi, Louisiana, Alabama and Florida. They had forecast a fascist devil-dust spraying attack on Norfolk, Virginia allowing the evacuation of the civilian population and warning the armed forces. However, San Francisco was not evacuated until after a deadly attack of devil-dust bombs were dropped by the Japanese flying from Mexico.*

As it was the naval dockyard had to be abandoned for month while it was decontaminated. In May they predicted a fascist thrust to Memphis, Tennessee from occupied Birmingham,

Alabama as well as major Japanese offensive from Los Angeles to San Francisco between the Santa Lucia range of mountains and the Coastal Range running south-east to north-west parallel to the southern coast. General Clark's 4th Army, desperately fighting despite heavy losses from germ warfare, was able to stop them at San Jose and with reinforcements struck back pushing the enemy back to Monterey. In the south-west a major cyclone was summoned which swelled into a hurricane. It bizarrely swept at terrific speed from east to west and back again across the Gulf of Mexico without warning and sank a convoy of German-Latin troops reinforcing the fascist garrison of Cuba from Venezuela. However a major convoy from Ireland of aircraft, munitions, equipment and troops did land at the occupied port of Nassau, Bahamas where it sheltered and waited out the storm losing three vessels to the weather and six to US submarines operating from Jamaica.

Gryffyd took the children for a walk down the steep lane from the cliffs to the beach for exercise before breakfast. He never ate until later in the morning and wanted to discipline his charges as he had been by his father David, the descendant of Druids from prehistoric times. David taught Owen that the ancient ways of Druidism were passed from father to son, and if necessary to daughters. This was not the relatively recent costumed pageantry of the Ancient Order of Druids actually founded in 1781 in Poland Street, London in the Kings Arms Public House, the revival of the society of Bards, known as the *Morganwg* in 1792 or the Welsh festival of music and poetry the *Eistedford,* as good as that was in extolling Welsh pride but removed from being schooled into understanding, nature, God's creation. David's Druidism involved a lifetime's dedication to working with nature and the latent physical and mental powers within each individual to be able to do great things, the incredible, that some would call magic.

In the early dawn walking to Wreck Beach they passed women of the Women's Auxiliary Air Force known affectionately as WAAFS and their Canadian equivalent, the CWAAFS. They sported dark blue overalls and were launching barrage balloons, great lumbering puffy white whales of silk filled with helium tethered by steel cables anchored to the ground protecting the docks and other targets around Vancouver. There were pods of them floating over Point Grey and Vancouver Harbour as a deterrent to enemy aircraft flying in low on a bombing run. Any pilot foolish enough to fly below them stood a chance of running into a steel cable and destroying his plane.

He hoped that his fellow clairvoyants and spiritualists could train these children to harness their mental and spiritual powers and direct them against the enemy, an ongoing operation codenamed Lantern. Owen and the children breathed in the ozone-laden air, a bracing sea breeze blew onto shore. He stood admiring the grandeur of English Bay, a magnificent panorama as he faced the Lions, the two distinctive mountains to the north of Vancouver whose snowy peaks resembled white lions reclining majestically gazing down upon the port. His gaze swept across the coastal range of mountains encircling Canada's major Western port on the coast of British Columbia. Then he gazed east imagining the deep blue water of the Pacific Ocean past Vancouver Island ruled, at this point of the war, by the Imperial Japanese Navy.

It is hard to believe, I would end up here on the edge of North America with nothing between me and Japan but thousands of miles of Pacific.

Exciting, but at the moment Japan is not a place I want to visit, maybe a lot of years after the war … if we win, he concluded.

A new voice nagged inside his head. His oracle. Something unpleasant was on its way. Air-raid. Owen looked for a shelter; he always trusted his inner voice. He called out, "Come on!" and waved the children, strung out along the beach looking for crabs, to him. "Let's have a run." He took the hand of the smallest child, Pyotor Troubetzkoy and swiftly led his charges along the beach to a half-built pillbox just fifty yards under the cliff back along the way they had come. Owen waved them into the concrete shelter, counting them in, "eleven … hurry, twelve. Good," then he followed them in and sat on an upturned wheelbarrow almost hidden in the gloom. Just then the air raid sirens made their banshee noise alerting Vancouverites to an air raid. In the east just above the horizon he could see specks coming towards them. The forty-two long-range Imperial Japanese Naval *Mitsubishu* G4M bombers nicknamed 'Betties' by the FAN air forces were escorted by squadrons of *Zero-Sen* fighters nicknamed 'Zekes' but usually just referred to as Zeros. They had taken off only forty miles from the southern shore of Vancouver Island flown from 'shadowed' aircraft carriers invisible to radar contact to all but the closest aerial or naval observer. The Betties had flown skimming the waves using usually effective radar jamming equipment utilizing the latest Japanese invention, transistors. These were mini-valves, minimizing the weight of equipment that would normally be so heavy as to prevent a bomber or fighter plane from making a long sortie.

Through the slits built in for machine-guns Owen and his young charges watched as a dramatic panorama unfolded in front of them. Scores of ack-ack guns opened up unleashing a barrage of shells aimed at the aerial invaders. "Children, this is our first chance to practice what we have tried in our sessions," Owen announced, "Concentrate on the engines of that Japanese bomber there," he pointed out one that had veered towards them. They could clearly see the large red circles of the Japanese Naval Air Force on its fuselage and upon its wings. "We shall put our minds in that other place we have been practicing, breathe slowly, apply willpower to make the engines seize up. Imagine the pistons inside the engine blocks sticking, unable to function, heating up to a very great temperature, melting, just like the car engine we stopped yesterday. It's much further than thirty feet away, about a half-mile, but we can try." The twelve children and one middle-aged man focussed on the bomber and concentrated their inner eyes with all their might on seizing the engines, stopping the enemy dropping bombs on Vancouver. Within seconds the bomber came to a complete halt in mid-air. It bounced backwards as if hitting a brick wall then fell straight down in a dive towards the water which it entered with a huge splash.

"You did it, you did it!" Owen cried. Then the realisation of what they had done flooded over him, their combined power had killed the crew of the bomber. They gazed at the broken bomber resting like an injured whale on the surface of the sea. A Royal Canadian Navy minesweeper headed towards two Japanese crew members who were pulling themselves out of the water and clambering on top of the wing lying on the water surface. Armed sailors were leaning forward to throw them a line. "Not all were killed, those will be prisoners," Owen told the children who were wide-eyed their faces filled with wonder that they had something to do with the bomber falling quite literally out of the sky. "We did that, but for anyone else watching they will see what they wanted to see, that the aircraft's engines failed or that a shell brought it down. We shall not boast about what we have done but we have defended what we hold dear and you can see the power that we can unleash. It's a fearsome responsibility and we must never use it except for very good reason.''

The flack was extremely accurate due to the close proximity fuses that were now standard issue for American, British and Canadian shells and air to ground rockets. Winning the war was becoming increasingly a matter of scientific innovation wedded with industrial production and quick, tactical application of new weapons in a fast-changing conflict. The close-proximity fuse was developed from the cavity magnetron, a British invention brought to the United States by a scientist in the 'Great Evac' in 1940 and given gratis to the 'arsenal of democracy' Roosevelt's America. For a few minutes it was left unguarded on a train at Euston Station by mistake. Its guardian, a scientist from the Ministry of Defence charged with taking the 'Tizard's briefcase' to New York via a ship from Liverpool waved a porter over telling him he needed to get his luggage onto the 08:30 Liverpool boat-train. He handed the black jappaned metal box to a porter to hold while he placed his luggage upon the porter's trolley but was shocked to see the man swallowed up by the crowd bearing the precious prototype of the cavity magnetron and his bags. Sweating with anxiety he darted after him weaving through the masses. He grabbed hold of the man's coat. "Wait! That box ..." He decided not to cause a scene and lowered his voice forcing himself to smile and calm down," I'll carry the box, my man, something breakable in it." Relieved, with the box once again under his arm, the civil servant tipped the porter a shilling

"Ta. Don't drop that tin, sir" the porter replied then muttered under his breath, "Anybody would think he had the crown jewels, I ask you."

*

A Betty bomber streaming smoke from both of its 1,850 horse power Kasei 25 radial engines dived under the majestic Lion's Gate toll bridge, which had been officially opened by the late King George VI and Queen Elizabeth in 1939. Built by the Guinness family it connected Stanley Park with the mountainous North Shore, where the Guinesses owned the 'British Properties'. Bofors and 3.5 inch guns by the docks opened fire. The enemy plane ruptured exploding into two fiery yellow balls speckled with flecks of jagged metal, within milliseconds of each other almost indistinguishable to the eye. The crew was about to release its torpedo at an oil freighter the Indiana Mercury, part of a newly arrived convoy from Seattle tied up at the dock. One explosion was from the torpedo affixed to its belly, the larger explosion was from the plane's fuel tank. Another *Mitsibushi* G4M was doing its best to avoid a Spitfire zooming towards it at 350 miles-an-hour chasing an A6M *Zero-Sen* fighter to sea level and pumping it full of cannon shells that were tearing great chunks out of its fuselage. The nervous Japanese bomber pilot steered too close to a barrage balloon bearing the black painted name 'Bertha'. He clipped his tail wing flying alongside the steel cable suspended from the balloon. Without stability provided by the wing the plane flipped over and fell like a spinning stone into Stanley Park sending up a plume of smoke over the centuries old pines and cedars towering hundreds of feet over the fern covered ground. Eagles momentarily deserted their eyries and flapped over the trees with a great kerfuffle.

Ten Zeros were shot down by ferocious Spitfire Mk. VBs which, in a straight dogfight could attack with two 20mm cannon and four .303 machine guns while outracing the enemy fighters through their maximum speed of 374 miles per hour. However, several of the green painted Zeros bearing the Red circles of the rising sun on their wings and their fuselages pursued a damaged green and brown camouflaged Spitfire hammering 20 mm cannon shells and 12.7 and7.7 mm bullets into it. Seeing flames coming out of his engine the South African pilot released his cockpit and flipped the machine on its back and bailed out. He pulled the ripcord and his white silk parachute spread out above him as he held on to the lines of the chute and saw himself landing him on top of Peter's Ice Cream Parlour on W. 4th as the enemy were chased away. He was helped down from the roof by a puffing owner putting up a ladder. Inside the parlour the airman was presented with the largest serving of ice cream he had ever seen in his life, the five large scoops of strawberry and chocolate had square wafer wings each with a cherry on top to represent the air force roundel of aircraft. The Afrikaaner pilot from Pardeburg declared in a strong accent; "Thiss my frrend iss the best sweet I hav ever had. I will be sure to brring the squadrunn heer be four wee go outt on the ttown." The one-off dish became a fixture known as the 'Spitfire' and became a popular item on the menu for the local residents in Kitsilano and 5 squadron of the Royal South African Air Force whose members enjoyed sitting in a row on the leather topped stools at the ice cream bar each asking at the top of their voices for "A Spitt and step on itt ice crream keeper!"

The three twin 5" barrels mounted upon the American destroyer USS Madison, escorting the convoy belched forth flames as shells fixed with close proximity fuses, triggered to explode when within feet of their target sped towards their target. As a result another Betty jerked out of formation heeled over and with a wingtip catching the water somersaulted once then smashed apart safely between two freighters containing ammunition and trucks from the United States. The dogfight between Spitfires and Japanese fighters high overhead moved west over the Pacific as the fighters and what were left of the bombers turned back towards their carriers.

The all-clear siren wailed and after looking out to ensure all was safe, Owen had the children follow him up the steep narrow path to the top of the cliffs and to their home and classrooms in a neo-Tudor home overlooking the sea on the corner of the UBC campus containing the homes of faculty members. They talked as they walked up the trail from the ocean. "Yes, Sir, we are part of the war now, it was what brought us together," Elizabeth from Colorado spoke for them, she was the oldest at sixteen. The rest of the children nodded or murmured agreement. Carmen Fado from Brazil uttered with a Portuguese accent, "that plane would have killed other children or our mothers and fathers maybe I think." That night before going to bed, Nicholas confided to Owen "I don't like killing people but there is not much choice is there."

"No, there is no choice. We had a chance to stop Hitler in 1936 or even earlier, we chose the easy way out. I am sorry my generation let you down. I am glad though," Owen Gryffyd responded, "that you did not enjoy it. If you did then I would think there was something wrong with you and send you home. It is not normal to kill, but we don't live in normal times and what would happen to civilization if we do not win this war does not bear thinking about. It is a paradox, we ask soldiers to kill, we train them to do it but if they start to thirst for it they are no better than wild beasts; worse."

"I know Mr. Gryffyd, I have talked it over with my family and I do understand although I am only eleven, I have read and seen films about what is happening in Europe and Asia, terrible things. I just want the world to be at peace so children everywhere grow up and have a normal life."

Owen put his arm on the boy's shoulder, "You are not only a powerful spiritual warrior but you are wiser than your years, Nicholas. Peace is what I want too. We all do."

The next morning at their isolated mock Tudor headquarters in Point Grey, a short curly-haired man with an upturned nose, chubby cheeks and a scruffy pair of brown corduroy trousers, open neck shirt and tweed jacket knocked on the door with one hand. In the other he clutched an unzipped brown attaché case carelessly stuffed with papers which appeared to be escaping, threatening to blow away in a gust of wind. A plainclothes RCMP officer opened the front door. The visitor had no way of knowing that the officer in front of him was armed with an automatic pistol in a holster under his arm beneath his jacket as were three other detectives guarding the children and their trainers while working as chauffeurs or gardeners.

"Ah, good morning I'm Mr. Thomas here to see Mr. Gryffyd. I'm expected," he proclaimed in the musical voice of a Welshman. He reached first into one pocket then another and eventually produced a wrinkled and stained stiff paper identity card indicating he was a scriptwriter with the Crown Film Unit.

"Come on in, I'll tell him you are here, he's just on the telephone at the moment."

He showed the scriptwriter into the living room "Make yourself comfortable. I'll tell him you're here."

"A cup of tea would be most welcome," the affable guest replied shaking a cigarette from a pack of ten Player's cigarettes decorated with a colour portrait of a bearded Victorian sailor bearing the name Hero on his cap band. He lit it with a wooden match that he blew out dropping it into an ashtray. He crossed his legs in relaxation looking around the room. Several moments later the head teacher poked his head round the door and glanced at the visitor who had a cigarette hanging from his cherub lips. "Hello, I'm Owen Gryffyd we have been expecting you and the film crew."

"Pleased to meet you," Thomas said taking the cigarette from his mouth with one hand and rising to shake Owen's hand with the other. Owen looked into the man's sensitive brown eyes

136

beneath the curly brown hair that was badly in need of a trim. Dylan plundered the papers in his attaché case. "Here is a letter from Colonel Le Meseurier, head of Canadian Military Intelligence giving the Crown Film Unit and National Film Board scriptwriter, that's me, and the cameram ... camerawoman clearance to travel and film the work you are doing here. She's from the National Film Board out filming some of the local area but will present her papers a bit later. I also have a letter here from Lieutenant-General Saunders, aide to Field Marshal Alan Brooke, giving me access to any or all help from all services for the film on Operation Lantern."

"Thanks Mr. Thomas, by the way I admire your poetry, your work makes me proud to be Welsh." Owen chuckled aware that the writer was embarrassed by his praise. "I know what young men are like, especially ones that love life. The best ones. And how you must write or else burst with frustration. Tell me did you manage to get your wife and child safely to Canada.

"Ah," Dylan looked at his crepe-sole desert boots, "You know about them."

"I make a point of knowing everything printed in the newspapers about the principality."

"Well there was a bit of a mix-up in Swansea, I was late getting to the ship, it was awful; crying children, people asleep in a line to get on, mayhem it was. I was told by a friend that Caitlin and Aeronwy were on board already so I lined up and got up the gangway one of the last on board. People were packed like sardines on the Scythia, which normally carried 245 first class and 350 second class passengers, all in all we were 900 living in overcrowded cabins or passageways. Anyway I got aboard, the gangway was wheeled back onto the dock and we headed out to sea. Then I looked out and saw my wife and daughter on the dockside waving at me. I can't swim but I did try to jump overboard but a sailor stopped me told me not to start a panic with any luck he told me, they would get another boat. So I left them. It was horrible."

Without saying a word Owen beckoned Dylan to follow him. Picking up his staff in the hall Owen led his guest through the green kitchen door and into the garden. He had fashioned it from an oak limb selected by his Druid tutor, his father, and carved under his tutelage during his apprenticeship during the First World War and the 1920s. Owen closed his eyes and faced east.

"To Wales!" he raised his staff and pointed it. A thin shaft of light pulsed down the staff and out across Georgia Strait towards the coastal mountains unseen by none but the most alert eagle over the Rockies, the plains, the great lakes and the ancient stone of the Laurentian Shield, the great moving depths of the Atlantic until it reached the British Isles and landed in Wales. It returned almost instantly at the speed of thought. "All's well, Mr. Thomas they are fine," he tapped his fingers on the staff.

Amazed, Dylan usually so glib and confident, fumbled for words, "Er, yes, thanks. You know only the Prime Ministers, Attlee, Mackenzie King, the combined war cabinet, President Roosevelt and his Chiefs of Staff will see this film, as well as yourselves of course. I was told to write a script for a film about your project to be a celluloid archive for the future. We were on the cliffs by Fort Camp at the university and got some great footage of the air raid. Did you happen to see that one Jap plane coming towards the cliffs it seemed to stop in mid-air must have been ack-ack fire? She remarked it was the most incredible footage she has ever shot."

"We saw the bomber, we were on the beach. It was our children that stopped that plane and sent it into the sea.''

The young poet listened with a look of incredulity on his face as Owen explained exactly what the children were learning in Operation Lantern. He spoke keenly about man's relationship with the earth he inhabited and how with true understanding and instruction anyone, particularly gifted children, could tap into the immense spiritual and psychic power within each of us, a secret passed on by his father to himself in Anglesey in Wales, the last redoubt of true Druidism after the Romans tried to wipe them all out. "Now, these children," Owen expounded, " have exhibited a natural skill and a high degree of power which we are teaching them to use and will apply to the war effort, keeping them out of danger as much as possible of course."

Fascinated, Dylan asked, "Who is teaching them? Just you?"

"The White Eagle Lodge of course, the members here are mostly from North America, witches like Christine Hollet for example; a clairvoyant from Vancouver. She is taking the class on prophecy as we speak. Every weekday the morning is split between spiritual classes and regular classes of English, History, Maths and Literature. The afternoons include psychic lessons followed by PE, Art or Music. Evenings there is homework-both kinds, spiritual and regular and occasional informal chats, talks if you like, from one of the Lodge. Tonight for example our speaker is Running Horse, a Lakota Red Indian who is just back from Colorado working on an antidote to the plague and influenza using natural medicines. He has been working with Brazilian scientists and shamans, learning about Latin American drugs and herbs. Red Indian shamans are like Druids or white witches if you like, not an ounce of evil in them only goodness and a love of God or Manitou's creation.

Eddie Walker Junior is a clairvoyant from Tennessee who has the ability to speed or slow down time, you will want to get some film of him working with the children. I must say the children are making very rapid progress in affecting the environment around them thanks to his methods. Their stopping and starting radios, clocks, telephones are a sight to behold, it will make terrific subject for your film."

Dylan Thomas leaned forward his eyes sparkling, "This is incredible Mr. Gryffyd. First you communicate instantaneously with my family in Wales, or if you'll forgive me for being a sceptic, appeared to do so, then you tell me that your children are gifted in performing miracles and that the bomber we filmed falling out of the sky into the sea was due to their efforts. It seems a bit surreal to be in 1944 talking about such things. Is it possible that there is a kind of warfare brewing here which is quite unique in history? It would seem that you are carrying on the ancient wisdom, in touch with the powers in each of us or God-given to the gifted, deep, wonderful secrets that may yet help win the war. The children are … "

Owen jumped in excitedly, "The children are the hope for the future, a spiritual, psychic future. A secret future."

"You must admit it is hard to swallow in one gulp but I believe you."

"I see that you do," Owen smiled as he looked the poet in the eyes and saw a man who loved life and had the sensitivity, energy and soul of a good heart. He also sensed in the small chin and sensuous lips a man who occasionally had trouble reining in his passions. "Now, since we are both Welshmen we do not have to be so formal, call me Owen and I shall call you Dylan."

There was the sound of someone clearing a throat, "Am I disturbing you, Mr. Gryffyd?"

"No. Your class must be finished early, Miss Hollet. Please meet Mr. Dylan Thomas he's making a film for the top brass about our work, it will also be an archive of our work for the future."

A look of delight ran across the lady's pretty face. "You're not Dylan Thomas the poet?" Dylan stood up and bowed.

"Ooh," the woman cooed. She offered her hand which Dylan took and she kept in his a bit too long. "Sorry, it's just that I am quite a fan of yours. The way you have with words ... I just love 'And Death Shall Have No Dominion' ...'though I sang in my chains like the sea."

"He has been cleared to write a screenplay for a documentary film being made about our work so you can talk freely about your work in Alaska." Owen turned towards the writer and explained, "She just returned last night from Anchorage by plane."

There was a ring at the doorbell. Dylan looked out of the bay window. "Our camera woman."

The 'doorman' opened the door and admitted a lady on barely out of young adulthood wearing a rucksack bulging with cans of film. Her curly blonde hair, decorated with colourful beads, was tied up in a ponytail and a red kerchief was tied around her head. She wore a worn leather pilot's jacket and pink jodphurs and a pair of riding boots. "I'm Marjorie Bresson, assigned to the film your project." She spoke with English with a tint of Spanish accent.

"You are Spanish?" Owen asked.

"I was born in Madrid and spent my childhood there, my father was American ambassador in the 20's. Until General Franco's regime ends Quebec City is my home when I am not on the road with the National Film Board. I am here to report to Mr. Gryffyd."

"That's me, Miss Bresson." He checked her letters of introduction and her identity card and ushered her into the library. "The children will be coming into the garden for a morning glass of milk and a cookie in a moment," he said checking his watch. "Let's go out into the garden it's quite lovely I'll have a pot of tea brought out. But first, come into the living room Mrs. Hollet was just going to tell us about her mission in Alaska." With that Owen led her back into the living room. Christine, a middle-aged lady with her hair tied back in a tight bun was talking to Dylan who was taking notes about her work.

"I was just telling Mr. Thomas about our time in Alaska scattering 'Go Away Powder.'"

Marjorie Bresson stifled a snort of derisive laughter, "forgive me, I should have told you I may have been assigned to film your work here with the children but I am somewhat sceptical about spiritual or psychic warfare. But feel free to convince me."

"Oh we will Miss Bresson and even if we don't I am sure you will not allow your beliefs to interfere with your professionalism. You come highly recommended by the NFB."

"You have my word Mr. Gryffyd. I apologize for being so cynical but growing up in Spain during their Civil War made me proud to be an atheist, but I want to see this war won as much as anyone so if the work here helps then I am glad to film it for posterity. I just need a few minutes to set up my camera and microphone." She busied herself and motioned Christine into a seat by the window holding the 16 mm camera steady with surprisingly strong hands. "Ready to record."

Christine broke the silence in the room, "I just returned from scattering 'Go Away' powder in Alaska. It is a uniquely North American compound made of Red Indian Shamanic items imbued with defensive energy by our group wielding spiritual energy held in our chakras as explored by the Hindu yogis and Tibetan mystics. We visited various strategic locations using a US Navy Grumman Goose flying boat. We were strafed by Jap fighters from the carrier *Soryu* while we were refuelling in Cook Inlet alongside a US Navy fuel tanker. Luckily we survived with just some holes in the wings. I was able to dowse the location of their carrier and we had enough fuel. We took off and flew after them.

"The Jap carrier was using its masking technique which makes it invisible to the naked eye and to radar waves. It is the strangest thing to get close and see puffs of smoke from its horizontal smokestacks appearing out of nowhere although I am told that the Japs are starting to pump the smoke, from oil burning boilers powering their propeller engines, into the water so we cannot even see that with the reconditioned ships. Anyway they have not yet been able to mask the smoke from their horizontal stacks but it is the strangest thing seeing planes instantly disappear as they fly into the masking bubble covering their ship. We radioed the naval base at and they directed a submarine to the position we gave. The amount of power the masking technique must use prefigures that at night they would turn it off so the sub might be able to spot it visually. Now we shall wait to see whether the Japs move onto the mainland from the Aleutian Islands or. Too bad the Axis are still in Southern California, they are giving the Yanks the devil of a time in the south-east and south-west. Perhaps there was something wrong with the 'go away' powder we distributed there.''

"Sceptics would say no matter what we do things happen as they were going to," Owen replied. "Attlee and his Brains' Trust think we have something which is better than nothing. Bertrand Russell is not too keen, in his own words, 'we may precipitate co-incidences that work more in the favour of the allies than not, so although illogical and so far unprovable the work of the White Lodge should continue and scientific measurements of their work with children carefully taken and reported to us. We cannot have the children mistreated or warped. If Operation Lantern proves to be a waste of time it should be stopped for the childrens' sake. Logic demands this.' He's right, of course, but yesterday these children proved they are a great hope in our war of minds. I hear the Soviets are using children in similar experiments but my agents apparently indicate that are concentrating on mind control on the populace by the children, in order to ensure everyone follows the party line rather than in a true military sense. I think we are on the right track but certainly we must ensure we teach the children how to protect their own minds and thoughts in case they ever come up against equally or even more gifted channelers of psychic energy who have been taught to take over free thought. In short they must be able to defend themselves from physical and mental threats.

"I will look after them as if they were my own, we have a doctor on staff, a psychologist and a nurse. They have two house mothers, both experienced school headmistresses, principals they call them over here. They console, tutor, make sure they eat and sleep well and write regularly to their parents. Now with your film of how we stopped that bomber and the documented reports of our successfully locating mines, submarines, controlling the weather to name a few, the proof is incontrovertible.''

143

After interviewing the staff and the children Dylan left Miss Bresson to film a class and walked along the cliff smoking cigarettes and thinking about his script. He found himself soaking up the beauty of Vancouver. "This is a beautiful spot it has a raw beauty which is even more impressive than the sands of Swansea beach. But Wales is still home. Oh, there's Dorothy," Dylan told himself, "working with the barrage balloon."

Dylan Thomas waved and Dorothy, wearing unflattering blue overalls, waved back cheerily and shouted something he could not hear. The girls were busy painting a silhouette of a Japanese bomber on one of the puffy tails of Bertha the Balloon. He walked over to the WAAFs. "Dorothy, I was wondering if I would see you. You were the star of the film of our 1942 film, 'Balloon Site 568'."

"It was a good performance of being me," she giggled. "And since then I have read your books. I've told the girls all about you."

Dylan smiled in embarrassment and only succeeded on lighting her a cigarette on the third match cupping his hands around the flame. "Thanks but I would give all my poems to be with my wife and daughter again." Dorothy puffed on her cigarette and squeezed his arm. "The war will be over one day and you can go back."

"It's what I am living for. It is hard knowing my family are still in New Quay overlooking Cardigan Bay in an asbestos-sided bungalow." Dylan continued in his stream of consciousness. He was full of emotion and sucked in the healing smoke before he spoke. "I was told they were on board the bloody ship that was leaving Swansea I jumped on board as it left the dock and after frantically looking for them it was too late I can't swim or otherwise ...," he wiped his eye over his round check and then smiled. "I wish I was there now mind, I would hold my Caitlin close, in a great hug like an overly friendly bear who was lonely then I would put my girl on my back and run down to the frothy sea and keep on going if it was warm and just run in or just get our toes wet if it was nippy, we would go for a fish and chip dinner and we would have a pint, or maybe two and a package of woodbines and then I would tell them stories until midnight or whenever the cat came in. Ah," Dylan sighed. "Caitlin and Aeronwy are probably watching the cousins of these seagulls in front of us, gulls perpetually criss-crossing the void split by the tide between green tree-gnarled land and the sucking salt waves of the sea.'' Dorothy stood next to Dylan they both looked out to sea in silence content to share the view as friends. Behind them the girls filled up Betty the balloon with helium and winched it up into the air.

CHAPTER TEN   PATTON'S THRUST

"Well they've given us a job to do. A tough job, a man size job.
We can get down on our bended knees, every one of us, and thank
God the chance has been given to serve our country.
We're going to go right in and kill the dirty bastards."
General George S. Patton

General George S. Patton, Jr. newly promoted to four star general rank was in an expansive mood. As he shaved his face covered by soap lather he talked to his aide. "Did I ever tell you about the 1904 Olympics in, er, St. Louis, Missourri? I was in the Pentathlon, ate raw steak every day for months and even injected myself with opium so I could handle the cross-country race after the tough competitions. But fencing was my favourite sport."

"You were a young blade General. Now the men call you 'Old blood and guts'"

"Yeah, now I'm an old cutlass. So watch out I don't cut you in two if you get out of line," Patton laughed. His batman put on a crisply ironed light brown shirt on the General's arms which were held out and back. He knotted his olive green tie himself ensuring the four stars on his shirt collars were shining and positioned his lacquered helmet bearing four stars. Looking grimly at himself the rough faced general looked himself up and down from his shined boots, spotless whipcord jodphurs, a reminder of his young cavalry days in mid-west forts. His gaze moved up to the Eisenhower style battledress tunic copied from the British but better tailored and not made of thick wool but a smoother wool. He wore his medals from the Mexican incursion 1916 and in France '17-'18." He walked downstairs and stood in the streets of Vera Cruz on the east coast of Mexico. His 6th Army had done the impossible, destroying a German-Latin army at the Battle of Houston, routing a Mexican army at Monterey and moving down the east coast to take Vera Cruz. It was an important city to take. He could move west to take Mexico City or head south through

146

Central America to reinforce the American forces in Panama who had taken back the Panama Canal from fascist control knocking out Guatamala, Honduras, Nicauragua and Costa Rica as participants in the Fascist Latin Alliance.

The old town's harbour at Vera Cruz was a hive of activity. Lean and tough veteran soldiers marched by or rode in a long line of trucks, M3 Grant and Sherman tanks. These were the long awaited reinforcements delivered courtesy of the US Navy out of Norfolk, Virginia and Philadelphia with six extra divisions including all-female regiments, Patton had fought to keep women out of his army, dubious about this dramatic change but circumstances, the need for many more hands to bear arms and Roosevelt's persuasive skills forced it upon him. His attitude changed when he visited a sweltering field hospital in Pachuca in Hildago Province. A mine had exploded as she drove a caterpillar bulldozer grading a road full of shell holes so a convoy could pass through. She died holding his hand and it was at that moment that he swore never to be anything but professional about the women in his command, he would protect them as best he could just like his men by ensuring his officers were good and his tough training regime applied even in the front line, giving a bit of extra polish to soldiers just out of training school. There were soldiers then there were Patton's soldiers, there was a difference, men or women they were the ones that were smartly dressed. The woman who died had joked she had one up on male soldiers, "I don't have to shave, sir."

"No, I should goddam well hope not and that gives you ten minutes extra to check your weapon and make sure it's loaded, right, Sergeant?"

"Right, sir." she said. He had attended her military funeral and ensured that three of the soldiers firing rifles over her grave were women his eyes filled with tears as he laid some flowers on her grave. He muttered some words from a poem he wrote in 1916 in Mexico, 'His eyes can see Valhalla   Where staring from the skies The men who fought for England Watch how their offspring

147

dies.' Then he strode off quickly, Willy his Yorkshire Terrier marching behind him. Despite his tough reputation he was a romantic, a poet convinced that he was the re-incarnation of great soldiers of the past. His wife, men, and now women, adored him.

In a sense he was the incarnation of Caesar or any great soldier, he took the art of war seriously and was the model of discipline and a sense of historical destiny. Every night, when not in battle he had 100 buglers play at 2200 hours to remind his army of thousands of years of soldiering. Coyotes howled across the two hundred miles of encampment joining in with the echoes of the bugle called across the Sierra Mojada and the Amnuilipas mountains all the way to the Gulf of Campeche. In the heat of New Mexico in his notorious manoeuvres in 1941, each soldier was restricted to one gallon of water and each vehicle three gallons. He continued this regime in Mexico but on extremely hot days where the temperature hit 120 degrees Fahrenheit he increased water rations to those in combat. In that one year of gruelling training his tanks clocked ten million miles so after that and over a year of heavy fighting his men were the most experienced crews in the world and more than a match for enemy tanks men.

His troops survived on c-rations of beef or chicken with vegetables in a metal tin cooked inside larger tins almost filled with sand, soaked in petrol and put on fire when campfires were impossible due to rain or battle conditions. Often Patton slipped into forward fox holes squeezing his six foot bulk into slit trenches as long as him just two feet wide chatting with his troops sharing a meal, giving out Hershey chocolate bars or checking on his beloved tank crews of the 2nd Armoured Division as they prepared to sleep alongside their tanks or in the early morning waking up to freshly brewed coffee courtesy of shipments from their ally, Brazil.

Even in battle he chewed out any officer of soldier he suspected of inept decisions or cowardice in his high-pitched voice believing that public humiliation worked much better than formal military charges.

General Arnold ordered Patton to move to the west coast in a lightning strike to take the important harbour of Manzallino which was being used by Japan to reinforce its forces in Mexico, then move to the centre of the country and take Mexico City which had been left almost undefended by competent troops which were heavily engaged in California. Roosevelt intended to set up a pro-American Mexican government as soon as Mexico City was in American hands.

After jumping out of his scout car to help direct traffic and unsnarl a jam in the army's move west leaving a garrison in Vera Cruz he climbed back in slapping the side of the vehicle in excitement. "Come on we have an appointment with the Jap army at the Aloyac River, can't keep the bastards waiting." As he said it he felt a premonition of danger, he was not afraid to die and he did not keep them waiting long. The five-mile long convoy rounded a corner of the rugged dirt road that barely straightened out in a wavy line through a deep valley beside a steep hillside covered with large rocks and cactuses. Reconnaissance scouts in armoured cars had not noticed anything untoward after chasing off a squadron of Japanese armoured cars at the end of the valley although they had radioed the convoy that it should come at high speed through this potentially dangerous corridor. Once the convoy was strung out in the valley moving quickly at 40 mph there a barrage of artillery shells from forty 75 mm Japanese mountain guns and 47 mm anti-tank guns was unleashed knocking out tanks at the head of the column, some artillery being drawn by trucks in the middle and ten ton GM trucks carrying troops at the rear.

Japanese tanks and German *panzers* crewed by Mexicans raced out of a maize field on the left of the road pumping shells into the column. Instantly American tanks slewed off the road and geared up racing towards the advancing enemy vehicles in squadrons taking out the enemy tanks methodically as they crashed through the maize stalks creating crazy patterns in the crop. Thousands of enemy infantrymen hiding amongst the rocks and brush of the nearest hillside on the right began firing into the column as male and female GIs tumbled out of the trucks and sought cover on both sides of the road. American officers began forming their men into skirmishing lines moving forward towards the infantry. Armoured cars began giving the American soldiers covering fire with heavy machine guns and shots from M-4 Sherman's guns smashed into the enemy.

"Let's help the infantry to our right our tanks can look after themselves. I want to know why our recce scouts and planes did not catch these guys," Patton yelled to the driver of his scout car. He drew the two pearl handled revolvers from the holsters at his belt and waited impatiently as the driver wheeled the wide bodied 7,000 pound Scout car off the road and into the rough ground being chewed up by enemy fire and shells. The Hercules 6 cylinder engine of the 4X4 M3 Scout car whined as the driver put it into the top gear, the machine-gunner at the rear let loose with his .50 cal Browning machine-gun ripping into the Venezuelan, Bolivian and Japanese troops that were firing at the General's vehicle with frenzied cries from their officers helping direct their fire. Patton's aide called up air support from the USAAF base in Vera Cruz.

Enemy Bullets shattered the windscreen killing the driver narrowly missing the General. Patton fired his Smith & Wessen .357 Magnum and 1873 vintage Colt 45 six-shot revolvers into the melee. His white Yorkshire Terrier Willy who accompanied him everywhere snarled, angry at the disruption of his sleep on the floor of the M3 scout car. The armoured Scout car skewed around and roared up the incline of the hill as GIs ran past it expertly attacking the enemy soldiers with companies leap-frogging each other as they over-ran the enemy positions. Double rotored Eagle helicopters on patrol with air-to-ground rocket projectiles mounted underneath their large fuselages were called down to help by radio operators in a Packhard armoured car accompanying Patton. M4 Sherman tanks began pounding the enemy artillery positions situated on the slopes and ridge of the southern hillside. Attacks by the Eagles and a squadron of Thunderbolt fighter-bombers dropping 500 pound bombs put paid to the determined fascist defence.

"Send the Sherman tanks and the infantry in to mop up," the General ordered and in clouds of dust the tanks roared away with G.I.s hanging on for dear life. They clambered off after getting a lift as the tanks clanked and squeeked up to the edge of hillside raising their 76 mm guns and firing in volleys. The soldiers took the crest in a screaming bayonet charge led by a battalion of US Marines. The olive green helmeted marines could be seen by Patton from the bottom of the hill fixing bayonets and tearing into the thousand enemy troops still alive. Japanese troops manning artillery and dug-in tanks fired back and the fight became a matter of hand-to-hand combat. Japanese soldiers fought like madmen until they dropped, only a few surrendered. Bolivian officers shot several of their men attempting to surrender to the *cringos* in an attempt to stop the panic. But it was too late the surviving Bolivians ran down the reverse slope throwing away their weapons and Japanese helmets allowing them to run faster. The Marines and infantry picked up the weapons and ammunition pouches to be used by themselves if necessary and kept helmets as souvenirs. They carried them back to the convoy in triumph. There would be other battles but there was no stopping Patton and his 6th Army. Within minutes the burning wrecks of tanks and trucks were bulldozed aside and the convoy continued towards the Pacific and more victories.

CHAPTER ELEVEN   BERGSHIPS

The bulk of the bergship HMCS Iroquois, approaching the Iberian Peninsula from the Azores in the mid-Atlantic, was so vast as to be beyond imagination as to how much it really weighed. It was made of an ice and pulp wood mix called Pykrite resistant to bullets and bombs and was developed in Hudson's Bay in Canada in a billion dollar secret project. Its man-made glacier hull of ice was able to absorb a large amount of explosive damage and had amazing powers to not melt excessively in the warmer waters nursed by the Gulf stream in the mid-Atlantic. Code-named, 'Lebanons' the three leviathans were created in Hudson's Bay. Each weighed an estimated 200,000 tons and was propelled by ten diesel fired engines. Insulated boilers condensed the steam to turn the sixty large propellers and drive shafts had been built inside an insulated core heated by excess steam. Steam pipes heated the insulated crew quarters and the two flight decks. Iroquios was a giant aircraft carrier. It might melt somewhat if it moved towards the equator and lose some weight but trials had proven that it would remain an effective platform for up to ten squadrons of aircraft as well as batteries of anti-aircraft guns or carry a smaller number of squadrons and a flotilla of fifty landing craft, one division of assault troops, and one armoured division of tanks and trucks with fuel and ammunition.

RAF and RCAF squadrons of gull-winged Chance Vought Corsairs of the Royal Naval Air Service and a Polish squadron of Sea Mosquitoes ensured defence from enemy attack. It did not have the masking technology invented by the Japanese but its icy bulk did not register as a ship on long range enemy radar screens but only as an iceberg. It did not produce smoke from its engines but instead pumped it into the sea with a reverse snorkel adapted from a captured new U-boat.

On board Z for Zulu, a four-engined Lancaster bomber of 100 Squadron RAF, was a tousle haired Flight Lieutenant navigator called Patrick Moore even then renowned for his eccentricity. Under his tunic and turtleneck jumper he wore his old school tie as a belt, as if playing cricket, a game of which he was inordinately fond. He organised matches aboard the bergship in a flat area playing cricket on the ice wearing spiked running shoes under their white outfits and shin pads and getting used to the hard cricket balls sliding across the deck as they were slashed by batsmen who crunched the runs making for a memorable voyage. He had been on a few missions flying from Iceland to Norway and Scotland to hit German and fascist military targets but this was the big show coming up. He contemplated the imminent invasion of Hitler's Europe in the biggest sea invasion in history three armies two targets - Lisbon and Cadiz.

He had seen the massive floating oil pipeline Pluto being towed towards the Spanish coast and the floating concrete docks, the Mulberry harbours, being taken to be temporary ports close to the beach heads. The Allied strategy was based on over a year's detailed preparation involving engineers, naval and military experts. Until Cadiz and Lisbon were taken and made useable as ports by the attackers oil and supplies would be guaranteed. Moore knew that he was one of thousands of airmen intent on keeping the enemy heads down and destroy their gun positions and any *Panzer* tanks rushing towards the beaches to stop the invaders on the first day.

Standing by his four-engined Lancaster bomber the amateur astronomer looked up at the stars that sparkled in a clear patch through the clouds, he could out make the Andromeda Constellation. He had no idea that his love of astronomy would one day make him the leading populariser of the future British-French-Russian space program with his long lasting television series 'The Sky Tonight' but then no-one knew what the next few days would bring let alone decades. Pondering the cosmos he recollected the book he had read when he was eleven, Last and First Men by Olaf Stapledon, a novel about voyagers to the stars. *When the war is done it will happen, hope I live to see it.*

"Come on Moore, the erks want to take the Lancaster down below deck to the bomber level. You can stay up and look at those precious stars of yours but the rest of us are going to the mess for a pint." His skipper said. "I'll be down in a bit, sir." be maybe two or three more years, I know there will be a future for me reaching for the stars. *They are my destiny. Although it may not be me who goes toward them but I can help build the rockets or plan the trip for my children or at least those who come after us.*

"Good, you owe me a one after that last cricket match with the Canadians. You told me that they wouldn't beat us then they showed up in hockey skates. Completely against the rules. Bloody brilliant. No wonder they took Vimy Ridge when one else could take it."

Patrick Moore was brought down to icy earth, "I have some double bladed ice skates for our cricket team's next match, after the big show!

"I like your spirit, Moore. We'll show 'em."

154

CHAPTER TWELVE   D-DAY

"Could you please oblige us with a Bren gun?"
Sir Noel Coward song 1943

The pre-dawn mist over the Atlantic just west of Cape Trafalgar shrouded and protected the invasion armada as if it was a shimmering swathe of ministering angels. John strained to see their objective from his landing craft Royal Navy LCI 561 through the early morning mist ten hours out from Tangier. Through the waves of nausea he felt a stone in his stomach knowing that he was part of the greatest invasion in history, one that would decide the outcome of the tumultuous global war. He was well aware that in these waters on 21st October, 1805 Admiral Lord Nelson decimated the combined French and Spanish fleet with his own led by his flagship HMS Victory. It was a victory that kept the Royal Navy as the supreme ruler of the seas for one hundred years. John was re-assured that ironically Nelson suffered from sea sickness as much as he did.

Their modern fleet comprising much of the Atlantic and Mediterranean squadrons of the Royal Navy coupled with the US. Seventh fleet was more than a match for any force the Germans, Italians and Spanish could put to sea.

D-Day, 1 May, 1944 the invasion of Europe by three armies sailed on unusually calm waters toward three beaches codenamed Gold, Juno and Omaha. High overhead in the dark heavens rumbled wing after wing of Lancaster, B-17, Liberator, Halifax and Marauder bombers each with black and white wing stripes indicating Allied aircraft to prevent anti-aircraft fire from the naval forces below them on the Atlantic. Also flying from Morocco, but at low level, the first wave of hundreds of fighter-bombers roared over the fleet approaching Europe on an unusually calm sea. Just the day before the weather was terrible, a strong sirocco, the warm wind blowing north from North Africa and a storm from the Atlantic made Bradley postpone the invasion for one day. Seasick troops in the holds of hundreds of troopships cursed the 'brass hats' who masterminded the operation as they finally approached the beaches.

The armada neared Juno Beach on the Spanish mainland on the east side of the port of Cadiz which lay on a peninsula reaching into the Atlantic. The mist dissipated and he could catch, in the dimly growing sunlight of early morning, the four grey landing craft of his force holding fifty men each dispatched from a troopship now a quarter mile behind him. For seconds the mist lifted and his view was broadened to allow him and his men to look around in awe at the scene before them. On all sides were landing craft heading for the target. Behind them were even more troops, the second wave, behind them the third wave were boarding landing craft for their return to the beach from troopships. Behind them were scores of battleships, cruisers and destroyers. He could make out pinpricks of flame from their guns on the horizon as they sent broadside after broadside of shells into the enemy defences. The invasion was on.

Looking ahead John could see explosions on the shore upon pillboxes and gun emplacements. He brought his binoculars up to his eyes and his mouth opened at the incredible damage being done to the Spanish and German defenders. *Remember* he told himself *they are well dug in, in their reinforced concrete blockhouses designed to withstand tremendous punishment. They will be firing back soon.* Each man was struck by excitement and apprehension knowing that this day would be remembered forever in history and was a turning point in the greatest war ever known.

I must look after my men get as many as possible through this bloody day and the campaign beyond. Then unaccountably, his mind jumped to Book Three of Homer's Iliad where the Greek ships land near Troy beginning their long siege. Unbidden the words thrust themselves to centre stage in his mind. "As when some mighty wave that thunders on the beach when the west wind has lashed it into fury- it has reared its head afar and now comes crashing down on the shore; ... and as they marched the armour

156

about their bodies glistened in the sun." *Stafford*, he told himself, *concentrate on the mission: 'Your troop will secure your section of Juno Beach by destroying any German gun emplacements not hit by our aircraft and overcome the first and any other layers of defence allowing the main force to land and move inland. Experience in the landing on Sicily showed us that camouflage can conceal emplacements only the man on the ground can see. Knock them out and you will save hundreds of lives. You will be the first on the beach, it is up to you to make the day a success."*

In the pre-dawn gloom the vista below was largely hidden by protective patches of mist. There were no lights showing from the amphibious force proceeding majestically towards Hitler's Fortress Europe. Two thousand ships: battleships, bergships, aircraft carriers through to destroyers, frigates, minesweepers, troopships and hundreds of landing craft loaded with tanks and anxious troops sailed towards their targets.

As the landing craft carrying the Commandos headed for Juno Beach the Spanish coastal that had survived aerial attack began firing salvos. Shells landed close to the LCIs manned by Royal Navy sailors the spray from the columns of water blown into the air by the explosions drenched the closely huddled Commandos. They were eager to jump onto the beach when they landed and the sailors gaped the mouths of the landing craft open.

A shell found its target and hit the front of the landing craft on their left. *God that's Aubrey's lot*, John thought in dismay as he stood at the front of his men waiting for the craft to stop and lower the blunt moveable ramp they would jump from in seconds. Bullets pinged off the ramp and zipped over their heads.

"Ready men," John pulled his sword out of his scabbard and brandished it tightly in his left hand. His mouth dried. Machine-gun bullets pinged off the sides over their heads. A whirl of Typhoon fighter–bombers screamed overhead letting loose a blizzard of rockets into the Spanish defences and the opposition fire in front of them became desultory. John wondered if Brock was one of the pilots. John had time to think *Thank you* then their landing craft crunched into the beach and the ramp lowered.

"Good luck lads" the crew shouted. John jumped off the ramp into the waist-high salt water, wading up onto the sandy beach in four-foot waves, his boots sticking in the sand. Splashing forward he pointed his sword at the enemy, his Sten machine-gun, its horizontal magazine sticking out strapped across his chest. He could distinctly feel the water soaking into the pack on his back. See the sword he held pointing towards the enemy. "Forward Red Dragons!" At least my beret is dry he thought bizarrely then a bullet whizzed by his forehead. He ran forward while all around him Commandos stormed the beach crouching firing, kneeling firing, advancing fast towards the enemy inexorably as they had been trained. They were not going to die on the beaches like cattle.

Corporal Williams his radio operator, carrying a heavy portable radio on his back and firing his Lee-Enfield rifle every time John halted, followed him closely then knelt with his C.O. by one of many anti-tank steel girder obstacles stuck in the beach, a towering letter X. Facing them were sand dunes covered with clumps of grass and scrub trees bent with wind from the sea. A hundred Spanish and German heavy machine-gunners, mortar crews and soldiers with sub-machine guns and rifles who had survived the seemingly cataclysmic attack by high explosive rocket projectiles fired from their still smoking trenches. Each one was intent on killing as many of the soldiers coming towards them as possible, firing at the figures scrambling up out of the surf onto the beach who staggering under the weight of their backpacks, ammunition, mortars and anti-tank PIATs as the sand sucked them into the beach.

"If we don't keep going we're dead," John shouted. He looked to his left and right. Aubrey's landing craft was on fire, there were dead bodies floating washed up and down by the surf as men were scrambling down the damaged half-open ramp at the bow. Duncan's LTI was on course for the beach

A swarm of machine-gun bullets buzzed around him like metal hornets intent upon boring holes into his body; one hit him in the chest and knocked him back. Dazed, John shook his head and groggily stood up still holding onto his Wilkinson sword. Corporal Williams helped pull him up. 'President' Lincoln led a knot of men towards the dune containing the culprit, a *Spandau* machine-gun crew. He fired his Bren gun 'Bertha' from the hip as he ran forward holding the weapon with his strong arms, switching from single shots to full bursts as he stood over the trenches, spraying them with bullets oblivious to the enemy shooting but incredibly unable to hit him. It was if the Goddess Juno had covered him with a magic cloak. Sixteen men closely following him fired and threw grenades into the trench and blasted the soldiers in the trench. It was over in seconds.

Commandos from two other landing craft to John's right splashed onto the sand and were led by Duncan who played his bagpipes. The stirring tune of 'Highland Laddie' joined the atonal symphony of war as the Scottish naval officer wearing the MacLeod tartan kilt, his badger sporran and RN blue jacket and green beret led his men up the beach defying the bullets kicking up the sand and mortar shells exploding. Lumps of sand were thrown up and fell down as if giant, crazed children clumsily created a sand castle. Taking the bagpipe from his mouth he took his Sten sub-machine gun strapped around his back and placed his pipes carefully into his pack. He began giving orders for the Troop's 3" mortars to fire upon the enemy trenches. Then he led his platoon forward against the enemy.

"Corporal," John shouted to his Welsh radio man, Corporal Williams above the sound of enemy mortar shells exploding around them "call up an air attack on the camouflaged gun position. Here are the co-ordinates," he scribbled them down in a notebook. "It's urgent tell them the first 'funnies' are landing with the Sapper mine detectors and the Beach Master in fifteen minutes." John referred to the fascine carrying tanks, adapted Churchill tanks and bobbin carrying tanks that could lay a stiff path for caterpillered Bren gun carriers and Australian armoured division tanks expected in the next wave of landing craft within the Black Watch infantry and Royal Engineer sappers.

Williams spoke into his round hand microphone attached to the radio by a cord. "Beach control. This is dragon 1 over."

"Dragon 1 this is control 1. Over." An RAF liason Sergeant from the craggy wind-swept coast of northern Cornwall at Tintagel on board a warship replied calmly. "Dragon 1. This is Control 1 receiving loud and clear. Over."

"Urgent. Request air attack on a camouflaged 8" gun on Juno co-ordinates are X Ray 20. Over."

"Roger Dragon 1 we will ask the brylcream boys to pay a visit soon as. Roger and out to you."

"Roger Control 1. Over and out."

Royal Engineers on the landing craft with John's men began sweeping the beaches with metal mine detectors and unwound tape to indicate safe paths for the next waves of troops to be landed, one stepped on one of the, luckily still rare, modern undetectable plastic mines and parts of him were scattered around, his helmet hit Corporal Williams in the arm almost knocking him over.

"The radio's alright, sir," he called to John through the noise of gunfire and explosions, "the air force will come but didn't say when like." A measured shot from the Spanish coastal gun plowed into the nearest of the second wave of landing craft approaching the shore appearing to stop it in its tracks. The Captain in the bridge at the stern amidst flames and smoke managed to keep one engine going and limped for the beach desperately trying to give the amphibious tanks a chance to get onto the beach before they sank like stones drowning their crews. Defiantly a sailor manning a Swedish *Oerlikon* cannon fired at the coastal gun. Just yards from shore the crew and soldiers managed to crowbar the shredded bow ramp so it could operate and the first amphibious Sherman tank sank into the water and bobbed its way towards the shore in a waterproof screen using its engine to power a powerful propeller fitted to its rear. It was followed by another and the tank landing craft kept going churning out smoke and flames until it could land the non-amphibious bobbin and fascine carrying 'funnies' which were to enable the oncoming vehicles to grip firmly on the sand by laying a roll of pliable track or fill up the anti-tank ravines dug out on land. The captain stopped the one working engine as the ship skewed onto the beach, another shell went into its side and out the other in-between two tanks but did not explode just plopped into the water. "Go off!" he yelled at the tank commanders. They needed no encouragement their diesel engines were switched on. The heavy tanks began chugging down the ramp as if all the devils in hell were after them.

"We'll get that bloody gun ourselves. We'll get over to Captain Hunter." Flail 'funny' tanks began moving from an LCT up the beach whirling metal chains around a forward drum exploding mines in their path. Royal Engineers lay tape behind them indicating a safe path oblivious to the fire coming at them confident the Commandos were tackling the enemy.

John encouraged the Red Dragons as he ran to Aubrey who had successfully led his platoon to the trenches to his front. He was leading his men as they mopped up despite his shrapnel wound. His battledress tunic was stained dark with blood on his shoulder. Oblivious to pain with the rush of adrenaline filling his body being in combat Aubrey ceased firing his Tommy gun and reached for one of the Mill's grenades in his gas mask bag. Then a German-made grenade whipped through the air towards him revolving like a juggler's pin. It was a wooden handled 'potato masher'. Adroitly like a championship batsman he swung the stock of his Tommy gun and whacked the enemy weapon back to the grey-clad German soldier who threw himself down uselessly into his trench just as it exploded over him. "Howzat!" Aubrey whooped like a crack Aussie cricketer.

John shouted at his friend. "Well done. I've radioed in an air attack on that that gun emplacement it could be a while though." He pointed towards an almost indiscernable low emplacement heavily covered with camouflaged netting five hundred feet along the beach perched on a recessed rock that had been somehow missed by air strikes. "Why not use some of your PIATs and some snipers to wipe the gun crew out? The rest of your platoon can join us in clearing out their first line of trenches along the dunes and go forward to check how deep their defences are." John suggested.

"Good idea, John." Aubrey shouted orders to his platoon and men carrying the new 'Projectile Infantry Anti-Tank' or PIAT, the British-Canadian version of the American hand-held rocket firing bazooka, scrambled into position surrounding the gun from the sides from the now silent Spanish trenches. The PIAT-equipped two man crews loaded the rocket launcher with one man loading and the other lying, or kneeling down firing off each rocket. The second rocket shot right through a narrow side slit and exploded, smoke poured from the strong concrete blockhouse, a third joined it and crack-shot comrades with Lee-Enfield rifles and scopes gave the PIAT teams cover moving up in the smoke. Time to deliver the coup de grace picking off choking Spanish soldiers who tumbled from the bunker guns blazing.

"You're wounded, Aubrey!" John said.

"Just a bit of shrapnel. Nothing serious, John."

They glanced at the landing craft heading sailing towards the beach. "Phew, they should be alright now," Aubrey said.

"Amen to that. Come on we have to go forward, take their second line of defence."

Seventy-five minutes later with the enemy troops holding a second line of trenches and pillboxes killed or captured the Red Dragons dug in one mile inland at a road junction. It was their main objective. *Mission accomplished.* John thought. He took a drink of water from his canteen and noticed a rip in his brown and green camouflaged smock. There was a hole over his heart that went through the woollen khaki battledress blouse just under his MC ribbon and through his khaki shirt. Smiling incredulously he reached into his shirt and pulling on the silver chain around his neck pulled out a cruelly bent angel coin. In its tight grasp was a squashed bullet. On his chest was a lacerated bruise. He showed Duncan. "Dunc if it had not been for my lucky coin that bullet would have drilled me!"

"You've got a guardian angel, literally," Duncan said holding the coin and looking at his friend in wonder.

"Yeah, I think I do." He and Duncan both took a drink of water from their water canteens. "Here's to guardian angels," Duncan said wiping the sweat from his eyebrows.

"Cheers," John said, glad they had come through. They talked together about casualties and John marked names down in his notebook, then they consulted a large ordinance map of the area.

"Only 1050 hours. We won the beach and set up a defensive position inland at the road within one hundred and forty minutes," John commented as Duncan took out a pipe and filled the briar bowl lighting it with a wooden match that he cupped in his hands while he puffed on the plastic stem of the pipe in his teeth.

"This will be the shortest and the longest day."

"That's good that, mind if I use it when I write my memoirs?" Duncan joked.

John had been surprised at the tenacity of the Spanish troops sprinkled with some veteran Germans. *Of course the Spanish nationalists did not win their civil war by handing out ice-cream to the Communists and anarchists that included visionary but naive foreigners like George Orwell, Ernest Hemingway and that Mitford girl.* One of the captured Spanish officers had told him that they had been told that the first to land would take no prisoners. It had not stopped a group of eighty unshaven mainly Spanish troops with a few Spanish and German officers being taken prisoner. RSM Lincoln had posted guards to watch them while the prisoners sat without their weapons behind some dunes at their rear until the Beach Master could direct some Military Police to escort them to empty landing craft and a troopship heading for a POW camp in Morocco.

The spring sun was already hot as John surveyed A Troop, his two hundred men minus sixteen dead and twenty three wounded in the assault. All but a few men with flesh wounds had been taken back to the ships by landing craft dropping off troops, tanks and lorries and returning with the wounded. Thanks to the Red Dragons their quarter of a mile section of Juno Beach had been secured in good time, allowing the reinforcements of a New Zealand armoured division and the Black Watch infantry regiment to land and move inland to take Cadiz from the north.

John walked over to Aubrey's position on the left flank and was dismayed to see that the Australian's battledress blouse was sodden with blood lying on the ground. Aubrey's face was white he smoked a cigarette, his back against a gnarled tree. He was gripping his pack containing grenades and his beloved didgeridoo as if the enemy had nothing better to do than try and take it from him. Some shell bandage showing under the white bandage wound around his shoulder was scarlet. "You need a doctor Aubrey. I'll have someone take you to the rear there might even be a field hospital set up by now. "

"Just need to ... rest a bit." Aubrey stated.

"You need a blood transfusion."

"Is that an order, John?"

"Yes, it bloody well is. Come back soon we'll look after your men until you return." John saw a Royal Medical Corps Corporal driving a jeep marked with a red cross carrying with some wounded men on stretchers coming along the road from Cadiz heading for the beach and waved it down. "Take Captain Hunter here Corporal."

"Yes, Major. The Jerries are putting up a bit of fight in Cadiz these are some of the first casualties. We need the ambulances, they haven't landed yet I don't think," The driver

164

said. Aubrey blacked out as they lifted him into the jeep in the right-hand passenger seat.

Duncan came up concerned for his Aussie friend that he loved to tease, "Make sure he doesn't lose that awful Aussie field hat or his pack," he said to the driver and they watched the jeep bounce over the hill making their own road to Juno Beach.

Although wounded Aubrey had managed to put the beach gun out of action, lead his platoon to take two lines of trenches several hundred yards inland and destroy several armoured cars. It had not been a pushover. Duncan and 'President' Lincoln and the men showed incredible bravery following John in a bayonet charge on Spanish positions at the last defence post. John's was proud of his men they all deserved a medal. He had cleaned his sword and placed it in the scabbard in his pack. You've served me well today, he recollected the Spanish soldier who charged at him when he saw his Webley had run out of ammunition. Two sword thrusts and the soldier was no longer a threat to anyone.

After ensuring the Vickers machine-gun positions, PIATs and mortars were properly sited over a defensive line running along the coast side of the road in a thousand yard curve. John sent a runner and a radio message to the bearded Royal Navy beach master informing him where he was and that he was dug in awaiting artillery support and orders. He had met and worked with the crusty, bearded Commander during invasion exercises. He chuckled to himself imagining him gesticulating with his walking stick shouting orders in salty language, his bulldog 'Winston' curled up in the sand happy to watch him instilling some order into the chaos of landed troops and vehicles jamming up the beach with only a few safe makeshift roads able to siphon off the pressure.

John took a long drink of water from his water bottle and with his binoculars studied the valley of dry Spanish fields which lay before him as he faced east. They contained tens of thousands of olive trees which grow well in the arid Spanish soil. He had ordered the men to grab a lunch of cold rations and water and apart from piquets on look-out take a few minutes to sleep if they could.

Friendly planes flew overhead and his men waved at them. They were flying south back to Morocco to refuel and re-arm, several were streaming trails of smoke. The Spanish Air Force had woken up. John thought they might have been Typhoons and wondered if Brock was flying one of them.

His request for an air attack was cancelled as soon as the PIAT rockets and the snipers did their work. A Churchill Bombard with a massive howitzer pumping a shell into the large concrete structure completed the job. The fighting over for the moment John looked to his left where Sergeant-Major Lincoln had taken command of Aubrey's platoon. He was cleaning his Bren gun with elaborate care. On his right flank Duncan was having a cigarette and talking to his sergeants and corporals.

John walked over to the Sergeant-Major. "Well done Mr. President or should I say acting Lieutenant Lincoln. I want you to continue commanding Duncan's platoon."

"I will but it's been an uphill fight proving myself as a Negro NCO in the British army. Imagine being a darkie officer! But I appreciate your faith in me." Modestly Francis changed the topic. "Phew, it's been hot work." Lincoln took off his beret took a drink then sprinkled some of his canteen water on his short curly black hair.

"You must be ready to be an officer 'Mr. President' I see one or two white hairs"

Lincoln's brown eyes twinkled, "Don't rub it in. I might have to give you a lesson in self-defence like in Scotland."

"No thanks. I have enough memories of being flipped over with the wind knocked out of me. I had to use that technique today when a German grabbed me from behind. We'll hold this position until we get orders to move on." John showed the acting commander of C Platoon their position on the map and possible attack points if the enemy was able to make a speedy counter-attack upon the beach-head. As they spoke there was an increase in the clank of caterpillar treads and the thrum of engines as a new

166

'road' began to disgorge Bren gun carriers full of Black Watch infantry joining the steady stream of Churchill and Firefly tanks of the New Zealand tank regiment kicking up dust on the dry Spanish road heading south for Cadiz. Some tanks and armoured cars of the Royal Dragoon Guards and a battalion of Green Jacket light infantry troops headed north riding on the tanks or in lorries. They waved as they set off a few miles north to reconnoitre and set up a northern defensive position to protect the beach-head. The Royal Artillery were expected to set up a battery of 25-pounders near the Red Dragons' position by 1200 hours and relieve a squadron of tanks and armoured cars that had been ordered to help defend the way to Juno Beach. Within two days two armies were to be on the offensive with oil delivered by the Pluto, the pipeline under the sea and munitions being delivered by ship docking on the temporary Mulberry concrete dock firmly anchored off Juno Beach and already in use and in the harbour of Cadiz after being swept for mines.

Major Stannard gripped his Garand carbine tight as the first open landing craft in which he crouched, left the destroyer U.S.S. Winslow crammed with the first platoon of his two hundred strong Ranger Company. General Bradley had ordered the Rangers to attack the Spanish naval base at Cadiz and destroy the fuel stocks to help the British who were under attack from a combined Spanish and German assault. "Taking their naval fuel reserves will take the pressure off the navy and provide us with extra oil. Destroying the dump is not a possibility."

He remembered the times he been in action, firstly with John Stafford as they landed at the beach on the south coast of the Isle of Wight and the second time when the Americans secured the beachhead west of Oran in Algeria. The first time he had been too excited to be scared. The second time he began to appreciate what a lucky shell and bullets could do to his men. The Vichy French were supposed to hoist the white flag at the first sign of landing American troops but the opposite was the case. He had lost two officers and fifty men within five minutes of landing the only explanation short of a traitor spilling the beans when they left from

Morocco was the unfortunate co-incidence of the usually lax Vichy troops holding anti-amphibious manoeuvres under the watchful eye of German advisors. A lot of good men had been lost. He felt nothing but professional regret. With his brother killed in Hawaii and his father dying of cancer, his mother long dead he had nothing to live for except to exact revenge upon the enemy who had taken his younger brother and do the best job he could as an American army officer.

A wave of two-engined Mitchell B-26 bombers and B-25 Liberators flew overhead to soften up the Spanish defences. He could not see them but he and his men could hear the comforting thrum of their   engines as they arrived from their bases in Morocco and dropped their deadly load of bombs on the Spanish batteries, pillboxes and airfields along the Andalusian coast.

The flotilla of grey LSIs - Higgins 'Landing Ships Infantry', launched from the surfaced Beluga submarines took the Rangers crouched in the vessels towards the Spanish shore. Their powerful inboard engines speeded them along and the US Navy crews expertly brought the landing craft towards the target in the pre-dawn darkness. They dropped their ramps as they reached shallow water and the Rangers jumped off them into the surf running in the sand and firing at the desultory resistance from Spanish positions dug into the hill overlooking the beach. "Get the mortars firing," Stannard shouted running up the beach waving his men onwards.

Mortar crews assembled their weapons quickly shoving mortar shells down the 2" tubes, the missiles arched towards the enemy positions. They continued firing as the rest of the Rangers ran through the holes made in the barbed wire by the U.S. Army Air Force and stubbornly overran the beach defenders.

From the higher ground Ben Stannard looked through his field glasses at the two hundred foot high round oil tanks three-hundred yards south nestled like giant building blocks amongst sand dunes. "Right that's our target men. Able Company stay here to secure our rear, I'll radio you in if you are needed. The rest come with me. We keep it or we blow it up."

In the fire-fight with four hundred German and Spanish troops and artillery assigned to guard the largest oil supply in western Spain John sustained a wound in his arm. A medic sprinkled white sulpha powder over the wound then bound it up firmly. "You'll have to keep your arm in the sling for a few days, Major."

"Guess I'll have to shoot my Garand with one hand or use my Browning," the Ranger replied. Dan recollected his Browning ending up being the weapon of choice until he ran out of ammunition for it. At the end of a maelstrom of fighting with all the enemy soldiers dead or taken prisoner Dan led a team of Rangers up the ladder winding around the tallest tank and took down the Spanish flag flying from a metal pole at the top. He reached into his pack and pulled out a large Stars and Stripes flag.

Colonel Derby, the founder of the Rangers, modelling the American 'first-in' troops upon the Commandos, had given it to him on board their troopship. "Dan I want you to make history. Here's a flag to hoist when you have the oil tanks, and here is a cameraman to capture it for posterity."

He waved over a reporter wearing olive green fatigues and baseball cap. I'm Abel Truman," the toothy photographer declared shaking Ben's hand, "I'm gonna make you famous son."

"Good but don't make me die while you do it," Ben responded dryly. The Colonel slapped his leg and laughed heartily. "We had better get a grip Major, serious work this invasion business. I'm sure Mr. Truman will excuse us while I meet with my officers in the wardroom."

Sure enough the cameraman from the *Chicago Tribune* was true to his word and name. He took the original photograph then, because that did not look 'dramatic enough' he had them restage the event for his camera. The second photo wired back home was published around the world, one of the iconic photos of the war;

four Rangers raising a flagpole bearing the blue, white and red striped and starred 'Óld Glory' flag of the United States on the top of an oil storage tank with smoke rising from the battle in the city of Cadiz behind them.

Ben did not know that today, he was going to appear on the front page Life Magazine most American papers including his own home-town 'rag' in Niagara Falls, New York. He woke up in a church in Cadiz at dawn and took a few seconds to remember he was in the bell tower. It all came back. Taking the fuel tanks after hand-to-hand combat, then fighting their way towards the harbour after Marines took over guarding the oil tanks. The German SS Division had unexpectedly arrived all guns blazing. He rubbed his stubbly chin, stuck an old cigar into his mouth and clamped down. With his good hand he grabbed his Garand rifle and straightened the helmet that had slipped back onto his neck, giving it a crick as he slept. Major Stannard crouched below the parapet overlooking the city and moved along to the company sniper who squeezed off a round at the enemy sniper."

"Did you get him?"

"Yeah," the private said in a Brooklyn accent as he sat with his back leaning on the wall cradling his rifle, "he's hanging over the window of that nice lookin' building over there." He jerked his thumb back to indicate the direction. They both moved and cautiously popped their heads over the wall. Sure enough there was a dead soldier hanging over a window ledge. Dan took out his binoculars and scanned the city. It was a sunny clear day but clouds were moving in from the Atlantic. It would rain later. There were tank shots from the streets below as Sherman tanks resumed fire against the German and Spanish soldiers still holding the docks despite being outnumbered. Tiger tanks fired back.

US marines and infantry had taken the docks and the southern part of the town but a German SS 16th Armoured Division had been twenty miles east of Omaha Beach and had swung into action against them just as they had mopped up the beach defences and moved north up the peninsula to take the harbour. Stannard knew that the US army was landing in force and would push east against the panzers while the British moved south to ensure the harbour was taken. Then the strategic plan to conquer Spain would click into place but to succeed they must get the harbour up and running.

"God damnit, the Krauts must have moved a bloody SS division here, remember we captured scores of SS swimmers minus their uniforms on the beach when we arrived," he said to the twenty men with him in the bell-tower. In his pocket, he had a coiled leather snake, a black belt with an SS insignia buckle he picked up on the beach. "They probably were resting them up before sending them over to Morocco. Well we beat them to it but they're hopping mad." In reality von Runstedt had decided to place the division near Cadiz for manouvers since the terrain was similar to that near the Black Sea in Russia but also because it was the only way he could get permission from Hitler to place an armoured division where he rightly feared an invasion. Hitler had reinforced Norway and earmarked panzer reserves for his attack on Russia.

The US and British troops had met Tiger tanks and some of the recently produced heavily armoured King Tigers. Either one was a formidable enemy. Dan's bazooka-bearing soldiers had managed to figure out a good tactic, two bazookas shooting at the same spot of caterpillar tracks and bogey wheels as the 68.5 ton tanks crunched their way through the streets blasting whole sections of houses and hotels with one shot of their formidable armament of an 88 mm gun. His men were in the church below and in the other buildings along the street overlooking the harbour sleeping where they had fought until morning had broken.

It was D-Day plus One, Ben could not shake yesterday's ghastly image of seeing a row of olive green Sherman tanks going into the city, each one wearing the white star indicating a US Army vehicle, all on fire from King Tiger tank. The shells from the Sherman guns had bounced off while the enemy tank commander calmly picked off one Sherman tank at time. *No wonder they nicknamed the Shermans 'Ronson Lighters'*, he had thought with a shudder, *they went up in flames as quick as a flicked cigarette lighter. Maybe that's why the Brits call them Fireflies.* But Americans learn quickly. A fresh squadron of Shermans aimed and co-ordinated their fire together at the rim between the turret of the King Tiger and the hull blowing the turret off. *Some consolation* Dan thought.

The Ranger unit commander had been awakened by a fascist sniper shot aimed at their observation position commanding a good view of the harbour. The bullet ricocheted off the bell and hit one of the Rangers in the leg.

The first twenty-four hours had been a blur of action, landing on Omaha Beach mopping up Spanish resistance, taking the oil reserves and marching into the ancient cathedral city that had been the site of many invasions including the one where Sir Francis Drake had set fire-ships into the harbour and completely destroyed one of King Philip's armadas, 'singeing the King of Spain's beard'." They had taken the harbour and made a defensive screen on the eastern part of the city as the SS division fought its way up the narrow peninsula fighting brilliantly against a growing but seemingly disjointed US army. Grim building to building fighting in the city and the closeness of enemy forces with American soldiers in the peninsular meant that Allied air attacks were limited to decimating the remainder of the SS Division which was fighting on the mainland. However, an estimated twelve King Tiger tanks were still roaming around the western part of Cadiz as well as 6,000 battle-hardened veterans of the *Afrika Korps*.

God, I'm going to need your help again today, please don't get tired of my leaning on you, Ben prayed. Then he turned to his men. "We've got the SS guys trapped there's no way home for them. They've got the British to the north and us to the south. Easy meat."

"Yes, sir," they shouted back. "Easy meat." And they went out and did what they had to do and by the night-time with half his men killed or wounded. The last of the SS resistance in the city petered out when the last soldiers in camouflaged smocks reluctantly threw down their weapons and were marched away with their hands over on their heads.

Major Stannard reported to his colonel that enemy resistance in the harbour, thanks to the massive influx of GIs from the beach head was no more."

"I want you to take a slug of this ten year old Irish Whiskey, Major before you dismiss and get your men some food and a rest. I am putting you in for the Congressional Medal of Honor."

"Every one of my men deserves one, sir."

"I can't recommend every one of your men to get this but I will mention your whole unit in dispatches and you can give me twenty names for various medals but I want you to accept the highest award America can give on behalf of the men that died and the ones that live. Will you do that Ben?"

Ben took the glass and drank it in one gulp. "That's mighty good of you, sir."

"No son, it's mighty good of you. Now see to your men get some sleep. We have some more campaigning to do."

*

In Lisbon General Harry Crerar met the new government of Portugal: Admiral Vasco De Silva the leader of the pro-Allied junta, an Army General and an Air Force Marshal. The Admiral was elderly but decisive. A professor of English from the Lisbon University translated beautifully for Crerar and the leaders of Portugal.

Ádmiral De Silva led the *junta*, wearing chests full of medals their shoulders heavily engulfed by gold braid, in embracing the dour Canadian and kissing him on each cheek. "Just like the great Duke of Wellington you landed at Montego Bay. It was there on 21st August 1808 he came with 10,000 troops at La Goa, the lagoon of blood. He used the landscape to hide and protect his troops a trick he learnt in India and continued to use up to and including his great victory against at Waterloo. But in 1808 his commander did not allow him to march to Lisbon which he could have done after decisively crushing the French army. And now a Canadian army is here to help us."

"Well, ahem," Harry Crerar uttered humbly. "I congratulate you on seizing power from Dr. Salazar and look forward to working with you as we establish freedom in Europe. I little thought when growing up in Hamilton and working at the General Electric factory as a researcher before joining the Royal Canadian Artillery in World War One that I would end up in this beautiful country." Inwardly his first impression was disappointing. *Surely these costumed dandies are more suited to be chocolate box soldiers than fighting a determined enemy but I will reserve judgement we need them and they need us. After all without their co-operation my losses could be much higher and time, a crucial commodity as Hitler could quickly move divisions from France south to Spain and Portugal, has been saved by the coup and its success.* By the end of his meeting however their common sense, charm and military acuity soon allayed his fears that his new allies would be more of a hindrance than help.

De Silva spoke sincerely through the interpreter, "We invite you and your army officially to our country. Yesterday you only spoke to our officers at the harbour under the white flag. We apologise on behalf of the Portuguese people that several thousand of our men decided to disobey our orders and sided with Hitler's aims rather than that of Portugal. They have paid the price. Portugal and England have been allies since the fourteenth century and it is only right that we fight alongside the English speaking peoples.

"Our people are united in supporting this temporary junta. We promise a free and fair election once Spain has been liberated. The people and your allied leaders will know this today it will be broadcast on the radio and published in the newspapers. All known Nazi sympathisers have been rounded up and the German

174

Embassy staff and spies have been put under guard and are now awaiting flights from the airport to France. We no longer want them here." Crerar nodded as he heard the translation. General, your arrival here ensures that Portugal shall not become a vassal to Hitler like Franco's Spain. In fact we will help you free our cousins. We will loan you some of our army and place them under your over-all command. We Portuguese value our freedom, yes we fear Communism but the educated among us have learned to also fear fascists, it is they who have plunged our world into this terrible war and threatened to drag us into it. Well, we shall fight but as part of FAN. We also want to join the Earth Government which has been discussed by President Roosevelt and Prime Minister Attlee."

"We must move quickly," Crerar warned, "Hitler will even now be ordering divisions from southern France to meet us. I must cross the *Torres Vedres* and drive into Spain. I must reach Badajos in five days. I need hundreds of translators who speak English, Portuguese and Spanish and scouts who know the mountains and Spain.'' He pointed to the spot on a large map his staff officers had pinned to the wall of the military HQ. We have, thanks to you, the great harbour of Lisbon. It is of inestimable value to the allies and our ships, aircraft and troops will help you defend it and Porto to the north. I suspect that Hitler will not invade Portugal but will concentrate upon Spain just as Napoleon did in the Peninsular War."

Crerar walked over the window. He admired the two mile wide mouth of the Tagus River as it met the Atlantic. Smoke still curled up from the ruins of buildings where die-hard fascists had been shelled into submission. "Let me share with you the situation, excellencies," the Canadian General asked. "My men, tanks, artillery and lorries have landed at Montego Bay and since last night at your excellent harbour. I have 80,000 men with more reinforcements expected. Our tanks and infantry are preparing to move towards the mountains tomorrow. Reconnaissance units have already gone east. I would appreciate Portuguese units to liaise with them. Our staff officers can go over the details. I would be glad to take several battalions of infantry under a commander of your choosing to go with us into Spain. I may ask for full divisions if I need them but for now I would ask if you could use your forces to defend Portugal in the north and along the coast. We can supply you with some tanks and aircraft as they come available until then we will help provide air and naval cover. This morning staff officers from Allied HQ in Casablanca will land by flying boat in the harbour to arrange the landing of Allied squadrons of aircraft and assignment of ships to protect Portugal from German and Spanish attack and sign the formal papers sealing the alliance. I am expected to meet them with your permission."

The Air Marshal standing next to Crerar announced in Portuguese, "I will be honoured to go with you. You shall go in my car and be escorted by my men. We shall take my aide-de-camp he speaks English. I shall bring them back to our palace."

As it turned out his aide-de-camp knew as much English as someone could who had never studied it but whose sole experience of it was sailing on a liner and staying in New York for one month to visit his brother in Boston in 1939. The Canadian was able to see the funny side as soon as it transpired that the Sunderland flying boat carrying the team of staff officers also carried five excellent translators.

CHAPTER THIRTEEN NAPOLEON JUMPS

D-Day plus Two 0900 hours. In the darkness that came quickly in Morocco at the French Airborne Battalion hanger Napoleon strapped on a parachute while his aide-de-camp Admiral Francois Roesch looked on in horror. *"Mon Dieu, mon Empereur* what are you doing? It was agreed zat after your escapade in North África you would not go into battle in case you were killed and our cause lost."

"Nonsense, if we do not win our cause is lost. If I join my troops zere is more chance of us winning. I jump. Now, help me with zis."

"Have you ever jumped before?"

"Once before ... twenty years ago. The chute looks the same; the pull ring to open it is very similar."

"I will have to go with you damn it. I hate flying as it is."

"Ha, good man Admiral you have great *courage mon brave.*"

The two men struggled into the harnesses criss-crossed over their chests each with a rectangular chute package sitting at the small of their backs. Strapped to each of their heads was a regulation British paratrooper's helmet covered with netting filled with green branches with leaves for camouflage. They looked at each other and roared with laughter. In the centre of their chests was a round metal release disc.

"Here," the Emperor picked up a Thomson machine-gun and threw one over to Roesch. "For you. I have a Browning pistol." Each was weighed down with a parachute pack, khaki back-pack, rations, shell bandages, torch, sheath knive and a map. As they walked out to the Stirling bomber that was to drop them they joined the line up of twelve Free French paratroopers. The men recognized the figure with the Van Dyke beard even though the rest of his face was smeared with camouflage ointment. *"Vive*

La France," Napoleon called out waving. "*Bonne Chance, mes freres.*"

"*Vive L'Empereur!*" they called back exuberant they were going into action with Napoleon. He grinned like a small boy climbing a mountain for the first time as he sat opposite his Admiral who did not feel anything like his emperor's enthusiasm.

One hour later nearing the drop zone just west of Malaga on the Costa del Sol the plane descended to five thousand feet dead on target for the dropping zone. The pilot drew back on the throttle of the four-engined Stirling bomber to slow his speed and he had his co-pilot switch on the green light by the rear door in the bowels of the airplane. Two rows of men stood up moved back to the doorway holding onto their static lines. The aircrew opened the hatch in the bottom of the fuselage of the converted bomber and the first man sat on the edge a sergeant gave him a sharp tap on the shoulder and the man dropped out into space. Quickly with much practiced speed one paratrooper after another left, then it was Napoleon's turn, he turned to smile at his aide-de-camp and disappeared into the night.

As he tumbled out of the plane at fifty miles an hour the French General counted to five and pulled at his ripcord handle; strangely he thought of his codename 'Porcupine'. His great-great-grandfather Napoleon III, had been depicted in a Punch cartoon as a porcupine bristling with bayonets, his father had shown him that caricature when he was six. *Strange he thought, I never realised the co-incidence. Well here comes the Porcupine!*"

He felt a terrific jerk as the parachute opened and slowed his descent. He looked around and saw most of the white mushrooms floating in a clump away from him and his aide. Some were already on the ground gathering up their chutes and setting up machine-guns in defensive positions to protect their landing comrades. There was no gunfire they had not yet been detected. He made a mental note to have dark coloured parachutes used in future by his troops. Bonaparte looked at the ground which he could see in the moonlight was rushing toward him very quickly. Forcing his legs together he relaxed them ready to land and roll as he had practiced when he got his wings and a red beret at the British parachute school in Egypt. He had been blown by a ground wind some distance from the main stick of men from his plane away from landing site to a Spanish guard post near a bridge. He could make out a Spanish flag with its eagle insignia on a flagpole. He pressed the release mechanism of his parachute harness and pulled out his revolver. A dog nearby saw him and started to bark. A sleepy Spanish voice called out, *"?Quien hay."*

Bonaparte fired in the direction of the voice there was a sharp cry and body fell to the ground. Another Spanish voice called out and rifles cracked as they shot at him. Scrambling down a hill Bonaparte made off into the night running behind a line of bushes. He ran east toward the target where gunfire now picked up in intensity. He stopped running when he saw his aide-de-camp hanging in a tree a prime target lit up by moonbeams. He was alive and literally kicking in his struggle to disentangle himself, from the chute which had wrapped around his legs. He was twenty feet up and unable to clamber onto a branch.

"Get me down quick, sir," he called, "I am a seeting goose up 'ere." Bonaparte chuckled and climbed up the tree and climbing along a limb, cut away at the tangled chute caught in the branches, using the knife strapped to his leg.

"Get ready to ..."

"Drop, I zink you mean," Napoleon declared as he fell to the ground. Bonaparte tumbled with squirrel - like agility that belied his extravagant lifestyle and forty years. He swam and lifted weights away from prying eyes to keep in shape and lately had woken early to go for long walks and think about the war and the future.

"Just winded, sir, thanks."

"Grab your weapon someone coming." They heard voices, dropping to the ground they crawled into a ditch. A Spanish patrol was walking towards them. They were jittery and fired at a cat that ran across their path. One of them made a radio report to his HQ "Only a stupid cat, so one of the conscripts shot at it. There is nothing out here. *Nada.*"

Bonaparte unclipped two grenades from his belt giving one to Roesch. They pulled out the pins and threw them at the patrol. While Napoleon's ADC sprayed it with machine-gun fire Bonaparte leapt out from their hiding place blazing away with his revolver as the grenades exploded. Satisfied the patrol had been wiped out Napoleon led his aide to find the main body of paratroopers who had made their way to the bridge and held both side.

Once he found them they consulted a map with an electric torch. "We make our way south on zis path for a kilometre then turn right and we should be by ze cliff overlooking ze Mediterranean where we believe zae super-shells are being shot from Big Bertha. See, a hill, inside zat hill eez the firing position. It ees now," he looked at his watch," 0015 hours, they often fire the gun at 100 hours then again at 230 hours. As you remember zey only fire ze gun at night. We zink they open a camouflaged side ze cliff and disguise the flash so it cannot be seen at a distance. We have practiced in Morocco finding four or five air vents three feet wide set in the cliff top going back one hundred yards, open only during the night time firing long enough for us to drop high explosive packs down ze shafts at the same time. Zen we detonate them from the side of the hill far enough away to not get blown up to ze sky when the gun and eet's ammunition go up. If anyzing 'appens to me Admiral Roesch has another radio control. Just like ze practice. *Allons-y!"*

One by one they killed the German guards patrolling the perimeter of the hill with crossbows or knives. Silently they crawled on top of the hill looking for the vents. They were open at an angle propped up by solid wooden frames covered in painted soil and grass allowing only a minimum of subdued lighting from the cavern home of the super gun below them, perceivable to only someone only on the hill. The faint light guided them. "Does eet look like the explosives will fall all ze way down?" He checked each of the vents even though they were fifty yards apart far below him he could soldiers preparing the gun for firing, twenty men were overseeing the lifting of a static crane in the rood which was lifting a heavy twenty-five inch shell to the breech of the super gun. At another vent he looked down upon the magnetic rings circling the barrel that speeded the shell punching it through the air on its supersonic journey to Gibraltar. Five paratroopers were placed across the black outline of the hill ready to drop their deadly packages at Napoleon's word. Each package was connected by a detonator wire to a group of paratroopers guarding the engineers with the detonator control. The French emperor blew a whistle to indicate it was time. Each man dropped his package and ran the hundred yards to the ravine side of the hill away from the road scrambling to safety of the side of the hill. Napoleon hit the red button on the radio control switch. At first there was only the sound of several small explosions inside the hill then there was a very large one that made the hill shake and the tremor made the men sway, then a chain almighty explosions as the stock of shells below made the cavern a molten horror of heat and rent steel. Smoke and flames poured out of the large open firing door.

"Now we make ze disappearing act and make for ze coast." He took out his compass from a pocket of his American style paratrooper jacket, a gift from Bradley, and looked at the ordinance map showing cliffs and beaches near Malaga. Our pick-up ees thirty minutes from 'ere."

"Motor Torpedo Boats are off-shore and are sending in men with rubber rafts to pick us if we are separated you have the maps and know ze pickup is between 0200 and 400 hours.. If we miss zose times we hide during the day and zey will try again the next night."

The MTBs were late getting to the rendezvous since they had to sink several Spanish E-Boats that gave battle. "We are glad to see you, *mes amis*," Napoleon said as they hauled him and his men up into the fast torpedo boats.

181

"Sorry we were held up," the Captain said, as the boats turned south and their bows lifted up from the sea cutting through the water as their powerful engines kicked into high gear, "some enemy boats got quite upset and started shooting had to put them straight it's bad manners to try and sink a chap."

CHAPTER FOURTEEN   THE ROCK

On the British island colony of Gibraltar, just six miles from Algericas on the Spanish south coast the garrison and population were in for another night of air raids. The Spanish were only sending a token bomber force tonight since most of the German and Spanish squadrons had been sent west to deal with the Allied beach-head. "This is a turn up for the books. The French have finally paid off a bit of what they owe the British for helping them in this war and the last. Apparently that Napoleon chap knocked off the gun with a squad of paratroopers," he told the Admiral commanding the Western Flotilla of the Mediterranean fleet as they finished a hurried dinner of corned beef and toast followed by strong tea and oranges. There were still fears that the Spanish might try a 'forlorn hope' attack on the island they claimed as their own ever since signing it over in the peace treaty of 1713.

"It's wonderful news. I shall tell my staff. Does James, the RAF commander know?"

"Yes, I phoned him. He said, "Good, my chaps can knock the planes out of the air but those Big Bertha shells were tearing up my runway, making it a bit tricky.""

"And knocking off some of the Barbary Apes on the slopes of the Rock , sir," the Admiral interjected.

"Quite right, we've had to hide them in their own air-raid shelters. Bit smelly I'm told. RSMs use cleaning it out as a punishment. Oh well, the apes will be happy to get out again and I am sure the Sergeant-Majors will find another equally horrible duty."

In the underground naval HQ hidden in one of the many tunnels bored into the rock of Gibralter a twenty one year old newly commissioned Lieutenant Helen Spencer Helen Spencer adjusted her naval jacket and for the fourth time that afternoon since arriving on HMS Cheshire from Capetown, checked her tricorn hat with the naval insignia on the crown in the toilet marked WRENS. She was proud to be a member of the Women's Royal Naval Service. She applied a little surreptitious light lipstick she had bought in Egypt in the Wren toilet at Gibraltar's Naval HQ. It was her first day at Gibraltar after spending a year delivering Convoy instructions to ships in Capetown harbour in a motorboat. Now she was to do help plot convoys in the Mediterranean RN command control room inside the Rock.

She decided to wipe all the lipstick off after all since it was drummed into them in training that they were not actresses but sailors. It did not stop girls on active duty sneaking it on to the obvious delight of the men they worked alongside. *Still one wants to make the right impression*, she decided finally. She straightened her stockings smoothed down her navy blue skirt which went below the knee and five minutes early, knocked on the door of her new C.O. Commander 'Sunny' Ray Boniface's office.

"Come," a West Country voice called out, Cornish, Devon or Somerset, Helen could not decide just from one word.

"Lieutenant Spencer from Capetown reporting, sir." He looked at her not unkindly she was old enough to be his daughter but he appreciated a fine looking lady and she certainly was that with finely sculpted features. His was a paternal interest however. I would have thought more like from Buckinghamshire."

"Er, of course sir," she smiled relaxing a bit. "You know the Spencer family?"

"Of course I would be a damn poor student of British history if I didn't know you are of a distinguished family, related to our royal family in quite a few ways. Besides Admiral Tennant in South Africa not only gave you a glowing report but mentioned your connection. Please take a seat. I am glad you are here but so apparently are the Admiralty in Halifax, Nova Scotia. You are to spend only two weeks here to get experience on convoy plotting and then you are ordered to Iceland for 'special duties to be assigned overseas' all top secret. They did tell me one thing, be prepared for a cold climate. I'm not sure whether they meant Iceland or somewhere else. I am sure you will find the suitable kit in Iceland to suit your new job."

"Well I have my trunk with me and that has my winter uniform."

"Take it with you and perhaps cadge a few warm things from the Wrens here they don't have much call for woollies. Now how about I take you to the plotting room and show you your duties? I believe they have you down for the dog watch 400 to 1000 hours, this week starting tomorrow but it would be a good idea to observe this morning until the end of the watch and see what my personal assistant does. Bascially it is ensuring that the WREN plotters keep up with the situation as convoys and ships report in and out by radio. The duty officers feed the information they receive by phone to the plotters who chart and mark the progress of each convoy and ship. Then grab some sleep in one of the beds in your barracks and a meals in your mess.

"Of course I took plotting training sir and got experience in Capetown in the plotting room when I wasn't boarding vessels coming in and out of port. I even did some piloting."

A red light glowed on the wall indicating an air-raid alarm topside had just sounded. The Admiral looked at her and calmly asked, "How was South Africa?"

"A lovely country, sir."

"Yes, isn't it. But I think they shall have trouble after the war between the blacks and whites if they don't bend a little. Excuse me I am a bit of an historical philosopher always twittering on."

"I think I know what you mean, sir. There seems a two tier system there. The native people I met were good people, but poor and without any privileges."

"Here's the plotting room, Lieutenant. I'll introduce you to my PA."

185

In London's Russell Square society clairvoyant Thomas Dixon Fairley was in a private session with one of his high placed clients, Lord Lancelot Eastbourne, Prime Minister of New Britain. Lancelot was unhappy and the strain of worry about New Britain's situation in a war that seemed to be tipping gradually against the Axis made him anxious. Worry lines creased his face. Dixon Fairley was, besides his wife who was suffering from cancer, the only one he could talk to about his inner concerns.

Dixon Fairley had silver hair despite being in his late twenties. Unkind members of the Mayfair cocktail set for whom he gave often accurate prophecies whispered darkly that he did things with bottles of bleach to give the right effect. "That monocle, the cape and hair is pure theatre, darling. He has the eyes of a cat my brother says and he was at school with him."

"Poor Fairley I think your brother is such an awful bully."

"At least my brother doesn't dye his hair, but he does have a receding hairline. I wonder if Dixie can change that?"

"No, he reads minds and the future with his extra-sensory perception he calls it."

"Well he does have extra-sensory sex appeal I must say."

"Hmmm doesn't he just?" So the conversations went.

There was more than met the eye with the mind-reader, he was in the service not of dark powers but Free London. C was his spy-master and looked forward to gleaning the chunks of information Dixon Fairley extracted from Lord Eastbourne's troubled mind without him even realising what he had lost. In return the clairvoyant gave him reassurance and bad advice that subtly influenced the decisions the New British Prime Minister was allowed to make in the Nazi run new order. Lord Eastbourne was already suspicious of his fellow fascist politicians but Dixon Fairley's predictions based on half-truths over the years had stirred up fantasies of epic paranoid proportions in Eastbourne's troubled mind. Above all Dixon cleverly worked on Eastbourne's fear that his Jewish ancestry would become known by the SD or Gestapo and he would end up in a KZ camp. "I sense Prime Minister," Dixon Fairley declared "that the Allies are drawing up plans to place all high placed British fascists on trail for war crimes if they win. Of course it is doubtful they will win such is the power of the *Reich* and New Britain but I thought I should be honest with you."

"Of course, I depend on you being honest. I am surrounded by Mosley's spies. I have to know more than he does to stay one step ahead of him and his Nazi masters." Beads of perspiration burst out on Eastbourne's brow.

Raising his arms from the table Dixon Fairley closed his eyes and proclaimed what he saw in the future and told the truth since it suited his careful handling of the Quisling leader. "I see a court and charges read out against prisoners accused of shipping Jews and political prisoners to camps on the Isle of Man and the Isle of Wight, of outrages against their own citizens using cruel reprisals."

"Good God. Do you see me in that court?"

Dixon Fairley concentrated. "I cannot see faces but there are hundreds of politicians and officials facing trial and the hangman is busy." Eastbourne swallowed. "Perhaps if one could prove one had tried to help some Jews or others being shipped off to a camp the judges would be lenient just let some live life in prison, working on a farm or perhaps a castle in Scotland where all is peace." *He's losing touch with reality* Dixon Fairley thought, *over the worry about over his wife in hospital. It's a fine line I don't want him to go over the edge or he will be replaced perhaps by a competent leader who may make decisions that will make it harder to win. We need Eastbourne to stay in power as an inept leader open to our suggestions. When the time comes it will be easy to get him to do our bidding and neutralise the loyalty of British fascist forces.*

"Of course we are both staunch fascists my lord. But I have seen that it would be a good idea to build up some credit as you suggested. It could be done secretly, you run the Gendarmerie and have a good relationship with their commander you told me. You could take an interest in some prisoners under Gendarme control and use your influence to have them 'eradicated' on paper but in actuality you could have them sent to safety. Should the worst happen and the outcome go against us you have evidence showing you were a just prime minister who was forced into the position but merciful, someone who did what they could to be noble in the face of adversity."

"I don't like being cruel Dixon. I like politics but I don't enjoy being a bully. Seems to be a lot of that expected. I'm sick of it." *I can't help feeling sorry for him, a bit. I shall finish up with checking on his wife. He had already harmlessly extracted information hidden in his client's mind about the tooling up of British factories for Tiger and King Tiger tanks with air conditioning units for service in the Americas and Asia, and the training of a New British army to fight in Russia and Afghanistan.*

"I want to check on your wife, sir. Do you have something of hers she has touched recently?" Eastbourne passed over a letter she had written to him from the clinic in the country. Dixon Fairley ran his hands over it and held it as he concentrated. He did not need to read it. "I feel it coming ... 'pictures' coming in about Lady Eastbourne." He saw her in bed but eating, getting stronger, coming home and then leaving her husband again and not coming back on a physical plane.

Lord Eastbourne finished wiping his brow and became alert, sitting forward listening. "Yes ... it is good news the doctor will say she is in remission. She will come back to No. 10 this week with her appetite restored and her energy. She will feel well for a month to three months but ..."

Eastbourne squeeked, "Tell me man I can take it." The seer decided to tell him the truth at least on this personal matter, although normally he did not share bad news that he perceived.

188

"She will be healthy and happy with you for a month, maybe three then the cancer will come back and take her quickly. I do not usually tell clients when a loved one will die but I know you are a brave man and my most important client." *All of which is true*. Dixon-Fairley stood up and walked over to place his hand lightly on the prime minister's shaking shoulder for an instant.

The Prime Minister pulled himself together. "I shall be brave like her." He stood up and made for the door, his chauffer and bodyguards waiting downstairs. "Good luck Prime Minister." Wordlessly his client attempted a smile and left. Dixon Fairley knew he would back there would be the regular phone call from his secretary, every Monday morning to confirm the Wednesday afternoon appointment at 2:30 pm.

CHAPTER FIFTEEN   UNCLEAN

"So this is *Der Gestank*, the stink I think it is called in *Englische,*" the German General growled while covering his mouth and nose with a handkerchief while flying over New Orleans in a reconnaissance flight in a Gross *Leibe*l helicopter. He was the commander of the 8th American Axis Army Group comprising the 10th German Army, the 3rd Latin Army, the 2nd Mexican Army and the 1st Confederate States of America Army. They flew over the low lying French Quarter of the city, there was no sign of life; unburied bodies lay in the street: people, cats, dogs –bodies and carcasses-tens of thousands of them as if they had crawled out to die in the open. The General knew that the bodies would have, in the first few days when recognizable, show bubonic plague symptons, swollen lymph glands, buboes, red spots on the skin turning black *This is war,* the General reasoned*, we are out to win this is happened in all the cities we sprayed with 'devil dust'. No wonder the Americans are not taking any prisoners. No more Mardi-Gras until we re-populate the city with Vichy French and Spanish colonists. A downdraft of air brought them closer to the city.* The General grabbed the air-sick bag that had been pushed into his hands by his adjutant who was alarmed at the green hue of his commanding officer's face. He retched into it and passed it to his aide who gingerly closed it and placed it behind their seats.

The General shouted over the sound of the rotor, "Roosevelt says he has cashiered his own officers caught shooting prisoners but he is out of touch from what is happening on the front lines in Tennessee and Mississippi no quarter is asked for or given. At least in North Africa when Rommel faced Montgomery there was some semblance of chivalry. What beasts have we become?" he lamented.

"But we must win at all costs," his adjutant countered. "If we do not, the *Fuhrer* will have us shot. Look what happened to Adaneuer who lost to Patton at the Battle of Houston. Besides it is the duty of the super-race to rule. It is a hard road but we must take it."

"Yes. I am sure you are right. I have had enough of New Orleans. Have the pilot take us to my headquarters in Vicksburg, I feel like a chilled bottle of Riesling. Wine will settle my stomach and I can plan my counter-attack."

*

At the White House, the Surgeon-General was briefing President Roosevelt and his Chiefs-of-Staff about the latest developments in the fight against the disease stalking America.

"In the 1330s rats from China brought to Europe in ships carrying fleas infected with plague bacillus to Europe, it was known as the 'Black Plague'. Twenty five million is our best guess of how many died in Europe. There were recurring plagues particularly in the summer of 1665 one can read Defoe and Pepys for their comments on the feared epidemic that was wiping out 1,000 Londoners a week with a peak of 6,000 a week in August 1665. Japanese scientists have found a way to sustain living plague bacilli and instead of using fleas have artificially spread them in a virulent, long-lived spray which infecting an estimated three to four million Americans, killing three million. Most of the deaths have occurred close to our front lines in California and in the southern United States, although bombers and agents have managed to infect some parts of major cities in the mid-west. Thanks to a potent antidote developed at Harvard University we are seeing good results on infected patients. Troops, nurses and doctors and industrial workers are being given two injections over a three week period which will make them immune to this plague. As more of the antidote is produced it will be given to men, women and children starting with those closest to the front lines, in line with Presidential Decree 310 in the Emergency Powers Act.

"Yes, it should have been Decree 10, if I had known the terrible effect of this 'devil dust' but a lot of decisions had to be made very quickly when we were invaded."

191

"Mr. President," General Arnold, head of the army said, "You have done more than any President could have done. Those that died did not blame you but the enemy that infected them. It has given us a resolve that is so strong it frightens me. If I was an invading soldier and knew how angry this has made every American and how we are squeezing all that that anger into cold steel resolve to rationally kill and destroy him them until there is nothing left, I would be quaking in my boots."

FDR wheeled himself over in his wheelchair and poured himself a weak drink of bourbon and water. "Ha, 'We have not yet begun to fight' you mean? Like Patrick Henry declared."

"No. We have begun to fight.' Admiral King spoke standing up and helping himself to a drink of water. "Norfolk has been successfully defended. Charlston is almost ours again. The offenses from Birmingham, Alabama and into Mississippi continues. On the west coast thanks to an amphibious landing by our navy of six of Mack Clark's Divisions on the Yucatan peninsula we have cut off the Japanese supply lines to their army in southern California."

"By God, so we have," Hap Arnold, the commander of the air force agreed. "Patton is achieving miracles in Mexico with few reinforcements and using enemy ammunition and vehicles. We shall continue to supply him with air-drops of supplies from Texas and by ship. Thank God we have held Texas throughout the invasion."

"Well now I know what my next speech will be about. I am grateful for that. I am also," he lit a cigarette in his holder and stuck it into his mouth at an outlandishly oblique angle, "indebted to Dr. Morrison here who has patiently allowed us to ignore his excellent presentation. "Pray continue doctor."

"Mr. President, gentlemen, the crux of the matter is this; we know how they make 'devil dust' we know what it is in it and we now know how to stop each of its deadly ingredients: bubonic plague bacilli, Ricin, a deadly poison, and a mutated influenza virus that until now has no real antidote. Their antidote we found in some captured Japanese field hospitals in San Diego is not very effective and next to useless."

"You mean they are using the Spanish flu germ that killed between twenty and one hundred million people around the world at the end of the First World War?" FDR asked, "surely the bacilli died with those victims?"

"We believe the Japanese thawed out the lungs of frozen cadavers loaded with the living virus and found a way to reproduce and change it. Many become ill but did not die from1918-1920 they developed an immunity to that specific virus. However, this influenza, although similar, is different and more virulent no-one has immunity to it, 60% die who get this Japanese flu with the Spanish flu virus 40% higher than the original Spanish flu. So far three million Americans have caught it with two million dying within two weeks.   Strict quarantine measures put into place immediately after the attacks have meant that a catastrophic epidemic of both the 1943 Japanese flu and plague have been avoided. The ricin poison, developed by the Soviet Union is not as effective weapon as supposed but is a deadly nuisance. Exposure to the elements reduces its potency, it is responsible for deaths in the thousands rather than the millions."

FDR spoke dramatically, "One of our subs picked up some interesting messages in Osaka that were deciphered. A deadly influenza outbreak in that city has killed many thousands and it is taking hold in Tokyo and spreading fast across the country. Now they are reaping what they sowed. To think they used the disease as a weapon without having a proper antidote. I pray that this may lead to the end of Japan's involvement in the war although they may accuse us of infecting them purposely although we have not. First Spain is on its knees, now Japan in trouble. There is unrest in Italy due to the length of the war and food riots due to poor crops. Mussolini is no longer a god to many Italians.

"I am not a fortune-teller just a Democrat but the future looks better." His Chiefs-of-Staff Admiral King and Generals

Marshal and Arnold laughed along with Roosevelt. "Now if you'll excuse me I have some phone calls to make and then my wife would like me to join her for dinner and I would be a fool to not do as Eleanor bids, besides I always enjoy her company. Thank you doctor." He turned to his Chiefs-of-Staff, "Gentlemen, until tomorrow at 9 am in the Pentagon."

CHAPTER SIXTEEN   ZULFIQAR

Half the world away in Jerusalem in the British protectorate of Palestine, Captain McDougall (retired) was opening his door to a young man in a dirty panama hat and a rumpled cotton suit twenty years out of date. The clean-shaven young man had a scar on his chin from a wayward hockey puck, light blue eyes, a tall athletic. It was Alan Stafford, John's twin brother. Alan was the younger by five minutes but far more athletic. He shared John's red hair and light blue eyes but had a more ample spread of freckles over his face which did not quite camouflage a maturity ten years beyond his youthful age which was one legacy from his days in KZ1.

A Captain in the Canadian Commandos, Alan, began special duties for Canadian Military Intelligence by impersonating an SS officer in KZ1 a concentration camp on the Isle of Wight in a successful operation in 1942 to free a Jewish physicist, Lise Meitner. After the trauma of his mission in a concentration camp he needed medical help for depression. A stay at the psychiatric wing of the Princess Margaret Hospital in Winnipeg did the trick and he volunteered for a special assignment in the Middle East. In preparation for his mission he was given crash courses in Arabic, Turkish and Iraqi and found he had a talent for becoming proficient in new languages at a phenomenal rate. He was ordered to report to a retired archaeologist living in Jerusalem who would be his commanding officer for special operations.

I still find it amazing that I am working with the famous Lawrence of Arabia, whom the world believes died in a car accident in 1935. But I am in on the secret and if anyone can help me strike against the enemy and wreck their evil plans it is him he reminded himself. Alan burned with a desire for revenge for the ovens and cruelty he lived with on the Isle of Wight. It glowed in his heart despite his best effort to jettison the sickening coldness of the feeling hate gave him.

He had spent months in the deserts of Arabia and Syria with Bedouin tribesmen. His mission from Sphinx was to track down a legendary sword called Zulfiqar by becoming invisible as a linguistically talented Canadian, able to slip into the role of a Muslim tribesman familiar with the customs of the Middle East and Asia. He had become as bronzed as a tribesman, adopting their dress and customs. He had heard only legends but no-one knew where it might be. 'Paradise' was a common answer. Then he was dispatched on a secret mission to neutral Turkey meeting the President and top members of his general staff. He made good use of his newly found expertise in learning languages. He explained to Sphinx how he had followed his orders and sounded out the Turks as to the possibility of them making a secret treaty with the allies against Hitler. Alan relayed the British position that Hitler would disregard Turkey's neutrality if he invaded Asia and found Inonu did not actively support them in his plan for world conquest.

"I asked President Inonu about the sword and asked permission to speak to their top experts about its possible location. He expressed surprise saying the German Ambassador had visited him the week before with an SS archaeologist who asked the same question. He mistrusted their motives and made only a cursory inquiry of Museum staff telling them what answer he wanted to hear, he told the Ambassador and his pompous SS officer that it assured it was a legend and only hundreds of copies existed but for me he made deeper inquiries. The experts revealed that it was possibly hidden in Asia during the Mongol invasions perhaps in a mosque or citadel. There were no records of it in the Hagia Sofia or the Blue Mosque in Istanbul. They took me on tours of those wonderful buildings but as they showed me, it would be impossible to find it without massive excavations, it could be buried in the foundations or in the walls, but they doubted it. Either way it was out of the reach of anyone. Inonu assured me that the Germans had merely been told that he did not believe the sword existed because the only record of it was from Mohammet's time, no mention of it since could be absolutely verified. He told me, "Captain Stafford, I don't want the Germans to find it, it could be used to cause an insurrection in our secular state."

"I liked the Turks and I felt at home in Istanbul thanks to my hosts. They are leaning towards joining the Allies. I feel I touched their hearts in expressing myself in Turkish, albeit with lots of mistakes, but they knew I was sincere when I gave them arguments for siding with us. Inonu was interested in the offer of a post-war defence and free trade alliance with the allies as well as a seat in the inner cabinet of twenty nations of the proposed Earth Government. His generals were more interested in the military aid we could supply and how long it would take to train their men. As you authorised I promised that such training could begin immediately once a secret treaty is signed. Inonu said he would contact our Ambassador for a meeting and give his answer.

"Antitkabir, the mausoleum honouring Kemal Ataturk, housing his body and honouring his memory was very impressive. I was treated like the British ambassador not an army Captain. We went on a night-time motorboat tour of the harbour in Istanbul and talked for hours. The moon shone over the Hagia Sophie and harbour. President Inonu spoke of how much he admired our generals Allenby, his adversary in the First War, and Montgomery in this one. He liked Churchill and wants to meet Attlee his successor. He expressed his disgust at how Lloyd George did everything he could to thwart Turkey in the 20s. He warned me that the Germans are aggressively courting Turkey. He suspects the Nazis are preparing to move against Stalin. He said, 'Tell Attlee, I am weighing up what is best for Turkey. We may not remain neutral if the Germans invade the Soviet Union and if they invade Turkey to get the oil fields at Mosul in northern Iraq. I am willing to meet Attlee in Palestine, Egypt or Turkey. I assure you that the alliance you propose informally could be received kindly depending on the circumstance when it is formally presented to me by Her Majesty's Ambassador to the Republic of Turkey.'

"They are already uneasy jumpy would be an apt term. All Greece except for Crete is under German and Italian occupation.

In return for signing a treaty with FAN they want a lend-lease for war material to the value of one million pounds, to be full partners in a post-war free trade and military defence blocks with Britain, France and the United States, guarantees of their borders, and a seat on any inner-council in the proposed Earth Government."

"Very good, Captain. I am glad you have their trust. I will report to Ottawa and mention you in dispatches. There is no doubt that Turkey could be a great ally, they are a secular state and stand against the *Wahhibi* movement of Suni Muslim radicalism begun in the late 1790s and now expressing itself generations later in nationalism which sympathises with anti-Jewish Nazism.

"The Germans are expertly playing the hatred card. The Muslims in the Middle East all the way to India are being set up by Nazi propaganda and promises of another Islamic 'golden age' to fight against our cause and support Hitler's. Hitler would like nothing better than to whip up Muslims in their tens of thousands in the Indian army fighting for Britain turn against us. It could result in wasting whole divisions into putting down revolts. Luckily Attlee has promised India independence after the war and on the whole Indians, both Hindus and Muslims believe him but that opinion could swing against us. The flames of revolt in Iraq against the pro-British Hashemite King we placed there would be fanned by the cry '*Jihad bis saif*'–'Struggle by the sword' and if that cry is taken up we will not be able to put out the fire easily across southern Asia.

"We must be on the look-out for anything the enemy is doing to rally militant Islamic feeling. Remember Alan, pre-1914 Turkey made a secret alliance with Germany and placed the Ottoman army under German advisors, it was only their adroit diplomacy and fight with Greece after the war that ensured that they did not lose as much as Austria and Germany did at Versailles. It was through their great General Kamel Pasha who named himself ... "

"Ataturk," Alan put in, "meaning 'I am a Turk'.

Sphinx nodded and continued, "In 1919 Churchill wanted Turkey as an ally but the PM Lloyd George did not, ironic since Churchill's big gamble in 1915 was trying to invade Turkey at Gallipoli since it was a member of the Triple Alliance, with Germany and Austria. If it had worked we could have marched on Constantinople, knocked Turkey out of the war and attacked the Austro-Hungarian Empire from the Balkans, in concert with the Russians attacking from the East bypassing the deadly stalemate of trench warfare in France and Belgium."

"But Ataturk beat our chaps at Gallipoli."

"We blundered. The timing of our initial attacks was faulty, they knew something was up due to our increased naval ops in the Dardanelles and we underestimated the strength of their defences and bravery of their army. We withdrew but only after horrendous British and Australian casualties over several ineffective months trying to take the high ground. We should have realized we had lost the element of surprise and not reinforced failure.

Churchill almost did not recover politically, many political observers said that his star had fallen and he would never again be a force in British politics. But he served on the Western front commanding a battalion of the Royal Scots Fusiliers before returning to the cabinet as a successful minister of munitions. As we all know he was the best man to be Prime Minister. Without him the war could have been lost in 1940, here we are in 1944 still fighting with a good chance of winning. I miss Winston. I wish he could have slowed down a bit and not died of that wretched heart attack in Australia in1941, but what he did before, during and after the Battle of Britain saved our bacon. He will never be forgotten. Two more years of war lie ahead if Hitler makes the mistake of invading Russia but it could be much more if he does not, maybe three or four. Hitler is beginning to lose touch with reality let us hope so."

Sphinx opened up a carved wooden box beneath his bed and lifted out an object wrapped in green silk.

He unwrapped an object twelve inches long and passed it to Alan. "Here, a small Persian version of the fabled Zulfiqar or Zulfigar as it's sometimes spelt in transliteration from the Arabic." Alan looked in wonder at the object and took the steel dagger into his hands. "If the Jerries get their claws on the original sword, of which this is just one of many fanciful copies, it would be a major propaganda coup for them. It may well have been hidden during one of the many invasions and incursions across western Asia. If Hitler, or even Stalin finds it, he would use it as to cause an anti-British uprising by young nationalist Muslims from Iraq east through Iran and across Afghanistan, perhaps even into India which contains large numbers of Muslims some of whom are openly anti-British and sympathetic to Bose's Indian Liberation Army already in existence funded and trained by the Axis."

Alan gripped the hilt which was decorated by an etching of a seated Iranian nobleman and pulled out the weapon from the wooden lining within its decorated steel scabbard. Bifurcated curved steel blades decorated with foliage were revealed. "Two blades!"

"Yes, replicas of the sword usually have two blades to symbolise the lightning speed and deadliness of the sword so sacred to the Arab world."

The Canadian held it in his hands balancing it; gripped it in his right hand and flashed it through the air. Its split blades curved to one end made it look like the talons of a bird of prey ripping through the air. "It is the most amazing weapon I have ever seen." Alan studied the upside-down emblem of a warrior riding a horse etched into the top of the blade beneath the hilt.

"It was made in the 1800s in Persia. The blade is of watered crucible steel called 'Wootz'. I believe the Prophet did give a sword to his son-in-law. Time and legend have made it a strong symbol in the Islamic world. Evidence has arisen that places it in Harat, Afghanistan. I heard rumours of Zulfiqar's resting place while travelling in Iran and western Afghanistan undercover as an archaeologist in 1938. Baghdad, Iraq; Kandahar,

Afghanistan, Damascus and Mecca were all locations that were bandied about. I and my agents searched and made inquiries but nothing surfaced. Now information from the Free London reveals that it is located in the Citadel, Qala-i-Ikhtiyar-ud-din built by Malik Fakhruddin in 1305 AD. It was built on the site of the fort built by Alexander the Great on his way to India. The fort was attacked repeatedly by conquerors like Genghis Khan, the Seljuks, the Ghorids, the Mongols, the Timurids and the Safavids. The walls of the citadel silently tell us the past of Afghanistan. One legend a librarian dug up is that it will be found, "In the mouth of the earth."

"Could be a cave, a spring-the head of a river," Alan interjected.

"Or something that every fort and castle has to withstand a siege," Sphinx tossed out a clue.

"A well, of course that fits with a Citadel built on the site of an ancient fort," Alan concluded.

Sphinx continued, "There's a Turkish archaeologist working on a dig near the old Mosque. His name is Murat Yilmaz a friend of mine. He speaks Pashtun and English. The Turkish government has asked him to afford you all the help he can in locating the sword. An SS expedition was sniffing around northern Iraq since I gave out some misinformation that led them there but they have left heading east and could be in Afghanistan; their researchers may found something in the German libraries which have excellent collections of material on Asian travels and artefacts and sent them on the right trail.

Yilmaz has been excavating Alexandrian sites all across Asia for decades and, as luck would have he was close to Herat when my message reached him. He should not be suspected by the Germans as looking for Zulfiqar. He has set up a dig at Herat's citadel with the permission of the Afghan King. It was a fort built by Alexander the Great on his way to India. A Turkish Airline DC-3 Dakota is flying out some archaeological equipment and supplies to Yilmaz, in exactly five days time it will land at Baghdad. You will board the plane at Baghdad airfield and which goes direct to Herat. Today I want you go to Baghdad your contact there is a remarkable lady, Freya Stark. She's in charge of British propaganda in the region and is a mine of information to help you know more about Asian archaeology.

"I will write to Murat to expect you, he and I have worked together on other little projects. With his help you will locate the sword and bring it back here immediately taking the plane back to Baghdad then take an RAF plane to Jerusalem. Here are travel passes cleared by Persforce. If you cannot find Zulfiqar he will use the dynamite he uses in blasting rocks to seal the well so no-one else can find it in this century anyway. We cannot take the risk of allowing the Germans any chance of getting it. They are hot on the trail."

"I hope I find it," Alan said, "it would be a shame to blow it to smithereens."

"If it **is** there, it has survived Genghis Khan's hordes and many other invaders whose power rose and fell. Herat is the crossroads of Afghanistan. I imagine it will survive us." Colonel Lawrence removed one of the two rings on the fingers of his left hand and handed it to Alan. It was silver and depicted a profile of the sphinx with small ruby eyes. "Show this to Murat and he will know you are sent by me."

Alan took the ring then noticed a photograph of Lawrence on a camel in front of the Great Pyramids. Lawrence talked about it. "That is my old self and Winston on camels in front of the Sphinx and great pyramids 20th March, 1920. His wife Clementine and his detective are there. Winston was Minister for the Colonies and I was his advisor calculating the new borders of the Middle East and deciding who should reign over them. Feisal should have been made King of Syria as well as King of Mesopotamia, now Iraq. I promised him the French Protectorate of Syria but his attacking French troops in Syria in the 1920s doomed his cause. Churchill was desperate to cut millions of pounds maintaining

202

British and Indian troops to keep the peace in what is now Iraq. We felt Feisal, an Arab Hashemite prince, an emir, descended from the Prophet, would have a chance at leading an independent Iraq and following British advice thanks to our support. Feisel was more energetic than his brother Abdullah II, who we chose as King of Trans-Jordan, a smaller territory north of this Palestinian Mandate the League of Nations gave Britain. Now Feisal's young son is King of Iraq.

"In 1924 Ibn Saud conquered the Kingdom of Hijaz in Arabia, displacing our choice, King Hussain. Overnight the reactionary Ibn Saud became Guardian of the Two Holy Places Medina and Mecca. This reinforced *Wahhabi* followers within Islam, they adhere to the strict form of the religion which is could become nti-western is anti-Zionist. In 1932 Ibn Saud named his kingdom Saudi Arabia and gave oil concessions to America and their company, Aramco. We should have promoted the Hashemite King of Hijaz because he was an ally. Instead we financially supported Saud. I am doing all I can to keep the Saudie-Arabians neutral at least, having them declare for our side may not be possible until we are close to victory.

"Now you must be on your way to Baghdad I have arranged an RAF flight to Baghdad this afternoon just report to the airfield commander he is sending a driver to pick you up. Good luck Alan. I am told by my confidants that Germans and pro-Nazi Muslim intellectuals are trying to find the sword. There are SS teams searching in Asia; the operation is led by an SS officer, Otto Von Darmstadt."

Alan looked sharply up at the sound of the name. "You know this man?"

Alan replied slowly. "Our paths crossed at KZ1 on the Isle of Wight."

"Tell me about it." Alan related the tale of his mission impersonating a British SS officer in KZ1, helping Lise Meitner escape while pretending to all the other inmates and the SS guards that he was a British SS officer, his subterfuge included shooting an escaping prisoner. He related how he had helped prisoners escape when John's Commandos and American Rangers who landed by submarine on the Isle of Wight after a fight with Otto Von Darmstadt during. "He's the nephew of Count von Darmstadt who my brother John tangled with at the Tower of London when they sprang Edward VIII and Queen Wallis."

The Sphinx listened and looked Alan square into his eyes, whatever he was looking for was not there.

"The shadow of what you saw may appear in your heart from time to time. It is the price heroes pay, the ones that live anyway." He looked out the window to the street below watching an RAF jeep park in front of a small cinema next door where lurid posters proclaimed the latest Egyptian film. "Your ride is here I shall see you off." Alan put on his panama hat and followed Sphinx down the narrow stairs to the street.

A few weeks later Captain McDougall sat in his favourite chair took off the silk scarf from his neck and used it dust off the cafe's round table then he placed his pristine white panama hat down and opened an Arabic newspaper. A middle-aged Turk wearing a fez and a drooping bow tie drove an ancient Ford taxi by the cafe, Pushing a young boy out his cab he lit a cigarette with exaggerated operatic movements that brought a smile to McDougall's long face. The boy ran up to the cafe looked at each of the patrons and stopped in front of him. The Sphinx politely gave him the Muslim greeting, "Assalamu alaikum."

"Wa alaikum assalam. Captain McDougall? I have a letter," the boy said in Arabic. The Sphinx nodded. The boy put an envelope into his hand. The man who was once Lawrence of Arabia reached into his pocket and pulled out a ten piastre piece and gave it to the boy. With a squeal of delight the urchin clenched the coin in his hand, turned on his heels and ran off. The Sphinx opened the letter and read.

Dear Captain MacDougall:

Freya Stark here in Baghdad has been a great help. She is doing wonderful work shoring up pro-British Iraqi opinion at a time when Nazi led agitation has increased in Bahgdad. She wonders if you could possibly arrange shipping some more sixteen millimetre films; the intelligentsia here and the royal family (all those wives in the harem) love everything, the one showing the shopping district of the Royal Mile in Edinburgh had to be shown three times! During the one about the Royal Navy the number one Queen, Freya assures me, stood up at the end she was so moved. She has never seen the ocean in her life. Anyway the British Council say they have sent everything they have so she is desperate for more.

I believe her when she says that opinion against the British is being fired up by Nazi agents and she fears that some Army generals have come under Nazi influence and may lead a rebellion against the king making things precarious for the British legation in Baghdad and the RAF base at Habbaniya. Perhaps you could mention this to anyone you may know who could share this with.

The architecture here is fascinating and Freya has been a good tour guide and host. She introduced me to several archaeologist who are members of the Friends of Britain Society she has built up to include about seven hundred intellectuals mainly in Baghdad and Basra. They were helpful about my area of interest-Alexandrine fortifications. Anyway next stop is where you suggested don't want to say much in case, doubtful since the war still rages, a rival archaeologist picks up our lead on Alexander's footsteps. She is knowledgeable and confirmed what we thought about the possible dig we discussed.

Yours,

Alan (apprentice archaeologist)

CHAPTER SEVENTEEN   JET FIGHT

The *Messerschmitt* 262A *Sturmvogel* jet fighter equipped with multiple cannons and a *Junkers Jumo* jet engine mounted under each wing, took off from the New Orleans *Luftwaffe* airfield in a cloud of dust and roared into the sky leaving twin vapour trails. The pilot watched the coast of the Gulf of Mexico on his left side disappear swiftly beneath him as he turned north like a screaming eagle to Memphis, to find some American planes to shoot down. "Nothing the enemy has can stop you," the pilots of the jet *Staffel* had been told. Confident, the pilot increased the speed of his plane to 500 mph it would not be long before he could see the Appalachian mountains to the north east and Tennessee ahead where the USAAF was throwing everything it could against the 15th German and 3rd Latin American Armies which had been thrown back along the Mississippi Valley by determined American counter-attacks.

He would have to slow down over suspected enemy areas to stalk his prey but could easily tackle any enemy interception. It was 'a piece of strudel' once you got used to the shark shaped nose's tendency to lift too soon on take-off and wiggle from side to side when you landed. That and the G force of gravity pushing the blood out of your head when you reached the maximum speed of 540 miles per hour, almost two hundred miles an hour faster than the Mark VI Spitfire, Thunderbolt or Mustang, was a challenge even to highly experienced pilots. But, once you had the hang of the power you were like a jockey successfully riding a temperamental and massively powerful racehorse.

A squadron of silver painted Mustang piston engine fighters on patrol saw a very fast object coming towards them, the pilots tried to face the *Sturmvogel* but the jet destroyed two before they could defend themselves and raced away before anyone could position themselves to fire.

"Control, T for Tango 212 Squadron, we've just been attacked by a very fast enemy aircraft, it shot down two of our flight. No propeller, possibly a manned rocket or jet plane, repeat possibly a manned rocket or jet plane. We didn't have a chance to attack him. Over."

"Roger, T for Tango. Over and Out."

USAAF women radar operators in Chattanooga picked up the fast moving blip heading north in the centre of Mississippi and contacted the station officer. He looked at the screen with professional interest, "This bogey is very fast, a German jet, we knew they were being tested in Germany but did not think they would be used in theatre ops for another six months. There are no British jets flying this afternoon and it would not shoot down our boys. Scramble 313 Squadron we'll see how those limey jets do in action."

When the call came through at 313 Squadron an RAF Meteor jet was scrambled. Gloster Meteor jets, made in Canada, had just been flown down days before to Little Rock, Arkansas. It had been test flown in desert conditions alongside the American jet prototype the Comet. However the Comet had run into teething problems just when designers succumbed to the plague in Seattle. It would be a few weeks until factory production could begin. In the meantime the British had agreed to help push the invaders out of the mid-west by sending their first jet squadron into action against the Axis air force.

The pilot clambered into his pressurised G-suit and ran to his plane. An 'erk' helped him into the cockpit where he lay prone on a leather-covered pallet contoured to his body. The sleek plastic bubble of the cockpit was closed over him. The Meteor had one Whittle jet-engine mark II, named after its inventor, Sir Frank Whittle. It was mounted inside the fuselage, its burner right beneath the tail painted with the RAF vertical colour bars, red and blue. The stubby wings were swept back and painted a sand colour. The Meteor sported an RAF roundel on both sides of each wing and one on each side of its fuselage.

The engine blew out flames, emitting a thunderous rumble as the jet flashed down the runway and lifted up into the sky. The pilot wore the pressure suit developed by Dr. Wilbur Franks of the RCAF. He asked the US Army Air Force control for instructions.

"Control , this is W for Whiskey am at 10,000 feet. Where is trade? Over."

"Control to W for Whiskey, bogey thirty miles south of you flying due east at 14,000 feet at over 500 mph. Over."

"Roger, over."

The Meteor pilot increased the amount of fuel to be burned by the engine and felt the pressure of the increased speed push him down into his horizontal cockpit seat as he sped towards his prey gaining altitude quickly. He spotted the *Stormvogel's* vapour trails below and scanned along them until he saw the dark object at its leading point.

"Control, W for Whiskey. I see the bandit. Over and Out."

"Roger, Good luck. Out."

The pilot held his right thumb over the cannon button in readiness and manoeuvred his plane into an attacking angle. The Meteor burned its way towards its target, as it reached cannon range he fired. The plane shuddered and the shells thrust their way past the nose of the *Messerschmitt*. The enemy pilot cursed, instantly jerked his plane to starboard thinking he could out-fly anything that had been lucky enough to get close to hitting him. He looked in the rear-view mirror above his head he was shocked to see what looked like another fast fighter, a single engine job with a rocket or jet built into the fuselage. He pulled on his joystick and spiralled vertically up into the sky increasing the fuel going to the two *Junkers Jumo* engines straining the *Sturmvogel* to the limit. Too late, shells chewed up his tail and it fell off.

Even though the plane had already slowed to three hundred and fifty miles an hour it was in an uncontrollable spin the Luftwaffe pilot fired the small explosive bolts unlocking the plastic dome over his head, pulling the ripcord. He was jerked violently then floated in air supported by the silk mushroom above him and watched as his wounded plane fluttered down into the desert and exploded. The first jet-versus-jet duel had finished in less than a minute and the German pilot badly breaking his leg landing was surrounded by curious GIs who took him prisoner. The Meteor pilot did a victory roll over the control tower letting everyone know he had shot down his first victim, boosting the moral of the Army Air Force pilots and ground-crew. "You know, waking up this morning I wondered if this war was ever gonna end but now," the commander of the air force base said. "Just wait until we get our Comet jets in action!"

In the White House President Roosevelt was told the news and chuckled as he inserted a Camel cigarette into his cigarette holder and waved it at his wife Eleanor in jubilation.

"Now Franklin, you must cut down on those cigarettes they play havoc with your chest."

CHAPTER EIGHTEEN   FISHING WITH HITLER

Adolf Hitler sat in a deck chair in the garden of Dumbleton Hall in the lush Worcestershire countryside lulled into calmness by the buzzing of bees. He read from a thick green volume with black and white illustrations of animals wearing English clothes, jackets, caps, scarfs, straw boaters, tuxedos.   Hitler read haltingly in English out loud to his creakingly ancient butler Marmaduke Mole. "Oh bo-ther, oh blow .. Oh, hang spring cleaning said *die* mole."

"*The* mole, sir," the butler gently corrected the *Fuhrer* so earnestly trying to be an English gentlemen. It was an idiotic idea. This dictator had as much chance of becoming a gentleman, the nimble minded Marmaduke knew, as a snowball flourishing in hell. However it furnished the long suffering butler with hours of amusement that suited his ironic sense of humour. He was having a 'good war' and when and if the time came he was in place to follow instructions from the SOE. It might mean killing his master or helping imprison him or just giving information as to his whereabouts or intentions, he was ready for anything.

The next morning standing in a shallow part of the river that ran through his Worcestershire estate in thigh high rubber boots, a tweed hat on his head and a country tweed jacket that was far too big for him Hitler flicked his fly-fishing rod as Mole had painfully told him and his fly shot out over the surface of the water and a trout made a half-hearted attack at it.   It lacklustre fish flopped back into the current. "Too bad, sir. I thought you had that one."

Hitler gave his open wicker creel a withering stare it only contained one tiny roach. He looked gloatingly at his butler's stuffed basket full of magnificent fish.

"Please Mole, could you please try, I am how should I say? Sad to go back *mit* only zis little fish." The servant took the rod from the German dictator's hands and cast it expertly once, twice. The line darted out in text book precision over a deep channel, a trout caught the fly and the servant reeled it in. Hitler quickly grabbed the net and succeeded in catching the jerking, gleaming trout in it, excitedly he plunged his hands around the trout and squeezed pulling it out and after inexpertly ripping the hook out of it's mouth stuffed the magnificent five pound fish into the basket where it continued to flip as he excitedly carried it home in triumph. Marmaduke followed his exultant master carrying the rods, nets and his own heavy creel. He dreaded the fishing tales to come when Hitler would claim he had caught a five, no fifteen pound trout, there would be no limit on the growth of the fish as he would regale his dinner guests with his lies.

The fish was dutifully gutted and poached and became part of the dinner that night, soup, fish with salad followed by pheasant, small potatoes, buttered peas and carrots then sweet, a sticky toffee pudding swathed in dollops of light cold, home-made custard or apricot surprise for the ladies watching their figures.

Hitler stood at the head of the dining table at the end of the meal. "*Ach* it is good to relax after my great speech Nurenburg. One of the fish tonight I caught in my own river, it was this long he stretched out his arms in exaggeration und it was five kilograms at least. That is ten of your imperial pounds. " There were murmurs of sycophantic admiration from the guests, fascist politicians, the German ambassador Ribbontrop and various scientists and military men invited to discuss the rocket program underway on the Isle of Wight, the Isle of Man and in Peenemunde in occupied Holland.

Werner von Braun, his top rocket expert wiped his mouth with a linen napkin then exclaimed; "They were stirring words *mein Fuhrer* I have committed them to memory. 'We are on the eve of the great victory against our enemies using secret weapons of immense power. I see a *Reich* of a thousand years one year to another victory and power to the Aryan race launched by the *ubermenschen* of National Socialist Germany. Nothing, not Roosevelt, Attlee or the other weak leaders of the democracies can touch us. We will wipe, we will crush, we will destroy any attack against the *Gross Reich*.' The way you timed it and jerked your arm up and down, in time to your delivery was a masterstroke. I watched it on my television live from Berlin while here in New Britain, there is no end to what German science can do."

"Thank you Werner, You are right of course and I am glad my practicing for hours in front of my full length mirrors paid off."

Lord Eastbourne thought he had better say something although he felt very tired and light-headed. "I too saw it on television at 10 Downing Street. Never have I seen such weeping by the women of the Nazi party they were hysterical and the roar from the ten thousand SS troops and 100,000 *Wehrmacht* soldiers would have put fear into the devil himself. I particularly liked the part where you accused the allied leaders and outlaw women like Queen Elizabeth and Madame Chang Kai Shek of being notorious criminals, pimps and prostitutes helped by a lobby of Jewish and Marxist revolutionaries. I am told that 10,000 British Black-shirts cheered in Trafalgar Square as they watched the speech on a huge television screen. They could follow along with subtitles of what you said in English." Lady Eastbourne kicked her husband's shoe to signal him to be quiet. Enough was enough.

*

In the scenic snow-capped mountains of Norway Manfred von Darmstadt lived in a chalet designed to accommodate his wheelchair as he supervised the creation of an underground city, Valhalla. He designed a lead impregnated liquid canopy to be sprayed on the interior of a huge radioactive caves carved out under the mountains during the subterranean testings of the *atombombe*. "It will protect the occupants of my Valhalla from radioactivity," he told his small army of engineers and scientists. There were three such caves, large enough to maintain a million Nazis. He planned a self-sufficient secret city that grew its own food, developed its own industry and could withstand attack by any weapon. In case of disaster it would be the last secret redoubt of the Reich, designed to last one thousand years or more. Everyone who worked on it, German men and women were destined to live and breed in it. Hitler, Himmler and his own nephew were the only ones outside of the working team who knew of the project and they spoke of it only when they were alone.

*

Aztec prowled along the beach on the coast of the Isle of Wight and spotted the body that was being washed up onto the sand. Carefully gripping his teeth into the man's coat collar he dragged it up as the surf pounded them, his powerful legs braced and dug into the sand. The water sucked back and he pulled the man up out of the waves in jerks. After a few minutes he had the body lying on dry sand. He licked the man's face and as if in reward he saw the man's hand move.

It was gripping a glove. Aztec pulled at it gripping it with his teeth and decided to show his master. He pounded up cliff scrambling up a narrow and treacherous pathway he knew running into the darkness making for his home.

He scratched at the back door and coughed. 'Aztec, what's up boy?" the cat dropped the glove at Marcus's feet. "A wet glove." Marcus squeezed some water from the leather garment and tasted the drops in his palm. "Sea water." There was some sand on it. "The beach." Aztec looked at him with large yellow eyes.

"All right Aztec we've got a long time before dawn and it's going to rain, no moon and no beach patrols tonight if I know the Jerry garrison. Let's see who this fellow is." Marcus grabbed his raincoat and made sure his *Luger* pistol had its safety catch on and was carefully tucked into the back of his trousers wedged in by his belt which he tightened as he stepped through the door.

Reaching the beach Marcus reached down to test the man's neck pulse as Charlotte had done to him in practice. As he did so the man groaned, Marcus put him on his side and putting his arms around him squeezed his chest, he had seen a fisherman do this once to a waterlogged yachtsman who had fallen off his ship. The man vomited some more and gasped

213

"I'll have to get him home or … that cave Aztec." *I think I can drag him there, there are some blankets and food.* While Marcus grabbed the man under his arms and dragged him Aztec picked up a trouser leg in his teeth to help and trotted alongside. The rain beat down upon them. After one hundred yards, exhausted, Marcus squeezed behind some bushes he had planted in front of the cave which had sand and stones glued to a wooden board to camouflage it. *Oh,* Marcus smacked his forehead, *'Idiot, got to check if he's on our side.* He finished dragging him into the cave replaced the board and lit a match. The man was still unconscious but breathing Marcus studied him, a sailor, British or American? If British was he a fascist?

He unbuttoned the sodden dark coat. Checking the pockets of his jacket he pulled out a sodden envelope containing photos of a large rocket being launched. There was no identification. *Probably he was rowing out on his way to a sub pick up off the coast and was attacked by an E-Boat patrol,* Marcus wondered. "Let's see if there's a boat somewhere?"

They went out into the filthy night, the rain slammed down wet nails hammering both the young man and jaguar as they looked for a boat or raft. "There it is," Marcus said under his breath the water running down his cheeks and chin. It was a rubber craft with very little air left in it. Marcus rubbed his wet fingers over some bullet holes. He carried the rubber raft and wooden paddles to the cave. "I'll patch it up sometime, could come in handy," the Isle of Wight resident confided to his jaguar.

"You stay here Aztec. I'll phone my Iron Duke contact they will want to see this man and his photos help him get to freedom."

CHAPTER NINETEEN   LION CITY

In Singapore two battalions, the 7th Rajput Rifles of the Indian Army, the Royal Sussex Regiment and a West Indian infantry battalion returning from duty fighting the Japanese at Kuala Lumpur were in for a treat. At the barracks were crates of bottled beer delivered from Ceylon by Beluga submarine and hoarded carefully. General Freyberg had issued a bottle to each of his 60,000 troops when Monty won the battle of El Alamein now with stocks up he could afford to issue two bottles per man to celebrate the success of the D-Day landings in Spain and Portugal. The men had switched with the Royal Hampshire Regiment and an Australian infantry battalion who were going to the front line that Freyberg's besieged army held despite ferocious Japanese offensives.

The news had come on from British army HQ in Calcutta by radio to Freyberg's underground HQ under the largest hotel in the Far Eastern naval base and redoubt of the British Empire. The radio room duty officer reported to the Kiwi C.O. "Good news, General. D-Day is a success, the allies have beachheads at Cadiz and Lisbon and are fighting making their way inland."

"Good news indeed, this will raise morale, have two bottles of beer issued to each man when off duty and start with the troops just coming in from the attack on Kuala Lumpur. We shall have another shipment of beer from Ceylon brought by Beluga sub, we'll need to celebrate again when Monty marches into Madrid."

At sunset a Sikh bugler of the Indian 4th Army division played last post as the Union jack flag that had flown at the governor's mansion since the siege began was hauled down from the last time and a new one made by the wife of the Bishop for Singapore readied to be hoisted in the morning. The siege was in the thirty-seventh month,

Incredibly they were able to hold against the best Japanese general, Tiger Yamashita who was on the brink of victory in 1941

215

when 20,000 of his veteran troops had been pulled out and sent to Australia. In return he had been given far fewer fresh conscripts. *With more troops and shells and air support I could have reduced this Lion City to rubble in weeks but damn this Freyberg who is able to not only survive but strike back up the Malayan peninsula taking back land we took from them. Singapore is rubble but they fight. The shame of it*, Yamashita thought at his headquarters at Kuala Lumpur.

In the infantry barracks which had patched-up holes in the roof from enemy bombing runs were cartoons and photos of pin-ups like Betty Grable, Marlene Dietrich and the singer Anne Shelton pinned up on the wall from magazines like *Lilliput*.

First lieutenant Rupert Wellesley, of the Duke of Wellington's Regiment, was just becoming used to his recently assumed position as the 8th Duke of Wellington on the demise of his father, of the 8th Duke-in-exile, the real one, not the fascist imposter a distant cousin set up by Lord Mosley in 'No. 1 London' Apsley House the ducal London home in 1941.

In the previous three years of exile the Duke in Boston working for the British Council had dispatched his personal standard to Queen Elizabeth in Scotland via a Queen's Messenger to carry on the tradition that for the anniversary of the Battle of Waterloo, 18th June, 1815 his standard was presented to the sovereign as a sign of fealty. This year the flag would be from the young Duke in the Lion City, Singapore.

The twenty-one year old peer of the realm stationed in Singapore carefully wrapped the Union Jack that had flown from the flag pole since the beginning of the siege. It was a mess, strips of ragged cloth faded from the tropical sun. It contained bullet holes from *Nakijima Ki. 84 Hayate* and *Mistibishi A6M Zero-Sen* fighter planes. Over the years crack pilots of the Japanese Naval Air Force had taken the risk to fly low in order to try and destroy the hated Union Flag, a symbol of the frustrating hold the British and their antipodean cousins, and Canadians, the ones rescued from Hong Kong, had on a naval base and city that should have

216

been theirs for the taking in 1941. Their shooting competition was won by an Army air force ace flyer who was shot down for his trouble flying down 'ack-ack' alley the line of Bofors guns protecting the city. They were using the secret Allied close proximity fuses that made artillery on land and at sea much more deadly than anything the enemy threw at them.

The British had held onto the fortress of Singapore and a large chunk of the southern mainland when the Japanese expected it to fall every day over the last two and a half-years. Thanks to massive US and British air-drops of supplies and paratroops and clandestine deliveries of reinforcements and munitions by a fleet of gargantuan transport submarines of the Beluga class and attacks by Chindit units, led by Orde Wingate, behind enemy lines. Success against the odds came at a price the new peer of the realm recollected as he tightened his Sam Brown belt another notch, thanks to the rations that were enough to maintain life and provide energy to fight but were not conducive to obesity.

The subaltern, Arthur Wellesley had permission from General Freyberg to send the flag to the Queen Regent in Scotland as the 129th annual tribute paid to the sovereign by the Duke of Wellington on the anniversary of the Battle of Waterloo, 18 June. In 1815 Arthur Wellesley the first Duke of Wellington defeated Napoleon Bonaparte in Belgium and gave Britain military superiority for one hundred years. Every year thereafter long-lived first duke presented a flag to George IV and the tradition began of a sumptuous dinner on the date held in the Waterloo Room in Windsor Castle.

*

In Tokyo Hirohito spoke to General Korechika, Kotohito and Nagona while they walked around the garden and over a bridge which the emperor's staff had checked for microphones placed by Tojo's secret police.

"General Korechika you will be my man on the army's general staff. Like me you see the Soviet Union and possibly Nazi

Germany as far greater future threats to *Nippon* than the United States and Britain. But I caution you to keep these thoughts to yourself. I want you to discreetly build support against Tojo amongst like-minded officers. I fear my prime minister may have to be removed in order to save our country from being destroyed, for taking on enemies that may soon outstrip us in technology and in strength.

"I want you to be ready with your supporters to oust Tojo and replace him with my trusted officials, Kotohito and Nagona. Korechika, I want you to sound out all general staff regarding their loyalty to me. I want you to cultivate senior officers who can be trusted who can take over the armed forces in Tokyo and Osaka, Manchuria and China on my command. "The codeword for the coup will be 'Three Storks'. The codeword may come next week, two years, ten years from now or never. If Japan can gain more from negotiated peace dealings with the Allies than fighting a war we have no hope of winning then I will give the order, if Japan faces destruction I will give it. If anything happens to me, if Tojo has me imprisoned or killed you will automatically put the coup against the government in immediate action and install my son as emperor under your protection.

"I am told that mutated influenza germs were lost on a train in Osaka three weeks ago, they were discovered by a child on the train and he infected his family. Within four days several thousand cases were reported but it was kept quiet, most died. By last week there ten thousand deaths in Osaka and it has spread to Tokyo, even Okinawa and Manchuria. A million now have the disease it is estimated. There is nothing in the newspapers and only a few know the truth but it is only a matter of time and unrest will begin as it realised that our antidote is ineffective and we are ill equipped to deal with a mass epidemic. Hospital staff are already straining to deal with hundreds of thousand of wounded soldiers our hospital system is collapsing.

"Our antidote fool-proof as I was led to believe. Apparently Tojo has withheld figures at the Ministry of War that

218

show that 3,000 of our own troops have died in California catching it from contact with infected American prisoners. I have given orders American prisoners are to be turned back to their own lines. I want to ensure we do not hinder any future conditional peace talks by being accused of breaking the Geneva Convention. It would appear that our treatment of the dishonoured enemy troops surrendering has been not up to standards upheld by the Geneva Convention. If diplomatically necessary I will arrange better conditions for the allied prisoners in our camps but my first priority is looking after my own people.

"Our agents in America know the Americans are devising an effective medicine to counter the influenza. I admire their ingenuity and skill. If we have a full-scale epidemic here in our over-populated islands we may have to sue for conditional peace and negotiate obtaining their help in combating the disease. I have a presentiment of doom-ever since we failed to take Singapore and having trouble in China and Australia."

"I asked General Tojo if he would consider negotiating to keep some of our conquests with the Americans via our Ambassador in Switzerland or Sweden but he said that this would be tantamount to surrendering when we are on the verge of victory. He believes we are the Asian master race and are immune to such germs. He forgets that 100 million people died in 1918-1919 in the Spanish Flu Epidemic and that included many Japanese. Here are lists of all the top commanders in the Imperial Navy and Army, alongside the names of my supports are stamps of yellow chrysanthemums. The names of my enemies are indicated by black chrysantheums. They are to be arrested when the time comes. Is all that clear? Swear your allegiance."

Each of the men solemnly swore the oath and bowed deeply to Hirohito.

"Good. Carry out my commands. Next I shall have the commander of the Imperial Guard brought to heel whoever commands them in the first 24 hours of the coup will win."

That night one of the Grey Foxes, Prince Konoye offered a prayer to his ancestors then picked up the black telephone receiver and made the call to the commander of the Imperial Guard that set in motion the journey of Japan back in time to the feudal period of Samurai warriors. But this was to be sometime in the future. First there would be setbacks for *Nippon,* but one thing was certain; there was no going back. The prince and the peace faction were committed. They would put an end to Tojo's war mongering and save Japan from ultimate defeat and humiliation when the moment was right and the message was sent from Hirohito was given to strike. *Isn't Hirohito's reign to be known for posterity as 'Brilliant Peace'? We must make sure that he be remembered for that not this terrible war. Hundreds of years from now my fellow Japanese will honour me.* He took a deep breath as he started to dial. "Is that the commander of the Imperial Guard? It's Prince Konoye."

*

The Avro Anson landed at Nicosia airdrome on Cyprus held by the British and populated by Greek and Turkish Cypriots. Control of Cyprus had been ceded to Great Britain by Turkey in 1878. On this beautiful island at the far eastern end of the Med the two engines were shut off and the two propellers of the small transport plane ceased rotating. Josef Comenice, the middle aged Romanian one of the passengers had noticed the Romanian air force Spitfire planes landing after patrolling the airspace to the north of the island, some had bullet holes visible in their wings or tails indicating a dog fight with *Luftwaffe* planes. He jumped down to the grassy airfield after an RAF aircraftman opened the door at the rear of the fuselage.

"Captain Comenice!" a young voice proclaimed as its owner strode towards the plane towards his moustached compatriot. Josef blinked in the blinding noon sun. "Is it you Your Majesty? Words cannot express …" Youthful Michael, the tall, exiled King of Romania, embraced Josef by gripping his fellow countryman's bear-like body and kissed him on both cheeks. Michael's smile belied the worries and torment he endured knowing that his father, Carol III a weak King, who had once abdicated in his favour in 1938 had taken his place as a puppet King in the power of the pro-Nazi Iron Guard party in Romania.

Michael had been ousted in a coup in 1943 but he had seen it coming despite being only twenty-two years old and had taken steps to ensure he and his mother and some trusted government officials and loyal segments of the Romanian armed forces could escape and wage war against the government which had taken Romania into the Nazi camp by smashing opposition and instigating a reign of terror against all who stood up for the rule of their constitutional monarchy. "At last, my Captain of the Palutal Victoriei Guard. Come, I have my car. I want to introduce you to my staff and talk to you about the operation we are putting into operation soon in our homeland."

As they drove to King Michael's HQ in a hotel in the city Josef studied his monarch. He had

matured, seemed much older for his years than in 1939 when he last saw him. His ears were still big, his hair short under the British officer's cap, but becoming a king and a man at the same time as losing his throne and his country to fascists had given Michael a serious manner. Working in the palace Josef saw the boy grow and become the hope for the future of Romania. Before the war his father Carol II, a philanderer and pro-fascist had abdicated, his place taken by the boy-king who hated fascism. Now his father was again monarch of a fascist Romania, an ally of Nazi Germany which was readying itself for the invasion of the Soviet Union.

As if reading his thoughts, King Michael spoke in Romanian, "I want to thank you for going to Paris and Berlin to be a bodyguard to my father. He did try to get French support for Romania before he turned to Hitler; who wooed him with false promises and protection from Soviet intentions in the Balkans."

221

"I know, sire. One day you shall be king of a free Romania." Josef had been a page to the chamberlain, then a footman in the palace. Aged sixteen he joined the army and obtained a commission by 1932 he was captain of the palace guard. In the turbulent days of the 1930s the exigencies of the world depression polarised the political arena in many countries particularly those like Romania whose democracy was young. Pro-German and anti-Russian nationalist feeling was whipped into an hysterical fear of instability and lack of faith in a multi-party system. Romania itself was a young country, formed out of the old Austro-Hungarian Empire set amidst a sea of old ethnic enemies, Russia to the west, Bulgaria to the south, Hungary to the north.

"Refresh yourself Captain with a bath before lunch. I have a uniform for you in your room upstairs. One of our soldiers will be your ... batman as the British call it."

A Romanian corporal showed him to his hotel room on the second floor. It was simply furnished with an old mirror over a battered chest of drawers and an ancient mattress on a bedstead which was old when the Titanic hit the iceberg in 1912. It had a lovely view of the Mediterranean from the open window. He washed using the hot water brought to his room in a jug pouring it lavishly into a chipped white washing bowl, then shaved using a cut-throat razor. Then he changed into the captain's olive green woollen battledress uniform that his batman had ironed. Its epaulettes each sported three pips. He put his large feet into the well polished brown officer's boots and tied up the laces tightly and placed the gaiters around his ankles securing the battledress trousers which he let sharply hang in its fold over his boots. He picked up the new Sam Browne belt and .38 Webley revolver in its holster and placing the diagonal holding strap across his shoulder tightened the belt. Checking himself in the mirror he turned sideways pressing in his stomach and twitched his large black moustaches. "Uhhm I need some exercise, running, swimming, action - killing the enemy. I wonder what King Michael has in mind for me?"

He was soon to find out. After an excellent lamb stew and a bottle of wine, he joined the king in the drawing room of the hotel, which had been completely taken over as the Romanian HQ. Officers representing the Romanian army, air force and navy and King Michael were volubly expressing their views of the best strategy of fighting a guerrilla war in a country which was surrounded by enemies: Hungary, Bulgaria and the Soviet Union on three sides and the Black Sea on the other.

"Quiet!" Michael commanded. "Let us be professional. Our British friends have offered us transport and help from the Turks to build a guerrilla army which will be a thorn in the side of the Germans who already have had to station several divisions in our unhappy country. Our enemy of course are any Romanians who oppose a free Romania, and I put my father in that category.

"Captain, I want you to go home and start a terror campaign. Your first mission will be the Iron Gates of the Danube. We need to know the exact location of flak guns in the area. Photo flights would reveal that we have an interest so the only time Allied planes will be seen will be the actual attack from Turkey by the RAF using special bombs. You will be taken in by Lysander aircraft at night with some radios, cameras and weapons and met by one of our partisans, an old soldier called Thomas Tallich. Once you are established we will parachute men and weapons to help you. You will eventually have an army."

Josef expressed surprise, "Army?"

"Yes, you will recruit Romanian patriots. It will strike from the forests, no Iron Guard or German will be safe. This is where I want you to go, I think you will recognize it, Badau." The king pointed with a finger onto the map before them.

"Badau my birthplace my family is still there," Josef drummed his hairy fingers on the table in excitement.

"Precisely you know it well, you often told me of your hunting expeditions going on long trips in the mountains with your father. I want you to stay in the hills, sink barges in the Danube, blow up trains, attack fascist convoys and arm and organize those Romanians who can be trusted.   The Turkish authorities are allowing the Allies to use secret airfields in Turkey on the Black Sea, transport planes will fly at night and drop you near here on the Romanian coast of the Black Sea, south of the port of Constantja, you will be smuggled up the Danube in a barge from the port and dropped off at Badau more weapons and ammunition will follow on other barges. You shall meet the unit that will follow you at the parachute training school tomorrow morning. Perhaps you would like to get your wings as well.   One week from today you return to Romania, an aircraft will take you from here to Turkey refuelling at Konya and heading north for Adapazan near the Bospurus straits between the Black Sea and the Sea of Marmera."

"That will be pleasure full," Josef said his eyes dancing. "I can start to kill the men who have polluted our country."

"You each will be given large amounts of Romanian money, weapons, plastic explosives, detonators, maps, compasses, radios, codebooks and of course instructions for meeting your contacts."

After lunch with the monarch Josef placed his cap at a jaunty angle and gripping his swagger stick skipped out of the hotel and walking on the beach counting his blessings. *It will be so wonderful to see my father again. I shall have a lot to tell my friend George Orwell when I see him next, I shall write to him surely if I address it to him poste restante BBC, Calcutta, India it will get to him. It may be months or years before I get a chance to tell him in person. What fun we shall have talking over bottles of wine and a roasted chicken, at least I hope they have such things in India.*

*

In Piccadilly at Fortnum and Mason's tea room Felicity could not believe her ears as she listened to Princess Chouku from gossip about the Buckingham Palace servants and her fiancee's odd relatives to something much more serious.

"You know Felicity I feel I can trust you and that is a wonderful quality in dangerous times," she looked at her with her large brown almond-shaped eyes, speaking English tinged with a curious mixture of Japanese the language of her birth and a French accent from her upbringing in Paris as the daughter of a Japanese diplomat who was a cousin of the emperor, Hirohito. "I am not stupid like Lord Eastbourne, the German governor and indeed, even Frederick my husband-to-be in a month. Although King Frederick is a kind man and I have grown fond of him, at least he would never claim to be bright. But I think there is more about you than most people realise. "I have noticed how you tense up ever so slightly, almost imperceptively when the conversation steers towards the North African campaign or now, the invasion of Spain. It is as if you have a loved one fighting there, perhaps on the other side?"

"My husband was killed! He was the captain of a frigate that hit a mine in the North Sea in 1939." *How could she know?*

"I shall tell that story to anyone who asks but I believe you are a spy."

Felicity's green eyes widened in shock, she shook her head and her long red hair tied up in a bun by a Knightsbridge hairstylist shone in the lights. *I must look suitably amused and dismissive,* Felicity quickly reasoned, *but not frightened as if I was a fascist lackey hurt by such an accusation.*

The princess who was the same age smiled sweetly and lit a cigarette. Pulling a bit of tobacco from her upper lip made cherry red by lipstick she daintily dropped it onto a plate of meringues.

"You're either a very good actress or I am mistaken. You should be in films or on the stage. Don't worry I am not here to inform on you. Just don't tell my hidebound, stuffy cousin Hirohito about me. I smoke and drink excessively, dress in the best clothes like a European princess and go to night clubs. He knows but he has a lot of other things on his mind. In fact he may find me an ideal device for his plans. I am persona non grata with any Japanese official here or at home. In Japan I am a monster, here I am just a terrible embarrassment to the Japanese embassy. I love being a rebel princess. King Frederick makes no demands on me, well just the usual and accompanying him to events I want to go to. I hate Japanese traditions: the ritual clothes, wooden sandals, the boring tea ceremony and all that stifling etiquette that never changes. You have hierarchy and quaint social rules here but they are amusing and I can choose what I like. It suits me very well. I won't be having any children I shall see to that. My first name is Chouku -butterfly child it suits me very well."

She leaned forward, "Felicity, I am a minor royal, just a niece to His Imperial Majesty. But the status of my family meant that my Tokyo childhood was so strict as to make a nun's training seem wild in comparison. But growing up in Paris, becoming a woman, my secret experiences, shall we call them, dropping the kimono for Picasso and Modigliani shocked my mother although I think my father secretly admired my bid for freedom. Formally he condemns my behaviour sending me to London out of his sight but he sends money to my bank account regularly and every birthday sends me a magnum of the best champagne. He cannot say things but I can read his heart. He no longer lives with my mother. She lives with me at the palace wandering around rather out of place in her kimono making small steps in her traditional shoes making tea for King Frederick. I prefer gin and tonic. She plays the koto for us, koto and sushi are the only Japanese things I love. She prepares us sushi, rice and fish dishes. It is so funny seeing him try to eat with chopsticks and sit on the floor, he needs two footmen to get him on his feet again. But he laughs at himself. I wish more people knew of his great sense of fun." Felicity did not voice her thoughts; *most Britons hate Frederick with a passion but it seems she really loves him even though he is three times her age.*

"That is why I was surprised to receive a message from a mysterious man from our embassy yesterday, at least that's where he said he was from. He came to the palace and asked to see me about a family matter and told me he had come direct from my uncle, His Imperial Majesty Emperor Hirothito." She wrote down a few sentences on a small piece of cream-coloured paper with the Buckingham Palace crest. "Read it and then we shall burn it in the ashtray, for fun." She giggled.

Felicity read it carefully. 'The Imperial Emperor wants to secretly open peace negotiations with the allies without the support of his prime minister Tojo but is ready to oust him and replace him with a 'peace faction' when the time is right.'

"You are showing me why exactly?"

"Because," she picked up her crisp linen napkin and slowly wiped her mouth so only Felicity could possibly hear her. Felicity glanced at her bodyguard driver who was slurping his tea loudly at a corner table facing them and the door momentarily distracted by a pretty waitress in knee length black skirt, white pinafore and1920s cap.

"If you are what I think you are. I want you to let someone high up on the Allied side know that they should have the Swedish ambassador in Switzerland contact the Japanese ambassador there about opening channels to explore a separate peace between America, Britain and Japan. Our new ambassador in Switzerland is my father who is loyal to the Emperor. He hates Tojo and war and what it has done to the world."

Felicity carefully ripped up the paper as if absent-mindedly getting rid of an old shopping list and placed it in the ashtray. Chouko O-No held the burning tip of her cigarette against the paper and they both watched as the message went up in a small spurt of flame and smoke.

The bodyguard lurched forward and muttered beneath his breath in Japanese as he slopped some cream from the cream jug into the ashtray. The princess laughed, her eyes sparkling with mischief. "I am always doing things like that it annoys him and my mother. That's why I do it. Neither of them can speak any English so they are easy targets."

As the future Queen of New Britain picked up her crocodile handbag Felicity reached for her bag matching her red two piece suit stood up saying, "It has been a lovely lunch, your royal highness,"

"Just call me Chouko . We don't pay - they will bill the palace and you won't forget what we talked about. We can drop you off on the way to Buck House."

I have to trust her. This is my job it is why I am here in London. If what she says is true it could shorten the war and save thousands, even millions of lives, including John's. "No I won't forget what you said. It is important," Felicity said taking the plunge. "I shall talk to you the next time you come for the wedding dress fittings, three days from now. I look forward to it Chouko."

"Good." She put her cigarette out by holding the tip in the cream. There was a sizzle and it was out. She left it on her napkin; she was not totally devoid of manners.

CHAPTER TWENTY OPERATION ANGRIFF

"Marshal Tukhachevsky and several other
Generals were sentenced to death by the Supreme Military Court
in Moscow on charges of espionage and high treason."

The Times June 12, 1937

Pock-marked dictator Joseph Stalin, the all-powerful secretary of the Soviet Communist Party was enjoying a picnic with the miniature, malformed chief of the Russian secret police the NKVD, Nikolai Yezhov. The five foot tall 'poisonous dwarf' as he was fearfully nicknamed began the Stalinist terror by writing about how treason and treachery would be the result of even the slightest hint of counter-revolutionary thought or action. Suspected Generals were forced to admit to trumped-up crimes of treason in places they had never visited or when they had airtight alibis. Those who could say otherwise were dealt with. A tailor was jailed for ten years for absently sticking his needle in a newspaper photo of a Communist official; a good 'comrade' notified the authorities that he was guilty of anti-revolutionary sabotage and there was no recourse to justice. In 1939 all the admirals and half the generals were shot, hundreds of thousands of other victims had been shot or sent to hard labour in the Siberian Gulag, a series of camps that made the softer Tsarist days of exile for revolutionaries and criminals seem positively benign and luxurious. Fear ate into the souls of Russians, no-one was safe from denunciation, the revolution had gone mad. Their power secure the dictator and his sadistic servant toasted each other with vodka in small glasses as they reminisced about the old days. They sat on a blanket in front of a packed wicker picnic basket at Yezhov's ornate dacha, a country cottage some ten miles outside of Moscow. They nibbled on blackberries they had picked. Stalin's very name was false, it was his *nom de revolution* from his youthful revolutionary days, it meant 'Man of steel'. He became the strongman who succeeded Lenin as the leader of the revolution.

The city of Moscow had sprawled out into the fields as more Communists were attracted into its orbit as the centre of power in the rapidly industrialising Soviet Union. They joked about their old comrades in the vicious civil war against the White Army from 1917 until 1924. Many of them who they had professed to love as comrades fell victim to Stalin's growing paranoia in the 1930s when, after killing off all his real rivals for power, he began imagining loyal officials and humble peasants guilty of devious and unlikely plots to get rid of him. His close partners in crime, Beria, second-in-command of the NKVD and Nikolay Yezhov had no scruple in helping the 'Man of Steel'. Yezhov wore a leather apron when he 'worked' in the prisons so blood and vomit did not soil his uniform. The revolution had caused ten million Ukrainians to die of starvation when their crops were sent to Moscow and other cities since the revolutionary steps taken to create giant commune farms from millions of small family farms created chaos in food production. Stalin cynically made peace with his enemy Hitler while he moved the burgeoning heavy industries east of the Urals, away from the *Reich's* reach and playing the part of the loveable father of the revolution to the uneducated masses. Most of the intellectuals had been wiped out or were in exile but there were some professionals in important positions who bided their time using their wits to stay alive forced to live a life of lies in obedience to the party's diktats and the party was Stalin. Today though was a time for sun, open neck shirts and laughter. It was just a days before Hitler would end their warped version of Marx and Engel's 'worker's paradise' in a cataclysm of hatred and fire.

General Zhukov came home from the army skyscraper offices in Moscow and felt twitchy and restless. He had made a decision to resign from the army before a subordinate eager to take his position informed on him. Even the ghost of a whisper was enough to have him trundled off to the green rooms of Lubyanka prison and if he was lucky be shot in the back of the neck and not put through the humiliation of a show trial and the torture behind the scenes. *This Stalin, this Georgian gangster and his gang are insane. The system is irrational at least in the Tsar's Christian Russia even though hypocrisy and poverty existed it offered a better world than the mad hell Communists created, where treachery is rewarded and everything is unpredictable, nothing solid. Is it normal for a huge nation to be cowed into terrified submission fearful of the slightest weakness in unswerving alliance to the great Stalin, the great defender of the revolution? The revolution has no meaning. Stalin is mad, he is a modern Ivan the Terrible. I would destroy him but he is too powerful I cannot do it alone.*

Restless he picked up a postcard from his friend Marshal Boris Shaposhnikov who was on holiday yachting at Leningrad. "Why not come and join us?" *Us? Other officers? It is unwise for us to meet outside of work. Hmm, I also liked the sound of the old name for Leningrad-St. Petersburg.* He rolled the word around his mind. He tutted. *No, the revolution has changed everything, things cannot go back.* On an impulse he packed a bag and phoned for a taxi to the train station. He did not want his army chauffeur to take him. He was in a hurry but no one should know. Zhukov put on a suit, wore his army boots underneath them and stuffed his uniform including his pistol into the bag.

Meanwhile Josef Stalin and his servant lay on their backs looking up into the clear blue sky, "Tomorrow morning I show some commissars visiting Moscow for their conference around the Kremlin. I love to show them the thirteen-foot thick walls of the burgundy fortress. I love to say, 'Ivan the Terrible lived here. Now I live here.' I take the armoured train with my family in the afternoon to our summer house for a month on the Black Sea." Stalin stroked his moustache.

"Lucky for some," Yezhov replied. "I have work to do." He licked his lips. Stalin tried not to think about what Yezhov was looking forward to. *It is hard being a leader one must be close to distasteful people, decisions and myself. But that is easier than my dismal fourteenth year in the seminary in Tiflis. So I must be strong*, he vowed as he dropped off to sleep in the sun.

*

In Berlin Heinz decided to phone his 'American Friend'. The brilliant translator had rung the number given to him in Sweden by his American spy controller only once before. This time he had momentous information to pass on. After leaving the *Reich* Chancellory Heinz took a tram along the *Unter der Linden* and got out by his favourite cafe. He ordered a pastry and coffee and thought about his wife and baby boy in Stockholm. He had married Ingrid an attractive blonde *Wehrmacht* secretary on Hitler's staff and he had convinced her that Germany was on a downward spiral of destruction and that eventually Hitler would invade Russia and that would mean the death of millions of Germans. Heinz felt himself to be a German patriot, his land was the land of Beethoven, Bach, Durer and Goethe – those names conjured up all that was good about his homeland, not death camps and armies. He had quit his job as head translator at the Chancellory in 1941 and taken his new bride to Stockholm. Sweden was neutral and he went into the exporting business with his uncle. While there he contacted the American embassy and offered to help spy against Hitler before the madman totally destroyed Germany. His contact, the 'American Friend', suggested he go back to his old job where he would be privy to important secrets that could shorten the war. Heinz agonised over his decision then went back to Berlin and explained that his business venture had not worked out. Luckily his expertise in languages fluently reading and writing English, Italian, Spanish, French, Russian and Japanese and his excellent work record assured his obtaining his old job as Hitler's chief translator. He felt reassured that Ingrid and their baby Osker were safe in Sweden but he knew that if Hitler won it would only be a matter of time before Sweden and Switzerland were no longer neutral but completely under Nazi direction. The *Fuhrer's* secretary, his boss, had not questioned his story and Heinz knew that any Gestapo inquiry into his life would find it pretty dull except for the,

232

hopefully secret, phone calls and occasional clandestine meetings and oh yes, copying important documents and handing them over to the enemy.

His hand shook as he lifted the coffee cup to his lips. Normally he relished the Colombian coffee he always ordered but today it tasted like swamp water. He left several Marks which included a generous tip and left. Walking quickly before he could talk himself out of his decision he went to a hotel and pumped some coins into a public phone that was in a quiet hallway. He dialled the number, wrong number. *Try again more slowly dumpfkopf!*

"This is Reynard phoning for Klaus," he said in German to the lady who answered. He could hear calling out and there was the crackling sound of the receiver being passed over. A gravelly voice answered, Heinz 's sensitive ears detected a Hamburg accent tinted occasionally by a very slightly American-accented word. This man had spent at least five years overseas a long time ago, probably as a child.

"Klaus, I am glad to catch you in. I have some good news perhaps we could meet and I could tell you about it."

"Yes. The Berlin Zoo at the lion house, there is very good ice cream for sale near there. and it is a hot summer's day." Heinz felt his forehead break out in beads of perspiration as he was reminded of the heat. *"Is tonight good 8 o'clock?"*

"Yes, we have a lot to catch up on. Auf Weidersehen." Heinz replied and hung up. The hall was empty no-one had passed by.

The lions had woken up from a nap and were pacing back and forth on the rocks inside the large cage. A sleek tawny female took a drink from the bubbling fountain at the top of a miniature lake. The male padded towards some meat that the zoo keeper had thrown in for dinner and tore at it, its tail swinging back and forth whisking away flies.

Heinz bought an ice cream and joined the man in a homburg hat holding a melting ice cream. He had a grey moustache in the style of Kaiser Wilhelm and looked like a strict school-master. In fact he was a dealer in rare books and prints. He was constantly buying and selling incunabula and rare modern books via contacts in Switzerland who maintained business relationships with book dealers in America and around the world. Before the war he was no stranger to auctions in New York, London and Paris. Now visits to America were impossible but as a spy for the United States OSS secret service he could still send messages in shipments to his contacts in Geneva several of whom were American agents. Heinz had been holding a first edition of The Three Musketeers published in Paris and signed by Dumas. He placed it on the park seat next to Klaus to look at it. "Page thirty-three has an interesting typographical error which was rectified in all subsequent French editions but has been repeated in every German edition I can find."

Klaus finished his ice cream, wiped his hands with the purple handkerchief from his suit jacket pocket ran his hands lovingly over the binding and opened the book to read.

Germany will invade the Soviet Union in mid-August 1944 - Operation Angriff. Atombomben will be dropped by aircraft on Moscow, Kiev and Leningrad to destroy the Communist party centres. Only three bombs are available until more are produced. Two army groups will invade. One will head south-east for the Caucasus and seize the oil fields the other will hold the left flank of the first army group and continue east to Iraq, through Afghanistan and link up with a Japanese army which will invade India from Burma. Von Paulus will command the Caucausus army group. Rommel will command the Asian Korps heading for India.

The book dealer blew his nose loudly. "This is very interesting I have some potential buyers for this book do I have your permission to sell it? I would charge my usual commission of 20% and you would get the rest of course"

234

Heinz nodded. Klaus made some notes about the book and its condition and wrote out a receipt for Heinz. "Phone me in a week and I may have made a transaction. This will be quite a find I think for the discriminating bibliophile."

Four days later the dossier from agent Klaus in Berlin via Zurich landed on William Donovan's desk in Washington marked 'Top Secret' and 'Most Urgent'. Within seconds of reading it the head of the Office of Strategic Service phoned the White House and asked to speak to the President on a very important matter. An hour later he was in the Oval office reporting to FDR. "I believe it, sir our agent in the Chancellory has given us some good information before but this is of immense importance. As incredible as it sounds it does explain a lot: why Hitler did not take Gibraltar when he could, why he has not thrown as many men and Panzer divisions into Spain even though we are firmly in control of southern Spain and have cut off Madrid."

President Roosevelt tapped a silver pen against his chin as he considered. "The worst news is that they have fission bombs they call atom bombs before we do. It could be months more before we have one that can be used but the thermobaric weapons we have are effective without any of the radioactivity that is emitted by fission bombs. I think we can use Hitler's crazy idea to invade the Soviet Union to our advantage. I shall phone Attlee and arrange a meeting immediately, I want you to fly to Ottawa and brief him and the Canadian-British war cabinet ahead of my arrival. I will fly up tomorrow for two days. This information is worth its weight in gold. Well done Donovan."

*

In Leningrad a civilian clothed Marshal Boris Shaposhnikov, Chief of the Russian General Staff took two men on his thirty foot yacht: Georgi Zhukov Marshal, Deputy Commander in Chief and General Alexander Vassilevsky. They talked in parables fearful of each other informing on them for lack of loyalty to Stalin. They worried about the threat from Germany and Stalin's lack of concern about reports of troop build ups in the East of the *Reich* and large manouvres in Prussia and Poland, reports of troop movements from France and Spain gleaned from communist agents. "I am ready for a return to Russian greatness, the old patriotism when going to Siberia meant temporary exile, coming back alive without being a broken man instead of the insane cruelty of the Communist regime. Even as he said it Vassilevsky knew he had signed his death warrant to the NKVD but he didn't care anymore, it would be better to die than to live in such intolerable conditions that Stalin decreed.

To his surprise Shaposhnikov and Zhukov agreed. After heated discussion that resulted in a drastic course of action on their collective behalfs they on the great lake adjoining Leningrad and they returned to their separate hotels each determined to support each other to end Stalin's rule and his reign of terror. Zhukov was the one designated to contact the American Embassy and get help for their coup d'etat, in return for money and support they could promise a Russian ally to attack the Third *Reich*. Roosevelt would be a fool not to take their offer with both hands. They would be in a position to strike by the end of July.

*

That next night Turing took the phone call on the secure line at Hamilton Hall, McMaster University in Hamilton, Ontario from General Alan Brooke, Commander of the Imperial General Staff who had spent two hours with discussing Hitler's future invasion of Russia with Attlee in his 'No. 10' offices in the Langevin block of the parliament buildings in Ottawa. "Turing. It's CIGS Alan Brooke here in Ottawa. Sorry to bother you so late. I am told you regularly work late."

"What's up, the Jerries haven't invaded Canada have they?"

"No, but I want you have some of your best cryptographers concentrate upon signals dealing with a possible German invasion of Russia. Our sources indicate it could be early August-Operation Angriff. There are possibilities of super bomb attacks on Kiev,

236

Moscow and Leningrad. Also, Japanese signals may be indicating increased activity in Burma regarding an invasion of India. American intelligence is convinced it is going to happen, two army groups will invade southern Russia with one taking the Caucasus and the other going to India via mid-Asia."

"I'll have our people get right on this. I take it the Yanks are also doing what they can."

"Yes, we are sharing the information as usual"

Turing ran nail-bitten fingers through his hair. "Could be nasty for the Russians, sir bit of a poser about how we use the information but then I have just have to worry about decoding things not what to do next I am glad to say. There have been a gradual increase in signals in eastern Germany and Poland but we have been concentrating on signals in the Spanish theatre. I shall assign a fresh team to look at them. I shall phone you with anything concrete and have important decrypts telexed to your office as usual."

"Thank you Alan, goodnight and pass on my personal thanks to all your code breakers."

It was two in the morning but Alan took the lift from his office down to the second floor of the basement of Hamilton Hall, the centre of Canadian-British decryption where his American assistant Kris Kowolski, a brilliant mathematician from Princeton was checking the output from the Cyclops computer Turing had devised to crack the modified German Enigma coding machine. "Kris, you had better come up to my office there is a bit of a flap, this time it is someone else who is going to get the chop!" Alan Turing filled his kettle with water and lit the gas ring in his office to make tea and explained everything to Kris who was momentarily struck dumb by the news so astounded was he. Alan unchained his tin mug from the radiator and found another for Kris and put a handful of tea-leaves into a large, brown betty teapot. He added milk and a large dollop of sugar and poured in the boiling water. "There's tea all ready to enjoy right from the pot!"

"Wow!" was all that Kris could say over and over. He sipped at some of the strong, over-sweet tea and gradually became his fast thinking, fast acting self. He said, "I'll take five decoders from 'Hut 5' to concentrate on Japanese signals in Siam." Kris had become used to the British tradition of naming things in honour of what had been. Teams of de-decoders, a mix of brilliant men and women mathematicians, chess players and logicians were named after the numbered huts used by decoders at Bletchley Park operating up to the evacuation from Great Britain when they were transplanted across the Atlantic to the heart of Canada.

"Good, watch for any messages dealing with movements in east Europe. Their code name is Operation Angriff. I also want some people who know Russian to monitor Soviet signals, we need to know if and when they become aware of what is planned," Turing asked his deputy.

Three days later Roosevelt chaired the FACE Inner-War Committee in Ottawa. "We have to prepare for this new Hitlerian outburst of evil, this attack upon the Soviet Union by an erstwhile friend which signed a peace treaty in 1938 is unconscionable. We have checked out the information and it is valid. As agreed we will operate from Iceland and Turkey, now it has signed a secret treaty of alliance with FAN, to set up a provisional government of Russian exiles in Leningrad or Sevastopol. The Empress Alexandrovna has asked that Leningrad be renamed St. Petersburg, as soon as possible. An agent of ours in Leningrad has picked up something about three generals sharing a sailing holiday. He was able to pick up some of their conversation with a radio receiver hidden in their sailboat and has made contact with them. They plan to kill Stalin and overthrow the Communist grip on their country. There is discontent and fear in the Soviet Union. One of them, Zhukov revealed their plans to stage a coup against Stalin. This plays into our hands and we have encouraged them to time their coup for the day of the invasion.

"For weeks after the attack comes Stalin and the Soviet leadership or what survives of it after the initial F-bomb attacks will be off-balance, an ideal time for us to take advantage of the German attack. This period could decide the war. If we have Russia on our side the end is inevitably a victory for us. Stalin has never been an ally but we have thrashed out the arguments about letting him know ahead of time or waiting until they are attacked and offering our help to a non-Communist Russian government. I believe the free world expects us to defend freedom not side with such a foul dictator possibly responsible for the death of millions of his countrymen and a sworn enemy of capitalism. We will do all we can to have these three Generals who have immense influence and include their Chief-of-Staff Zhukov, to prepare a coup and lead their armies against the Germans and Communists in the name of the Empress."

Mackenzie-King spoke, "Franklin as usual you have concentrated the essence of the problem into a few sentences. Clement and I agree that our intervention is necessary to ensure Russia has a chance of becoming a free country. We do not want to support any Soviet government but we should support any pro-allied government and indeed we should be ready to set in place a White Russian government able to take control and direct the anger that will tear across the country. It is cynical but necessary I fear," the wily Canadian Liberal Prime Minister continued, "if this Operation *Angriff* is successful, these super weapons we have not yet perfected, will wipe out the Communist leadership and its control from Moscow and Kiev. There will be a vacuum, a lack of organised government which must be filled by leaders who support an end to Communism.

"We don't want to win this war and end up facing another monster waving instead of a swastika flag one bearing the hammer and sickle. Hitler may well be making his greatest mistake invading Russia. The size of their country and the millions of men Russia can put into action once galvanised is staggering. Our military advisors believe we can spare some air and naval support in the early stages and we have had success persuading Grand Duchess Olga, youngest child of Tsar Alexander III and sister to the last Tsar, Nicholas II, to become Empress Alexdrovna. She was in Denmark after the revolution but came to Canada settling on a farm in Campbellville, Ontario leading a simple life.

She would prefer to remain living anonymously but is willing to become a constitutional monarch, like our sovereign, of a free Russia and hold elections for a freely elected Parliament or Dumas as soon as possible because she sees it as her duty to her fellow Russians who have suffered badly under Lenin and now Stalin's deadly rule. She will lead the fight of the Russias against Germany when they invade. She told me that "I will be hard on my enemies but fair to my peoples. I do not want to be feared like Stalin but respected and loved because of what I do. I will safeguard Russian interests and ensure we defeat the Nazis as part of the Free Alliance." This message will be broadcast by the BBC World Service as soon as the German attack. She is willing to meet with us tomorrow and to that end she is staying incognito at Rideau Hall with the Governor-General. She wishes to discuss piecing together a provisional government that can be set up quickly in Russia perhaps in Sebastopol or Leningrad, whichever can be held by sympathetic Generals willing to fight Germans under the figurehead of a Russian Empress rather than a cruel dictator.

CHAPTER TWENTY-ONE   "YOUR RAVENS, YOUR MAJESTY"

Queen Elizabeth was on a royal tour, but not one with crowds and hoopla. This was an underground tour of her occupied dominions, risky but a great morale booster for loyal Britons. It was to be the second and last one of New Britain before the longed for liberation. After this she would stay in Scotland moving when necessary. She had been to Londonderry, Liverpool, Cardiff Castle, Leominster, Salisbury, Norwich and Coventry where she visited a private school cheekily posing as a Ministry of Education political advisor ensuring school boards followed Fascist guidelines. She wore dark glasses to cover her bad eye and looked suitably glum until she gave a speech to the six formers who were sworn to secrecy. She was shuttled with her aide and military bodyguards in civilian clothes from 'safe cottage', 'safe house' (domestic or public), once a nunnery, hotel or stately home depending on what the local resistance movement had organised.

Heading north, tonight she was at Howarth House, the 'safe stately home' of the Earl and Duchess of Harewood for a week. He was ostensibly a member of the fascist House of Lords but rarely attended pleading ill health. In actuality he was the Red Rose resistance leader.

After dinner Elizabeth, in a dress with a simple strand of pearls and a Stuart tartan sash spoke to the family and servants. "I think it is appropriate that we meet at this magnificent home of the Earl of Harewood we thank him and his family and staff for your hospitality. It is our hope that Britain will be liberated within three years. Of course the strategic direction of the war could change that prediction for good or ill. For instance Germany invading the Soviet Union this year has already weakened them and given our troops in Spain a great advantage. If White Russia becomes a strong ally and the campaign continues to go well in Spain in Portugal it may be sooner. However, if Hitler does secure the oil fields of the Caucasus strikes successfully to Suez and seizes the

241

Iraq and Saudi Arabian oil fields the liberation might be pushed forward into the future. However, it is possible that Hitler is attempting to do what Napoleon dreamed, striking for India. He wants to link up with Japanese forces coming from Burma and not concentrate on the oil in Iraq. That would be a grave mistake on his part and a stroke of luck for us." She spoke with knowledge of military strategy. Hardship had not eradicated her naturally optimistic nature but served to deepen her understanding and adaptability sharpening her facilities as a commander of the Scottish Resistance movement, the Black Douglas.

"Whatever happens we will be ready. Supplies are being stockpiled in secret locations in throughout Great Britain, Northern Ireland and the occupied republic of Ireland. Agents with radio sets are being dispatched and put in place to specifically train resistance cells in the techniques of urban and rural resistance fighting supporting the Allied invasion forces. The railways and telecommunication centres in enemy hands will be prime targets. Everything will be done to reduce civilian casualties but they will occur, but we must keep in mind the greatest prize of all, freedom for our people and of our Irish friends and eventually of all Europe."

Eight days later the Queen arrived in a car with one bodyguard at Jack Gaitskill's farm near the village of Goathland, Yorkshire just north of Harewood House en route to the ruins of Whitby Abbey to meet resistance leaders and take a fishing boat to Aberdeen. Welcomed by the Gaitskills and their wartime guest Charlie Gates, they offered tea and home-made scones and jam and marmalade and had a merry time as Charlie insisted on pouring out large measures of Irish Whiskey for everyone toasting her Majesty. "And here's to Jeremiah and Croakey, Your Majesty! They are waiting in the barn if you would like to inspect 'em."

"To Jeremiah and Croakey, Raven Master!" the Queen beamed, draining her glass her round face animated in the warmth of their welcome. "Yes, we shall visit the ravens before we take our leave, Whitby awaits us."

As they went out into the night Charlie supported her past puddles. "Forgive me for asking   Does your eye hurt, Ma'm? Charlie asked with concern on his face.

"No," she smiled at him "I thank you for your concern Mr. Gates. It is well healed and I still have my other eye but shall tell you the worst of it is that I still miss Bertie, my late husband but I feel he is with me when I   am tramping over the heather in the highlands he loved or when I go to sea. He was a sailor you know."

"Yes, I know he was a midshipman at Jutland in 1916. I lost my older brother at Jutland in HMS Indefatigable"

"Oh yes that was one of the battle cruisers that blew up when the magazines were hit, an awful business."

Charlie cleared his throat. "I have the ravens to show you Ma'm. It will cheer them no end to see you."

"Lead on Raven Master!" Charlie puffed out his chest with pride and squared his shoulders as the five- foot five-inch Queen Regent followed him to the barn where Croakey and Jerehmiah looked at them quizzically from a large metal cage in the corner.

"I'll let them out if that is all right Ma'am?"

"Yes, let them walk around a bit as if they were on Tower Green their wings are clipped are see."

"Of course just like they would be in the Tower. We look forward to seeing you and the birds back where they belong."

CHAPTER TWENTY-TWO   CYCLOPS

Alan Turing stood in front of his first creation the Turing Bombe now the standard tool for allied decoding of enemy coded messages. The bombe, a heavy calculating machine on wheels, was first developed by the Polish Intelligence Service at the outbreak of war in September 1939 to unravel the coded messages sent by the German armed forces. The coded messages were typed on a special typewriter developed in the 1920s to code business documents and until 1939 there was no known way of deciphering an enigma message so effective was the German invention. The Poles captured an actual enigma machine while attacking a German convoy advancing into Poland and set fire to the vehicles giving the impression that the machine had been destroyed. In Hamilton Hall one of the female operators was checking the three double rows of twelve coloured wheels that were spinning as they made their calculations. She wearing Canadian olive green summer cotton WRAC uniform, light brown blouse and khaki tie, light brown jacket with brass buttons and skirt to the knee, sensible laced brown shoes and stockings.

Alan was nervously chewing the skin on his right thumb near the nail as he and his assistants toured Clement Attlee and Mackenzie-King and the US Secretary of State for War through Hamilton Hall, McMaster University in Hamilton, the city known for being the steel producing centre of Canada. Stricken with a bad cold he sounded as if his nose and throat were stuffed with cotton wool. "Dis is our standard decoder, until last year id was able to cope wid decoding most enemy messages.

"We do not think they know that we can read their Enigma messages. In fact we are sure of it as I wrote in my report which I submitted to the combined war cabinet. The enemy code-makers decided to avail demselves of the fourth Rotor wheel option increasing the complexity of the encryptions," Alan sneezed violently and slipped out a sopping wet handkerchief from his trouser pocket with which to wipe his streaming nose. "Sorry, bid of a cold", he spluttered. P'rhabs by assistant Kris Kowolski can carry od the story." He looked at the tall American Mathematician who stood beside him, wearing a natty brown pinstripe double breasted suit and colourful paisley yellow tie in sharp contrast to Turing who wore a white shirt that needed a good wash, a soup stained tie and barely covered by a too tight knitted cardigan missing two buttons and wrinkled wide whale corduroy trousers. Mackenzie-King noticed the sixth finger growing out of Kris's left hand and wrote a note to Attlee which he showed him in his notebook. "I think he must be descended from Anne Boleyn. Look at the extra finger." Attlee read the note smiled and resumed paying respectable attention to the man who was speaking confidently with a Boston accent.

The American beckoned them to follow him to the lift where they passed armed two Royal Marines on guard and had the lift operator take them down to the third subterranean level under Hamilton Hall. The basement had been secretly extended and two levels of offices and computer rooms added since 1940. Showing his identification to the guards Kris ushered them into a large machine in a room all by itself. It took up as much room as a small truck. "Behind these metal covers lies Cyclops. The operators are constantly checking that the hundreds of vacuum tubes storing and relaying information are working and the paper coming in and out is not jammed. Professor Jack Good has taught us to use sounds and smell to pinpoint a problem, he and Max Newman pioneered its technology with Alan Turing's guidance of course." Turing shook his head in embarrassment and blew his nose.

"Excuse me Dr. Kowolski but why has someone painted a picture of one large closed eye on the side of the machine. Shouldn't it be open to indicate a Cyclops?" the American Secretary of State asked.

"Someone painted it on after a few drinks celebrating D-Day, the shut eye indicates that this the first reliable truly electronic automatic computer looking inward and figures out, contemplates if you like, what we feed into it. It is focussed on the problem and not distracted like humans who look away so easily, distracted by the call of nature, the need to eat or be distracted. Six years ago a computer was anyone making numeric calculations sometimes using now obsolescent mechanical calculating machines. Today we have machine computers. Cyclops can decipher 1,000 characters a minute and print out the plain messages here," he stood in front of a solid teletype machine looking like a solid manual typewriter. It began to type out a message as the impressed visitors looked at it.

"We started work on Cyclops last year when the Jerries began using four rotors in their enigma machines, the Turing bombes using cribs of known mistakes by German operators were not efficient enough to keep up with decoding the thousands of signals we were being asked to decode. The first machine we developed was unreliable due to the paper tapes we fed into it breaking and vacuum tubes burning out it also needed a lot of statistical work from us at the same time. This was the 'Heath Robinson' named after the cartoons of that wacky professor who cobbles together all kinds of strange everyday objects in fantastic inventions. Also the OKW, the German Army High Command's Lorenz code was giving us headaches. The Lorenz coding machine uses pin patterns made by wheels which were changed every so often we needed a sophisticated machine capable of 'pin breaking'; the message is broken up by nonsense digits and letters selected in a pseudorandom nature. If it was truly random we would not have a hope of realistically keeping up deciphering them but there is a system and by using statistics we can pinpoint things fairly accurately.

Max Newman came up with the idea of using paper tape, two loops, one showing the coded message, the other tape loaded with the pseudorandom sequence. Each time 'Heath Robinson' was fed the first tape the second was moved by a position. Possibilities were then scrutinised and scored, the one with the highest score is then decoded. Keeping the two tapes in synchronization and not breaking was a challenge. Tommy

246

Flowers figured it out by using electronic valves rather than paper, so Cyclops does not have the old problems of paper snapping or getting out of synch. Having valves for digital switching is working brilliantly and makes Cyclops very fast. It is the fastest and first electronic computer in the world. ENIAC in the States is good but not as fast and this Cyclops was first. Now there is just one but we are building another. Now I'll take any questions and we can go to the canteen and meet some of the team."

Later sitting next to the American official Mackenzie King over a mug of cocoa Kris talked about his Boleyn ancestor with some pride with the Prime ministers and General Alan Brook and Turing. "...so you see without Anne Boleyn there would have been no Reformation and more importantly for the English speaking peoples, no Queen Elizabeth, a great Queen who was her daughter with Henry VIII. Every two generations or so one of us sprouts the extra finger. I never think of it anymore but it is a good conversation piece."

*

In Kandahar, Afghanistan Otto von Darmstadt had a nightmare in his tent under the stars. He had spent months looking for the sword without any luck now a jaguar lurked under his seat in the cinema here he had wandered trying to get his mind off his failure, the doors are locked and he is strapped down. His hunting rifle is hanging from the ceiling by a rope but no matter how hard he strains he cannot reach it. He tries to will it down to shoot off the restraint around his arms. He woke up pulling his *Walther* out of his holster. There was no sound except for their horses startled by his crying out.

"*Was is loss?*" a voice came from the tent next to his, one of the archaeologists a Nazi Professor.

"Nothing just a bad dream." He fell asleep again and dreamt of an antique shop in Berlin that he knew, he walked in a bell rang jangled by the opening door, a voice asked, "Looking for a sword-an ancient Asian sword?" He could smell a rich burning smell of best pipe tobacco, there was a figure covered in smoke behind the counter, it was furiously smoking a Meerschaum pipe. The only thing he could discern of the face was a wild moustache. Was it the Kaiser? No those were just wayward individual long hairs-whiskers-like. *Mein Gott*, a cat. He could see two eyes glowing like emeralds boring holes through the smoke and they were looking for Zulfiqar.

"Do you know where the sword is?" he asked.

"I do but I am not telling you." The next thing he knew it was morning. It was on to Herat with their Afghan guides. They had a clue, a story picked up in their investigations and confirmed by librarians in Berlin studying Asian tomes of folk-lore, that Zulfiqar was swallowed up by the 'earth's mouth' at the crossroads of Afghanistan where many invaders had come and gone. It could only be Herat. The city was the first one taken by Alexandria in 330 BC. *It won't be long and Germany will take Herat and follow Alexander's route onto the plains of India but I will find the sword first.*

CHAPTER TWENTY-THREE   ATOMBOMBEN

"I go with the certainty of a sleepwalker along the path laid out for me by Providence."

Adolf Hitler 14 March, 1936

The three wide-winged Heinkel 177 *Greif* bomber planes each with a bulbous glass fronted nose for a machine-gunner and bomb aimer, were warming up their engines in western Poland, each was loaded with an 7,000 kilogram *atombombe*. The two large propellers, one on each wing whirred on the *Luftwaffe's* only heavy bomber, were aided by a rocket engine mounted under the back of the fuselage giving it an extra boost. The twin double wheels began to roll along the concrete runway as each Daimler-Benz engine churned out 2,950 horse power. Each wing was 103 feet and two inches in length. Originally it was slow, with a maximum speed of 295 mph but the Messerschmitt rocket engine gave it an extra 180 mph for the final part of the flight. It made the plane shake like crazy and very difficult to control but they held together. It had to it was the only plane capable of carrying the squat, heavy weapon to its target. Plans were afoot for delivering the bombs in rockets but that would not be possible for a decade. It only needed to hold together one way the planners thought but this was withheld from the crews. The crew were told that they had the power to destroy a whole city and bring the Communist regime to its knees by leaving a circular scorched wasteland with a diameter of at least eight kilometres. The pilots quietly talked with each other. They were rigid in their determination to help destroy their mortal enemy but knew that the weapon they were to drop had such awesome power it was unknown whether the planes would survive the shock waves. Each bomb was to be dropped by parachute as they had practiced and film taken of the event as the plane circled above the blast zone.

"Too bad we are flying the Griffin the 'flaming coffin' surely there is a better aircraft? How about those new American bombers, B-29s, what a plane that is?"

"Be fair, the engines have been improved since the first ones in 1942 and they don't heat up as much now we have the help of a thrust engine to get our speed up. They sure as hell are tricky to fly but this is the   only bomber capable of carrying the *atombombe* until the Arado four-engine jet bomber will be ready next year, we will be the first squadron to fly it."

"Don't worry," the *Geschwader* leader said in his final words to his *Staffel*, "We will be flying at a great height and have the element of surprise. Their radar is primitive. On our way back there will be little resistance because our glorious *Luftwaffe* will be destroying the planes on every important airfield in a dawn raids jus as we drop our weapons. This is a great chapter in the history of the *Reich* we have the honour of writing the first page by blasting Bolshevism out of existence. If we come back we will be honoured by our *Fuhrer* as great heroes, women will throw themselves at your feet, you will have everything you want as long as you live. Statues of you will be erected along the immense Victory *Strasse* to be constructed in Berlin, the capital of the world, when this war to end all wars ends and we have a Nazi peace."

Early the morning of Operation *Angriff* Nikita Khrushchev was duck hunting north of Moscow and looked towards the city as some flying teal as the bomb exploded and was blinded by the sharp points of light by the exploding *atombombe*. Bubbling at the base of a large mushroom cloud filling the sky was an incandescent hell. Word slowly came from fleeing Muscovites who had survived the initial blast and resulting firestorm. One was the factory manager of tractor factory No. 3 whose clothes were smoking his face was seared and sagging, who had been seven miles from the blast point above Red Square driving out of the city. He jerkily drove his truck into a tree near Khrushchev who was slowly recovering partial vision. The man recognised the

Politburo member responsible for Moscow and shouted, "You are in charge of nothing anymore!"

Six square miles of the capital were utterly destroyed. The cauldron of fire dried up the Moska Reka that once flowed alongside the warped and broken and towers bricks of the Kremlin fortress and St. Basil's Cathedral. The first television in Russia, a German model owned by Communist *apparatchic* Mikoyan with a viewing screen that stuck out at 45 degrees and reflected the televised picture, reflected the image of the fireball outside then melted milliseconds later as a mushroom cloud slowly built up over what had been the capital of the Soviet Union. Yezhov died in the prison along with his prisoners, the air sucked out of the jail by the firestorm then burned up in the fire that raged for two days. Forewarned by American agents three men had made sure that they were with their armies away from Moscow, Kiev and Leningrad. Marshal Shaposhnikov was inspecting army troops in Stalingrad, General Zhukov was twenty miles from Leningrad on manouvers with his army Vassilevsky was in Vladivostok inspecting his new command and had taken the Admiral of the Soviet Pacific fleet, a school-friend into his confidence and convinced him to join them in fighting the Germans and restoring sanity to Russia by destroying the Communist regime.

The Griffin heading for Leningrad had difficulties with its rocket assistant, it went out of control and the aircraft's speed increased beyond what the wings could stand, they were torn off as it crossed the Polish border and it crashed boring a hole into the ground but its *atombombe* did not explode. Leningrad was saved with far reaching effects.

CHAPTER TWENTY-FOUR   STALIN'S LSD

"By raising their hand against Comrade Stalin
they raised their hand against all the best humanity has,
because Stalin is hope ...Stalin is our banner.
Stalin is our will, Stalin is Victory."
Nikita Khruschev January, 1938 to 200,000 in Communist parade
in Red Square

Stalin was at his dacha on holiday by the Black Sea with his staff, daughter and son. He had brought his favourite Hemingway and James Fenimore Cooper books to read. Last summer he had read the Forsyte Saga, that very British story of the upper-class, now it was time to read the work of American writers he admired. He had a cough the last few days he always suffered from sore throats when overworked so he was glad to have the waiter on staff bring him another glass of mineral water. It contained LSD a new drug slipped into the glass by a sous-chef to the moustached chef, Putin. The man was bankrolled by Hirohito's Grey Foxes who wanted Stalin out of the way in case he sided with Hitler against Japan. Stalin took several gulps and opened the *The Last of the Mohicans* to the first page but was interrupted by his secretary.

"An urgent phone call from General Konev he says the Germans have invaded it is very serious. There have been massive air attacks on Moscow and Kiev and on scores of airfields." Stalin ran to the phone imagining himself as a gazelle on the veldt in Africa. He looked at his hand to see if it was really a hoof.

A voice he recognized as General Konov in Ukraine was speaking quickly, it sounded like a squirrel trying to talk Russian, trying to impress people with its military knowledge by giving out rapid fire commentaries on some kind of invasion. But if what was a squirrel talking to him it could not be real invasion. Squirrels were not the same as his army generals, they spoke slower, they did not have fur suits. The thought struck him as funny and he began to giggle, a horrid gurgling sound. The creature was still talking "... Germans sweeping all before them ... reports of Moscow and Kiev being totally destroyed by some kind of super weapon. Cannot go back to Moscow." The line cut off but Stalin kept holding the phone laughing until he wept trying to remember what he had been told in case it did have a bearing on reality. But what was reality? He bounded towards his garden chair. *What an amazing piece of work this sitting piece of wood.*

He sat down. It was very hot and bees droned in the flowers in the garden. He wanted to be with his roses andmarmosas sitting down reading a book falling asleep. *I don't care anymore about government.*

By the second day of the invasion Stalin's bodyguard and secretary were frantically relaying telegram and phone messages to him in the garden but the more they told him the less he responded. "Comrade Stalin. Armies under Zhukov have taken Leningrad, and proclaimed an end to the Communist regime and declared it is St. Petersburg the home of a provisional government that has invited Grand Duchess Olga to return as Empress Alexandrovna, declared war on Germany and joined the Free Alliance of Nations."

"Kiev and Moscow have been utterly destroyed, all but Khruschev in the politburo are dead, he is flying here to see you. He has been partially blinded by the bomb dropped on Moscow."

"Rumours are flying, that you are dead or driven mad by the invasion. Comrade you must speak to Russia by radio."

"The Siberian Soviet has appealed to you to come to them and lead them."

"Yezhov and Beria are dead. There is confusion everywhere. The Germans are over-running eastern Poland and will soon be in Ukraine."

"The generals in Ukraine and Siberia are loyal to you and the revolution."

"The armies of Generals Shoposhnikov have taken Stalingrad for the provisional government."

"Vassilevsky's army is fighting in Sebastopol for control of the city. It is the civil war once again and this time we may not win."

"A German army group of three armies has crossed the Romanian border and is heading south-east towards us on the Black Sea."

"Enough," Stalin said stroking his thick black moustache. "I have my boots on but that is all I need to walk. I shall walk to Siberia. It is my penance and shall be a monk forever." He admired the beautiful blue sky and stared at his toes as he stretched his booted legs out from the chair.

White Army generals had every soldier remove the red stars on their helmets or caps and wear the Free Russian patch of white and blue. Their mantra became - 'kill the invaders' - 'A free Russia for all Russians'' - 'No more fear. No more paranoia'. They turned their armies into patriotic killing machines heading south to destroy Hitler's legions, and any Reds who stood in their way. Allied money and support was beginning to pour into northern Russia; the troops would be paid well. There was hope for the first time in a generation that a better world was coming once the Reds and the Nazis were defeated.

In Iceland preparations by Britain and America to help the White Russians proceeded at a frantic pace. The framework of naval and air assistance was in place. The Empress was in Iceland determined to Duchess Olga lead her people and destroy the Bolsheviks who had massacred her beloved brother Nicky and his family. She had escaped by a British ship in the Black Sea now she was to return in a British flying boat to the north. She was staying as a guest of Dowding in Rejvakic and was to be flown to Leningrad where she would proclaim it to be known as its old name, St. Petersburg on the White Sea.

Squadron Leader Bob Farnham was just sitting down to a roast beef sandwich slathered in mustard and horseradish after a particularly gruelling patrol looking for U-Boasts in the Atlantic when a Wing Commander commanding RAF squadrons in Eastern Iceland sat down opposite him and offered him a cup of tea from his black bakelite tray. This usually meant an interesting but demanding mission. Suspiciously curious Bob asked "Very good of you, sir. What are you doing to ask me?"

"You know the Germans have invaded Russia?"

"Yes, Hitler thinks he can take everyone on."

"Exactly, it could be the big mistake we need Hitler to make. But Hitler's learnt from Napoleon. He is not heading for Moscow. There is nothing much left by all account. His armies are mainly heading south-west. This gives us a chance to move into northern Russia and help the White Russians fight the Germans. We are sending the first load of laison officers and Russian exiles to set up the new government we need them in Archangel where you'll refuel then you fly them south to St. Petersburg."

Bob looked up, his eyebrows quizzically arched as he cooled his tea. "St. Petersburg, don't you mean Leningrad, the Reds changed the name."

"It's being changed back. Officially it happens when the Empress arrives on Russian soil and you Farnham will be flying her. She is a very straight-forward woman, her English is good. She was the younger sister to Tsar Nicholas II who was assassinated in 1918. She escaped from the civil war that rent Russia and went to live quietly in Canada via Denmark. Some Soviet generals have defected with their armies to the White Russian government, one of them, Zhukov, is in St. Petersburg. You are to deliver your passengers to General Zhukov and representatives of the provisional government. If there is any sign of trouble I want you to take her back to Archangel where we already have a naval and air presence which is growing daily. You leave tonight so you will flying in the dark for most of the 1,200 mile flight until you reach your passengers will be at your mooring at 1800 hours.

"I don't have to tell you, you are responsible for a VIP. There will be four Sunderlands flying politicians, laison officers and shipments of gold, printed roubles. You leave from the airplane base at Thistil fynordhur, fly around Norway and Sweden refuel at Murmansk, it is in White Russian hands and fly south to the Ladozhskoye Ozero near St. Petersburg. You will also be taking Prince Troubetzkoy, an aide to the Empress. The squadron adjutant is looking after the details. The planes will have several hundred passengers, gold and printed Roubles in the new Russian currency to be divided up. There will be a briefing just before you leave with the latest weather report. You did a good job taking Attlee to Casablanca last year."

Pleasantly surprised by this unusual mission and honoured to take the Empress, Bob agreed. "Sounds interesting, sir." *Isn't life unpredictable?* He thought of the submarine he had sunk on dawn patrol that morning after not even sighting a U-boat for a month. Bob reached for his bowl of sweet hot custard over tinned pears and enjoyed his cup of tea, even though it did come with a price-tag. Still it was a chance to be part of history, bit of a coup that.

*

As dusk came Stalin finished the water with great satisfaction as he read. His large head nodded as he sat in the wicker chair and he slept and dreamt then awoke hallucinating the same story in his head. He was in the angel air force gliding the way from Poland to Siberia, it was wonderful. He could count all the trees they all loved him they were dependable these trees they had no words they could not betray him with tongues or weapons. He would look after them and they would look after him. He knew he was an angel who had hidden his soul for the sake of revolution and power, the true soul the one God gave him and had tried to get him to commit as a priest but he had become an atheist and then a killer, a revolutionary. *Oh what a fool. When I could have been flying like this. Siberia. That is where IT is at. The great forest and swamps. I need to traverse them to meet and help the people there as a priest, as an old believer, a staretz. Rasputin walked from Siberia with powers to heal. I will go to Siberia and walk around it until I die. I will find those powers, make myself worthy, prostate my cowardly body in the dirt and ask God for the power to do good. I will need stout boots, one change of clothes and a few books that is all. Rasputin never worried about how he smelt and women did not mind.*

The next day at his Black Sea resort Stalin continued to act strangely. He let the telephone dangle and sway on its connecting line whenever it rang in the still summer air. He walked sideways and did a little dance through the back kitchen door and into the garden after getting a drink or some food. His doctor believed he had suffered a mental shock due to the news of the attack and would recover with time. He was wrong.

A frantic visitor came, Stalin's overseer of Moscow, Nikita Khrushchev. He spent five minutes with his boss and came out of the garden shaking his head. He grabbed Stalin's daughter Svetlana by the arms, baring his gold teeth he brought her close to his round face so he could see her eyes. "Your father is insane. He is no longer capable of any decisions. The other leaders are dead. In the name of the revolution I proclaim myself First Secretary of the Communist Party and pledge my life to defeat the traitor White Russians and Hitler's legions. I spoke to 200,000 party faithful in 1938 in -27 degree weather and proclaimed 'Stalin's life is our life our beautiful present and future.' Planes flew over in formation making the word 'STALIN' in the sky. We shall say Stalin suffered a heart attack passed power to me and died. He's just a character from *Alice's Adventures in Wonderland* now, quite mad. I brought my pistol it would be a mercy to put him out of his misery." He pulled it out of his suit pocket. Svetlana was horrified and shrank back in shock.

"I brought my pistol as well," said a drunken young man in olive air force uniform. It was Stalin's oldest son Yakov. He was holding a half-empty bottle of vodka leaning upon the doorframe of the dacha pointing a pistol steadily at Khrushchev. "You are not going to kill him. My father is happier now being mad than he ever was in Moscow. He may have killed his second wife, he may be a monster but he is my father!" He sobbed, "He loved my mother. You would rather kill your fellow Russians than just Germans. In the name of Russia!" He squeezed the trigger. The bullet went in the front of Nikita's large peasant forehead and out the back of his head. The man who killed off the last serious hope of Soviet revival staggered out onto the lawn and found his father's bodyguard passed out from drinking with him earlier. He said goodbye to his father who sat reading in the garden more bothered by wasps than the sound of gunfire. Standing in the sea up to his knees the waves lapped around him as he guzzled the rest of the bottle. He tossed it out to sea then shot himself falling face down in the water that gently rocked him into death.

Stalin with three days stubble on his face sat docile in a chair puffing on his pipe. He had spent three hours on his knees in prayer to a crudely drawn icon of Mary and baby Christ in gold paint he had ordered to have made and placed on the wall of his bedroom. He had a drink of water and said he wanted to think about their future. His daughter tried to bring him back to reality. "Father we are under attack we need your orders. You must not let the Marxist revolution fail now!"

"I am no longer Stalin. I am God's child, his pitiful servant. These flowers in the garden are children all Russians are flowers. I cannot cut them down any longer. I must go to Siberia and grow flowers and be one with the trees. It is His will I should be a priest. I thwarted him once when he wanted me to be a priest, and now I shall be. I am now a holy wanderer. Come with me on a train to Siberia let me grow a beard," he pleaded.

"If that is what you truly want father. I will shoot anyone who stands in our way. We shall go to Siberia immediately we shall take all the money and jewels we have."

"Bring the books, daughter. There will be lots of time to read."

CHAPTER TWENTY-FIVE   WHITE RUSSIA

During the first act of Operation *Angriff* the political leaders of the free west and the wives of President Roosevelt and Prime Minister Attlee were together in Detroit. Attlee and his wife Violet, FDR and Eleanor Roosevelt and the bachelor Mackenzie-King made a cosy scene in the best hotel in 'the motor city' as they sat before a roaring fire to take an unusual August chill out of the air.

The Canadian Prime Minister was tied up quite literally by a ball of wool that he was helping Violet unravel to the commands of Eleanor to untangle it.   His hands were held out stretching the wool and Violet was winding a string of blue wool into the ball in her hands.   Clement Attlee and Roosevelt were smoking and discussing the rumours coming from Russia. An aide came into the room and gave FDR a telex from General Marshal in the Pentagon, the armed forces HQ shaped like a pentagon. He took the telegram then exclaimed, "My God Clem, the Germans have done it just like we suspected they have dropped super bombs on the Soviet Union and invaded.   Here." He passed it over to his ally and friend. Attlee tersely read it out loud.

GERMANY DROPPED SUPER BOMBS ON MOSCOW AND KIEV LAST NIGHT. NO CONTACT WITH EMBASSY STAFF IN THOSE CITIES.   GERMANY HAS INVADED RUSSIA. SOME SOVIET GENERALS HAVE DECLARED A FREE WHITE RUSSIA IN LENINGRAD. SOVIET UNION COULD BE DISINTEGRATING. DETAILS TO FELLOW.

GENERAL MARSHALL. PENTAGON.

The inner cabinet of the Free Nations Alliance met. Mackenzie-King took the chair. "Thank goodness we took measures to be ready for this moment. The situation in Russia is chaotic." He went on to give more details as had been relayed to them.   Officers were constantly coming into the room giving memos to their respective leaders or having hurried whispered discussions.

Lord Beaverbrook asked, "But surely Stalin is directing strong counter-attacks?"

The British Prime Minister answered. "I have just heard from our ambassador who was not in Moscow when the bomb dropped, that there has been no statement or radio announcement by Stalin he may have been killed or is ill." There was complete silence then the rush of air being sucked into amazed mouths then expelled as they took in the news.

"Perhaps there is hope for a counter-revolution with Stalin out of the way if that is true but he would have killed a lot of Germans," Harold Wilson said in his Mancunian accent while he lit his pipe.

FDR jumped in waving his cigarette holder in excitement smoke trailing from his Camel cigarette in circles. "The White Russian government we are setting up now stands an immeasurably stronger chance of surviving and leading the fight as our ally without Stalin. I would like you Clem to send someone you trust to St. Petersburg as our Ambassador to the court of Empress Alexandrova who is in on her way from Iceland by air to her capital St. Petersburg.

"We have a golden opportunity to ensure that a liberal government is established in what was the Soviet Union. It will join us in our fight against fascism. As the details filter in from our ambassadors and agents, and the decrypted signals it appears there is a strong chance that the Soviet hold on Russia is fragile. The entire upper hierarchy of the Politburo may have been vaporized in the F-bomb explosions. Is Stalin really dead?"

Attlee looked up from decoded Russian signals brought to him by General Alan Brooke received from Hamilton Hall minutes before. "Not dead but insane. Decrypts from Sevastopol show he was on holiday in his dacha at Sosi on the Black Sea and was drugged by an agent in the pay of Japan with a chemical that has made him seriously deranged."

"Excuse me Prime Minister Mackenzie-King said laconically, "more deranged than he was before the German attack?"

"Point taken" Attlee said with a laconic smile. The best part is coming … He is constantly hallucinating and has now convinced himself that he must become a wandering monk in Siberia like Rasputin.

There were murmours: "What?", "You gotta be kidding" amongst the august group of Canadian, American and British politicians and officials.

"Nevertheless it is true. We decoded messages from the Japanese ambassador sent to Vladivostok to replace his predecessor killed in Moscow."

Harold Wilson took his pipe out of his mouth and wagged it at Attlee making is point, "This is preposterous the man hated, hates, religion, he is an atheist Bolshevik whose cruelty and ruthlessness is a byword and if anything is even worse a dictator than Hitler. He killed many millions by letting them starve to death in the Ukraine to force through collectivisation in the 30s, his purges killed off hundreds and thousands and he ruled through fear, inspired by the French Revolution's Reign of Terror but on a massive scale."

"I agree, Harold it is preposterous but he is out of the picture. But there are still Communists. They have set up a government under a commissar called Tchakovski in Novosibirsk, Siberia. He has managed to gather at least four armies loyal to him and has named himself Secretary of the Politburo and Soviet Commander of Chief. The Admiral of the Pacific Fleet has declared loyalty to him but most Generals and their men in western Russia have followed Marshal Zhukov and declared they are no longer fighting for a Communist Soviet Union but for Russia. The Zhukov declaration in St. Petersburg proclaiming the Empress's arrival was relayed by radio throughout Russia. He stated that the Germans would find Russia a deadly enemy but Russians would fight as free men and women not slaves of a tyranny under men like Stalin. He asked true Russians to rise up against the Soviets who sold out to the Germans in 1917 and killed the Tsar and many millions in a terrible civil war. Many Russians have voted for him with their feet and have flocked to join armies whose Generals have declared themselves under Zhukov.

Harold I propose you go to St. Petersburg as our representative as a liason with Zhukov and the Empress let us know what is happening, encourage them and promise them as much as you think you can. Franklin perhaps you could send a good man to work with Harold, someone with experience in Russia.

"I know just the man, he will be on his way to St. Petersburg in days," Franklin said decisively. His mood had lightened. "You know with Hitler invading Russia we really stand a good chance now by golly."

Eleanor and Violet clacked their knitting needles making a soothing accompaniment as Clement Attlee spoke for all of them in the room, "Franklin, you hit the nail right on the head." .

"Gentlemen you should know," General Alan Brooke spoke to the leaders at the behest of Attlee, "Our intelligence reveals that Hitler is not heading for Moscow or what's left of it but is heading south-east to the oil fields in the Black Sea region destroying any Soviet opposition left in the way. Just as our agent in Berlin said would happen. They are proceeding at a very fast rate."

A phone call was put through to President Roosevelt. "Well? Ah Admiral King....What? The commander of the US Mediterranean Fleet has relayed a message from our Ambassador in Istanbul?" FDR excitedly put his hand over the phone receiver and called out to everyone in the hotel room. "We've got more good news coming in" "Sorry Admiral, go ahead ... hmm you

263

don't say. Keep me posted make sure the Foreign office is informed, the vice-president and the Pentagon. You are aware about Russia .... good. Good. I shall phone you tomorrow morning and be back in Washington tomorrow night. Goodnight." He turned in his wheelchair his face creased in a charming broad smile, "A celebration drink. Turkey has declared war on the Axis powers and is now an active member of the alliance. Elements of the Turkish army have moved north and attacked Von Paulus's army that is pouring into south-eastern Russia."

CHAPTER TWENTY-SIX   TRAVELLING

The bells of the Cathedral of the Transfiguration in Archangel, northern Russia rang out in their bright tinny fashion, tinny to ears attuned to British bells that unique to Europe rotate all the way round and give rise to a distinctive peal. Word had reached the bell ringers that the town was flying the old Tsarist flag with the double headed eagle. It signalled that Empress Olga had arrived on Russian soil, or to be precise Russian water.   A squadron of Yakovlev 9 fighter planes from the Soviet Air Force, which had defected to the White Russian leadership headed by General Zhukov in league with the Empress, escorted Bob Farnham's squadron of Sunderland flying boats as they flew from the White Sea to the great lake near St. Petersburg carrying their important passengers the Empress and her government.   As Bob brought his large flying boat into a graceful landing despite the choppy waters of the Lake Ledoga the Empress excitedly looked out of the round windows as he taxied the aircraft to the docking area near the new capital.   Before she walked onto the dock she went to the cockpit and thanked the pilots.   Full of joy she gripped both hands of Squadron Leader Farnham.   "Squadron Leader, you and the men will be our guests at my palace here in St. Petersburg once we are organised until then I will ensure you are treated as honorary members of the Russian Air Force. Please stay for a few days until I can repay you."   Tears ran down her face.

Farnham a man of calm and good sense replied, "Thank you Empress, it has been an honour to fly you back to your motherland.   We are honoured to be invited."   A crewman showed the Empress the ladder to the dock and helped her down.   An honour guard from Zhukov's army came to attention and sixty Cossacks on horseback wearing red long skirted coats with pouches for bullets drew their swords and waved them in the air cheering.   Wearing a white scarf that blew in the wind, Alexandrovna inspected the men who wore a white patch indicating they were part of the White Russian army.   Already a million men and women had joined up and were being trained and kitted out by British and American instructors. Successes against German Army Group Four were becoming more common as they became adept at destroying German tanks and vehicles with bazookas and artillery. Four armoured divisions of the Red Army equipped with the recently manufactured JS2 heavy tanks had defected to the White Army. Originally intended to be called Stalin tanks they were renamed *Pyoter* tanks after the great eighteenth century Tsar Peter the Great who westernised Russia. These divisions attacked Von Paulus's men who were at the gates of Stalingrad and halted their advance. American and White Russian paratroopers landed in Stalingrad and took the Soviet commanders captive and inspired the population to support the White Russian government in St. Petersburg. Stalin's Russia was melting like the snow in spring.

*

Owen Gryffyd tucked into fried eggs and toast in the cabin of the small motorboat that was chugging up the west coast of mainland British Columbia and then turned his attention to a cup of coffee which he almost filled with sugar. "You know Chief this stuff is worth its weight in gold where I come from, rationed in Wales, it is."

"The Germans and their friends take it all for themselves?"

"Yes, that is precisely what I mean. Now in return for your taking me to your village for a weekend and telling me about your healing plants and the ways of your tribe allow me to tell you about the Welsh druids."

"I am listening," the Haida Chief said solemnly as he turned the wheel of the boat slightly to miss a dead-head that had escaped from a raft of logs being taken to a sawmill on the Gulf Islands.

"A Roman historian, Tacitus, wrote about us."

"I heard of Caesar and his writings but not Tacitus."

266

"Oh, I brought a book of his for you, anyway when the Romans came to Anglesy in Wales, my birthplace, about one hundred years after Christ Tacitus says they found a fanatical band of Druids shouting curses at the invaders. Julius Caesar wrote that my ancestors the ancient Druids made wicker statues and placed people inside them, then set fire to them as human sacrifices. I am not sure if this was true, I was told that we used to make wicker statues and set them on fire but not with living people inside them. Either way we no longer do that, although my father did teach me how to weave twigs to make a human shape.

"But what of Stonehenge, your rings of stone totem poles? Isn't that the most important place to Druids?"

"Yes, to modern Druids, the amateurs pretending to be Druids, the ones that are either retired eccentric doctors or the easily impressed it is very important but it was John Aubrey in the 1660s who wrote about a connection of Stonehenge in Wiltshire with the Druids. The modern Druids, the fake ones, started in the 1700s based on his writings and those of other antiquarians who were not real Druids. Since the blue stones making up Stonehenge were probably quarried in Wales the home of Druids, chances are my predecessors had something to do with Stonehenge, probably a lot. All I know is what my father taught me as his father and their ancestors had passed down for over a thousand years. These are the ancient ways of Druidism, living with the earth not just on it, wielding the power within our bodies and minds and inherent in nature to do what otherwise seems impossible. To flow with the inner stream of energy inherent in living things, people, animals, trees, plants, fish even the sea, rivers and mountains."

"This sounds very similar to what we believe the spirit of Manitou in his creation here the fish, the sea, the forests and its animals, the bears and deer, mountains, eagles, ravens, hawks and sky. We hold these creations sacred and full of power. Let me tell you about my son Charlie. He's a fighter pilot in the RCAF flying a P-51 Mustang fighter in California. His tribal name is 'Raven's Eye' because as a baby he had black eyes. He has shot

267

down fifteen enemy aircraft. He is coming home on leave soon. He will survive the war but he will come back with a wound maybe inside or outside or both. I had a vision of this but I could not tell for sure the water was murky when I looked down for more details.''

'But he will come back. We are going to win you think?''

"Yes, we shall win but many and much will be lost. However, that is things stand now, they can change but right now we are flying faster and faster and getting close to the top of the mountain. As long as a stone does not bring us down.''

"What kind of stone?''

"A stone big enough to kill any bird in the sky.''

"Then we shall smash the stone."

There was a comfortable silence for some fifty minutes. Then the chief spoke. "We are almost at our village, another hour or so. I want to show you the face carved in a tree many years ago when Sir Frances Drake sailed up here, our legend is that his face was carved into a cedar by a totem pole carver and of course it became covered with moss but we recently cleaned it up.''

"Chief, in Drake's time," Owen related, "there was an astrologer, a medicine man, who advised Queen Elizabeth, I his name was Dr. Dee. He prophesied that she only needed twenty good galleons and she could rule the world and begin an empire which would be greater than that of the Romans. She sent Drake on a mission to plunder gold from the Spanish in Latin America by attacking them in their undefended towns on the West coast of Central and South America. He followed Magellan's course sailing around Cape Horn and up along the west coast up to this area of Canada, your land. He may have gone further, maybe he had secret orders to find a way back to England above Canada, a North-East passage. He may have gone as far as Alaska but this is just my fancy I have no way of knowing for sure.''

"There is a legend of a white man in a hard hat going north, past the Fraser River to the south and further north than where we are, probably it is Drake."

"A Druid knows when a thing rings true or if it is a lie. It is my job now to train psychic warriors and the best hope we have is with the children."

The Chief replied, "the young have unlimited energy I can understand that they have special powers. I think you will enjoy your stay in our village and go back to your work refreshed."

"Thanks Chief Jimmy, I am looking forward to it." For the rest of the trip they said nothing but enjoyed watching the green forest of large firs and cedars growing along the stony shore until Jimmy Seaweed turned into a stony inlet and a village of tents and wooden houses guarded by several totem poles against a background of mountains loaded with tall green firs and cedars came into view. "This is majestic," Owen said over and over.

CHAPTER TWENTY-SEVEN   IN THE 'MOUTH OF THE EARTH'

Alan had shown Sphinx's ring to Murat Yazil the Turkish archaeologist who greeted him when he arrived dressed. Murat was tall and thin with shoulder blades that stretched the spotless tight double breasted suit he wore despite the heat. Like Sphinx he wore a panama hat. He had a well-trimmed moustache and was deeply tanned by the sun. The disguised Canadian seemed the even taller than his normal six feet thanks to the turban wrapped around his head, part of the native costume Freya Stark had given in Baghdad for his role as an Iraqi dig foremen sent from one of Yazil's Baghdad digs to help in Harat. They conversed in English interspersed with Turkish as Murat showed Alan the workmen working with spades and trowels in the dig inside the fortress that Alan was to supervise during the day while at night they tried to find Zulfiqar themselves with the help of Murat's most trusted assistants . Alan followed as the Turk led him up onto the ramparts. They looked at the desert around them and saw a man in robes and round Pushtan hat leading a donkey laden with food into the gate, they were both tan coloured from the light Herat dust.

"The fortress needs some repairs but is still being used. The tribesman hired by the King to man the citadel have gone off to arrest some bandit or other who's been disturbing what usually passes for peace here. They have left me in charge since I want to protect the place and I speak Pashtan and Persian Of course my men and I are armed. This works out very well for us and our search. I am doing some investigation in the old well to the left there. It dried up in the 1500s so they dug another one on the other side which still works, it provides the water we drink here."

"That sounds promising. I shall start work on the dig and tonight we can begin our search."

"Yes, Captain Alan that was precisely what I was thinking, only a few trusted men will be with us tonight as you descend into the well. I will show you the winch we have set up. It's perfectly safe, it can hold two of me, which is about the same as you. I tried it already." Murat smiled.

"I am glad you have such confidence."

"Come let us get some refreshment and I can show you your daytime duties. You can fill me in our mutual friend, Sphinx, he is the most amazing man I have ever met even though we were on opposite sides in the war."

That night, with the fifty local men employed in digging and scraping out the foundations of the citadel inside the fortress and in the outlying area sent home Alan, Murat and a strong assistant entered the unused stone well room. It was cool as they entered through the Moorish arched entrance. The Turkish archaeologist held a flaming torch of pitch that he stuck into a rusted metal bracket on the wall near the well's mouth. The light from the flames flickered and created large shadows on the wall which had once boasted fine green and white tiles which were now cracked and faded. Alan lit a paraffin camp lantern and held it as Murat's assistant wrapped a rope, attached to the winch set up on a wooden frame over the well, around Alan's body and securely under his arms. "We have five hours until the guards arrive for their morning check, I have two armed men outside in case those Germans searching for the sword find us."

Alan sat on the edge of the circular stone wall that was just two feet above the ancient tiled floor holding up the lantern with one hand and holding onto the wall with the other, his feet dangling over the edge. He looked down into the dark hole below him. "I see why this could be the 'mouth of the earth. OK I'm ready. The spokes of the wooden wheel controlling the rope on a metal drum above them began to turn as Yazil's assistant in workman's clothes strained. Alan was lifted up into space then the man slowly lowered him one foot at a time.

Alan studied each square inch of each layer of bricks calling out to be lowered another foot. The stones were quite large, about three feet square. *This is tough work* Alan thought.

"Nothing yet," he told Murat who was not expecting anything quickly if at all, he had been disappointed too many times in his career to think anything of such great import could be found in weeks let alone minutes.

There was nothing to indicate any object hidden inside or between the bricks. They were almost seamless. The only marks were scratch marks from buckets used over hundreds of years and some splashed bat droppings. Take the lantern Murat and lower it down to my level with a rope there's a good chap. Murat did so an Alan felt into the bag around his waist pulling out a chisel and hammer to experiment to see how strong the bricks were. He hammered at the fourth level of old bricks, the thin seam of mortar in the old well was powdery but the bricks were tightly fitted together. After five minutes struggling with a chisel and hammer swaying violently in the basket his vision Alan was frustrated. The job seemed impossible, *Perhaps Zulfiqar is buried at the bottom that will entail heavy work that could take a week. Still, his men are trustworthy. I suppose I shall have to go down to the bottom. Murat said it was fifty feet.* Then he remembered what the Afghan tribal chieftain had told Lord Roberts. "Seven layers down you will be in inside the mouth. There are thirty two large stones in a circle. The stone facing due east has a metal ring attached. Pull on the ring, twist and the stone below is pushed back. Reach in and pull out the sword."

Murat had heard the sound of hammering echoing up the well from twenty feet below. It had stopped. now there was an unbearable silence. No, something outside perhaps, Murat looked over his shoulder then convinced himself it was his imagination. Alan pulled on the ring. Nothing happened he tried again there was a slight movement or was it his imagination. He felt places for fingers in the ring pulling the lamp to shine over the object he could see it was designed for a left hand to grip it properly. He switched the torch to his right hand and gripping the ring and with the added traction due to the grip pulled and twisted his feet held hard against the wall of the well, his knees bent as he tugged. He felt a stone in the well wall pull back. He shoved the lamp up against the open side of the well. He knew would have to reach in his arm and feel at the back of the other stones. Imagining terrible things, rats, a ball of snakes, a sprung knife trap he started to sweat.

There were muffled shouts and shots that made Murat peer down and hiss, "There are noises outside it is the Nazis."

Now or never. Alan concentrated pushing his hand first into one side behind the wall. *Nothing.* Then the other-*something solid*! He fastened his hand around it and carefully drew out a long object wrapped in a faded rotting silk green flag the material fell apart and dropped down the well. Despite the urgency he could not resist pulling the sword out of fabulously jewel encrusted silver scabbard. *Zulfiqar!* Even in semi-darkness he could tell that was a weapon fit for a prince. He reverently touched the blade with his thumb. *A miracle it's still sharp, an even bigger miracle I found it.*

He shoved the sword into his bag. So fixated was he that on succeeding in his mission that it took several seconds for the struggle above him to penetrate his consciousness. Murat was calling out "Help!"

Looking up he could make out, in the flickering flame of the blazing torch held up by a newcomer, a cruel face looking down upon him, it was a face he recognised - Otto von Darmstadt. "Ha, we have you! Come on up and we shall take what Hitler wants."

Alan knew his only hope was to act in a split second and use the sword. He slammed his feet on the rock he had pulled out. *Would it ...? Too late to question.* His gymnastic skill from army jump horse competitions guided him as he nimbly launched up towards from the darkness of the well towards the mouth of the well. Alan shot up five feet balanced his body sideways for a second teetering on the stone mouth of the well, then pulling the sword out of the scabbard in his bag cut the rope and dropped onto his feet holding the sword. Von Darmstadt fired his *Walther*, the bullet ricocheted off the Damascan steel of Zuliqar hitting the SS officer in the shoulder and knocking him off balance. He fell against the stone wall at the top of the well. Murat kicked the gun out of the hand of the SS guard distracted by the struggle and wrestled him to the ground pounding his head on the stone floor of the well room until the man groaned and was still.

Alan slashed at von Darmstadt as the German raised his pistol for another shot and the weapon clattered down the well. "Know who I am Von Darmstadt?" Alan ripped off his turban and rubbed the back of his hand over the dirt that covered his tanned face. "Alan Stafford we last met at Kz1."

"Stafford!" his enemy jeered. "Now you are masquerading as an Arab. You and your brother are irritating but hardly warriors! You cannot stand against the SS!" The insult made something snap inside Alan and all the hate that he had surpressed transferred itself into energy as he leapt like a tiger onto his prey. OttoVon Darmstadt gripped Alan's sword arm and the blade grazed the SS officer's face as they struggled. The German SD officer had made a cardinal error while stationed in London, the physique he had once nourished with gruelling exercise, marches, horse riding and miles of swimming had become slack as he became satisfied with hunting and golf as recreation. Alan on the other hand had hardened himself in body and spirit so that he could exact revenge on those who had created the hell on earth called Kz1.

They rocked back and forth locked in combat breathing hard into each other's faces. Murat held his breath; it seemed the antagonists would both fall into the well breaking their necks together as they hit the dry bottom a hundred feet below. Then Alan twisted and shoved decisively pushing the German over the brink and the Nazi was swallowed by the abyss which was the 'mouth of the earth'. For a split second the SS officer's hands reached up to grab the sword but Alan drew it back and the hands followed Von Darmstadt's body out of sight as he seemed to be sucked away to the centre of the earth, a scream filled the well and echoed around the room . There was a crashing sound far below and silence broken only by Alan's heavy breathing as he helped Murat get up from the tiled corner of the well room where he had been thrown.

"My friend you did it. The sword helped you."

Alan fell to his knees exhausted. Holding a pistol Murat limped out into the corridor of the citadel leading to the old well to see his guards. He came back in a moment. "My men killed von Darmstadt's team but one of my staff was killed and one wounded, I have sent someone to wake our doctor. He is conscious and says the bullet went through his arm. He should be o.k." The Turk sighed taking off his panama hat and fanned himself with it. "I am sad in my heart for my foreman. I know his family, they will be devastated."

"I am sorry too, Murat," Alan said switching to Turkish. "Look, do you think this is the real thing?" He offered the sword to the Turkish archaeologist who put on his glasses and took the proffered weapon and studied it in the light of the torchlight. "It will need proper study with a magnifying glass and chemical tests and the opinions of sword experts but ...." He held it up and turned it, professionally examining the blade and jewelled hilt. "It is magnificent. It is the finest Muslim sword I have ever seen, the blade is superb and the rubies in the hilt make it priceless let alone for its religious value.

"You must leave with it with my wounded assistant. You will leave at dawn which is not far off. I do have some boxes of artifacts to send back to the Museum at Istanbul as well they are already on the plane. The pilot can drop you at Baghdad when he lands to refuel for the last stage to Istanbul. Our friend the Sphinx wants it yes? He is an amazing fellow we worked together before the war on shall we say other adventures." Murat said putting his forefinger to his lips.

"Yes, he will find a safe place to keep it for the duration. I will ask him if it can be given to the Afghan King once the war is won since we found it here in Herat, in his kingdom."

275

"That is what I would do Alan. It is the proper thing to do but it may not happen that way. You know the way of the world is sometimes cruel."

"Yeah," Alan agreed with his Turkish friend. "I'm learning. Thank you for everything."

"Come my friend," Murat insisted. "I will have my friend and colleague buried in the local cemetery and arrange for the bodies of our enemies to be disposed of. The 'mouth of the earth' will still have its secrets." Holding him up and carrying the sword they stepped over the dead body and into the night. At dawn a red blood sun rose from the direction of Kabul over the Afghan desert. Alan embraced his friend and stepped up the ladder in the fuselage near the tail of the American transport plane. He holding a large leather bag, inside was a new Herat woven Afghan carpet wound around a wooden box containing the sword that could start or step a revolution. Murat waved as the Turkish Airlines DC-3's two engines whipped light brown dust and sand as it gained speed and took off heading west.

Alan unshaven and wearing a badly fitting suit sat with his precious cargo in a bag next to him fell asleep minutes into the flight. Underneath him as he slept were thousands of miles of rock and desert, mountains, valleys, rivers, ruins, sheep, tribesman, the old Silk Road travelled by merchants on camels for more than a thousand years, the route Marco Polo took to Cathay and back to Venice.

In Baghdad he took a taxi to the British Legation and the first person he saw outside the building was Freya Stark who smiled broadly as she saw her young friend then looked concerned as she noticed his rag tag appearance. "Young man you need a bath and a shave then I am taking you for lunch and you can tell me as much of your adventures as you are allowed to."

"Yes it sounds good but I have something to give to the Ambassador first to keep safe until I get a flight to Jerusalem."

"Well I just had a chat with him he's having his morning cup of tea and biscuit. I'll wait for you in the lobby of the legation."

Back in Jerusalem, dressed in linen trousers and a fresh open neck white shirt and a panama hat Alan walked with his bag on his back, containing the precious item. *This is very strange walking the streets of Jerusalem carrying Mahommet's sword on my back, to be walking in the same city where Christ walked and through which he carried a heavy cross on his back. Come to think of it, it will be a relief to give it to Sphinx. Still it has been my protector.*

"This is wonderful," Sphinx said impressed. "We shall have it cleaned by an expert and find a hiding place. Any ideas?"

"Hmm. Mecca?" Not the Grand Mufti's palace.

"Where is the last place the Nazis will look?"

"New Britain-London."

"Exactly. I know just the place," Alan said. "I was always impressed by the Wellington Peace Monument at Hyde Park Corner near Apsley House there would be room inside one of the horses pulling Victory's chariot it must be hollow. But I think it should go back to Afghanistan once the war is over and the danger past."

Sphinx looked oddly at Alan. "I could pass that idea on but I have learnt in my years at the top and the bottom of things that some things are beyond our control." Then the frown on his forehead left him and he grinned. "I like your hiding place idea of course we shall never know where they pick. You have done well. I want you to pick out one of my books to keep as a memento of your mission, a thank you."

Alan was hesitant. "I insist I am an old man, I have no wife or child to pass them on to, it would be doing me a favour, I have too many. Ah, good choice." he proclaimed as his protoge pulled out a first edition of Winston Churchill's book about the Afghan campaign, *The Malakand Field Force*.

CHAPTER TWENTY-EIGHT   PARTY AT THE CASTLE

The Waterloo Chamber at Windsor Castle was the site for the '1944 Engagement Party at the Palace' hosted by the swaggart of bacchanal, King Frederick and his bride-to-be Princess Choucu O-No. It was, and is, a magnificent room but it was soon to be desecrated by a hundred especially invited toadies and informers who made up the upper crust of the rotten pie known as the fascist court. Bewigged footman in heavy gold encrusted uniforms with tails, silk stockings and shiny black shoes with silver buckles circulated with trays bearing glasses of martinis and flutes of champagne. Already the noise was rising as the guests slurped greedily.

King Frederick, despite a diet imposed upon him by his new advising doctor Mr. Crusoe still needed two footmen to help him climb up on a short ladder and step onto one of the highly polished mahogany table in front of the massive painting depicting Wellington's infantry formed into squares as waves of French Curaissers hurled themselves and crashed upon the bayonets and muzzles of the red woollen coated British.

Beneath him the red woollen Axminster carpet. Weighing in at fourteen stone King Frederick was the largest King since George IV in the Regency, indeed during the war with Napoleon whose defeat this chamber celebrated. But unlike that flamboyant bon vivant, the Prince Regent of the early 1800s, Frederick was a fascist puppet, set up and maintained by Adolf Hitler and his British Nazi minions such as Lord Eastbourne, Prime Minister of New Britain. At least George IV was a monarch who followed the advice of his Prime Ministers and like his father before him was a constitutional monarch even if jealous of his prerogatives and eager to spend any and all monies Parliament voted him.

He held up a hand for quiet and waved it at his fiancée, who wore a flame red cocktail dress modelled on a flamenco dress by Felicity who stood holding a glass of Pimm's lemonade and sliced cucumber at the back of the room. The guests hushed and the King, his chins wobbling as he spoke, as if he was a ironically saturnine Buddha, addressed the throng, "Your Royal Highness," he nodded at his gorgeous young fiancée who smiled coyly back at him behind her fan revealing only her large almond eyes, "My Lords, Ladies and gentlemen. To coin a phrase, this year our Waterloo party at the palace, har har, is at this lovely if chilly whoop up at Windsor Castle. I chose the appropriately named Waterloo Chamber for our engagement party since the carpet matches the lovely dress made for my princess of the Japanese Imperial family by one of our talented New British workers in the Aryan state. This Briton, who is giving the French fashion designers a run for their money, is standing at the back in the chic black number, a bit shy I think, but let us recognize the brilliance of her work which is putting our style and fashions on the map within the *Gross Deutschland* headed by our *Fuhrer*, Adolf Hitler. Regretfully he could not come this year due to other commitments. He has sent the German ambassador to the court of St. James in his stead. A toast," the King leaned over and nearly slipping off the table was pushed back by some alert footmen, another footman passed up a flute of champagne and the king raised the glass high into the air.

"To Chouu my lovely wife to be. You are all invited to our wedding at Westminster Abbey, we shall be mailing you the invitations as soon as we have got over our hangovers. Now let the festivities continue." At this a chamber orchestra began playing and footmen circulated with plates of hors d'oevres before the dinner began.

Lord and Lady Eastbourne were standing together slightly uneasy at the obviously rabid Nazi court. "Every year this event gets more bizarre and fin de siecle, as decadent as ancient Rome under Nero or Caligula" Lord Eastbourne had mentioned to his wife as their chauffered Rolls Royce drove them with an armed escort of machine gun motorcycles and two armoured cars alongside the Thames to Windsor. "Remember how the Lord

Chamberlain threw up all over my back as he stumbled into me in the lavatory."

"I remember you telling me dear, luckily I did not see it but I can still picture it ... unfortunately. "We shall stay only for an hour and then I shall 'get a headache'."

"All right." He patted her hand. Her hands her face, her entire frame was emaciated she had cancer but the doctors had given her some of the latest radiation treatments and lately she had begun to put weight back on and be more energetic but still. He worried about her, he had begun to tire of Parliament, he had his majority every MP under him was a member of the British National Socialist party elected form a list of local riding fascists he had a lot of power, as long as he did not cross Adolf Hitler or Lord Moseley in the House of Lords. His boundaries were clear. He fought for what he saw as the New British corner within a Nazi Europe but not a day went by when he did not fear the knock on his door in the middle of the night and the revelations in the newspapers that his mother was a Jewish maid impregnated by his father. The maid was in Wales pensioned off handsomely he had visited her once and the whole affair was secret, he had not even told his wife.

It was time for another meeting with Dixon-Fairley he was the only one he could talk to him, who understood his fears and girded him to carry on in slippery times, his spiritual adviser, the clairvoyant who understood him. He had no idea that the friendly man in Bloomsbury who guided him in along his tortuous path was working for the resistance and pulling all sorts of interesting information out of his head without his knowledge every time they met which was at least once every month or two.

After the King and his fiancée had retired, she to her room at the Ritz and he to his bedchamber on the second floor of the palace overlooking the magnificent gardens, the party degenerated. Footmen were picking up the politicians who had drunk too much and were now forming teams shaking up methueselas of champagne and spraying the guests as if they were at an automobile racecourse at Brooklands, Nurburgring or Le Mans.

*

"Your Majesty, the Duke of Hamilton has agreed that Lennoxlove House will be the HQ for the resistance uprising in East Lothian during the liberation and he has invited you to visit him when you are able in a clandestine visit."

Queen Elizabeth finished feeding her corgi dog at the crofter's cottage she had been living at for the past four weeks in the western Highlands. "Hmm I used to think the Duke of Hamilton was rather pro-Hitler until he pledged his loyalty, told me that he made some ill-judged remarks before he realised the true ambitions of the Nazis. I accepted his apology and told him to stay in Great Britain, that he may be useful one day. He agreed."

"A good thing, Your Majesty," he offered.

The Queen Regent agreed wholeheartedly as she cleaned her revolver at the kitchen table then carefully inserted bullets into the spinning chamber. "When he is given the signal by the Black Douglas he shall do what is necessary. For now he sits in the House of Lords with that odious fellow, Mosley and his minions just to fool them."

Her aide-de-camp Colonel MacRae noted, "Rudolf Hess thought he was the man to negotiate a peace with Hitler when he flew over in a Me 110 and parachuted out in 1940 attempting to meet him."

"Yes, he was embarrassed with that so he wrote me the letter to explain we could count on his loyalty. We shall visit him and his family. Do make the arrangements while I do a bit of shooting practice."

A few weeks later as the Queen and her aide and guards were settling in for a long stay at the Duke of Hamilton's castle The Queen's messenger arrived dressed as the mailman delivering parcels to Lennoxlove the 16 th June two days before the anniversary of the Battle of Waterloo. "Special delivery for Mrs. Stuart." The butler looked surprised that this man was aware that the name of the special guest was Mrs. Stuart but recovered himself.

"I shall see she gets it."

"I must deliver it personally please tell her one her Royal Messengers is here. I shall wait."

The butler's thick eyebrows which were badly in need of a clipping as if he were some kind of Scottish terrier raised and put his whole brow into motion. "Certainly, would you like a cup of tea in the kitchen?"

"After I have seen Mrs. Stuart and handed this package to her."

"I shall inform His grace the Duke and his guest that you are here." He went to the drawing room where the Duke and Duchess and the Queen, 'Mrs. Stuart', were having a cup of coffee.

"Ahem, your Grace a Queen's messenger has an important parcel for your guest Mrs. Stuart."

The Duke looked over at his guest. "Well Ma'am, shall we see him?" She nodded.

"Very good, show him in."

The messenger was shown into the room nodded to the Duke of Hamilton and bowed his head to Queen Elizabeth. He opened his hand to reveal his badge a silver greyhound. "Your Majesty I bring you the Union Jack that flew over Singapore from his grace the Duke of Wellington."

"Ah yes, the young man with Bernard Freyberg in that awful siege." She took the parcel. The Duke passed her a pair of scissors with which she snipped the string that bound the brown paper parcel and opened the thin cardboard box and packing paper that surrounded a red, white and blue object. She carefully pulled

283

out the flag and raised her eyebrows she saw the bullet holes. A note fluttered to the floor.

The Queen's Messenger picked it up and read it. "The holes are from Japanese fighter planes Ma'am.

The Duke says they have been have been told they practise their shooting skills on it. The last was shot down moments later."

"Good, he made a terrible mess," she held up the flag and counted the holes. "I shall treasure it and tomorrow it shall grace the Waterloo dinner our host is preparing for us. I would be grateful your Grace if you would see that our messenger here is allowed to stay for the dinner."

"Of course he is most welcome," the Duke agreed, "Please join us for some coffee." He rang for his butler and asked for another cup and extra biscuits and scones.

"What is your name?" Queen Elizabeth asked of the messenger.

"Jonathan English. A week ago I took delivery of the flag with the crew of a fishing boat out of Oban that picked it up from a submarine HMS Scimitar off the Isle of Skye. Its trip from Singapore began with a Beluga cargo sub HMS Cormorant that flew it on its conning tower into Kandy harbour, Ceylon. It was taken by air to Cairo via Iran by the RAF then taken by a Motor Torpedo Boat into action near Gibraltar then taken by submarine to Iceland where Air Marshal Dowding himself hoisted it up the flagpole at the RAF airfield in Rejvavik."

"We have not knighted anyone in six months but I shall knight you for what you have done. Could you pass me a sword please," she sweetly asked the Duke of Hamilton.

He looked up at display of muskets, Scottish claymores and shields on the wall between the bookshelves. *Ah, this should do* he pulled a thick bladed claymore with a large basket hilt off the wall and offered it hilt first to the Queen. She took it and asking the messenger to kneel holding the sword with two hands around the handle gently tapped the man upon his left and right shoulders. "Arise, Sir Jonathan English."

The following night in the dining room the royal party were led in by a piper, a retired Pipe-Major of the Argyll and Sutherland Highlanders. After a sumptuous meal of roast beef, roast tatties, carrots and peas the Duke of Hamilton rose and gave the toast to the sovereign. "Your Majesty you are the monarch who stayed to share our troubles. I pleaded ill health and no longer attend the House of Lords but look forward to attending a cleansed House once the war is over. May it be quick and may your forces be blessed with victory and your peoples with courage. Let us stand and toast ... the Queen. God bless her." The Queen remained seated but the Duchess, the Queen's retinue, the Chief Ghillie of the estate and Sir Jonathan stood and lifted their glasses echoing, "The Queen."

She stood up and looked over them with her one good eye the other hidden tactfully by her pink eye patch matching the pink dress she wore tonight. In her handbag however she kept her revolver. "Tonight we remember an Irishman's victory over Napoleon at Waterloo in 1815 in Belgium whose army included Scots, English, Welsh and Irish just like our forces today. We were unable to commemorate on the anniversary June 14th but we are grateful to you the Duke and Duchess of Hamilton for taking us into your home for this important occasion. I would like to read the letter that came with the Union flag we have on display courtesy of the Queen's messenger here this evening, Sir Jonathan English.

"*Your Majesty,* Since I am now the Duke of Wellington on the death of my father, this is the first year in which I have the honour of continuing the tradition begun by the first duke, Arthur Wellesley, to give you a flag on the anniversary of his great victory at Waterloo, one hundred and thirty one years ago this 18th June. Circumstances here in Singapore have not allowed me to deliver my personal flag in person but you will I hope understand that as a lieutenant in your Horse Guards I am pleased to be on active service, accordingly with the permission of the commander of our *force here, General Freyberg, VC, a most courageous and noble officer, I am have dispatched to you a Union Flag that has flown over the unconquered Lion City of Singapore.*

The courage and dedication of many men will hopefully see that this is delivered safely to you in Great Britain to help you in your remembrance of the Battle of Waterloo.

Yours very sincerely,

Rupert Wellington, 1st Lt. Royal Horse Guards,

Singapore Garrison

CHAPTER TWENTY-NINE   ARCTIC EXPERIMENT

Lalitha, a Brahmin East Indian scientist comforted her husband who entered their quarters with a raging headache, she caressed his temples with her long cool loving fingers. Subrahmanyan Chandrasekahr was a brilliant Fellow of Trinity College, Cambridge in 1934. He had been brought up in Madras and had happy memories of escaping the pre-monsoon heat on the twelve-mile-long Marina Beach near Chennai on the Indian Ocean. Aged 19 he attended the Paris Conference on Novae and Supernovae-white dwarf stars and begun his meteoric streak to fame. Ironically his genius now meant he was working on something so secret that he could never tell anyone about it save for his wife, Attlee and Mackenzie-King, authorised members of the scientific brains trust, the Bridge Club and of course his own team in the Who Project. Their assignment was to determine if time travel was possible and master it, money and resources were unlimited and there was no time limit. "It may take ten, fifty or one hundred years or more but you must find out if it possible and how time travel can be utilised, it will be our ultimate salvation if the Nazis win. Even if they take over Canada they will never know about your research laboratories with its own underground village designed to be self-subsistent in the Arctic. If we win we may have a crucial trump card to play if we are ever threatened again. I don't even know exactly where you will be only those who have to know will be told the secret in case I am taken, tortured and drugged."

Subrahmanyan had agreed and moved his wife and army of researchers first to Winnipeg then flown almost 2,000 miles north to Prince of Wales Island where engineers constructed an underground complex of living quarters and laboratories capable of supporting hundreds of scientists and their families with huge stocks of food, wood for ingeniously efficient wood burning stoves, powerful radios, their own school, an airstrip for deliveries and ships for summer use. Arctic Rangers, the local Inuit tribes militia were asked to watch out all along the mainland and in the islands for any enemy submarines or agents looking for anything on the islands. They had been there for three months and already the air was becoming cold, the very brief summer would soon turn into the long night of winter so far north.

Now there was no sun just icy cold air. "It's going to be so cold, so bloody cold Lalitha, It will be unbearable.''

After telling him that the modern wood heaters radiated five times more than traditional fireplaces and would use up one tenth of the wood she tried to distract him, "how is your work going? I must go over some of your ideas, I am a scientist too you know, at the moment I am just setting up the equipment you and the others order."

The East Indian suddenly looked interested, his work was everything but his wife made it all worthwhile. "I told Attlee last week that I did not think time travel was possible but you told me something that changed my mind so you are already crucial to our work. You said that all the power in black holes was enough to turn the universe inside out if the hole was big enough. That is what we have to do, turn matter inside out and release the energy and direct it to move back in time. Doing it is a massive job and doing it with a person and coming back to their time without vaporising them is the challenge of a lifetime - several lifetimes.

"But we can do it, I am convinced. We have to replicate the conditions of a black hole or travel to one and link up with its energy. The first is more immediately possible space travel is decades away unless the war ends soon and we concentrate a lot of money and effort on that. I will recommend travel to the nearest black hole as a future project but I am starting with building a huge cyclotron on King William Island in case there is an uncontrolled explosion. I want to smash atoms into their smallest parts and investigate the power that is inside them like a fission bomb but use that energy to open a rift in the universe and move in time.

"Another idea is something Einstein has talked about. He went over it with me in Boston before we came up here, that is gravitational waves we will be investigating that in fact perhaps you would like to be on that team dear. Apparently there are even psychics trying time travel through purely spiritual or mental effort, some are able to, so they claim though of course I am highly sceptical. Our team will investigate their techniques but it is erratic and their physical bodies do not go with their thoughts, feelings or souls and it is uncertain so far as to whether in such a state change can be affected. That is the point: can we go back in time or into the future and change things and if we can how much changes? It is a whole new science.

"As Hindus we know about the spiritual possibilities but as scientists we also know about other possibilities." Lalitha posited. "The Ashkaric Record is what we were told about as youngsters, Gee," she called him by her pet name, "the print of what has gone on before that is inside us. Interesting how our Indian culture is of interest to the west now. Remember we met Robert Oppenheimer in North Dakota as he toured us around his Operation Wyoming site where they are working on the fission bomb. He is learning Sanskrit so he can better understand the *Bahgavad Gita*."

"Yes, it describes the Mahabharatha War of 2,800 B.C. where a terrible weapon was used killing fourteen billion in eighteen days so it tells us, supposedly, according to archaeologists, leaving what now makes sense because strata of clay and green glass found in some ancient ruins matches what a fission bomb leaves behind. Strata of clay and green glass were found in F-bomb test sites in North Dakota. Our direct ancestors probably walked in the ways where we are now walking we shall just have to watch our step. What else can we do? But they would be surprised at where we have ended up at the very end of the world! And I don't think the Aryans conquered time, now that is the ultimate challenge." He spoke in precise cut-glass tones of an upper class Englishman the product of a British education in Madras and England which often shocked those meeting him for the first time.

"Here my love have some hot tea, I think it will keep us warm here for many years to come."

*

Von Flaut, head of the KZ1 rocket factory and firing range on the Isle of Wight had been invited with Lord Eastbourne by Werner von Braun chief scientist of the Luftwaffe rocket program to the east coast of Ireland to watch the first launch of the S4 *Arien* two stage, double-engined supra-ocean missile carrying a two ton high explosive warhead towards New York. Every day several would be launched at the eastern American and Canadian seaboards. The rocket stood eighty feet high supported by a steel gantry that was pulled away. Its engines were ignited and it began to spin on its own axis and lift off with a great roar. Flaut held his hands over his ears despite them being in a concrete observation post with a foot of reinforced glass protecting them. As it lifted into the sky and arched over the Atlantic von Braun assured his guests; "When the first stage's fuel is used up the empty cylinder will fall into the ocean, the solid fuel in the second stage is ignited and the warhead is taken to its target to explode at supersonic speed, they will have no idea what hit them. Goodbye Radio City Music Hall or the Statue of Liberty, we shall get rid of it all."

Twenty minutes later a screaming sound came out of the eastern sky and descended upon New York, radar operators had no time to scramble fighter planes, shore flak guns were useless. The missile exploded at the base of the Empire State building and erupted, causing the building to shake off its windows and office workers into the streets below like a weird ticker-tape parade. The largest skyscraper in the world creaked and leaned in on itself, then half of it collapsed in a slow motion disaster of dust, concrete, sheets of paper, filing cabinets, chairs, desks, telephones and people.

Roosevelt took the call in his bedroom. "I am sitting down Hap," he told the commander of the USAAF. "You mean the Empire State building is gone, most of it you say? You think it was a German rocket capable of being fired from Ireland?" The

President blinked back tears sad for the city he loved. "Here's what we do Hap. You get a jet squadron of Comets flying off the coast trying to intercept these deadly rockets. I want floating radar posts set up in mid-Atlantic telling us their course, speed and altitude. You will make sure we find from where they are being launched and plaster them with thermobaric bombs. They are not going to get away with this. Get on it Hap I am going to New York."

"Oh, I'm coming too Franklin," Eleanor said, at the bathroom door listening, "There's a Red Cross convention at the Rockefeller Centre I will go."

FDR phoned Herbert Hoover head of the FBI and arranged for a train at Washington to New York for him, his wife and FBI bodyguards. They arrived at Central Station to cheers from the dazed commuters and made their way to the site of the explosion. Both the President and his wife comforted the wounded victims then Eleanor made her way to the Rockefeller Centre and spoke calmly to the Red Cross officials who were crammed into the air raid shelters below the building. "We shall get through this, every major city in Europe and some of ours have had worse, it is our turn. But one day we will not have to be fearful any more we have to go on and live for that day. Now we know about first aid so I think I shall take one hundred volunteers with me to help the hospital staff closest to the Empire State building, the rest of you can disperse with the executive members to other hospitals in Manhattan. I am told that they are all demanding nursing staff."

CHAPTER THIRTY   UNDER THE WAVES

The message reached John as they prepared to attack the Fascist Spanish and Germans holding Saville. 'Sub-Lieutenant Duncan MacLeod to report to HM Naval Base Cadiz for flight to Iceland. Immediate. He is seconded to British naval legation going to Russia. Major-General Waughburton-Lee, Royal Marine Commandos.' So a surprised Duncan, who had thought he would finish out the war as a Commando took a plane from Cadiz to a bergship then a transport plane to Iceland arriving on a clear, windy day. He began his war as a junior officer on a destroyer hunting U-boats, attacking the German navy and narrowly missing death at the hand from Stuka dive-bombers. He was ordered to report to a Rear Admiral being transported to Murmansk on HMS Sturdy and had two days to get ready on-shore helping the Rear-Admiral organise a complex convoy system ferrying supplies from Iceland to Murmansk and back.

WREN First Officer Helen Spencer docked at the Royal Navy base at Iceland and reported to the base administrative office. The officer of the watch took down her details while she sat in his office her kitbag at her feet. He looked her up and down admiring her trim figure in blue, he was a sailor who did not mind women in the service one bit.

"Ah yes, here we are, you are going to Murmansk, bit of a rush I'm afraid. The submarine Sturdy is taking you and others in the navy mission to Russia to set up their end of the convoy system we are setting up to supply the White Russians. Have a look at the map if you like see where you are going while I phone for transport for you and your kit"

She stood up and looked at the huge nautical map that took up the whole wall of his office. She noted that Murmansk was close to the Finnish border at the very top of the peninsula, made up of Norway, Finland and Russia, that was on the Barents Sea at almost 70 degrees north of the Equator. *Gosh that is far north. Oh well it will be a bit of an adventure.*

"No cars available I'm afraid but we do have a courier on a motorbike who can get you to where is berthed she is leaving at 1600 hours so better get a move on. He'll meet you outside." He opened the door for her and helped her with her kitbag. "Good luck say hello to Russia for me a wonderful travel opportunity," the veteran of countless days on frigate duty in the Atlantic said optimistically.

Helen did not have to wait long, a sailor in an open navy blue greatcoat, bell-bottoms, white and blue naval shirt and rating's round hat drove up on a noisy 650 cc Royal Enfield motorbike painted blue with a sidecar. He expertly eased himself off the bike took off his black gauntlets rested them on the seat and opened the hinged top of the side car open for her. "I can take the kitbag on the pillion, Ma'am. I'll strap it down if there's nothing breakable in it."

"Thanks, I must get to the sub HMS Sturdy before she casts off so if you can put a spurt on," she said smiling at the handsome blonde sailor, she guessed he was about nineteen and having the time of his life in Iceland. He gallantly tried, and failed, not to look as she daintily hitched her naval skirt up to sit in the sidecar. He was rewarded with a flash of thigh and black stocking top that made his afternoon. He had conveniently forgotten there was a side door that opened.

He looked away reluctantly and put on his gloves kick-starting the bike and shouting over the noise of the engine, "hang on!" After a fast ride weaving past cables, bollards, sailors, workmen pushing wheelbarrows and squawking sea gulls at high speed that made her giddy passing a flotilla of blurred grey naval vessels of every size and description the courier brought her alongside a dock which had a submarine moored by bow and stern cables. It was flying the Royal Navy ensign a white flag with St. George's cross with a Union Jack in the fly. Painted on the conning tower just aft of the deck gun were white silhouettes, two aircraft, a cruiser, three freighters and oddly enough a train.

293

"However did they sink a train?" she asked the motorcyclist who was carrying her kitbag on board for her.

"The captain is a dab hand with the gun he can have that three-incher cleared away and firing with the water still draining off the deck when she surfaces, they got a train as it went along the Italian coast blew it to pieces in six shots, every one hit home. I'll stow your kitbag for you Ma'am, I'll just ask where your bunk is." He disappeared down the stern hatchway which was open revealing a narrow ladder going down into the 872 tons of floating submarine. She followed him and slipped a florin, a two shilling coin into his hand, "Here have some beers on me sailor,"

"It's a pleasure, no need, Ma'am but since you insist. Have a safe voyage to," he lowered his voice, "Russia, don't worry I know everything that goes on in the dockyard."

"I'll be back no doubt as a block of ice." He shyly saluted with the edge of his hand to his forehead, naval style and left.

She found the captain on the bridge with several other passengers some wearing more gold braid than she had seen since Gibraltar's underground naval HQ. "First Officer Spencer reportin, sir."

"Good, wondering where you were you must have just got in from Gib. You'll be with the other plotter WRENS in the stern mess, they will be your ratings to look after Lieutenant here and in Murmansk, the five day voyage will give you a chance to get acquainted and go over your orders. This is Rear Admiral Johnson who will be in charge of all convoys going in and out of Murmansk you will be reporting to him."

The rear admiral stepped forward in the cramped space and held out a hand. Helen shook it, "I'm looking forward to working for you, sir."

"Good, that's the spirit, we'll talk at dinner about the work we've got lined up for you and your WRENS who are all highly qualified and experienced as you are. Have you been on a submarine before?"

In Capetown, sir in a South African navy one for a trip around the harbour, it was an old one not like this new one. Matter of fact it had a few leaks."

The captain snorted, "there are no leaks on this vessel lieutenant" the way he said it implied that women had no place on a serving submarine in wartime.

"Of course not, sir, if you'll excuse me I'll check on my ratings."

"Before you go you may as well meet this Scotsman behind me," the submarine captain said, shifting to one side of the periscope which took up the central section of the bridge as it thrust down from the conning tower. A few drops of rain came down the conning tower as a squall picked topside. "Duncan MacLeod is believe it or not a Sub-Lieutenant in the Royal Navy although," he said distastefully, "he is still dressed as one of those piratical Commandos one reads about.''

"Good to meet you lieutenant," Duncan said to Helen, "I do have a proper uniform I just got here and will be changing you won't recognize me once I swap this kilt and jumper for the proper rig. I am going to help you with convoy checks, crews and cargoes incoming and outgoing, docking and loading and unloading. I blew up some dock derricks in North Africa so the Admiralty must think I am ideal for the Murmansk docks."

"Quite lieutenant,'' the captain snapped, "Gentleman and er," he couldn't bring himself to say lady, "I will ask you to go to your quarters. I have to set sail. You are invited to the officer's mess for tea at 0500 hours and dinner at the start of the second dog watch, 2000 hours in case our Commando sailor has forgotten." As soon as his passengers had left the bridge the captain began giving orders to his crew, "Prepare to sail in fifteen minutes on the tide, He spoke to the engineer in the engine room asking for a last fuel and battery check. "Number one last torpedo, shells, food and water check, then cast off and batten the hatches." Within minutes his orders were obeyed sailors ran up the ladders and closed the hatches and watertight doors tight, tightening and locking them on the inside. The diesel engines began to thrum. Speaking to his first lieutenant the captain ordered, "Signal the harbour master we are departing." He gave orders by radio phone to the engineer and to the sailors in the bridge responsible for trimming the submarine keeping it upright and for diving and surfacing, respectively filling up and jettisoning ballast sea-water. The Sturdy still on the surface headed out to sea then submerged into the grey Atlantic beginning its voyage to the north of Russia.

Over the voyage Duncan began to feel more of a sailor as he accustomed himself to being an active part of the senior service after four years as a Commando exercising much more freedom than he did as a young ship's officer in the North Sea and now. But he was enjoying working with the Rear-Admiral and the pretty WREN officer and her young lady ratings planning a huge operation in a northern port only the admiral was familiar with. Helen, for that was her Christian name, had confided in him over a mug of cocoa one evening that she was actually a titled lady, 'Lady Helen' but had sworn him to secrecy since she did not want her WRENS to think she was a toffee-nosed aristocrat. He agreed with an alacrity which alarmed him, he did not seem able to say no to her. *Worrying,* he decided. Usually Duncan felt better keeping women at a distance, they were alright to dance with, go to the pictures, but that there had never been anything serious. *I'll concentrate on the big job ahead, there will be one convoy coming in and one going out within days of each other, a constant stream of PQ convoys.* It was a very big responsibility but he felt they had a good chance of pulling it off. Rear-Admiral Johnson really knew his stuff and was wonderful with the WRENS his other staff were going ahead by cruiser in the first convoy.

In return for her confidence two days later he told her that he had been heading for medical school but joined up but had to fake his eye test when the doctor wasn't looking. "That's why I wear glasses, not common in the navy,'' he told her. "so that's **my** secret." He found himself pleasantly surprised every time he bumped into her which was often since the submarine was crowded and their quarters cramped.

One morning she told him about her experiences taking a launch out to convoys coming into Capetown to drop the pilots and check the manifests and loads of each ship and dealing with many comments from merchant sailors who had never seen a woman sailor. "Some of the phrases they used were quite disgusting but I learned to find something wrong with their manifest and made them dock last, they soon learned to keep quiet the next time they dropped anchor. But I loved South Africa. You must go and see it one day." She decided to take the plunge. *It must be being cramped in this sardine with someone handsome who seems very compatible.* "Maybe we will both end up posted there. I am staying in the WRENs after the war and going to the top but there is no reason why I couldn't have a male naval friend to share our career highs and lows with, that is if you wanted ..." The Captain sat down and asked Duncan to pass the salt for his pie and chips which prevented him from replying. He looked at Helen his face red so she looked down and then made spirited small talk with the Captain who eventually began to warm under her considerable charm despite himself. Duncan excused himself and sought the company of the torpedo men in the bow who had remarkable stories to while away the hours.

Duncan had never felt like this, expectant, tongue tied, alternatively reckless and reticent. *When I am near this lady I am no longer responsible for my actions, usually so careful so Scottish, so middle-class. What is this am I in love?* He answered himself. *Yes, you idiot. You are in love with Lady Spencer and you have only known her for six days of course being in a submarine squashes everything together so let's say twenty days. This is ridiculous. A few weeks ago I was with John and the Red Dragons on the way to Saville then I was ordered to Iceland flown out via a bergship and assigned as a naval lieutenant to accompany Lady Spencer to Russia as a naval laison officer to the White Russian Navy. And I don't even speak Russian. Nyet. Well one word.* He threw his pocket Russian-English, English-Russian dictionary at the steel bulwark covered in large bolts that was the wall of his bunk on the crowded submarine.

CHAPTER THIRTY-ONE   ROMMEL'S *ASIA KORPS*

Afghanistan "A Kingdom N.W. of India. Chief industry is farming.
A country without railways."

The Triumph Stamp Album. Nineteenth Edition. London: G. F.
Rankin Ltd., 1959.

The last of the super tanks nicknamed 'Adolfs' by the least generous of the German tank men, which was most of them, conked out just outside of Kabul. The phrase employed with a chuckle was 'No coolant big plans - that Adolf!' "It's no good, sir," the panzer engineer in charge of the four massive U-Boat diesel engines driving the super tanks reported to his superior. "It is just too hot, it is 60 Celsius inside and it is only early morning, the combined liquid and air cooling mechanism keeps breaking down we'll have to wait for some new refrigeration systems.''

"Rommel is not going to be happy the Fuhrer is always going on about how important they are. We have left twenty of them in a long line of wrecks from the Black Sea, where the Turks got the first four, to god-forsaken Kandahar. Still, you have performed miracles getting this one here. But we are almost in India. Only 85 kilometres to New Delhi," the Major said confidently.

The Engineer *Hauptman* did not share his optimism he had seen too many campaigns and was looking forward to an end to the war. Still he was a professional soldier so he squared his shoulders covered by sweat stained black overalls. "*Jawohl, Herr Major.*" But he was thinking *Only 85 kilometres through some of the roughest mountain reaches in the world, not tank country. Not even close.*

Feld-Marschall Erwin Rommel, hero of the *Reich* and victor of three terrible tank battles with Russian forces on his long march through the Caucausus and onto the plains of Asia,

299

shrugged when he was told of the last super-tank giving up the ghost within sight of the walls of Kabul. "Build a camouflaged defensive position around it, use its 105 mm guns as an extra flak battery in case the RAF noses around as they seem to be doing with impunity. I am most upset with the *Luftwaffe*, Galland's promise of two *Luftflotten* supporting us every kilometre on the road to New Delhi was an empty promise but I suppose our factories and training schools are having trouble keeping up with its losses. I am down to two and seventy eight tanks, three hundred artillery pieces, five hundred other vehicles, 180,000 men and one month's supply of petrol. *Gott in Himmel* one King Tiger tank alone has a V12 engine that sucks up 500 litres of petrol every 100 kilometres. Our supply line for lorry transports is thousands of miles long and constantly being attacked by British and Russian planes and guerrilla Persians and Afghans. No I know what the British had to put up in the Afghan Wars.

"Von Paulus's army was supposed to take the Iraqi oil fields but no he follows Hitler's second set of orders orders gets entangled with the Turks and the Russians in the Caucausus. We were lucky to get through relatively unscathed considering. If the Japanese army gets the finger out and takes Calcutta we might just do it but it is only a slim chance. I am a good general but Montgomery is facing me and he beat me at El Alamein because he had a better air force, more petrol, tanks and men and his strategy was faultless. I must do everything I can to keep my army alive and beat him. I am waiting for him to make a big mistake, it is my sole hope. Our agents in India report increases in glider training and large numbers of parachutists are making practice drops. I suspect he will make long-range attacks on our staging posts, strategic spots, rivers or mountain passes and then rush his ground army in a strike across Afghanistan pushing us back linking up with his airborne forces. He has the air power to do it and I can do nothing to stop him. We may have to winter in Kabul and build up our strength, send raiding parties against the British at the North West Frontier. My hope is that he will try to hold a pass too far."

"Your orders, *Feld Marschall*?"

"We take Kabul, leave a small garrison and push on to the Khyber Pass. We lost four hundred good men trying to locate the right pass thanks to the British magic tricks but it showed the worth of our mountain troops. Hitler wants us in New Delhi by Christmas. I will try but God knows he is asking the damned impossible. Now I must write a letter to my wife and children, writing to them is the only thing that keeps me sane, the *Luftwaffe* air-mail courier plane leaves within the hour."

Rommel and his arch-enemy General Montgomery matched each other in experience both were infantry officers on the Western Front in the Great War and built upon their experience to reach the top of their profession of arms. Each became a master in tank warfare, Rommel as command of a Panzer division in France then made a general in command of the 4th Army Group in the Battle of Britain. They opposed each other in the see-saw battle of Hayward's Heath which saw Monty seriously wounded and Rommel as the victor. Two years later they were opponents in North Africa and it was the Englishman who once lived in Australia as a child to be the victor. One all. Now in Afghanistan they faced each other again with India in the balance.

One week later Rommel his trademark plastic sand goggles around his *Wehrmacht* cap wearing shorts and shirt watched from a vantage point on a mountain in admiring the columns of infantry trucks, tanks armoured cars with aircraft screaming overhead on the lookout for any resistance patrols to eradicate. "The cream of the *Wermacht*, Fritz," he said to his aide Colonel Fritz Anheim. "Not a great deal Montgomery can do against our lot until we get onto the plains of India. Finally we have proper *Luftwaffe* support and our engineers have coaxed twenty one more *Elefant* tank destroyers and King Tiger tanks to life."

"*Gut*, but The RAF can do a of lot damage, they have learned *Blitzkrieg* too well, their fighter-bombers are superb."

"Yes, we must be careful of air raids but our mobile flak units are first class and the jet fighter *stafflen* can knock these Tempests and Typhoons out of the sky once we spot them with our mobile radar. But they come in at impossibly low heights through cracks in the mountains our troops swear they are magically appear. We shall see whether I or Monty are the best conjurors.

Rommel did not know that a real magician, Meskelyne, who had disguised the Suez Canal with mirrors and made German bombers unknowingly jettison their bombs thousands of yards from their intended target to harmlessly explode in the sand, was at work. Over three months he had achieved what many thought was preposterous, he had established an elaborate system of mirrors and fake mountain passes to mislead German planners. Photos taken by recce flights over the Khyber and other mountain passes showed one thing for every pass, ordinance maps showed another. *It is not possible. Every one of the passes incorrectly mapped?* Impossible!" snapped Rommel. They showed him the proof and he stayed up all night examining the photos and comparing them with the maps with his intelligence officers.

"Well what do you make of it?" he asked wearily as the sun rose outside his command vehicle.

"The British are trying something very strange, they may have used unlimited Indian manpower to physically change the routes of the traditional passes. It is possible but improbable. The only way is for us to send raiding parties and check the ground for ourselves."

Rommel replied tersely, "But that will hold up our invasion of India."

"That is their intent and who knows what they are planning in the meantime. Montgomery will be on the offensive before winter.''

When, when? Rommel asked himself dreading the answer but not getting one.

CHAPTER THIRTY-TWO   GLIDERS

"Here out of one brigade we have lost in a fortnight 245 killed and wounded and nearly 25 officers."

Winston Churchill in a letter to his mother
Lady Jenny Randolph Churchill from Afghanistan
Winston S. Churchill, 1: Youth 1874-1900

In the western Indian state of Baluchistan several hundred miles south of Afghanistan John Stafford was introduced to the glider pilot who would fly him and his men to their target north of Kandahar at Jaldih where the road from Kabul began to descend to the lower altitude of Kandahar. "Ah, Major Stafford," Colonel Waddington of the 1st Airborne Division I wanted you to meet the glider pilots who will be flying the eight Horsa gliders carrying your Commandos." He introduced each one and ended with, "Flight Lieutenant Dene Vander Meulen, a Canuck who is piloting the lead glider which you will be in at H hour to your position at the end of the road to Kandahar. Rommel's men will be retreating down it from Kabul."

"You're from Canada aren't you? Your parents must be Dutch were you born there?"

"Regina, Saskatchewan, major, my parents immigrated in 1910. I wish it was as flat as the prairies at Jaldih the landing strips we will use will be marked by the Special Air Service but I am told there is little margin for error, at least we are landing by day. A night landing would be suicide."

With a grim laugh John looked at the maps pinned up in the Airborne Division HQ, the glider pilots discussed the landing details with John who was reassured by the energy and focussed attention to detail of the young men who had the lives of all two hundred of his Red Dragons in their hands. He and his men had spent a month practicing take-offs, flights and landings in the twenty-five man Airspeed Horsa gliders in all weathers at night and in the daytime. John with his love of history was fascinated that it was named after one of the Anglo-Saxon brothers hired by the English King to fight the Picts, Hengist was the brother and there was another glider named after him. Of course the mercenaries and their men came in the sixth century they settled and never left. History or not, the first time aloft his stomach felt a strange twinge as the 67 feet long metal aircraft with an 88 foot wing with huge flaps to control its glide to the landing target was left to glide on its own power. The cable connecting it to a transport aircraft like a Dakota DC-3 or a Stirling bomber was released and they were on their own piloted by two men in the cockpit who only had so much altitude and time to put the glider down and screech to a sliding halt on the ground.

The sound of the whistling wind as they were released and the drone of the transport engines disappeared was all that could be heard as the helmeted men linked arms and firmly placed their booted feet on the floor of the craft ready for anything. Every time he could almost hear the intake of breath of twenty-five men as the pilot warned them.

'Landing. Brace! Brace! Brace!'

There had been accidents, one Horsa glider carrying Red Berets, armed paratroops of the Airborne Division, had slid into a large rock killing the pilots and ten of the crew, injuring the rest. A cable broke one morning just as the transport was lifting its Hengist glider to five hundred feet and something happened to the flap controls, the pilot could not control his craft and it spun out of control killing everyone on board. It was a sobering experience but it had its compensations. John felt the thrill of exhilaration every time they took off, were released into space and landed with a crunch and screech of metal on the ground at sixty miles an hour. The tricycle undercarriage of the glider was released once they took off so the landing was a glide on land literally. It was, he decided, a bit addictive. He began to look forward to it with a strange mix of trepidation and excitement that dared him to keep doing it.

The colonel continued, "As you know Major, General Montgomery has attacked Rommel and prevented his army crossing the Khyber Pass pushing him back to Kabul. He will continue the offensive with the 8th Army and with air support forcing Rommel to either make a stand at Kabul with limited fuel or take the chance of saving what's left of his army by retreating to Kandahar which will receive reinforcements. Chances are Rommel will decide on retreat and try again next spring. Now it is our turn. Operation Rose Garden means that two parachute drops and a mixed parachute and glider drop will be made at three strategic points along the road from Kabul to Kandahar. Your men will land by glider as well as four hundred Kiwi paratroops in gliders, twenty jeeps, mountain guns, flying flea motorbikes, PIATs and mortars. Two thousand Red Berets will parachute in just before you land they will be met by local tribesmen who will show them the lay of the land and the best places to set up defensive positions. H hour is in three days time.

"Monty is taking a gamble but he thinks he can roll up Rommel's army by land along the one road from Kabul to Kandahar and dismember it by air attacks and cut off the supply of fuel, ammunition and rations along the road reaching the *Asia Korps*. You just have to hold and beat off any attacks from the south west or from the north east.

"Or both, correct Major. We will be dropping ammunition and rations every second day until you are relieved."

As they walked past a row of Dakota transport planes camouflaged in a light sand colour a voice called out. "Why all that's wonderful! John Stafford," John turned and saw his old air force friend, Brock Badger. "Are you a glider pilot these days Brock?"

"I'll leave that to the young daredevils, I've swapped my Typhoon for a DC-3 for this operation. I'm pulling a Horsa in fact

305

it might be yours." He looked in his notebook in his air force jacket pocket, "H 19 target Jaldih"

John looked at Dene who nodded, "That's us."

"Well," John said, "let me tell you about the chap who is going to pull us into Afghanistan." He proceeded to give a lurid account of his friend's flying antics from a helicopter in Wales to an Italian bomber stolen from Cornwall and flown to Gibraltar.

"Just don't let go too early, that's all we ask," was the lieutenant's earnest request. "Don't forget we're right behind you."

"Have no fear, Dene. How could I forget I am tugging a whole load of red dragons through the sky?"

Dene invited Brock to join them as they climbed into the side door of the glider and looked at the cockpit with its large plastic windows supported by a metal framework allowing the pilot a good view.

"Interesting we don't have such a good view just a few portholes," John noted.

Brock looked knowingly at the glider pilot, "It's best the passengers not see too much of what is going on. But don't worry these are designed to be used when at night or by day with fighter escorts which we will have in this case since it is a day drop."

Dene observed, "the big advantage is that there is no risk of running out of fuel since there is no engine at all, the fun is manouvering to find a nice little patch of field to land in. It's vertical darts from 4,000 feet up in the dark and trying to land in the bull. But I love it. Here, try out the pilot's seat and I can explain the controls."

John briefed his men going over the details of the jump. "We have our orders to board our glider H19 in fifteen minutes and take off at 0700 hours. We have good pilots, nothing to worry about getting there just the enemy we have to worry about." The men laughed, they were in fine fettle they knew they had an important part to play. John stood in front of his men clustered around the nose of the glider whose wings were emblazoned with a blue and red RAF roundel and white strips of paint to indicate to friendly aircraft that they were on their side. They all wore camouflaged Airborne Division smocks and airborne regiment rimless helmets and brown woollen trousers, puttees and boots. John's green Commando beret was in one of his smock's pop-button pockets.

CHAPTER THIRTY-THREE   OPERATION ROSE GARDEN

'Es lying on the dead with a bullet through his 'ead'
'Soldier Soldier' Barrack-Room Ballads Rudyard Kipling

As the sun rose the paratroopers known as Red Berets because of the winged badge and red berets awarded them on completion of their parachute training and the Red Dragons woke to a rosy glow that lit the black sky in the east until it was purple then dark blue and orange on the horizon. As they looked east from their vantage point in the mountains they could see for fifty miles it was so clear. "To think that Alexander the Great came this way thousands of years ago," John mused out loud. President Lincoln said, "Amazing to think we are in such good company. Didn't he carry a copy of *The Iliad* with him just like you John?" When out of earshot of the men the two soldiers used their first names

"Francis for a guy who left school early you know a fair bit," John kidded him.

The Nova Scotian chuckled rather pleased to be complimented by a historian who had gone to university but John as always treated him as a human being so knew he was not being patronised. "For a darkie I've done pretty well but it hasn't been easy. John, I've been thinking about what you said about applying for officer training. I would like your recommendation to get in the course."

"It would be a pleasure. I shall file it when we get off this mountain, you will have no problem getting in or I'll eat my beret."

"Thanks, John. I should check on my NCOs."

"And I should consult with our Kiwis on our left and the paratroops on our right. I want four good riflemen and a radioman on the reverse slope keeping an eye out to the south. I'll check it out myself right now." John scrambled to the top of the hill and finished scanning the horizon to the west and then the east with his binoculars there was some dust from the north-east. I think Rommel is coming or part of his army anyway." He brought his binoculars down to rest on his chest held by their leather strap around his neck.

As John walked along the bottom ridge of the hill 317 he could see the five thousand men of the 1st and 2nd battalions of the 1st Airborne Division digging defensive positions on both sides of the pass. Squadrons of jeeps and Diamler armoured cars landed by glider were reconnoitring the area for twenty miles.

He knew that this pass was the quickest way for any army to move from one part of Afghanistan to the other. It was impossible for Rommel to leave a force defending every such pass in the country. He had relied on the German air force and the distance from India to be his best defence. Also, John considered he probably did not think he would ever have to dispatch troops to his rear to deal with bold enemy parachute drops at three strategic points along a three hundred mile stretch that could only be militarily viable along with a massive frontal assault rolling up his forces into headlong retreat and relieving the paratroopers and destroying the *Asia Korps* at the same time. Monty's Operation Rose Garden was a calculated risk. If it worked Rommel's army would be no more if it did not there was a chance they would all be dead or prisoners.

To the north of the hills were the gliders left where they landed but covered with light brown camouflaged netting to disguise them from air observation. This morning though since there was a parachute drop there was an X marked out in white tape. As soon as the men and 25 pounder guns and ammunition cases floated down on panniers supported by several parachutes everything would be quickly arranged to look as if nothing happened, tracks covered up and parachutes buried. The guns would be installed in positions covering both entrances to the pass.

They did not open fire until the first section of the four mile column of tanks and vehicles had snaked along the rough rocky road entering the ravine. They would have held their fire for longer but German mountain troop patrols checking on foot walked right into their forward positions and paid the price. The Paratroop colonel commanding the force gave the order to fire and the German vanguard came under sharp and accurate fire from all the weapons the airborne troops had brought into battle. John ordered his men to attack the column and they opened fire with machine-guns, rifles, PIATs and 3' mortars. Wielding his long-barrelled Webley revolver John led his A Troop out to the foothills and his Commandos, marked out by their green berets, fanned out into two platoons taking out tanks and lorries as the confused drivers were momentarily without direction since their commanders had been destroyed by a devastating fusillade of artillery shooting with open sights, the 25 pounder batteries were firing on the column which had halted in disarray desperately trying to regroup and counter-attack.

John supervised the destruction of some twenty tanks and lorries then, as the enemy counter fire became

Intolerable, ordered a fighting withdrawl to their defensive positions in the hills. The first day the enemy attacked five times and each time was repelled by the defenders. King Tiger, Tiger tanks and *Elefant* tank destroyers used their powerful armament to blast away at the British and Kiwi positions. 88 mm. artillery began methodically blasting away at whole sections of the hills. 'There were casualties' as the British commander later laconically reported, to be exact fifteen men of each platoon of one hundred were wiped out then night fell. The Jerries did not attack that night but held defensive positions a mile back up the road to Kabul but the British did. This time it was the Red Dragons, several platoons of the paratroops led by the irregulars, the Afghan tribesmen across the difficult terrain of the mountains to the rear of the German position causing mayhem with grenade and Bren gun and rifle attacks keeping the Germans uneasy. But some did not come back and one of them was 'President' Lincoln, he had gone close to the enemy positions to bring back a wounded soldier and then gave Bertha to another Commando allowing him to retrieve the precious PIAT the soldier had left behind. Lincoln crept forward in the darkness and shot off the rocket in the PIAT magazine then a star shell illuminated the one hundred yards stretch of rugged terrain in front of the Red Dragons, Lincoln could be seen zig-zagging towards them the Bren kicking in his hands as he fired as enemy bullets followed his trail, then as quickly he disappeared, the flare fell hissing to the ground its bright light gone out. They waited for what seemed an eternity but there was no noise besides the occasional shot from the Germans. No movement could be discerned in the gloom.

Grabbing Bertha John went ran forward dodging shell holes to try and get him but could not find him in the dark, Williams and two other men came up beside him. Then a red flare shot up from the British lines, the signal to return. "No sign of him, sir. We looked right across the area." Williams reported. "Stay down here I'll just look ahead for a few minutes," he ordered. "Take this I might have to carry him back if he's wounded."

Disgusted with himself for not finding his friend, John crawled then ran looking behind rocks that he could barely see in the darkness in shell holes and behind burnt out enemy vehicles. He came across dead bodies from both sides, but no wounded and definitely no Sergeant-Major. He heard a commotion coming forty yards to the left so he edged up listening to Germans talking to each other as he edged sideways gingerly looking for him then backed away taking a different route in order to continue looking but gave up after twenty minutes. He finally found a burnt out German Tiger tank that gave him his bearings and headed reluctantly back to his lines hoping against hope that Lincoln had made his own way back and was ready to give him a hard time about being lost in no-man's land like a green soldier fresh out of infantry school.

Sleeping badly he was up at dawn sweeping no-man's land with his binoculars but there was no sign of Mr. President Lincoln.

John could barely look at himself as he shaved but he did notice his watery blue eyes were bloodshot with dust, exhaustion and helplessness. He asked permission to lead a patrol that night to find Lincoln but was told, "John, he might be a prisoner, he might have been wounded and found by some Afghans. I'll check it out but I don't want to lose you or any other men, we need everyone because they are coming back again and again. No more night attacks."

"Perhaps you're right, sir. He's tough as old boots."

"That's the spirit John. Is that his famous Bren gun, Bertha you're carrying?"

"Yes, he said it was the one in a million perfectly made in the factory, sir."

"It is in immaculate condition, your Sergeant-Major was a damn fine soldier I watched him in action. You've got a replacement senior NCO?"

"Already got my best Sergeant as acting SM, sir."

The next day hundreds of British paratroopers descended on the north side of the mountains along with one of the first drops of panniers supported by four parachutes of 25 pounder artillery guns, Matador quads to pull them and shells. The artillery, with the help of the Afghans and Red Berets, were with difficulty hauled up to positions on the ridges of the mountains and began firing salvos at the German artillery batteries. After two days of this the Germans tried an unusual, for them, night attack which was heralded by blue star shells fired into the desert heavens. An artillery barrage followed and King Tiger tanks came up with infantry jumping off and scrambling uphill and taking the first line of trenches. Then the Kiwis counter-attacked and took them back. On the third day the colonel and Alan scoured the horizon for the relief column but all they could see were German tanks lagaared out of range of their artillery. "Well John we've held them up but taken some losses. Thank God their garrison in Kandahar has not arrived up the road from the south-west. Monty said he would be

312

here in four days it is now the sixth day. We are the third and final drop furthest from Kabul so he is dealing with the brunt of Rommel's force, this force was sent here expressly to get rid of us it is not the whole retreating army" the colonel confided in his Commando commander.

"It's a big force, a division, we should be flattered," John grimaced. "We're running out of PIAT rockets and rifle ammunition, sir. Only enough for a few hours fighting."

"No more parachute drops the last radio transmission said, the RAF is busy reinforcing the other two drop-zones but they are trying to get some Eagle helicopters here with supplies from their forward airfields, they are leapfrogging from one fuel cache to another put there by the Long Range Desert Patrols to get to us. They hope to be here later today. If not ..."

"I'll tell the men to make every bullet count, sir."

As he made his way back to the Commandos' positions he saw the Maori paratroopers in a line, a Kata, he had been told by the Kiwi C.O. to watch for it. "Kata Hata, that is the traditional dance of gestures and shouts to show defiance before a battle and sometimes after, if it is a victory that is. Traditionally the Maoris went to war with the idea of eradicating everyone in the enemy tribe so there would be no survivors to carry on a vendetta."

"No wonder they are so fierce, right up there with the Gurkhas for bravery, they scare the enemy silly!"

In his caravan ninety miles to the north Monty had leapt out of bed at 5 am as his batman brought him a mug of tea. As usual he had retired early and was up early. "Bit rainy today, Sir."

"Hmm, unusual after the heat and dryness of the last few weeks." He could hear rain splattering in great drops on the roof of his caravan, there were flashes of lightning and loud cracks reverberating outside like a battle in the heavens. He lifted his white tin mug to the photo of Field Marshal Rommel which hung on the wall next to a detailed contour map of Afghanistan and a larger map of Asia including India. His aide de camp had stuck black headed pins in the Afghanistan map indicating Rommel's positions and that of his known supply points, airdromes. Red headed pins indicated British and Imperial forces in Afghanistan. Monty was dressed casually in grey jumper, black beret with its Royal Tank Corps badge and general's insignia, brown corderouy trousers and thick woollen socks tucked into brown walking boots.

ADC Freddy de Guigand knocked on the door and entered. "Morning Freddy. Today is the day we smash Rommel, it is day five of Rose Garden so it has to be today. What are the latest reports?"

"We relieved the second drop zone yesterday morning and as of last night the forward armoured division had fifty five miles to relieve Hill 317. The CO there sent a radio signal last night."

"Well read it Freddy while I shave."

Freddy, the 8th Army Chief of Staff read, "We are holding but have a lot of casualties fighting a whole Panzer division and elements of the Kandahar garrison are attacking from the south. The artillery that was dropped has been helpful but the Army Air Corps helicopters have to get through. Need ammunition and rations earliest only enough to repel one more attack before it is hand-to-hand."

"We have to get through," Monty said his bright blue eyes turning to Freddy were penetrating and combative. "The cloud cover is higher and the rain is letting up a bit. I'll phone the RAF to get some strikes on the forces giving our boys trouble at Hill 317."

"Already phoned them. They are sending some bombers as soon as possible. The *Luftwaffe* has shown some surprising resilience and sent some jet squadrons from the Caucausus to help Rommel. We only have one squadron of Meteors and they are doing their best to take on the Jerry jets who were pummelling our Mosquitoes and Lancasters. Now we have Uhuzal the RAF can help the third drop and once Rommel's army is boxed in they will have him. Rommel really made a very efficient withdrawl despite our air attacks and losing thousands of troops and scores of tanks at each drop zone, not to mention what the main army has done to him."

"Get me the Air Marshal on the phone. I'll give him a rocket." Montgomery only spoke a few sentences and got what he wanted. "Thirty Dakota DC-3s with the reserve battalion of the 2nd Airborne Division Red Berets are now being dropped at Jihal at 1200 hours no matter what the weather. Let's hope they are not too late the outcome of Rose Garden depends on it. I would feel better if I knew where Rommel is." Monty said.

"With the rearguard we are pursuing down the road to Kandahar or even flown to Kandahar," Guigand ventured.

Monty responded briskly, "My instinct tells me Kandahar, he will take command of the situation at Jilhal and try and turn his pending defeat in one last gamble."

"If he gets close he might be shot by one of our snipers or more likely by one of those Afghan they are absolutely deadly shots and some of them have captured German sniper rifles I am told."

"That would really be the icing on the cake. We won't count on it of course," Monty said as he

gobbled up a plate of fried eggs, sausage and fried bread and tomatoes with toast his batman had brought him and stood up.

"Now to get the 8th Army moving we have eighty miles to go today." They climbed into Monty's tan painted Humber Sedan and his driver put it into gear and they headed south to catch up with the 8th Army, the race was on.

Erwin Rommel looked through the clouds and mist casting gloom upon the foothills of the mountains that were planted around Jihal and brought down his binoculars holding onto them tightly in frustration. He had not shaved for three days, he felt badly leaving the bulk of his army eighty miles north by a *Fiesler Storch* plane flying low and evading enemy fighter planes but he knew that pushing up from Kandahar was the only way to rescue them. New petrol supplies and reinforcements, replacement Panther, Tiger and King Tiger tanks, two Spanish divisions, and an Italian armoured division were en route from Herat to Kandahar and he would be ready to attack in two days. He snapped at his staff, "These foreign mercenaries, the Ghurkas and New Zealanders and airborne soldiers the *Rot Teufellen* put the fear of God into our men. They have lost confidence. We need a victory or all is lost."

"This weather should keep the RAF at home" his adjutant prophesied.

"*Nein*, Montgomery has to reinforce his paratroops or they won't last another day. They will come today but if we are lucky a lot of them will crash the weather is terrible. Drive up closer I want to see their positions closely and supervise the *Gebirgsjager* troopswe are sending in to root them out of the mountains otherwise the *Asia Korps* is *kaput!*"

He got his wish and in one of those uncanny moments of war when the situation changes in an instant the clouds parted and the sun lit up the road along which Rommel was driving in his *Volkswagon kampfwagon* staff car just as two snipers positioned on opposing sides of the foothills at Jilhal were looking for targets along the road to Kandahar as the visibility improved. Two shots came heading for Erwin Rommel at the same moment, one from Corporal Williams of the Red Dragons using a Lee-Enfield No. 4 Mk. 1 sniper rifle with a telescope fired from the north side of the ravine overlooking the southern approach to the British position. The other came from the south side of the ravine by a Pashtun chieftain who was the grandson of the man who met Lord Roberts in the century before and told him of his dreams. Both the Briton and the Afghan knew instinctively that they had hit their target, through their scopes each had seen the important officer jerk and snap forward, they had seen the officer sitting next to him throw himself over the man shouting at the driver to speed up but they could only see his mouth opening then they could see the staff car pulling out of the convoy and putting up a cloud of dust as it went at top speed to an ambulance in the convoy marked with a red cross in a white circle.

"Got him, wouldn't that be amazing if that was Rommel?" Corporal Williams excitedly said to John.

"It would be and if it is Rommel I'll move heaven and earth to get you a medal. That was an incredible shot it must have been a mile. I wanted to promote you to Sergeant anyway since Sergeant Bradshaw is Srn't Major but the extra stripe is yours."

"Thank you, sir. Do you want me to carry on as batman?"

"I'll get a Lance Corporal to do that once we get into barracks again but thanks for all you've done ... Sergeant." John grinned glad to know that he had cheered Williams no end. "Now go back and see who else you can knock off."

On the other side of the hill overlooking the road to Kandahar the robed and turbaned Pashtun cleaned his state of the art sniper's tool and carved a notch in the butt, "That was a general maybe even the Rommel himself the way the man with him threw himself over him to save him meant he was important. I got him with one maybe two bullets. He's a dead man," he told his warriors who were preparing to move east to the next point good for an ambush. "By the time we and the British have finished there won't be an *Asia Korps*." Muhammed Khan the chieftain spat fiercely.

That afternoon as dark rumours flew through the German army about Rommel being wounded perhaps dying in a hospital in Kandahar the twenty American Eagle helicopters manned by RAF aircrew had flown through the storm and landed with ammunition and rations that were eagerly taken from the craft. It had been the longest mission ever by helicopters, four hundred miles of perfect navigation finding four fuel caches en route with the loss of only three craft due to mechanical breakdowns.

Next morning a state of numb confusion lurked beneath the usual military professionalism the

German army prided itself upon. The Desert Rats had arrived from the north-east to relieve the troops at Jaldih and on the way had destroyed the *Asia Korps*. Rommel was dying in Kandahar. He had gone in and out of a coma and his last words were to his aide. "Richard the Lionheart and Saladin were like myself and Montgomery, adversaries who respected and even liked each other. Richard met his end when a lucky crossbow bolt hit him in the neck and his inept physician allowed it to get septic so he died of poisoning a few days later. I feel like he must have ... I am dying."

"*Mein Feld Marschall,*" his right hand man said emotionally, "Do not even contemplate that you will die, you cannot die the *Asia Korps* needs you. Germany needs you. Your men would follow you anywhere you could be another Julius Caesar."

"Vanity," he croaked in a barely audible whisper, "on my deathbed I cannot be tempted by such vainglorious words, tell Montgomery he is the greater general, I salute him and wish we were able to meet. Tell my army that it was the finest Germany ever produced and most important see my wife and children personally and tell them my last thoughts were of them. Good luck. I am tired of what Germany has become, but only you must know that old friend."

"My lips are sealed, rest now sir there is still a chance you will live." But Erwin Rommel had dropped into a land of unconsciousness that was dark and deadly.

His second-in-command Major-General Eindorff was capable and already throwing himself into solving the desperate military problem that faced him but the spark in his men so vital to victory was extinguished by the double blows of their leader's death and the crushing arrival of Monty's army with massive artillery bombardments, air attacks and a tank onslaught by two armoured divisions of Churchill and Firefly tanks. The Fireflies were American Shermans equipped with the larger British 17-pound guns that decimated the tanks of the *Asian Korps* which

318

were down to their last litres of *benzene*. Operation Rose Garden was a total success. The Germans sent envoys with a white flag to arrange a truce for burial of the dead and treatment of the wounded. Montgomery assured the Germans that if their field hospital could not cope in Kandahar he would look after their wounded a gesture that Rommel would have appreciated. He also sent his condolences and sent several officers with a wreath to see his body and pay the respect due to a worthy opponent. The body was to be sent to Berlin for a state funeral Monty was told and the General who had just won his second tumultuous victory had to step outside and walk by himself to regain his composure. It was as if a bit of him had died with his arch-enemy but he could not tell anyone, perhaps his son when he got home when he was old enough to understand. He missed his wife so very much she had died before the war of an infected insect bite. *Bites and bullets. It's a funny old world* Monty told himself and blew his nose with one of the white handkerchiefs he always carried.

Victory is a mighty tonic and John and his men were exuberant despite being dirty, achingly exhausted and unshaven. To the victors the spoils in this case souvenirs of German weapons, *Asia Korps* hats and helmets and a feast with many roasted goats were provided by their Afghan warrior friends. The British paratroopers provided an amazing measure of scotch whiskey from various hip flasks hidden in packs while the thirty Maoris in the Kiwi unit stripped down to their underwear and gave a Hata that brought goose bumps to the skin of all who watched. The whites of their eyes were exposed as they opened their dark eyes wide, stamped their brown feet and brought up their arms in perfect unison shouting and fiercely grunting. They ended their victory dance by stamping while squatting slightly, pressing their hands on their knees and sticking out their tongues in defiance.

They were magnificent but victory for John was bittersweet, he had lost Francis Lincoln, a great friend and soldier and the band of brothers was broken and scattered. He turned away and let his men enjoy themselves while he sat in solitude racking his brain as to what he could have done to save Mr.

President and the other missing men. He would make inquiries himself – the wounded, Afghans, the Red Cross. Then he got up and visited the wounded in the makeshift field hospital the flying nightingales had set up after flying in that day while the German army still shelled their positions. His spirits were uplifted by the voice of one of the nurses. The matron, a Captain was in khaki uniform with the insignia of the Queen Alexandra's Royal Army Medical Corps, her blonde hair done up in a bun.

"Susan Day," John noticed her Captain's pips on the epaulettes of her open neck cotton shirt. 'Captain Susan Day. I would know that voice anywhere even here. Congratulations on the promotion" John said reaching out to gently pat the woman who been the only one to get through to his brother Alan and help him recover from his mission at Kz1 and would one day, God willing become Alan's wife.

"John, it's wonderful to see you. I heard you were on Hill 317 I did ask and was told you were alright. Sorry I did not have a chance to see you. I was going to look for you as soon as I was off-duty. As you can see it's been crazy as the Americans say." She checked a German soldier with a leg wound and turned towards one of the nurses in the large tent, "This man needs his dressing changed, Sister" she ordered as she moved on to inspect a Ghurka infantryman who had a bandage around his eyes.

John put his hands in his battledress trouser pockets starting to relax after the hyper-tension of the battle. He watched her absently rubbing his ginger moustache and the bristles on his chin. "I'll come back later when it's a bit quieter. I'll have a shave and a wash and something to eat."

"Good, you look all in, get some rest and we can catch up later I'm off at 1600 hours. It has been a bit of a tough time hasn't it?" she said as she expertly re-bandaged the soldier sitting up on the folding cot.

"Tough, yeah, that's a good word for it. Keep a lookout for our President Lincoln you met him in Gibraltar he's missing. I am hoping he'll turn up alive."

An hour later he returned cleaned up, shaved re-energised. She gave her a friendly peck on the cheek and they went in search of a canteen tent serving sandwiches and tea. They stood in line with Afghans, E. Indian soldiers with the 8th Army and paratroopers then sat and talked for hours catching up. They watched the sunset and in the distance heard the rumble of artillery.

"It's Monty attacking the remnants of the *Asia Korps* in Kandahar. John's ears still buzzed from the noise of battle within the same twenty-four period which felt he was firing his revolver into a knot of German mountain troops who had scrambled up the precarious heights of the mountain to attack the Red Dragons and Red Berets in a last desperate charge.

"I ordered the men to fix bayonets and was going to lead a charge using the last of our ammunition when the troops facing of us hoisted the white flag. They knew the 8th Army had taken sealed them into the ravine, surrounding them." They talked about Alan and what they would do after the war. Susan told John, "I got a letter sent to Peshawar last week from your brother, he is well, very tanned and getting a bit of excitement in his job he says and was recently in Afghanistan himself if I read between the lines correctly. He says he picked up a bit of Pashtun and a lot of Turkish."

Susan heard a snore coming from where John's red haired head had slumped over, his back to a rock. She got a blanket and covered him and listened to the sounds of the night within calling distance of her Field Hospital then fell asleep herself and dreamt vividly of a mist covered world, quiet, calm and mysterious.

CHAPTER THIRTY-FOUR   CHARLIE'S WAR

"Nihil Domestica Sede Jocundus
An inscription on brass letter box in a second floor door
without stairs on an ancient house in York, England.

It was early morning in the ancient Cathedral city of York once the prime target of Viking raiders coming down the River Ouse and before that the birthplace of the man who would become the greatest Christian Emperor of Rome, Constantine. Charlie Gates and his friend Jack Gaitskill were delivering a note from their Red Rose cell to an address in the medieval Shambles still a home to several butcher shops. The note confirmed that they were to be at Horcum Hole in the Moors the following night to help pick up a big drop of weapons and radios by plane from Iceland. They had stayed in a friend's house then taking advantage of a lull in patrols enforcing the curfew snuck out into the night. They found the home but could see no stairs leading up to the second floor room just a letterbox high above their heads. Charlie swept an electric torch quickly over the white door and read the inscription on it in black paint in gothic script.

"We can't reach the bloomin' letter box," Jack groaned. "There's no ladder in sight and the Gendarmes patrol this part of the Shambles in a few minutes. I'll have to stand on you, kneel down Charlie."

"Why me?" Charlie shaking his white beard in indignation

"Because you weigh a lot more than I do besides I'm taller."

Grudgingly Charlie obliged and braced himself on all fours as Jack stood on his back and shoved the note in its envelope into the box.

"Now let's get home," Jack declared starting to run.

"There's no place like it," Charlie said catching up having had time to translate the Latin motto while Jack played postman.

The next night right on time at 0212 hours Commando transport planes from Iceland dropped supply canisters on parachutes that floated down upon the eerily wild great depression in the Yorkshire moors south of Goathland known as 'Horcum's Hole".

Charlie, Jack and one hundred other resistance men and women spread out around the drop-point area of ten square miles of wild, solitary heath to quickly gather them and hide them where they fell in secretly marked caches dug into the ground or take them to pre-determined hiding places. Charlie and Jack drove a red lorry picking up some items in their area and taking them to Gaitskill's farm to hide.

Jack happily recounted the legend of Horcum Hole to Charlie as the truck rattled and rolled throughout the night on a lonely B Road through the desolate moors to home. "You may not know the legend Charlie since you are a Lancs man. Horcum's hole was created when the Giant Wade was having a bit of a barney with his wife Belle, he must have been losing the argument 'cos picked up a huge clod of earth and threw it at his wife."

"Now why does that sound familiar? Don't tell me she ducked and it went around the world and hit Wade in the eye?"

"That's not in the legend but you speak like a married man Charlie, I'm surprised you being a bachelor."

Charlie chortled, "I've learned a thing or two living with you and the wife, but by God, if you don't mind me changing the subject we've done it again Jack."

"Think we have Charlie. We'll hightail it for home, hide the goods and tomorrow night boy…"

"Tomorrow night " Charlie repeated.

"Tomorrow night Charlie, a few pints at the Goathland Hotel pub."

"More than a few to celebrate this." Charlie grinned and rubbed his hands together.

In the months to come Charlie and Jack would sometimes go out in the truck and threw rats stuffed with explosives and timers off their favourite railway bridge always ensuring that no Gendarmes were near, choosing the filthiest weather to ensure they would not be interrupted. They would aim at open railway cars filled with coal dug from the Yorkshire pits on their way to the munition factories of Bolton or Huddersfield. Once they were chased by some unusually eager Gendarmes when they failed to stop at a roadblock. As shots rang out Charlie set the timers on three rats to four seconds and chucked them onto the road as the fascist police car caught up. Charlie could see yellow flashes as the rats exploded beneath the patrol and car and it spun off the road as its tyres burst at high speed. The patrol car shot off the road and went over an incline into a river.

"Bad place to have an accident. Shame that." Charlie said to Jack whose hands were drumming on the wheel excitedly and they careened down the hill to home through torrents of cold rain.

"Best not go back lad. By Gaw I don't think there'd be any survivors after that and if there were I don't think they'd be happy to see us."

CHAPTER THIRTY-FIVE   WESTMINSTER WEDDING

King Frederick waddled down the long nave of Westminster Abbey. Normally he was befuddled by history and dates by today he was unusually belittled by the brass plate in the floor honouring the Unknown Soldier whose unidentified remains were brought back from the western front at the end of the Great War and buried with great honour. As he continued alongside his best man, Lord Mosley in his Blackshirt uniform, Frederick was for the first time impressed awe by the memorials and statues honouring great men and women of British history. He knew that one of the side chapels contained the remains of both Queen Elizabeth I and Mary Queen of Scots by the time he got to the high altar by the coronation chair built for the with his best man Lord Mosley at his side. He had been crowned here in 1941 and had enjoyed it all but somehow his perspective had changed and he felt history would remember him as a weak usurper unloved by his people except for the black clad fascists who held the power thanks to Hitler.   Perhaps O-No could help him redeem himself somewhat after she was married to him then crowned with an Art Deco tiara rather than a full crown. *But there would be lots of time for romping and partying. perhaps that is all I am good for*, Frederick concluded as he waddled.

He wore a dark grey morning coat with tails, striped trousers that were forty-three inches in the waist and held his grey top hat in his hand. To the congregation of fascists and their hangers on the round figure with the wobbling chins seemed a bulky and ponderous version of Fred Astaire. Even honoured guest Adolf Hitler sitting in the choir in a carved wooden seat surmounted with the coat of arms of the Duke of York was surprised at how much weight the king had put on during the round of parties leading up to the wedding of the year. Strangely enough at that moment Frederick was imagining himself at the reception dancing the waltz with his bride and then dancing with her in bed, horizontally. What a day, lots to eat, gallons of champagne for his guests- Hitler, Lord and Lady Eastbourne, all the other peers of the realm and the Japanese, Italian and Spanish Ambassadors. Lord Eastbourne seemed pale and uncomfortable sitting in the right hand pew with his wife, Lady Eastbourne. He wiped his sweating forehead with his starched handkerchief. Frederick began to feel apprehensive as he realised dully with the shock of self-recognition he had had all kinds of relationships with women in his forty nine years but this was a real commitment. He knew his wife would allow him his dalliances but funnily enough he knew that they would be only occasional from now on. *It's time finally settle down.*

Kneeling on the cushioned marble floor made in the thirteenth century before the high altar the King and Princess were married by the fascist Archbishop of Canterbury in his robes and mitre decorated with a cross made of lightning bolts a fascist symbol of power and energy. The Archbishop then placed a light modern crown on the Princess's head and proclaimed her Queen of New Britain. She stood in her white wedding dress with a train held by pages and bowed to her husband. He smiled and bowed back. They signed the register in Henry VII's Lady Chapel, on the way they passed Saint Edward the Confessor's Chapel behind the altar, there Frederick pondered what King Edward the saint-king would think of it all, let alone the other royals buried within feet of him: Henry III, Edward I 'Longshanks', Eleanor of Castile, Edward III, Philippa of Hainault and poor Richard II and his queen, Anne of Bohemia. The new Queen took her husband's hand and pulled him to see the tombs of Elizabeth I and her nemesis Mary Queen of Scots in death in the same room although they were enemies linked by blood and ambition. Together they looked at the marble effigies stretched out on their respective tombs. "Maybe we shall be allowed to be buried in a similar chapel, not here of course," the new Queen said, we are not worthy of that I know, but a little church in the country here or in your homeland Germany. I don't want to be buried in Japan I am westernised now. I cannot go back. I will not."

"You will always be with me. Now we must get back, hmm." He nuzzled the back of her neck.

"Stop it Frederick I am coming. You shall have to wait you wicked king, there's a bit of Henry VIII in you."

The wedding luncheon was at Kensington Palace at the request of Queen Chouku No because she particularly liked the palace which was welcoming and more intimate than Buckingham Palace. She had begun working on him to switch the nuptials from Buckingham Palace months before. "I particularly like the Dutch style that King William's architects used and the fact it has small gardens and is right next to Kensington Park. Oh Freddy, please say we can have the wedding luncheon there after that stuffy Westminster Abbey for the stuffy ceremony for two hours." She weadled expertly. "We can send my mother back to the palace as soon as the lunch is done. She does get in the way when the party gets going. And I love that painting of Charles I on his horse by Sir Amberly Van Dyke, in the east end of the King's Gallery."

"Very well," the soft-hearted King Frederick agreed, his chins wobbling. "It's Anthony Van Dyke my dear not Amberly but it is impressive the way he painted a silk dress or a cavalier's silk clothes. There's non-one to touch him."

"Yes, that's it. Anthony. I must remember that. I want to have the lunch and the wild party afterwards right where that painting hangs. It has a strange attraction for me. Are you descended from Charles I?"

"Well, I suppose I am descended from the Stuarts. I can have my archivist check into it and he can let you know."

"I do love you," the Queen said and, what would be a surprise to those who knew her, she meant it.

*

On the same day to the south on the Isle of Wight two not so loyal subjects of the puppet King and Queen also were getting married. The vicar of St. Mary the Virgin, Brighstone used the

327

traditional Anglican ceremony with readings from the Stuart king, King James's Bible in stirring tones in the small stone church which contained a small knot of villagers and several of Charlotte's friends from the New Land Army. Marcus replied "I do," in a strong voice ringing with sincerity.

At the appropriate moment Charlotte agreed to 'Love honour and obey' by declaring "I do." The vicar concluded the service and ended "You may kiss the bride.' They needed no urging. Charlotte had no veil Marcus held her face in his hands gently he was a thin, handsome young man so full of love and life kissing the woman of his dreams. Little did they know that almost a hundred years later their descendants would be called upon to help the sovereign of the United Kingdom. As they stepped out into the sunshine the best man and bridesmaid threw rice over them and the local photographer took photos of the happy couple and their friends.

"You are all invited to the pub for a lunch," Marcus called out, "Please join us." After several hours of songs, ale, sandwiches and a two tier cake with white icing surmounted by a licorice black cat the bride and groom took their leave and the vicar dropped them off at their home.

Marcus picked up Charlotte and carried her through the front door, "Hey Aztec, look who I found at the church in a pretty white dress?" They heard a soft thump as Aztec woke up and landed on the floor and saw his whiskered face looking up at them, he licked their hands."

"It is a perfect day husband."

"Yes wife. And you don't have to work until tomorrow."

"Nope. I'm all yours. Well after a cup of coffee I need a pick me up before anything you might have in mind Marcus."

"Who me? OK I'll get the coffee ready."

*

By 3 pm Queen Chouku was sitting on a stool in the east end of the King's Gallery of Kensington Palace admiring the large portrait of the Stuart King Charles1 on a magnificent white horse in armour bare-headed with long hair parted in the middle and what became known as a Van Dyke beard since the King and his aristocrats he painted sported the small pointed beards on their chins with a long thin moustache. At one point Charles wore the fashionable long hair on one side and half-length hair on the other and an ear ring but that was in his younger days. The 1944 King and Queen's intimate guests had gone into the garden for a giddy game of 'blind man's buff' and inebriated croquet with the additional rule that you could go through the hoops in any order you wanted. By tea time guests were passed out, draped over sofas or lying flat out in the gardens with pigeons cooing next to them, squawking peacocks strutted by raucously calling them awake to no avail. Hitler and Lord and Lady Eastbourne had excused themselves after the luncheon as it seemed the King and Queen were hell-bent on getting smashed with their close friends. She was draining her glass of champagne toasting Sir Anthony Van Dyke with a suitably squiffy King Frederick, four footmen lifted a Nebachunnezer of champagne and poured them full glasses of best champagne courtesy of Pierre Laval the Vichy Premier. They lifted their glasses together. "To King Charles!" the newly crowned Queen proclaimed loudly with a Japanese accent.

"To my ancestor!" her husband the king shouted. "Should we try and have children my dear?" Frederick leaned over and asked her.

"I do not think we, Your Majesty," the Queen said leaning on the King's broad shoulder, "are going to be King and Queen for long. We are going to lose this war, so no" she whispered "we should not have children."

"But I love you so much," King Frederic pleaded on his knees.

"In that case let's get to bed but no babies. Bring a manageable bottle of bubbly," she asked. "I had some beds made up. Come and have me on our wedding day Frederick," she implored a as she wiggled seductively in her tight 'going away' dress although they were going nowhere.   Frederick needed no urging, he trotted after his wife besotted with the Japanese woman less than half his age. *Can I keep up to her? I am having a lot of fun and if I die trying it will be a good way to go. Who will miss me? Not my people. Not even me.* He giggled at his paradoxical insight. "Coming my love," he wheezed.

CHAPTER THIRTY-SIX   INSIDE THE HORSE

The constable on duty in the second smallest police station in London beneath the Wellington Monument in London at the corner of Hyde Park Road, Park Lane and Piccadilly kept watch for the Free London workmen who were expected. They drove up in a van ostensibly to repair the bronze four horses of the Quadriga statue of Peace. The bronze robed female figure of peace was alighting upon a chariot of war. The two workmen set up ladders from the walkway on the flat roof of the memorial arch. The triumphal arch had been completed in 1826 just south of No. 1 London, Apsley House the home of the Duke of Wellington. The arch originally supported the largest equestrian statue in the world which depicted the Duke but it was moved to Aldershot after much debate. In 1912 Adrian Jones was commissioned to super-size a cake decoration that impressed George V. It was of the Angel of Peace holding a wreath and lilies alighting upon a young charioteer driving galloping and rearing horses. The horses, the charioteer and Victory were larger than life and impressive to pedestrians walking alongside the wall to the back of the Buckingham Palace gardens coming from Hyde Park or approaching down Piccadilly from the east. Standing next to the statue was even more impressive. The resistance men cum workers on the roof were overwhelmed by it.

Dennis, a bus conductor from West Ham and Fred an electrician and boiler-maker from Peckham erected a tall frame of plywood and sacking screens around the statue. This was their most interesting assignment so far although the most exciting had been back in 1941 when they posed as workers on Tower Bridge to look for Edward VIII's signal from the Bloody Tower, that he was ready to be rescued. "Cell leader 6 says this blessed statue is a Quadriga" Dennis said knowingly.

"What's a Quad-riga when it's at home, Den? Oh I get it," Fred said answering his own question, "four rigas." He found this very amusing and was chuckling and repeating his joke to himself as he lugged the oxy-acetylene cutting and welding equipment up the ladder from inside the monument that had taken some time to bring in from the London Works lorry parked neatly below them. It was behind an orange sign that declared 'Men at Work' and took up one lane of the thoroughfare that ran through the arch.

"This 'ere statue of the Angel of Peace landing on the chariot driven by that young lad holding on like grim death to them two gallopin' horses in the middle was put 'ere in 1912 once the king decided what he wanted to see on top. He saw the idea in miniature form on top of a cake." Den told Fred.

"It's impressive I must say," Fred declared breezily as it began to spit rain, "I reckon I can open up one of the horse's stomachs get that object we have to hide inside it and weld it up again. Anyway there's an expert coming any minute from the Victoria and Albert Museum who's a bronze sculptor to give us some advice. 6 says that he already has researched the original plans and says the horses are hollow, about two inches thick. He says we could pick which rearing horse we like. I think the north horse would be good, the one on the right as you face them."

"Fair enough," said Den agreeably as he closely studied the horses running his hands along their large sides.

Fred asked, "Have you got the box?"

"Oh I left it on the landing I'll just run down and get it," Den said and ambled down the ladder and into the arch through the open skylight. Two minutes later he returned holding the box. "Got it, wonder what's inside?"

"Not for the likes of us to know, come on get a move on, there's the expert coming up the ladder. Get the equipment over by the north horse" Den said. After a consultation with the expert invisible from anyone below thanks to the screening they began their work. After two hours of careful work the box was safely inside the horse, the 'incision' welded neatly shut and the 'scar' painted over by the curator with bronze paint to match the dark green patina of the sculpture.

"Right men, it's done only an expert could tell the horse has been repaired. You can take your equipment away and forget the job. You've done well. We needed to hide something for a bit perhaps after the war one day we'll find out what it is."

With that he left and Fred and Den put away their tools and the ladder, closing the skylight as they left packed up their road sign, waved at the bobby and drove off mission accomplished. They would have been surprised to know they had sealed up a sword called Zulfiqar from a disused-well in Afghanistan for safekeeping so the enemy could not get their hands on it.

*

In Vancouver Princess Elizabeth lined up at the armoury of the Sutherland Highlanders and spoke to the men, women and children waiting to see the sword of honour. Modelled on the royal sword of state in the crown jewels and crafted in Canada it was a gift to the new ally, Russia. Before it was taken to them it was exhibited in major cities until dispatched by sea. "I have been up to my elbows in engines and sump oil so I am glad to get away," the eighteen year old princess in WRAC uniform of khaki, skirt, jacket, cap and shoes said to an elderly couple who stood beside her. After a few minutes as the queue shuffled forward, she looked behind her and asked the name of the man standing with an oaken staff behind her.

"Owen Gruffyd? You must be Welsh," the eighteen-year-old heir to the throne asked. She had just joined the ATS, the Army Transport Service, and was taking a driving and mechanics course in rainy Chilliwack in the Fraser Valley.

"I am, your Royal Highness," Owen bowed.

"You *have* come a long way. Did you come before the war?"

"No, like you I came in October 1940."

"Will you go back after the war?"

"God willing and may He bless you, ma'am."

333

"Thank you" princess with hair pinned up in a bun beneath her army cap, smiled and spoke to a small boy holding the hand of his mother as he passed to the end of the line to marvel at the jewel studded scabbard on display alongside the silver hilted sword with its engraved inscription Pro Valore on the blade. Elizabeth moved with the line to the table upon which the gift to Russia lay. She gazed at the sword in wonder. It sparkled under the lights above it as it lay on a wooden dais draped with the Canadian Red Ensign. Its steel blade was simple but elegantly engraved with maple leaves. "Do you like the sword?" Elizabeth asked in an awed whisper of Owen who stood next to her.

"It's like ... like King Arthur's Excaliber."

"Yes, it is wonderfully stirring, like Arthur's sword in the stories isn't it, maybe it came out of one of the Canadian lakes held up by the Lady of the Lake?"

"Very much so, one wants to reach out and grab it if one felt worthy enough," Elizabeth suggested.

They stood in silence for several minutes. The young boy, at whom his future Queen smiled, never forgot and told his grand-children of that moment with pride.

CHAPTER THIRTY-SEVEN   AUSSIE URANIUM

"Worra Worra"
Aborigines imploring British colonists landing
at Botany Bay, Australia on 29th April, 1770 to 'go away.'

Aubrey had almost fully recovered from his wound, but the scar on his shoulder still ached all the way down his back every time he moved quickly. He was as the vernacular put it 'fair crooked' every time he went to bed or moved his back. Several large fragments of shrapnel had been taken out of him in the hospital ship moored in Cadiz harbour on D-Day and since the wound refused to heal in Morocco he was sent back to Australia with a leave promised as soon as he was discharged from the military hospital in Adelaide. Now he was on his leave with a friend heading for a bevy then he was going to find a way to visit his girl, Victoria Greenham a Women's Auxiliary Air Force sergeant. He had managed to get a phone connection to her in Darwin on the northern coast unofficially using an RAAF phone connection while an air force mate in the Adelaide RAAF HQ left the room 'just for a few minutes' after he had connected his office phone to the radar post in Rum Jungle where Aubrey's 'squeeze' was by luck, on duty.

"Hello, Sergeant Greenham here," the soft voice stated confidently. Fourteen hundred miles away Aubrey felt himself melt, she really sounded like a million dollars, his million dollars.

"Victoria, it's me, Aubrey. I got your letters at the hospital, now I'm better. I'm coming up to see you."

"Oh Aubrey, I have to speak quietly don't want anyone to know this is a personal call," she whispered as the line crackled fiercely, "It's is lovely to hear your voice. Glad you're better but you'll have to wangle your way up here if you're on leave. We're on the front lines. But I'm not planning on going anywhere soon. I should go."

"Wait, first I have to tell you I love you and second, reserve a table for two in your favourite restaurant Vickie for Saturday night." The static became overwhelming but Aubrey thought he heard her say 'Love you. Bye.' and then there was just a dial tone.

"Thanks Jack, I owe you one," Aubrey told his blue-uniformed friend, "any chance of arranging a ride to Darwin?"

After taking Jack out for an American style meal of steak, mushrooms and chips washed down with copious amounts of beer and taking in Laurence Olivier's new film *Henry V* at the cinema Aubrey found he still owed him a favour. After all the ride the next morning in an Anson aircraft ferrying pilots was a big gesture of friendship and he did not begrudge that.

They landed at Alice Springs for fuel and Aubrey bought his fellow passengers a beer, then just one hundred miles out of Darwin they were jumped by a Japanese fighter plane who ran out of ammunition just as he was about to give them the coup de grace. The pilot waved at them sportingly as he zoomed off. His shots had damaged one engine and it began to smoke with flames fanning back as they lost altitude over Arnhem Land.

The pilot calmly told everyone he was going to put it down and this he did with dispatch, the undercarriage had been shot up and would not lower so like a glider pilot he told his passengers to brace for a crash landing and the sturdy transport hit the stony ground that was touched with the red colour of kurrajong flowers that went whizzing by underneath them as they skewed and slid on the dirt and into a gorge. The plane came to a screeching halt, a wing broke and everyone was tossed like dice in a cooking pot. Aubrey was the first to come to, for once his first thought was not his back but his head which felt like someone had cracked him with a plank in a particularly nasty bar brawl, one where your opponents are sober rather than a bit wobbly on their feet to make it even. He looked at the pilot, his eyes were shut and a large amount of blood was pouring out of his head, his two fellow passengers were just coming to life.

Aubrey helped get their pilot out of his chair and out of the plane, one of passengers applied a bandage from the first aid kit and staunched his head wound. Sitting on the side of the gorge they took stock. Aubrey looked over the map from the cockpit and picked up a coil of thin wire he saw at the back thinking it may come in handy. "I think we are here," he showed his fellow passengers, "maybe a day's trek east of Pine Creek in Arnhem Land we flew over Katherine just before we got shot at." The two pilots agreed he was probably right.

The senior passenger, a Wing Commander spoke up, "I say we rig up a stretcher and take the pilot with us as we walk to Pine Creek, we can take the compass in the plane."

"No need, sir," Aubrey said.

"Why," both RAAF officers asked together.

"Two reasons, first I know how to get there without a compass just using the sun and stars and secondly we have company and unless the Japs have taken to riding camels, they are on our side and will save us a long pull of the stretcher."

The two men stood and looked to the north as Aubrey was doing with hand over his eyes and could see a group of dark blobs coming towards them on camels. The air was shimmering in the heat of the afternoon and made the sight a vision in growing liquid blurs.   Aubrey had, while convalescing, read T.E. Lawrence's book *The Pillars of Wisdom* about fighting with the Bedouin in Arabia and was reminded of his lucid descriptions of the desert. After a few minutes the vision congealed into figures, Aborigines in battle dress with rifles and machine-guns were riding towards them on descendants of camels brought to Australia by the British in the 1800s who used them for exploration in the arid outback since the beasts could easily carry them and supplies and go for five without water. A thought flashed through Aubrey's mind that he must write this up in his diary to be the basis for a book in the future. Victoria, a librarian before joining up, was his inspiration for reading voluminously and stirring a growing interest in writing.

The unconscious pilot began to groan in pain and brought the incredulous passengers back to earth. "I can speak their lingo, had a bit of walkabout experience before the war," Aubrey said modestly as he walked toward the visitors. He waved and spoke to them in rusty Aborigine when they got nearer. He spent a few minutes explaining who they were and the corporal commanding the troops had his men dismount and tend the injured man. "We spotted your plane coming down, thought we would help," the Corporal spoke in English introducing himself as Corporal Ronnie Munarryu leading a unit of 'Nackaroos' the irregular rangers of the North Australia Observer Unit. The irregulars were comprised mainly of Aborigine 'Jackeroos' expert horsemen, cattle-hands used to guiding immense herds over long distances from ranches as big as European countries to ports like Darwin for shipping to urban centres. They were joined by native and mixed-blood trackers, prospectors and young adventurers.

The Wing Commander was pleased with the arrangement that was decided upon . The Nackaroos on camels were to take the injured pilot and the two RAAF officers to Pine Creek while Aubrey was to accompany Ronnie and two of his men on foot to continue their mission to check out the area for a reported Japanese patrol probing Arnhem Land as the battle raged far to the southeast between the Japanese invading army of 110,000 men who had occupied most of Northern Territory and the top part of Queensland to the Barrier Reef and were fighting for every yard gained by Eisenhower's smaller, but increasingly successful American-Australian force. The American with the German name had learned to prepare his men with excellent training and maintain large reserves of tanks and vehicles so that the thrust of offensive operations could be sustained after the disappointment of his initial operations which failed to stop the invading army.

Aubrey who was wearing a cotton Australian army uniform of shorts and shirt with his favourite Digger wide-brimmed bush hat, socks and boots and a belt with a holstered pistol was content to let Ronnie call the shots. The Aborigine knew the country and the Aussie knew that if he could not have the Red Dragons with

338

him then these men were as good, in this case even better, for the job in hand. As they walked through the bush Aubrey and Ronnie talked. Ronnie told about his life in the Wangari Tribe in Arnhem Land and how he and many of his tribe had been active in tracking and killing Japanese patrols or lost soldiers, crashed airmen or naval personnel stupid enough to land on the northern shore and end up as fodder for salt water crocs. His stories of surviving on 'bush tucker' wallabies, white witchchetty grubs and by the ocean on turtles, oysters and 'sea cows', reminded Aubrey of his year with his Aboriginal teacher Nelson. They had hunted kangaroos with boomerangs, lived off the land. Aubrey had learned to deal with dingoes and wild pigs at night while they slept in the open, it was the only time Nelson let him use his firearm.

"The Japs," Ronnie, told Aubrey "especially do not like us and shoot or bayonet our wounded and behead any of us taken so us Nackeroos always use up all our ammo and then go for them with a knive, if you've got a spear then you use that, you don't let yourself be taken alive and we don't let them get away. Over a hundred years ago our ancestors told your lot to 'go away' and you didn't there was no stopping you except for in the outback which we can live in happily but you can't." Ronnie the Corporal looked over at Aubrey the Captain, to check his reaction but he did not have to bother he instinctively knew that Aubrey understood, he said he had gone walkabout with his 'Abbo' friend Nelson Pilgrim and been made a blood brother of one of his own. He believed him. The serious expression on Aubrey's face changed and he laughed "You know Ronnie, we're both saying Worra, Worra to the Japanese."

"Yeah, neither of our tribes asked them to come, that makes us allies but it's good to have at least one of you Aussies knows we are not just ignorant 'Abbos.'" Aubrey was going to reply 'Smart Ábbos' but the words never surfaced. Ronnie froze and waved his hand to make them sink quickly to the ground effortlessly and blend into the arid landscape. "Over there," one of Ronnie's men said they looked at the southern horizon. There was a very slight smudge of smoke or dust. Ronnie peered intently his dark eyes

339

taking in the vast distance in a split second. Aubrey took longer to focus and was still trying to pin down anything out of the ordinary in his vision. "Jap patrol Captain, fifteen men. I recognise the helmets." Ronnie had become formal. Aubrey returned the compliment. "Right Corporal, do you reckon we should track them see what they are up to or just kill them?"

Ronnie's face lit up with expectation of action and Aubrey began to feel the excitement of battle well up in him. "We could get right up to them no problem and catch them before they do any damage and then get their maps and orders to our HQ or take a prisoner if there any left after we jump 'em."

"What sort of civilians live around here?" Aubrey asked.

Ronnie replied, "Most of the farmers have left the area but the enemy have been known to strike on the other side of the big road south to lower morale. As for my people we know when they are coming and deal with them."

Aubrey considered and made up his mind as a flock of egrets flew overhead. "I think we should take them on right away."

"I was hoping you would say that."

The tracker led them up to the Japanese patrol which had brewed tea and were now heading west keeping hidden by the terrain as much as possible. They were good solidiers and were expert at keeping low but they were not native to the country like Ronnie and his men who knew every fold of the land. "Sir, one mile up is a valley with a path with a sandstone escarpment running along it covered in Cyprus Pine trees they will be making for that if they are heading east to cause trouble probably hold up there then move on at dusk as they get closer to any type of settlement." Aubrey nodded and they moved quickly and effortlessly. Though Aubrey felt his back telling him to rest, he put it out of his mind.

They headed for the escarpment and hid in the trees it to be in position before the patrol arrived. When it came they waited while the officer had two soldiers look for firewood and the others take off their helmets and drink from their canteens. Then Aubrey said "Now!" and they opened fire. The enemy in the horrid heat had forgotten to have lookouts, fatally careless.

Aubrey shot and killed the officer who was in the act of drawing his straight edged sword while Ronnie used his Lee-Enfield to shoot the Sergeant who managed to let loose one pistol shot which hit one of the Nackaroos in the stomach. Aubrey picked up the Owen sub-machine, with its uniquely Australian design of a vertical magazine above the breech, from the man as he sank to his knees dying. He sprayed bullets at the rest of the patrol and moved forward with Ronnie who was throwing Mill's grenades. Paul, the other Nackaroo, was wielding a Bren gun to great effect. Even taken by surprise the Japanese soldiers were no push-over the five survivors took cover and began disciplined firing. Aubrey and Ronnie picked up a Japanese rifle each as the Bren gunner kept the enemy's heads down and they withdrew disappearing into the trees. They ran two miles east and climbed a hill near a spring where they washed and drank as Ronnie scaled a tree and looked out across the escarpment. "They are coming they are pretty confident they can kill us usually they go back the way they came if they are lucky enough to escape. Oh they have two wounded they are not leaving them behind. So just three able-bodied men."

"Any extra grenades, Ronnie?" Aubrey asked. He remembered the wire he salvaged from the plane in case they had to make a stretcher or catch some tucker to eat. Fifty feet of it was coiled and squashed into his pocket. Ronnie helped him stretch out wire and tie up the grenades' safety pins between six trees across fifty feet of path and back again just above ground level in the brush while the Bren gunner kept watch. "They might be making for here the spring is on maps."

The Japanese moved quietly and very cautiously two soldiers went ahead to check the area around the spring. Aubrey decided he could drive them into the trap and waved at Ronnie and

Paul to follow the enemy patrol as they moved to the grove of trees around the spring. The scouts tripped the wire seconds later the grenades exploded killing them and forcing the other three soldiers to the ground. In two minutes it was all over. They had three prisoners one of whom was quite angry - he wanted to die with honour. Ronnie offered to help him out but Aubrey dissuaded him. They took their prisoners and the maps from the officer's uniform to Pine Creek where the wounded were given medical care and all three questioned as to the intention of the patrol. Then the trackers and Aubrey enjoyed some tucker, a dinner 'on the house' at the town pub. The settlement was a ghost town with only soldiers and Nackaroos in sight. The hotel owner was effusive, "Thanks for getting rid of that patrol they could have ended up here, nuisance raids trying to put the wind up us. There are no families around here anymore they have all been sent to Perth. I just didn't want anyone else looking after my hotel been in the family for generations." He pointed to the Lee-Enfield rifle and a Lewis gun hanging on the wall and winked.

Victoria had booked the best restaurant in Darwin not that there was a lot of choice. The small port had found itself growing in leaps and bounds after it was attacked and became the primary port of supply for reinforcements and supplies heading for the Northern Territory forces hammering at the Japanese from the west. But the main force fighting the Japanese were in central Australia and Queensland, never-the-less Port Darwin was now heavily defended and no longer an easy target. Victoria's job as a radar operator just outside Darwin was still important, new airfields had been built for the USAAF and RAAF around Darwin and Victoria now supervised twenty WAAFS on different shifts in the larger radar post at Rum Jungle that replaced the one which was bombed while she and Lieutenant Sarah Churchill were on duty and Victoria rescued the daughter of Sir Winston Churchill, winning a Military Medal. It was an award that in her humility she forgot. Only the occasional letter from Sarah or finding it under her blouses in her chest of drawers reminded her.

The restaurant did have small tables, candles and cocktails it also cost the earth so no matter what the food was like they could pretend to be living the high life. To be truthful she did not care if she was going to sit on a stump and nibble on an apple as long as she could be with Aubrey. "Oh, great to see you Victoria" he uttered tongue-tied as he took off his bush hat. She leapt up and they hugged and kissed. He shoved his hat into the hands of the hovering waiter and kissed her again. He held her hands over the table as they talked. The waiter had to cough several times before they picked up their menus. It was a memorable meal, the fish was overcooked the potatoes were not cooked at all, there was one carrot each unsliced but the coca-cola was cold and the newly imported American delight, cheesecake, a response to the demands of thousands of American soldiers and sailors asking for American food. They had two large slices each at the exorbitant price of two shillings apiece but Aubrey with a new haircut, a bath, and a borrowed dress uniform and Susan in a new, expensive flowered cotton dress, matching flat hat modelled on one of Felicity`s designs, and wedge shoes, were in no mood to do anything but renew their romance in style.

CHAPTER THIRTY-EIGHT   RANGOON

George Orwell was happy to see a blue airmail letter from his friend Josef Comenice sent from Cyprus months ago. It was covered in forwarding addresses from Cairo to New Delhi to George Orwell c/o BBC Calcutta. He took it then dashed out of his apartment and took a lurching tram to the Calcutta radio station. He read it as he went to work.

Dear George.

Cyprus is beautiful, lots of sun and sea. I have been swimming like some kind of whale but soon I have to squeeze into an aircraft and go back to a place which is very dearest to me. I am hoping for to see you in the Far East whenever I have a leaves from my duties. You can write to me here at my Cyprus address and it will eventually get to me. It is my hope you are not only doing radio work but writing as well as you do.

Your friend,

Josef

Orwell sat in the BBC World Service studio room 101 testing the studio microphone prior to his daily radio broadcast to the Crown Colony of Burma. He introduced his guest Dr. U-Phant a twenty-two-year old Burmese secretary to the Health Commission for Eastern Burma who had escaped from Rangoon by hitch-hiking to Mandalay after remonstrating unsuccessfully with a Japanese officer who had the Burmese not moving quickly enough from their home which was needed for Japanese soldiers and began roughly prodding an old woman with the flat of his sword, kicking the men who were not moving fast enough. He shouted at the U-Phant who remonstrated with him. "Go to the British if you don't like, this is liberation whether you like it or not. We are the Asian masters, better to agree with us." It had shocked him. Asians being just as, no more arrogant than the British. That had started him thinking. Finally he had made a decision whether to be neutral and see who won the war or support one side or the other, already the Japanese had formed a nationalist Freedom Army of Burmese. The Burmese suspected, rightly, that they would just be cannon fodder for the Japanese who had no intention of giving Burma real independence any time soon. But George did not know which way his guest would jump.

Checking to see that the Burmese translator was ready to repeat his words from the typewritten scripted comments and questions Orwell, the veteran of the Home Guard fight in London in the Battle of Britain and once an inmate at Kz1 until he had escaped with Josef Comenice waited for the red light to light up. Room 101 was on-air. "This is the BBC World Service to Burma from Calcutta. Today I have a guest Dr. U-Phant a refugee government official who last month was forced to leave his home in Rangoon due to the Japanese occupation of the city. He is a Burmese nationalist and is at the moment wearing a traditional Burmese costume. I welcome you to the studio Doctor." George nodded to his guest as they had agreed.

"Mr. Orwell last week in a conversation we had here in India you asked me what the ordinary Burmese could and would do at this time of crisis in Burma. I have thought deeply about it and consulted friends in Burma on both sides of the argument as to whether my people would be wisest to fight with you British or against you. Today I am here to say I have made my own mind up without any coercion and I shall say it in English to you and afterwards in Burmese for my people to hear."

"And what have you decided?" Orwell waited for the translator to finish. He knew that his job was destined for the dustbin if U-Phant said he was going to ask the Burmese to be neutral or if he went all the way and said that the Japanese were the best hope for his county's future. *I could be charged with aiding U-Pant's treasonous remarks* Orwell thought, *getting a shorter jail term than my Burmese colleague who would get the book thrown at him, but jail never the less. I'll be ruined. But I must let him speak not cut him off.*

There was a dreadfully long pause as U-Phant gathered his thoughts. George spoke encouraging his guest to speak. "The BBC is here to tell the truth, as much as wartime allows, which is more than the enemy does. So please be honest with me and all who are listening in the towns, oil fields, plantations and jungle outposts in Burma." George's words were translated while he could see the producers in the control room ready to switch off the broadcast. He kept his thumb on the on-switch the only way to stop them was to pull the plug and the ramifications could be used by Japanese propaganda. George covered the mike and held it away from him and hissed at the producer, "Cut him off and we lose the propaganda war the Japs will use it against us. Let him speak his mind and either way we come out as allowing free speech. For God's sake they will get their freedom soon anyway, let him use it now."

The head of the Burmese broadcasts mouthed a swear word and pointed at the Burmese who took a deep breath and finally spoke. "The best hope for Burma is to side with the British against the Japanese aggressor. We are on the verge of gaining something we have not had since the British defeated our army in the last century, our freedom. The British government has told the world that we shall have our independence within three years of the war's end if they are victorious. They will adhere to that or go down in history as worse than the fascists and I do not think Mr. Attlee or President Roosevelt will rest until that promise is fulfilled. There is talk of an Earth Government in the near future I want Burma to part of that but it will only happen if the Allies win. If we sided with the Japanese we would be supporting a new invader, it would be at least another one hundred years to gain any freedom if at all.

"The ones who join the Free Burma Army are still are Burmese but they are ignorant and misguided, do not be one of them. Thank you Mr. Orwell for giving me this opportunity to speak freely."

George had lit a cigarette when U-Phant began and smoked it down to the end in record time as his guest gave his speech and reiterated it in his native tongue. He stubbed it out energetically in the ashtray on the table on which the microphone sat as he continued in a much more relaxed manner. "What would you like to say as a Burmese in Calcutta to those in Rangoon who are now occupied until we return. Please tell them in English and Burmese."

U-Phant had become a friend to George out of the studio. He helped him relearn and surpass the amount of Burmese Orwell had forgotten from his days in Burma in the 1920s when after Eton College he had joined the Burmese Police. In those days he still used his real name Eric Blair and had been unusual in taking an interest in the Burmese and understanding their feelings. He started using the pen name when he wrote his novel *Burmese Days*.

CHAPTER THIRTY-NINE   TOLEDO

Toledo was the home of the Spanish Renaissance's greatest artist El Greco, who really was Greek. The old city was beginning to feel the cool winds of Autumn change it from an oven in summer to a bearable spot.   Ben Stannard walked through the shadows of the Cathedral and the home, now a museum, honouring Theotokop known to the Spaniards as El Greco.   The painter had moved to Spain as if drawn like a moth to the over-heated intensity of its religious fervour fed by the flames of the inquisition.   Ben was spiritually and sensually moved by the large paintings in the Cathedral and in his house, they were in electric blues, purples and browns, grippingly tormented portraits of Christ and saints with elongated bodies, long fingers and stretched legs that came from a pressurised imagination dripping in condensed droplets from each hair in his brush, like perspiration.   Frenzied heated air no longer distorted the Alcazar, the turreted fortress and the cathedral as it had done just a few months before.   Storks perching on trees or tall buildings seem to unfold as they took off in the thick air.   The inescapable heat of central Spain in their fight to take Madrid was still vivid in his memory he thought as he slowly walked to the Taverna where he was to meet his Ranger officers. He walked gratefully through shadowed, cool narrow stone alleyways made by white houses with roofs orange clay tiles and wrought iron balconies facing each other.

Reading a guide book as he slowly meandered he noted that each church in the city , except one which was a synagogue, was once a mosque erected with keyhole windows, cooling tiles and fountains during the Moorish invasion but taken back during the *Reconquista* in the 1200s. "Toledo, world famous for its sword making, sabres are fashioning here for West Point military academy in America.   Many invaders have come and have gone out: Phoenicians, Hannibal's army from Carthage, Romans and Visigoths.   These last ones named converted to Christianity. Then we have coming to Toledo, Moors from North Africa. Lastly we

348

had Napoleon's French but they did not stay long." *Now the Germans and Americans*, Ben added. He recollected how much fighting there had been since August. Now it was the last push to take Madrid. *It's going to be a push-over or hell. I hope the former.*

He came onto the main road dodging between jeeps, tanks and GIs on leave and found the `Hapsburg` Taverna with its painted wooden sign hanging from rusty hinges showing a crowned, black two-headed eagle. It was in the shadow of the Alcazar which had been the site of a brutal one week siege in early October. Thanks to his Rangers the Allies had taken it. It was odd coming back, the forbidding turreted castle now looked quiet and innocent, much smaller than it had loomed then. A crowd of Children played with hoops and dogs happily near its still damaged main gate.

The drained Major looked at his officers their faces strained and smeared with dried sweat and dirt, with four days of stubble happily gulping red wine served by an energetic young Spaniard. Ben was glad they had a week before they were in action again this time it was the turn of the Marines and Commandos to probe the Madrid defences. The gangly waiter responded to a conversation about Franco at their table as he brought more wine and some tapas, telling them in English, "I am no friend of Generalissimo Franco." He spat dramatically into the gutter. "In '36 when the Nationalists took Toledo my father was shot and his head used as a football in a game by the victors. Terrible things were done by both sides but now it is clear cut. We kick off the Germans and their friends then we are Spaniards worthy of the name." Today I am a waiter. Tomorrow I join the people's army *Espana Libertad* with many young other men, women. I fight alongside you in Madrid."

"We shall drink to you. What is your name?" Ben asked.

"Xavier," he pronounced it in the Castilian manner pronouncing the X as H.

Ben copied it exactly, "To Xavier. May he come home back to Toledo safe!" Ben toasted. The officers joined him and the waiter bowed his face beaming and rushed off to get more wine for them.

CHAPTER FORTY   WREN

Empress Alexandrovna welcomed Harold Wilson to her temporary palace in a hotel in St. Petersburg. Outside flew a huge white flag with the X of the light St. Andrew`s Cross emblazoned upon it. She had chosen the traditional flag of the navy as founded by Tsar Peter the Great as the flag of the new Russia. She intended to emulate her predecessor Tsar Peter the Great, as much as possible in modern times incorporating liberal values that would preclude any future revolution. She remembered too well the upheaval and tragedy of the Bolshevik revolution and civil war, she wisely worked to heal the wounds and look to the future. Already thanks to her leadership and the victories won by her generals under Zhukov`s brilliant strategy had made inroads into German and Communist attacks, she was already consolidating her control of northern and central Russia down to Sevastopol which her forces had recovered from the Nazis after the largest tank battle in history which the Russians had won forcing Hitler in his HQ in eastern Prussia in on the `Wolf`s Lair` to leave for Dumbleton Hall in disgust to shoot clay pigeons in preparation for the `glorious 12th August` shooting red grouse which he told Lord Eastbourne declare two weeks late so he could partake with Marmaduke being his loader.

The Mancunian socialist said, "It is a pleasure to meet your Majesty" bowing his head slightly.

"You are very welcome to Russia Mr. Wilson and if there is anything we can do for you, please let me know. By the way I know you are a socialist, not a Communist, and I respect you for that. I also know from my ambassador that you are a good man and I trust you, if you are a friend and confidant of Mr. Attlee and Mr. Mackenzie-King and you are you are my friend and confidant." Harold smiled amazed and warmed by her direct friendship.

"Empress." He found himself unexpectedly emotional. *Control yourself Wilson, this is the sister of Tsar Nicholas one of the most autocratic rulers in history, pig-headed and reactionary. Deadly.* But another voice spoke but he tried not to listen; *this is a different person his sister and you are under her spell admit it. This confounded monarchy business, it s all very well striking out the idea of monarchy at a party conference or a smoke filled back-room party meeting but when you had a fine woman or man on the throne it makes a difference. And isn't that what we all want to do, make a bloody difference.* He brought out his pipe filled it full of tobacco and lit it with a Swan Vesta wooden match and puffed away as she showed him some of the Vermeer and Rembrandt art works she had brought from the Hermitage until that palace was again fit to house the magnificent collection paintings mainly amassed by her ancestor Catherine the Great.

"'Mr. Wilson I want you to be the first non-Russian to know that for the first time we have discovered what was left behind in the building that was called the 'House of Special Purpose' in Yekaterinburg. This was the building in Siberia that my brother and his family were sent to as prisoners and it was there that they were murdered by the Bolsheviks. Hundreds upon hundreds of holy icons, crosses, books belonging to each member of the Royal family and their friends, personal clothing items and precious gifts presented to each member of the Royal household that they received while under house arrest... all in this hot, closed-up house that no one could see in to or see out of, the windows were painted. The royal martyrs spent their last months at this house before they were shot and bayoneted and their remains dumped into a well with acid poured over them All we have to do is to read the horrific accounts of how each member was treated, and we begin to realize that behind these walls was so much suffering and hardship which was certainly not deserved by a Tsar, a Tsarina, a Tsarevich, or the Grand Duchesses and their friends."

Harold Wilson found himself sympathising despite himself, "Empress, don't distress yourself" He broke protocol and offered his arm to her as she stood. She took it. "I think you would like to smoke your pipe please do, anytime you are with me, this will be your special privilege." That night Harold wrote to his wife and

352

said, "Forgive me I am in love with the Empress, I mean of course that I have fallen under her spell and hope that you will be able to join me in what I am finding is a most interesting posting here in Russia!"

Some miles north Lady Helen Anne Spencer was working sixteen hour days setting up the convoy HQ under Rear-Admiral Waddington's calm guidance, her WRENS were settling into a routine of plotting in a large room with a gallery where her girls and various male officers supervised the large wooden map on a huge table which showed exactly where every ship was to and from Iceland. Huge clocks on the wall showed the time zones from Iceland to central Russia. Telephones, radio and telex reports were constantly monitored to insure the naval headquarters was up-to-date with developments. The Rear-Admiral and his staff were able to call on Royal Navy and White Russian Navy and Air Force help it was just a phone call away. The first convoy heading back to Iceland with lumber, oil, aluminium, wool and leather from Russia was safely on its way. Helen had spent a week with Aubrey checking hold manifests and ship safety and crew lists for PQ 5 in Murmansk Harbour. Supervising pilots for each vessel to take them safely to the Barent's Sea had taken a lot of time as they learnt about the harbour and Russian shipping customs. They had dressed warmly in duffel coats with hoods up, scarves and gloves going out to the large freighters and oil tankers in a large tugboat that wallowed sickeningly in the often rough waters of the harbour. The weather was becoming increasingly bitter and often snow began to fall down in large snowflakes or drive like needles into their faces if there was a northerly wind. Their working relationship was a good one but there was no doubt, at least in Duncan's mind that there something more sparking between them. There was indeed but Helen had not yet succumbed to Cupid's arrow.

In the newly built NAFFI hut Aubrey and Helen sat down for a hot cup of cocoa and a few shortbread biscuits. They made small talk then Helen spoke of her childhood and visiting Althorp she pronounced Altrop, the ancestral of the Earl Spencer her relative. "You know we have to be on duty in thirty minutes, some VIPs coming so we had better pick off all the lint off our uniforms" Helen suggested.

"Is that code for dandruff?" Duncan suggested and started to laugh, "like a couple of chimps grooming each other." Helen also found the idea amusing and started to chuckle then choked on her biscuit. Duncan patted her on the back and the idea fitted into the joke of grooming that it made her laugh and cough even more. After she settled down to change the subject and stop the giggles he asked her about the silk stockings she had been given and donated to the navy to be auctioned in a fund raiser to build the frigate Wren in 1940.

At the Royal Navy station at the naval base at Polyarny just north of Murmansk after a lunch of vodka toasts interrupted by courses of food; borscht, salmon and venison the Russian commander of the northern fleet had one arm around a dignified, sober Finnish general and another holding a vodka bottle. In atrocious broken English he did manage to convey his thoughts, with the help of dramatic mime actions, "This Finn, Marshal Manneheim is my friend now ... we were at war in 1940 and he fought and the Finnish men and women fought us with the courages bears as do his .... General here ... meet my friend the great British-Back Admiral Lemmington to help tanks and planes. I am thanks." He took another swig. Helen and Duncan both in lint free naval uniforms, buttons and eyes shining stifled laughter as their eyes met.

The Rear-Admiral adroitly explained his mission to the sober Manneheim. "I have one hundred men and women, WRENS we call them, helping me organise the PQ convoys here in Murmansk. Moveable counters represent the ships in each outgoing and incoming convoy, each has number indicating the name and type of ship. Known enemy vessels and aircraft are also given counters on the map. As you can see PQ3 is just nearing the Barents Sea, it has been attacked three times by U-boats, once by a cruiser and destroyers out of Narvik and twice by the *Luftwaffe*.

The escorts have sunk two U-boats and shot down five aircraft with a loss of two freighters containing tanks and trucks.

Her Majesty's submarine Sturdy had arrived at Murmansk with a strange load of passengers, gloomy Russians and the first WRENS the sailors had ever seen on board. Leaving Murmansk harbour and diving as they cleared it the Captain shook his odd thinking about their current odd passenger they now carried. In one of the compartments were two young reindeer happily sleeping on a bed of hay, a gift of the Empress to the Royal Navy to help with Christmas 1944 celebrations in Iceland. *This will become a part of naval folklore, some ships had cats or parrots, once a donkey he had read. But this must be the first RN ship to have reindeer. The Russians had insisted it be taken to Iceland and the Rear-Admiral had told him that if his crew did not mind Sturdy could take it. The crew had taken to their mascots readily, not grumbling when mucking out their 'stall' they had named them, Ivan and Suomi in honour of their new allies, Russia and Finland.*

CHAPTER FORTY-ONE   STOPPING CLOCKS

Owen was on deck getting some sea air and looking at flying fish leaping across their bow as the Benson Class destroyer USS Wilkes cut through a path to their destination two hundred and fifty miles off the New England coast. They had sailed from Boston in the new warship with the latest long-range radar fitted to enable the USAAF and the Civil Defence authorities along the east coast to give them some warning about S4 rockets on their way from Ireland.

The 250 crew members were excited about the mission for every rocket they tracked could save a lot of lives, thanks to other destroyers spread out on stations across the Atlantic. Accurate plots could be made of their targets giving precious minutes to scramble aircraft fitted with air-to-air rockets although there had been only limited success shooting them down with the Comet jet fighters. At least more people were able to make it to shelters in New York, Boston or the other cities under threat. More powerful jets capable of breaking the sound barrier and catching these supersonic weapons that shot out of the sky and left four square blocks a smoking hole, were being developed but something was needed now and one of them was Owen and his band of spiritual warriors. He had asked for adult volunteers in his group to come with him to help supervise and lead a group of children from Vancouver and try stopping the delicate mechanisms in the rockets themselves, but his hopes were largely on the children who had much more energy. He had chosen five aged thirteen to fourteen, the most powerful mentally energetic and disciplined kinetic in his youthful group in the Lantern Project. He had contacted the parents and spoken to them of the great need to try out an experiment explaining that there was no stigma in saying no and that he would use those children on land. All but one set of parents had agreed and some had asked to go with their children on the ship. Owen had dissuaded them so the children would not be distracted and they had agreed.

The children had enjoyed a tour of the ship and were now practicing their tele-kinetic skills moving objects and stopping mechanical devices at large distances. Ships and pilotless aircraft launched from other ships at differing distances from the Wilkes were their targets. At ten to one hundred miles plus, more and more success was attributed to the children whereas the adult psychics were more 'hit and miss'. The youths were able to stop boat or aircraft engines from operating and disrupt compass readings or gyroscope functions for seconds at a time, enough to cause a plane to crash or bring a boat to a temporary halt, certainly enough to make an S4 spin out of control or sputter to a crashing halt if they could concentrate upon the path the rockets were travelling upon. They had been practising and honing their telepathic skills for months and were ready for tackling a much harder task than stopping sub-sonic aircraft as they had done so dramatically over Vancouver.

"Right," Owen told them in a room set aside for them. Armed guards stood outside the door. "We have tried this out of doors and indoors the effect is the same; you are capable of knocking down aircraft, stopping ships, tanks and small rockets. We just have to apply ourselves now to concentrating on stopping gyroscopes and engines in larger, faster S4 rockets bound for North America with warheads that cause a lot death and destruction. Even one of you getting through to the rocket as it flies over us within range and locking up its mechanical and electrical systems means it will fall far short of its target probably harmlessly at sea. Hopefully not on us," Owen smiled and the children laughed. "I am told that the chances of that are less than us being hit by lightning so you don't have to worry. I and my colleagues are right here with you. Together we can do this. We shall just wait for notice that they are on the way."

They did not have too long to wait, a phone rang and Owen picked it up. "Captain, here. We have an S4 from Killarney seven hundred miles away, its course takes it forty miles north of our position, and will be at its closest in four minutes. Altitude is 20,000 feet. Owen used a pointer to indicate the projected course of the rocket on a map of the eastern Atlantic. "This is it, just like in practice breath in relax, concentrate completely on the rocket each of you is focussing on the gyroscope the compass the engine - you are sending out the immense psychic energy you know is inside you. You know how to control and direct it." he continued in a low voice, the young adults had their eyes closed their faces a picture of studied concentration   They kept up their energy barrage upon the rocket on its mission of death for five minutes.

The phone rang again. Owen deftly snatched the mouthpiece his heart pounding with anxiety, a voice would tell them it had worked or that the missile was still on course without deviation. He listened to the incredulous Captain explain, "It worked! I don't know how. I don't believe it even but not only our radar operators but others indicate the S4 is heading for the sea in a steep downward trajectory. Wait ... It has vanished off our radar screen the closest vessel will try and find any wreckage but it looks like your gang of kids are hot stuff. They shot it down with their minds."

Owen breathed out and thanked him. "Just as well I can't breathe a word of this since it so secret, no would believe it," the Captain replied.

The druid turned to his young charges. "You've done it. Oh well done. You have made history!"

The teenagers looked at each other in bemused amazement. Twice more they succeeded that day. As the children slept Owen and the White Lodge adults channelled their energy towards a night launched S4. They did not bring it down into the ocean but they did succeed in nudging the internal computer adjusting its gyroscope so it went off course and it exploded in a field in New Jersey instead of a populated area. In the debriefings most of the adults and children knew instinctively they had succeeded.

*

Visiting Kz1's underground rocket factory on the Isle of Wight Werner von Braun sat on von Flaut's, desk while the director of the factory sat uncomfortably on a small shiny chrome Bauhaus chair with a black canvas seat. "If I say the word Asgard does that mean anything to you?"

"Asgard? *Nein.* Sounds Norwegian."

"Well you are busy with rocketry, so I forgive you the lacuna in your knowledge of Aryan history. You must learn to mix a dash of National Socialist philosophy with scientific facts – we believe the Norse Gods and their mythology to be correct." Von Flaut shifted uneasily. *Folk tales and old wive's stories are for children for goodness sake, not scientists*, he thought. He did not however utter a word.

"All will be revealed." Von Braun leaned against his desk. "First you must know that Asgard is one of the three worlds in heaven atop the tree of life, Yggdrasil."

The factory director could not stop himself looking quizzically at his boss the head of the rocket program in the *Reich*, the only such program in the world.

Von Braun continued, disregarding his subordinate's gaze. "The tree of creation," he continued, "Asgard houses the races of the Nordic Gods, the Gods of the Teutonic tribes on Germany, our ancestors, the two God races being of course, Aesir and Vanir. Asgard is now the name for our space exploration program."

Flaut almost fell out of the chair but was prevented by his bulk. *Into space? We are planning such an immense program before we have even won? It's madness.*

The chief of rocket projects answered his unspoken question. "Of course we have almost unlimited resources, we have all of Europe. The S4 *Aesir* long range rockets now carrying high explosive, germ and napalm bombs to America will carry *atombomben* and will be the basis for the *Asgard* space program. Three-stage S5s will take a *raumann*, a German into space. Eventually we shall have *raumannfahrzeugs* able to travel to the moon and the planets. Even now we are launching small animals, rats, dogs and monkeys from a launch site in the Paraguayan jungle

359

into space and have brought them back alive. Next month we send a rocket with a dog around the earth."

"But how can we do all this and defeat Russia? We should be concentrating on that."

"The *Fuhrer* has every confidence that his super tanks will enable Rommel to be in Delhi by Christmas. He has told me personally that because of the superior organization skills of National Socialism and the German spirit we can do in one generation what would take the Americans or British three generations to do even if we are fighting a global war. By the way the *Venir* nomenclature will be for the space rockets."

"I see, *Herr* von Braun. I am dumbfounded by these developments. To put a man in space in our lifetime. It is wonderful."

"Yes, you have a part of this you are like a god yourself. We are the super race."

"I shall work hard to be worthy, *Heil Hitler!*" Flaut attempted to hoist himself out of his chair to stand and give the Nazi Aryan salute but managing only to fall forward but the head of the German rocket program caught him and jerked his subordinate up.

"Let us hope your rockets get off the ground a little steadier shall we?" Von Flaut laughed nervously thrust out his suited chest flung out his right arm stiffly and tried again.

Von Werner kept a straight face until his underling left his office then he burst out laughing, thinking *the man may be a genius in rocketry but his body is less than intelligent.*

He did not laugh when his assistant director informed him that in the last three days only six of ten S4s reached their targets in North America. "I fear there is a mechanical or fuel failure. Back to the drawing boards something is wrong we must check everything perhaps we have rushed production. I cannot see how the Allies are shooting them down their anti-rocket defences are primitive, years behind us!"

*

In Kansas City at a dinner for local officials after a day of medal award ceremonies and meetings with military leaders FDR was feeling particularly exhausted but perked up when Harry Hopkins, his friend and advisor gave him the good news about the S4 rockets "four days of success stopping many Sieg 4s landing but wait there's more good news Mr. President! The results are in from the vaccines for the plague and the new J40 type of influenza we are calling 'Japanese Flu'. Success! 91.2% of the two thousand test patients have shown marked improvement.''

"This is wonderful news, telex me the details and my press officer will inform the newspapers. We shall have immediate mass production and distribution of the vaccine. I will give an interview first thing tomorrow to the journalist boys. This will really buck up America." *Good and bad news comes in threes*, FDR thought as Eleanor helped him by taking his trousers, underwear and socks off his legs emaciated by polio. Continuing the nightly ritual she patiently and gently put on his striped red and white cotton pajama bottoms as he lay luxuriantly in bed in their hotel room. *Maybe there will be more uplifting news but by God the events this week are miraculous* was his last thought as his head hit the pillow and was out like a light.

361

CHAPTER FORTY-TWO LOOSE ENDS

It was the report from his Health Minister that finally made up Hirothito's mind. The expected losses to the influenza germs on the rampage in Tokyo to Okinawa were expected to be from five to twenty million over the winter since the US sinking of food convoys to Japan were increasing and the population was undernourished and easy victims of the killer germ. The troubled ruler went to his Shinto temple and prayed. When he got up from kneeling he knew it was time but one last check was needed. He hated confrontation only if it was absolutely necessary did he push things. *But now maybe is the time to push.* He would phone one of his family a senior civil servant who worked at the ministry of health and asked him to see him about the officially secret influenza outbreak. The minister's view was verified in a visit that evening by his cousin as he feared it would be. It was a disaster. The entire medical system was collapsing, in a few weeks the fabric of society, millions of Japanese weakened by war and rationing would succumb to the disease.

"Thank you. I am afraid I am going to have to make some radical changes but I will do my best to save as many as I can. Have faith in me." Hirohito asked his relative. The nephew bowed and keeping his body bent stiffly at the waist withdrew backwards until he was ushered away by the Lord Chamberlain. The emperor spoke to his chamberlain, "I want you to take to go to the head of the Tokyo radio station and bring him here right away." He ordered the commander of his Imperial Guard to bring three of his most trusted officers to his office as soon as possible. He sat down and wrote two words each on four letters and sealed them with wax using his seal of a chrysanthemum, he did not address them. Instead when the Chamberlain reported the officers were waiting outside, asked that each officer be let in one at a time and told each one to speak to no-one about but immediately deliver the letter he was given. The recipients were to be the Grey Foxes phase one of the seizure of power from Tojo. As the three officers took royal cars driven by chauffeurs to their different destinations Hirohito told the head of his Imperial Guard that General Tojo was guilty of treason and along with his supporters in the military and government was being arrested. He ordered him to put his troops on alert and have a senior officer with a Lieutenant and detachment of men to take his Empress and the Crown-Prince to their country home and stay with them.

"Early tomorrow morning I go to the radio station in Tokyo, a squad of your men will accompany me."

"I will be up all night early ensuring your safety, sire and will accompany you to your appointment. I shall alert all the guards and double the number of sentries. They will be armed with live ammunition with fixed bayonets. I shall set up machine-guns at strategic points in the palace. We also have some mortars for just such an emergency and a squadron of armoured cars which I make ready. We also have ten anti-aircraft guns that can be depressed to fire over open sights if the traitors attempt to take the palace. I shall place four of them and armoured cars to cover the *Nijubashi* the double bridge leading from the Mikado, the main gate. We would all die ten times over if we could for your Imperial Majesty."

"Good."

Within the hour, each of the three recipients of the message from their emperor opened their letter and read the words that galvanised them into frenzied and dramatic activity, 'Three Storks'. They had their plans in place and now they initiated them. General Tojo was preparing for bed as soldiers loyal to the emperor overcame his guards, roughly bound him and took him to the capital's strongest prison, Tojo supporters in his cabinet were also arrested and dispatched to military or naval prisons. Overnight Tojo's star had been extinguished fallen. Hirohito was ready to bring a new dawn to his country of *Nippon*.

At dawn knowing that Tojo was imprisoned he phoned Prince Konoye and sent palace officials with guards to bring him by car to the palace. Once he had his former premier's pledge of loyalty and agreement to form a peace government Hirohito accompanied his new prime minister to the radio station. Both men were immaculately dressed in morning coats, top hats, charcoal and black striped trousers, black shoes. Hirohito wore a chrysanthemum boutonnier in his buttonhole. Received by a bowing station manager still shocked at the visit by the rarely seen Emperor he guided Hirohito and Konoye into a small studio and politely asked the Emperor to sit and speak clearly into the microphone when the red light turned on. It was to be the first time his people had ever heard his voice on the airwaves.

My people this is your Emperor speaking to you from Tokyo. I have acted as the father of our nation to save it from destruction.

Premier Tojo and those who supported him in the government, the armed forces and the police force have been arrested in my name as traitors. He is guilty of keeping me ignorant of the spread of a deadly disease a modern version of the Spanish influenza which was designed to be a weapon against our enemies but has become a weapon against ourselves. I will tell you the truth but in return I want no panic, be mindful that the loyal Japanese is courageous and will follow my new government's laws to quarantine the cities where the disease is loose and rest assured that we are working upon obtaining the antidote even from our enemy the United States of America. This is an honourable decision that I have struggled to decide but it is final.

I have ordered my armed forces to halt operations against the Allies unless fired upon as I ask my new prime minister, Prince Konoye to negotiate a ceasefire and possible negotiated peace that will included our obtaining the chemical formula the Americans have developed to combat the new killer influenza that mistakenly began to infect the population on one of our trains in Osoka last month.

My premier is guilty of prosecuting a war begun in China in 1936 which is no longer in the best interest of our nation. Our resources and population need peace so that our children and grandchildren may live and prosper and follow our traditions. I have asked Prince Konoye of the Fujiwara clan, whose members have advised the Imperial house for 1,300 years, to open negotiations with the United States to seek an end to hostilities and medical help with the epidemic. We have lost many sons of Japan, disease is stalking our land and already stricken one million of our countrymen, many of whom have died. I am dishonoured and ashamed of the sorry state to which Nippon has been reduced.

The blame is mine, I have failed to bring us total victory and for this I am sorry. As soon as my son Akihito is of age he shall become Emperor. Why do I say this now? I say it because the Showa reign is 'heavenly peace' and I have to act before my reign is remembered as one of destruction. We do not lack bravery our soldiers are feared but there is no honour in fighting a war which has no end and will result in the end of our country. We shall not be occupied I shall fight personally to prevent them landing here but I seek an honourable end to the war.

My ministers will negotiate a peace which protects our nation. Japan will protect its sacred past and turn its back on the modern direction of science and industry that have brought us so close to the reefs of destruction. Our victory will be restoring the honour of Nippon. We shall become as we were for so many centuries, independent and oblivious to the troubles of the world outside our shores. Those that are loyal to me, the divine descendant of the Sun Goddess will accept this. All others are against me and will be outcasts to be expelled from Nippon."

"*Banzai,*" the announcer said wishing Hirohito long life and victory. "You have heard the voice of His Imperial Majesty who sits on the Chrysanthemum Throne. His new premier, Prince Konoye, will now speak to the nation.

*

365

In Spain another emperor, one without his homeland, had words to say though of less dramatic import. Napoleon IV sat alongside the American Ranger Ben Stannard in front of a blazing campfire on a cold mountainside in northern Spain. "It eez o.k. Major only me. Ah, my cold, weary bones," he sighed. "When you reach my venerable age after a day of zee combat I feel like zee board of wood-steef! Now tell me a beet about yourself."

Stannard was honoured that the Free French leader had chosen his campfire to warm himself. "I'm just a police sergeant's son from Niagara Falls in upstate New York who joined the Rangers one day because I read about them in the paper." He told him about growing up in the industrial town, playing baseball in the Little League and football in high school and his experiences in the Rangers. "May I ask a question of you sir? How did you get to be Napoleon IV why not Napoleon V? Colonel Darby told me that your ancestor Louis the Prince Imperial was never crowned but his followers called him Napoleon IV. "

"The difference *mon ami*, ees zat 'e never was officially proclaimed as Napoleon IV in France but 'e did become a soldier, a brave one. His first visit to the army was as a young boy dressed as a member of zee Imperial guard complete with a small sized bearskin hat. He was fourteen when he came under fire at zee beginning of zee Franco-Prussian War in 1870 riding with 'ís father, my great grandfather, Napoleon III. Ze war was lost and 'e and 'is family went to Britain where zey were warmly received by Queen Victoria and ze British. Not surprisingly 'e trained as a British army officer at Aldershot, in zee Royal Artilleree."

Stannard interrupted, "Artillery, a Napoleonic tradition."

"*Mai oui*, I carried on also zat but I jump ahead of ourselves."

"Myself"

"*Merci*, 'myself'. You Americans are very honest, not much finesse but," Napoleon said noticing the Major's red-rimmed eyes open in surprise, "refreshing to us jaded Europeans. Let me *continuer, s'il vous plait major?"*

"Fair enough, sir."

"At twenty Louis the Prince Imperial graduated and made ze clamour for action. 'E was attached to the Royal Engineers and sent to Zululand as part of Colonel Buller's army fighting King Cetewayo's revolt. Before he was killed he met my grandmother, Contesse Emma they 'ad secretly married and she bore his son, my father, eight months after he was killed. Louis joined a scouting party as General Buller advanced to ze Zulu king's village, the commander of zee party had orders to look after the prince who was still a young officer. But when they stopped for lunch they neglected to order a piquet to watch for Zulu warriors who were able to move unseen towards them while zee officers ate and drew in their sketchpads. As they mounted up Zulu warriors opened fire and advanced shouting the word *'uSuthu'* which means 'kill!

"The Prince's horse was frightened and Louis was not fully mounted as eet ran off, he held onto the leather holster attached to the saddle and was pulled along. Its strap broke and he fell, so the horse smashed his right arm. He stood up and drew his revolver with his other hand and faced the enemy. A spear lodged in his upper leg. He fired at the warriors as another struck his shoulder; when his body was later recovered they found eighteen *Assagai* wounds all in his front. 'E died honourably wearing the sword that Napoleon 1st wore at Austerlitz."

"What about the soldiers with him?"

"To their shame they watched from a distance doing nothing. British honour was redeemed when ze officer in charge was, thanks to Victoria and my great-grandmother, Empress Eugenie, never socially spoken to again. He died a broken man in India six years later. The Zulus said that if they had known who the soldier was zey would not have killed him. Empress Eugenie made a pilgrimage to Suhuzas, the kraal near where he was killed. The Prince Imperial's body, what was left after the tropical heat, was shipped to Britain, where she had eet placed in a mausoleum near her 'ome in Kent. Zobanga, the warrior responsible for 'is death, died later at the Battle of Ubundi."

"What happened to his sword?"

"I have it. It is hidden in the grounds of my home in Nantes on the coast. My father was zee son of which the countess gave birth when she came back to France and was sheltered by her family in the country. He was brought up not knowing he was a Bonaparte until he was twelve when he was given the sword. It was not the time to be publically revealed as the long lost heir. I too was told when I was twelve and given the sword and again eet was not zee right time to tell the world who I really was. It was in 1943 once I launched my coup d'etat against the collaborators in French Indo-China."

"What a great story,"

"Zee best ees yet to come," he said confidently, "we should get some sleep tomorrow is a great battle, another time you can tell me about ze American milkshakes and ze girls of New York."

*

Harry Hopkins opened the door to the Oval Office without knocking and almost slipped over as he ran up to the desk where the President was signing a stack of documents. FDR looked up first in shock then his face softened as he could see Hopkins was alight with good news. "Franklin, momentous news! Hirohito has engineered a coup and arrested Tojo! He's set up Prince Konyoe as his prime minister and ordered him to set up peace negotiations with us."

Roosevelt gripped the wheels of his wheelchair and vigorously wheeled his six foot three inch frame using his well developed upper body and halted in front of his desk clapping his hands together. His black cigarette holder was clenched upwards in his teeth at a crazy angle. He removed the cigarette holder from his mouth with a flourish. "Well I'll be a son of a bitch. This is the best damned news we have had in this war." Hopkins elaborated what he had gleaned from the Reuters teletype. "There's more. Hirohito's called a cease-fire and wants our help fighting the influenza epidemic, apparently the bacillus got loose there and is causing mayhem killing hundreds of thousands with millions expected to die soon as the epidemic takes hold."

FDR bellowed triumphantly "First get on the phone and tell the Chiefs of Staff what you know and tell them I want them in my office pronto. Get me Clement on the phone. I'll leave a message for Eleanor in New York. Come on back once you have Attlee on the scrambler line and pour two stiff glasses of Bourbon. We shall toast the end of half of this Goddam war and a speedy end to the other half!"

*

In Kandahar it would take several days for the story of the cataclysmic events occuring in Japan to reach the British army but meanwhile John was catching up on events in a week old newspaper with photos and details of the successful attack by Alexander's armoured division against overwhelming odds against the Germans in the Pyranees. General Horricks, the British X Armoured Corps commander had persisted in attacking and as luck would have it succeeded when it seemed that enemy artillery on the higher ground was going to wipe out his thin green line of 200 tanks. Disaster had been averted by clever spotting by American Rangers radioing down hundreds of allied fighter-bombers of the 2nd Tactical Air Force to wipe out the German gun emplacements. John wondered if his American pal, Dan Stannard was one of the spotters and whether Napoleon IV was getting into mischief eager to be on his way to France.

John bent to leave his tent and straightened up to walk outside. His thoughts were as cold and clear as a rushing mountain stream. *I have been fighting this war for five years and now finally in 1944 we have more good news than bad. But I know there will be more missions, more deaths, more killing, more living. Give me strength for I have to go on, to lead my men, for Felicity, for our yet unborn children, for Alan for all I care for. We are scattered*

369

around the world; will war or peace bring us together and how many of us will be left? Francis is out there somewhere maybe in a Prisoner of War camp in eastern Afghanistan. I refuse to believe he is dead.

Resolutely John turned on his heel knowing he was a small human locked into big events in one small part of a globe hurtling through space amidst a million galaxies. He walked into the desert under a cold dark blue sky that so clearly exposed the cosmos as to make him feel he was falling into it as fast as thought.

AFTERWORD

The idea of Hitler looking for Zulfiqar was inspired by my visit to the new and splendid Royal Armouries Museum in Leeds, Yorkshire, England. In one of their superb displays of weapons and armour through the ages was an eye-catching eighteenth century Persian steel weapon with a steel scabbard as described as being shown by Sphinx to Alan Stafford in the book. The dagger has two blades and multiple blades in between them and was probably inspired by the legendary twin-bladed sword Zulfiqar given to Ali by Mahommet and reproduced by Arab armourers over the centuries. In World War Two the Grand Mufti of Jerusalem was a friend of the Nazis and the German SS recruited Azerbaijanis as soldiers to fight against the Soviet Union but by far the majority of Muslims in the Middle East and Asia remained neutral. There was a Nazi inspired revolt by pro-Axis Iraqi generals against the pro-British regent in Iraq in 1942 but this was put down by the British army.

The stories my father and grandfather told me as a boy about World War Two made me want to be a soldier. I became a librarian but I did have a go as a teenager in the Royal Canadian Engineers militia unit in Vancouver. Those tales gave me a lifelong interest in military history and the 1939-1945 global war in particular. My grandfather and father both served in the British Army, the former in the British Expeditionary Force sent to Archangel to help the White Russians fight against the Bolsheviks in 1919. In W.W. II he served in the Home Guard in Bristol and one night commanded a unit guarding Queen Elizabeth. My father was in a Royal Engineers Territorial unit and called up just days before war began on 3rd September, 1939. He was a Bren gunner at Chatham Barracks in E. London in the Battle of Britain and then served in the 14th Army as one of Brigadier Wingate's Chindits operating behind Japanese lines in the Burmese jungle. It is said one should write about what one knows so I have tried to do that, not that I am expert by any stretch of the imagination, but I have enjoyed reading a variety of books on the topic. The first adult non-fiction book I remember reading on 'the war' as people still refer to it seventy years after it started, I remember reading was a Pan paperback called *Cockleshell Heroes*, about Commandos paddling kayaks to attack German ships in a French harbour.

Those wonderful black and white 1950s British films about 'the war' were lapped up by ex-servicemen (and their sons and possibly daughters) who had only been out of uniform for a few years. Here's a list anyone of them is worth watching: *Reach for the Sky* (about legless fighter pilot Sir Douglas Bader who makes an appearance in *Napoleon IV*), *The Wooden Horse* (about a mass escape by British POWs in a German prisoner of war) both of these are based on books of the same name by Paul Brickhill. *The Cruel Sea*, based on the book by Nicholas Montseratt, *Ice Cold in Alex* starring Sir John Mills and Sylvia Simms, and *The Long, the Short and the Tall*. Interestingly the 'Tall' actor in that film lives in the same town as I do, a gangly figure, of African ancestry walking quickly his coat flying behind him. *Sink the Bismark* starring Sir Kenneth More, who also played Douglas Bader in *Reach for the Sky*, still is a gripping and moving film after over fifty years.

The Dam Busters starring Richard Todd is a superb film about 617 Squadron RAF, the Lancaster bomber squadron tasked with destroying German dams with Sir Barnes-Wallis's amazing skipping bomb. Sir Michael Redgrave masterfully portrays the eccentric and likeable inventor. The play *Breaking the Code* was made into a good film about Alan Turing starring Sir Derek Jacobi and is recommended. Horowitz's splendidly written scripts for the TV series *Foyle's War* about a detective solving mysteries during W.W. II in the coastal town of Hastings, England comes alive with a terrific cast including Michael Kitchen as Foyle. They are worth watching just to see the 1940s clothes and uniforms and scenes of still unchanged parts of Hastings and Eastbourne. In a comic vein the BBC TV series *Dad's Army* about the Home Guard was compulsive viewing in the 1960s and early 1970s by the Queen and millions of others. Now on DVD they are still being watched around the world.

The most famous 1950s colour film of W.W. II is the 1957 Academy Award winning, *The Bridge on the River Kwai*, from the novel *The Bridge over the River Kwai* by Pierre Boulle. There are two films in the 1960s and one in the 1970s that give you the feeling of D-Day, the Battle of Britain and the tragic paratroop Battle at Arnhem respectively, they are *The Longest Day* (1962), *Battle of Britain* (1969) and *A Bridge Too Far* (1977). These are epic films. *The Longest Day* and *A Bridge Too Far* both began as fast-paced non-fiction accounts by Cornelius Ryan.

All British boys in the 1950s and 1960s read comics such as the famous *Eagle* that once featured a series on Winston Churchill illustrated by Frank Bellamy that is still treasured by me and is now hailed as a masterpiece of graphic art. Most featured fictional strips on W.W. II exploits, graphic stories they would be called today. *Victor* comic's cover stories often featured V.C. winners. *War*, *Commando* and *Battler Britain* comics from 1959 on were in a new comic format, small and thick like mini-paperback books. Battler Britain -what a great name for a handsome RAF hero who could do anything? He could use his Spitfire to shoot down any enemy aircraft (or ten), fly a helicopter or even ride a camel shooting a Browning .50 machine-gun. The adventures of US GIs in the American Sergeant Rock and other comics were available in the UK and made interesting reading. The Biggles books by W.E. Johns, himself a pilot in the First World War, were voraciously read by three generations. Biggles was a veteran pilot hero of the First and Second World Wars and even into the Cold War. He and his comrades, Algy, Ginger and Bertie never aged.

Many young Britons in my generation born just after 'the war' were rather disappointed we missed what was obviously the most important experience of every adult we knew who served or just lived through the air raids and tribulations and excitements of the time. As we grew up we also, amidst the excitement of playing soldiers, realised we were lucky not to have been in the last war but saw the very possible war coming with the Russians as a serious but exciting prospect. Youth is without fear. We practiced dealing with invading Russians in games roaming through woods, unused railway lines and farmers fields in the early 1960s. As young boys in the 1950s of course one played soldiers and fought first against the 'Germs' that became the 'Germans' as we learned their proper name -at eight or whatever it was. Of course as you mature up you realise that there are good and bad people in all nations and that the ideal is that we all live in peace and work and pray for that. You also realise that if the bad people take complete control the good 'uns have difficulty preventing bad things happening and it goes on from there. That is why I respect the armed forces of the Commonwealth countries who have to fight when and where they are ordered but in the main the correct decisions have been made e.g. W.W. I, W.W. II, Korea, and the first Persian Gulf War. They have fought well whether it is a just war or the result of a morally wrong decision by the government who gives the orders. Luckily in our parliamentary democracies such unjust wars are rare but cogent arguments could be made that the second Persian Gulf War was unjustifiable and weakened the rule of international law. It seems to have been planned on the basis of incorrect intelligence reports which were knowingly exaggerated to convince politicians and the public that a quick decision was necessary in the name of the 'War on Terror'. One positive benefit however was relieving the Iraqis from the rule of a harsh dictator.

I have been asked by some readers to note some books I would recommend about W.W. II. I highly recommend Sir Winston Churchill's History of the Second World War (five volumes), it is fascinating reading and his prose really sweeps you along in a grand style that makes history come alive with passion and a warm and firm touch and understanding of how history is made by someone who did indeed make it. Peter Townsend's *Duel of Eagles* is an excellent account of the Battle of Britain.

The best novels I have read about 'the war' are Evelyn Waugh's superb trilogy: *Officers and Gentlemen, Unconditional Surrender and Sword of Honour*. A 2001 TV film version of the trilogy called *Sword of Honour* stars Daniel Craig (later of 007 film fame) playing the main character, Guy Crouchback, the humble and 'good man' to whom the war happens and yet he survives it. *Catch-22* by Joseph Heller is the best American novel of W.W. II I have read and satirises the cynicism and craziness of war. It was made into an interesting film of the same name in 1970. Earl Birney's novel *Turvey* is a well - written, humorous novel about the Canadian army.

Freya Stark's *Dust in the Lion's Paw* is a fascinating account of a British woman in Iraq for much of the war who describes what life was like in Baghdad before during and after the revolt of the Golden Triangle of generals when the Nazis seemed poised to take over the country.

One of the interesting revelations of writing this series is thinking of something that could have happened, incorporating it into the book and then reading that hitherto secret documents have been made public that substantiate my thoughts - which is fun and pleasantly surprising. For example a few months ago I wrote about the fictional deception plan to make Hitler think that the Allies were intending to invade Norway from Iceland rather than Spain. Apparently Hitler really was convinced the Allies would attack Norway in 1944 and sent agents to Iceland to spy on British and American forces based there. Icelandic sealers found the agents who were caught and false information sent back to their controllers. When I was writing the first book, Saving the King, I imagined that Churchill and his aptly named home defence commander General Ironside, prepared a corps of resistance fighters sustained by secret locations of weapons and ammunition, subsequent revelations revealed that this was the case. There is now a Resistance Museum that deals with the preparations to repel the invasion in 1940 and continue the fight if Great Britain was occupied.

In reality of course D-Day, the Allied invasion of *Festung Europa* occurred on 4 June, 1944 in Normandy, France. There was an actor who impersonated Montgomery to confuse the Germans, a story made world famous in another 1950s film *I Was*

Monty's Double. The actor was recruited by the film star David Niven who served in the Commandos. Niven was the only man to kneel to say his prayers nightly in his Commando unit except for the night before D-Day when every man, including the atheists, followed his example.

The Germans were planning to test an atomic bomb in 1944 and over the last few years some have proposed that they did test small bombs in northern Europe. In reality Hitler invaded the Soviet Union in 1941's Operation Barbarossa and fell into the same trap Napoleon did, making for Moscow and getting caught in the terrible winters with supply lines that were incredibly long and hard to defend. I have imagined that he over-extends himself in a different way through central Asia and Afghanistan.

The role of Emperor Hirohito in the Second World War is a controversial one, did he know what was going on in his name and if so did he agree with it or try to change things? It is documented that in one case he reduced the number of American prisoners to be executed. I have fictionally portrayed him as a man who saw drastic action was necessary to salvage what he could of the Japan he loved and personified once he perceived that disaster for his people loomed on the horizon. Japan did test germ warfare agents on prisoners in China so it is entirely possible that large scale germ warfare could have erupted in W.W. II.

Churchill met with President Inonu of Turkey in 1943. In reality Churchill lived well beyond the war but in my alternative history he dies in 1941. Inonu attended two Cairo Conferences during W.W. II but Turkey did not join a defensive organisation until 1952. In this book I have Turkey sign a secret defensive treaty with the Allies. Lawrence of Arabia (Colonel T.E. Lawrence) did die in an accident in Dorset, England in 1935 while riding his Brough motorbike and there was a reported black car that was never traced that possibly caused his death. I don't subscribe to conspiracy theories but in terms of the novel I thought it would be interesting if such an accident had been engineered by Churchill and his supporters in the establishment to look like

Lawrence was dead so that he could be used in the war that even then was looming in the future with Hitler. The Nazis were interested in mythological artifacts such as the Holy Grail, because of the symbolic power it would give them if people believed it was theirs. Finding the real thing of course was crucial. I extended this idea to the hunt for Zulfiqar which no doubt the Nazis would have used to gain power in the Middle East and Asia if they could have found the sword. As far as I could tell no one knows where it is. It lives on in such places as the Saudi Arabian flag and a tank in Sadam Hussein's army was named after the mythical sword. It is a potent symbol of Islamic history much as Excalibur, King Arthur's sword, has assumed mythological status.

There was a sword presented to Russia in W.W. II by the British people since they were their ally in the war against Hitler and it was put on public display before being sent to the Soviet Union. Evelyn Waugh describes it in his book *Sword of Honour*.

In terms of spiritual war Winston Churchill did convene white witches and clairvoyants to be the White Eagle Lodge in the Battle of Britain to protect Great Britain. I have merely expanded that fact to include the use of adults and children in tele-kinetic warfare from Canada and have a society clairvoyant in London working for the resistance movement.

The juxtaposition between what really happened and what I have created as an alternative 'the war' sometimes gets jumbled in my mind which can make for some interesting thoughts where fact becomes fiction and vice-versa although usually I can keep the two separate as parallel universes that sometimes intersect.

Robert Oldham

CHARACTERS

Fictional descriptions are shown in *italics*.

Alexandrovna, Empress Olga (1882–1960)-Youngest child of Tsar Alexander III sister to Tsar Nicholas II who was murdered with his family by Bolshevik executioners in 1917. She was raised at the Gatchina Palace near St. Petersburg. She escaped Russia during the civil war and was taken to Denmark by a British battleship via the Black Sea. Later she settled in a small town in Ontario, Canada *never thinking that in 1944 she was called upon to become Empress and lead her unhappy country at its direst moment invaded by the Germans, its capital city destroyed and the brutal Communist government trying to reassert itself from Siberia. She earned the respect and love of Russians for her modesty, simple life and courage. In her time not spent in official duties she painted.*

Arnold, Henry 'Hap' H., General-Commander of the U.S.A.A.F. (United States Army Air Force) born in Pennsylvania and a graduate of West Point, he was taught to fly by Orville Wright, one of the two brothers who pioneered powered flight. In 1938, FDR appointed him as commander of the American Air Force and member of the joint Chiefs-of-Staff.

Attlee, Lord Clement-(1883-1967)-Born in London, taught at London School of Economics, served in British army in World War One at Gallipoli, Mesopotamia (Iran) and the western front. First elected as a Labour Member of Parliament in 1922, in 1935 he became Labour Party leader. He joined Winston Churchill's coalition government in spring 1940, *asked by Queen Mary acting on behalf of the Queen Regent, to take position of Prime Minister of the British government-in-exile in Ottawa on the death of Winston Churchill June 1941. Attlee skilfully directed the British war effort for the rest of World War Two. Princess Elizabeth made* *him an earl in 1948.* He liked crossword puzzles, was quietly efficient and learned Arabic in his army days.

Aztec-Male jaguar born on the Isle of Wight, left behind by the animal trainer of a circus during the invasion. The big cat was looked after by Marcus Jeffries, becoming his inseparable companion, killing the occasional German sentry on Marcus's orders. The ancient Mayans believed that the sun god became a black jaguar at night.

Badger, 'Brock' Harold—*Thirty-year-old RAF Flying Sergeant sent to New Britain to help steal a German Liebel helicopter. Helped Alan fly to Gibraltar in an Italian bomber. Nicknamed 'Brock', due to the streak of white in his black hair, giving him the appearance of a Badger. Became a radar operator in a Gibraltar night fighter squadron while recuperating from a wound which prevented him from flying planes. Flew a Typhoon on D-Day*

Banerjee, Darjit-Twenty-one year old RAF Flying Officer in RAF born in Lucknow, India, one of three million Indians to serve in WWII, posted to Gibraltar in a Beaufighter night fighter squadron. Flew with Brock Badger but was killed in action while with him after they shot down three enemy aircraft in one night.

Beaverbrook, Lord (1879-1964)-Born Max Aitken in New Brunswick, Canada became a British Member of Parliament 1910, knighted 1911. He purchased the widely-read newspapers *The Daily Express* and *Evening Standard.* He became Minister of Aircraft Production in Churchill's wartime coalition government in 1940, and Minister of Supply in British *Government-in-Exile in Ottawa 1940-1945. Appointed Governor-General of Canada 1946-1949.*

Bohr, Neils-Danish physicist *captured by the Nazis and taken to Kz1 to work with Lise Meitner on their atomic weapon research program, sent to Kz2 on the Isle of Man and took his own life to avoid helping the Nazis.*

Brooke, Field Marshal Sir Alan (1883-1963)-Born in Ulster (N. Ireland) an artillery officer in World War One. In 1937 he commanded the first British Mobile Division. His Second Army Corps fought well in France in 1940, he was promoted to General and made Commander-in-Chief, Home Forces. In 1941 Churchill made him CIGS (Commander of Imperial General Staff). *Attlee kept him in that position.* He was made a Viscount in 1948.

Brylcream Boys-Nickname for RAF, whose members had a reputation for being glamorous and well groomed with Brylcream hair cream.

C- Codename for Anthony Smythe Armstrong the senior Free London resistance leade, who dealt directly with top level agents Felicity and Dixon-Fairley. C worked in the British Museum and mingled with the intelligentsia of New British society. He was an actor before the war, and was chosen by Churchill to assign agents to take places in important British institutions as Resistance controllers whilst London was evacuated in October 1941. An eccentric character he is known for his long eyebrows and tufts of hair growing out of his ears and his habit of wearing a monocle.

Carr, Evelyn-U.S. Army driver from Nantucket, Massachusetts, aged 19, assigned to drive American and Allied officers around Toronto. She met Alan and John Stafford at Union Station, Toronto in August 1941. She helped Alan switch places with John in his bid to go to Kz1 in his brother's place.

Chanrajekhar, Subrahamanian (1910-*1995*)-Groundbreaking astro-physicist born into a Brahmin family in Lahore, part of British India's intellectual elite. His uncle was a Nobel Prize winner and he won one himself sin 1983 for his research into the evolution of stars. At 19 he attended Trinity College, Cambridge on a scholarship while en-route in the Arabian Sea he pondered what happens when stars run out of nuclear fuel. His mentor Eddington publically criticized it but others like Bohr supported it and Chanrajekhar was proved right. His reputation outstripped his critics in the field of theoretical physics and his ideas became the foundation of black hole research. *In 1940 he came to Canada and taught and researched at Queen's University. Attlee recruited him as the head of the ultra-secret Operation Who time travel research* *project in 1943 in an attempt to give Britain and Canada the ability to send people into the past or future to change the present in case the fascists could not be defeated by other means.*

Churchill, Sir Winston (1874-*1941*)-Greatest Prime Minister of Great Britain; soldier, statesman, orator and historian, son of Lord Randolph Churchill and the beautiful American born in Brooklyn, New York, 'Jennie' Jerome. He fought in the last major cavalry charge at the Battle of Omdurman in the Sudan and became a war correspondent in the Boer War. Captured by the Boers he escaped, becoming world famous, then helped the British win the last decisive battle bringing the Boers to the peace table. He was first elected to the British Parliament as a Liberal in 1900, but later became a Conservative and ironically negotiated peace terms with the Boers with whom he shared mutual respect. These resulted in self-government in a few years and their support in two world wars for Britain. He was an inspiringly efficient First Lord of the Admiralty before and during World War I but after the debacle of the Gallipoli landings in Turkey he resigned and received a commission as a Colonel in the front lines in France.

As a back-bench Conservative in the 1930s he wrote a history of the Great War and spoke out against his government's policy of appeasement and German re-armament. Became First Lord of Admiralty again at outbreak of World War II, replaced Chamberlain as Prime Minister in May 1940.

He led the British Commonwealth alone against the Axis powers, authorizing the evacuation of British and French troops at Dunkirk June 1940. *He masterminded the 'Great Evacuation' of over one million allied soldiers and government personnel from Great Britain in mid-October 1940, set up the British forces and government-in-exile in Canada and established the British resistance network.* He worked closely with President Roosevelt on strategy, *persuading America to provide ships, troops and planes fighting under the Union Jack, to defend Hong Kong and Singapore; set up a volunteer U.S. army in Canada* and forged the *North Atlantic Defence Alliance (NADO)* with Canada and the U.S.

382

He encouraged Roosevelt to establish the 'Defending Attacked Ships Policy' under which the U.S. Navy protected British and Commonwealth shipping anywhere it was attacked, by sailing alongside convoys.

He allowed the U.S. ownership of airfields and naval bases in the Caribbean, Newfoundland, Fiji, Ascension Island and Ceylon for 99 years in return for rifles, machine-guns and ammunition for British defence in 1940, and fifty obsolete destroyers to protect convoys across the Atlantic.

His inspiring radio speeches during 1940-1941 kept freedom and hope alive. *Churchill died of a heart attack from overwork in Sydney, Australia on 5 June, 1941 the day the U.S.A. declared war on Germany.*

He was the first person to be awarded a posthumous knighthood (baronetcy), by Princess Elizabeth in Ottawa in the New Year's Honours list 1942 which was accepted by his widow, Lady Clementine Churchill. The United States Congress made him a posthumous citizen of the United States and the new tank, produced in Canada in 1943, was named the Churchill in his honour. In 1958 the newly built Australian capital was named Churchill to immortalise how he encouraged Australians to stand against the Japanese Empire.

Comenici, Josef-*Captain of the Romanian Palace Guard born in 1910. Hearty, large man with a round face and a large black moustache. Befriended John after he saved Prince Michael. When King Michael became a prisoner in his own palace due to a Fascist coup, he sent Comenici to England to wait until the time was right to encourage an Allied thrust through the Balkans. Josef fought alongside Royal Navy staff at Greenwich Naval College in the Battle of London. He was sent to a P.O.W. camp from which he escaped. He was sent to Kz1 where he and George Orwell escaped during the raid on the camp factory. They ended up in Gibraltar after signing up as sailors on the Spanish freighter Don Quixote. Assigned to Romania by King Michael to help the resistance movement in Romania.*

Crusoe, Jerrard-*Middle-aged surgeon at the Royal London Hospital and Harley Street consultant, less of a fascist than an amoral opportunist.*

D'Allaincourt, Charles Albert Louis *see **Napoleon IV***

Day, Susan-*Born in Leatherhead, Surrey the hazel - eyed nurse joined the Queen Alexandra's Royal Army Medical Corps in 1939 and served in France. She was posted to Gibraltar where she met Alan Stafford. She accompanied him on the voyage to Canada where she was assigned to the same military hospital in Winnipeg. She served in Alexandria, Egypt and treated Napoleon IV. As a Sergeant nurse she volunteered for the 'Flying Nightingales' and helped wounded soldiers flying with them from the front lines to hospitals at the Battle of El Alamein.   In 1944 she is promoted to Captain and assigned to Afghanistan as a Flying Nightingale flown in to the battle zone with her nurses providing initial care and flying wounded soldiers to hospitals.*

Darmstadt, Count Manfred von-*Born an aristocrat in 1911 in the German state of Saxon. Attended Heidelberg University, joined the SS in 1935. Led successful attack on the Belgian Eben Emaul fort in May, 1940. Awarded Iron Cross with oak leaf cluster by Hitler. Commanded Operation Checkmate, the capture of the Duke and Duchess of Windsor from the Bahamas August 1940. As Sturmbannfuhrer led paratroop attack on Windsor Castle 20 September, 1940 and escaped with half of the Crown Jewels. Promoted to Gruppenfuhrer when appointed Governor of London residing in the Tower of London during the occupation. Apparently killed during Operation Lion Heart when the Commandos rescued Edward VIII and Queen Wallis, January, 1941. He survived thanks to the surgical skill of Mr. Jerrrard Crusoe.*

Darmstadt, Otto von-*Nephew to Count Manfred Von Darmstadt, born in 1919, attended Oxford University 1937 and was given tour of Tower of London by Charlie Gates. Joined the SS in 1940 and assigned to the New British office of the SD in 1941 with the rank of Hauptsturmfuhrer.   His office was in the New Scotland Yard* *building in London. He vowed to kill John Stafford, who attacked his uncle.*

Dietrich, Ingrid-*One of Hitler's Wehrmacht Secretaries at his Chancellery in Berlin. A beautiful blonde born in Vienna in 1920, she fell in love with one of Hitler's translators, Heinz Erhardt. She married Heinz and moved with him to Stockholm, Sweden.*

Dixon-Fairley, Thomas-*Silver-haired society clairvoyant and medium in his late twenties, once consulted by Queen Wallis before her demise and other members of the elite in New British society. Recruited by C as a resistance member. Lives in Bloomsbury near the British Museum where Prime Minister Lord Eastbourne regularly visits him as a client.*

Eastbourne, Lord Lancelot (1879-1949)-*Fascist Prime Minister of New Britain appointed by Hitler after the defeat of Great Britain in October 1940 on the advice of Blackshirt leader Lord Mosley. He collaborated with the Germans convinced that he was saving Britain from Communism and moving it into the future where the Third Reich, Italy and Japan would rule the world. Became interested in spiritualism and was the regular client of Dixon-Fairley, a clairvoyant working for the resistance.*

Elizabeth, Princess (1926-   )-*Born in London 21 April, 1926, eldest daughter of George VI and Queen Elizabeth, survived kidnap attempt at Windsor Castle 21 September 1940 by German paratroopers, evacuated with her younger sister, Princess Margaret, first to Wales, then Scotland and to Canada in October 1940.*

She lived in Ottawa with her sister and grandmother, Queen Mary, in the Chateau Laurier Hotel in Ottawa, overlooking the Ottawa River by Parliament Hill, for the duration of the war. She visited Australia accompanied by Mrs. Clementine Churchill and Prime Minister Attlee in June 1941 to attend Winston Churchill's funeral in Sydney. A year later she and her sister Margaret made a successful state visit to Washington D.C. as guests of President and Mrs. Roosevelt. She became Queen Regent at the age of eighteen in 1944. At that time she began training in the ATS as an army driver in Chilliwack, British Columbia.

Elizabeth, Queen (1900-2002)-Born Elizabeth Bowes-Lyon, the daughter of the Earl and Countess of Strathern on his English estate, brought up at Glamis Castle, Scotland. As a teenager she nursed convalescing officers at the castle during World War I.

After twice turning down his offer of marriage Elizabeth married Bertie, son of George V and Queen Mary at Westminster Abbey 23 April, 1923 in the wedding of the decade. She left her bouquet of flowers at the grave of the Unknown Soldier (the body of an unknown British soldier was buried inside the cathedral near the entrance with full honours after World War I). The tradition of brides marrying at the Cathedral leaving their bouquets continues to this day. She despised Wallis Simpson who caused her husband Bertie to become King George VI. She supported him and helped him not only to cope but excel. She loved Canada, which she toured with George VI extensively in May-June 1939 just before the outbreak of World War Two. She swore never to leave Great Britain during the war and in fact never did leave during that time.

Wounded by a piece of bomb shrapnel she lost the sight in one eye during the Blitz attack on Buckingham Palace which killed George VI, 21 September. She was hospitalised in London then evacuated to Edinburgh where she made a rapid recovery. She was made Queen Regent by order-in-council 24 September until Princess Elizabeth became of age at eighteen.

When Churchill asked the Royal Family to go into exile to Canada she refused. She did give permission for her mother-in-law, Queen Mary, and her two children, Princesses Elizabeth and Margaret, to leave from Liverpool on the battleship HMS King George V.

Living 'underground' in occupied Scotland, she became a legend as the head of the Scottish Resistance, wearing an eye patch over her right eye and proving herself a crack shot against German and New British Fascists who attempted but failed to capture her.

Erhardt, Heinz-*One of Hitler's translators in Berlin, the son of German diplomats in China. Born in 1916 in Shanghai he was studying German literature in Berlin when he was called up for Wehrmacht service. Assigned to translation duties since he spoke eight languages including: English, Arabic, French, Russian, Chinese and Japanese. A German patriot not a Nazi, he feared a total war that would destroy the Fatherland. He married Ingrid Dietrich, a secretary at the Reich Chancellery and with Hitler's blessing they began a new life in neutral Sweden where he has a job with his Uncle who owns an export business. He becomes a spy for the Americans and returns to his job in Berlin.*

Farnham, Squadron Leader Bob-*RAF Sunderland flying boat pilot based in Iceland who flew microfilm of Axis plans to divide North America to Canada. Pilots a Sunderland to Casablanca carrying PM Attlee and British commanders. In 1944 he flew Empress Alexandrovna to St. Petersburg.*

FDR-Initials of Franklin Delano Roosevelt.

Franco, General Francisco (1892-*1946*)-Fascist Dictator of Spain known as El Caudillo, who gained power as the leading general opposing the leftist Republican government elected in 1936. Beginning the counter revolution in Teneriffe, he led the fascist Spanish forces to victory with the help of Germany and Italy in 1939. *In 1941 at the Madrid Conference he signed the pact allying Spain with the Axis powers and secretly prepared to invade Gibraltar. He attacked Gibraltar in 1942 and then found his country invaded by General Bradley's American army once they had helped defeat the Afrika Korps.*

Fraser, Peter (1884-1950)–Prime Minister of New Zealand from 1940-1949 attended Imperial War Conference *Sydney Australia, flew back to New Zealand with Princesses and hosted them in one week visit before they returned to Canada.*

Frederick of Hanover, King Joachim (1895--1956)-*A Hanovarian aristocrat selected by Adolf Hitler to be a pro-German King of New Britain. He took up residence at Buckingham Palace in New*

Britain in February 1941 and kept busy enjoying good food, wines and women. He married Princess Chouko in Westminster Abbey in 1944.

Freyberg, General Bernard C. (1888-1963)-English born but raised in New Zealand his nickname was the ironic 'Tiny' since he was a gigantic man with courage to match with tree-like-legs and a head the size of a giant's. He was a swimming champion, rower and boxer. In 1914 he joined the Royal Navy Division raised by Churchill, First Lord of the Admiralty and fought at Antwerp. At Gallipoli he won the first of four DSOs (Distinguished Service Order). He swam the Hellespont, like Leander, while serving in the Dardenelles. He won a V.C. (Victoria Cross) at the Battle of the Somme.. He was a pallbearer at the funeral of the poet Rupert Brooke. Churchill once counted twenty seven shrapnel scars on his body calling him 'the salamander of the British Empire' since the creature was once believed to survive fire unscathed. In 1939 he commanded the 2nd New Zealand Expeditionary Force and served with distinction under Montgomery in North Africa. *In 1942 he was sent to command the Singapore garrison and arrived just in time to prepare for a Japanese attack and lead a successful campaign to prevent the Japanese taking the important harbour and city.*

Gates, Charlie (1878-1960)-Born in Chadderton, Lancashire, England in 1878 served in the Royal Scots Fusiliers in World War One. Sergeant-Major Gates later served in India, after retiring from the army as a Warrant Officer he became a Yeoman Warder at the Tower of London in 1934. In 1937 he became Raven Master. In 1940, aged sixty-two, he fought in the Battle of London, was wounded but went back to work in the Tower as the last Warder for the Nazis, as a member of British resistance. He took the last two ravens and some turf from the Tower to Yorkshire for safekeeping during the occupation.

Greenham, Victoria-Freckled and petite, brown-haired Australian librarian in Sydney who became Aubrey Hunter's girl in 1940. She joined the WAAF becoming a radar controller near Darwin.

Awarded the Military Cross for staying at her post sending information to the Ops HQ under enemy fire and then saving Lieutenant Sarah Churchill by pulling her away from a delayed action bomb.

Grey, Phil- *British SS Rottenfuhrer, non-commissioned officer batman and driver for Otto von Darmstadt in the SD, at Scotland Yard. He is a member of the resistance from Leeds and assisted Alan in impersonating SD Storm Band Leader Hattersly.*

Gryffyd, Owen-*Welsh Druid born in 1901 on the day Queen Victoria died and Edward VII became King. In 1940 he was summoned to London's White Eagle Lodge of spiritualists convened by the government to spiritually defend Great Britain. He took charge of proceedings and saw success in their 'Go Away Powder' ensuring the defeat of the German attack upon Dover. He and most of the White Eagle Lodge were evacuated to Canada where he was made head of the spiritual war effort. His Operation Lantern project based in Vancouver incorporated children and young adults with strong psychic powers used in the war effort.*

Guingaud, 'Freddie' de-Monty's hand-picked Chief of Staff, a Brigadier who handled all General Montgomery's major administrative details.

Himmler, Heinrich (1900-*1996*)-Second most powerful Nazi after Adolf Hitler. He was made head or *Reichsfuhrer* of the SS on 6 January, 1929. By 1933, this elite Nazi bodyguard was two hundred and nine thousand strong.

Hirohito, Emperor (1901-1989)-124th Emperor of Japan 1926-1989, believed to be a descendant of the Sun Goddess Amaterasu, he opposed war with Great Britain and the U.S.A. but was not able to overturn the decisions by the military junta that took over the Japanese government in 1931. He tried to avoid war with China in 1937, but was overruled.

Even though he was worshipped as a god by followers of the Shinto religion, he was told what to do by his fascist Prime

Minister, General Tojo who advocated militarization of Japanese society and aggressive expansion in Asia.

Hirohito did manage to postpone hostilities with the Americans in early 1941 when an embargo was put upon oil exported to Japan by the United States. However, Tojo and his military junta had their way when the Japanese attacked Hawaii and San Diego, California on 25th December, 1941. *He secretly organized a group of family members and sympathetic peace faction generals and admirals called the 'Grey Foxes' to negotiate a peace for Japan, at the opportune moment, that would stave off the complete destruction of Nippon which he feared would be the result of attacking the powerful United States.*

Hitler, Adolf (1889-*1947*)-Born in Austria, an artist and would-be architect who joined the German Army in 1914, and served on the Eastern and Western fronts in the infantry. He became a corporal and was awarded the Iron Cross first class for bravery.

He led an aborted *coup d'etat* to seize power in post World War I Munich in Bavaria (Munich Beer Hall Putsch November 9th 1923). He was jailed and there wrote his manifesto Mein Kampf (My Struggle). He joined the National Workers Party and took it over creating the Nazi party in 1925, an ultra-right wing, patriotic and anti-communist political organisation which combined bully tactics; mesmerising, well-delivered speeches and ruthlessness in a time of great inflation and uncertainty in Germany. His fascist party was inspired by Mussolini's Blackshirts in Italy. Through intimidation and a groundswell of support he was elected *Riechkanzellor* (Chancellor) of Germany in 1933, and established the Third *Reich*, making himself and the Nazi party dictatorial rulers of Germany. He proceeded to swiftly re-arm Germany, put the unemployed to work, and manoeuvre to gain back what Germany had given up by losing World War I, blaming that loss not on defeat 'in the field' which was the truth, but unjustly upon Jewish treachery, and defeatism by the German leadership in 1918.

By 1936, he had taken the Rhineland unopposed by Britain and France, and continued building the most modern armed forces in the world. By 1938, he had absorbed both Austria and Czechoslovakia into the Reich. His plan was to create a world dominated by Nazi Germany in partnership with Fascist Italy and Japan. (see also Nazi, Third Reich, Treaty of Versailles)

Hunter, Aubrey-Australian Army lieutenant, born in Perth, Western Australia on 11 November, 1915. He was one of five children, the youngest son of third generation Australians of English heritage. Unhappy at school, he ran away and worked in the outback as a sheep shearer, then lived with Aborigines who taught him to live in the desert and play the didgeridoo. He worked his way up through the ranks after joining the Royal Australian Artillery as a gunner in 1937.

In 1940, a Lieutenant in the Australian division stationed in Britain he volunteered for Commando training and met John Stafford, Duncan MacLeod and 'President' Lincoln who become his comrades-in-arms. His distinguishing features were a shock of blonde hair, an irreverent attitude and a didgeridoo, the Australian Aborigine musical instrument in his kitbag.

Inonu, Mustafa Ismet (1888-1973)-Second President of the Turkish Republic which replaced the Ottoman Empire. As a General in W.W. I he lost the Battle of Megidda in Palestine against General Allenby the conqueror of Jerusalem in 1918 but destroyed the Greek army in Anatolia during the Greco-Turkish War. As a negotiator at the Lausanne peace conference he frequently turned off his hearing aid as Lord Curzon the British Foreign Secretary spoke against Turkish demands of territory, then he would turn it up when it was his turn to speak and carry on as if Curzon had said nothing. He became Turkey's second President in 1938 and ensured Turkey's neutrality at the beginning of W.W. II but leaned towards the Free Nation Alliance. Inonu feared a Nazi or Soviet incursion into Turkey. *He met Alan as emissary of Lawrence of Arabia and later signed the secret Treaty of Ankara in 1944 promising to join the Allies if Hitler invaded the Soviet Union or Turkey in return for membership of the Free Alliance of Nations and a seat on the Earth Government security council.*

*Jeffries, Marcus-*Born in 1927, his parents were Christian missionaries in Assam. They and most of the village in which they lived died of smallpox in 1933. An orphan aged six, Marcus was taken to Madras by a surviving Sikh friend of his family, who set up a cobbler's shop. Marcus became his apprentice and carried on the business when his guardian, Deepak Rachindra, died of a heart attack in 1938. In 1939 Ron and Phoebe Jeffries, a couple from England on holiday in India, took Marcus back to their cottage in Brighstone, Isle of Wight. In 1940 they were shot by Germans who suspected them of being members of the resistance. He looked after a baby Jaguar he named Aztec left behind during the invasion of the Isle of Wight. He often walked with the beast at night wearing a navy blue Macintosh coat and school cap. After killing a German soldier Marcus became a messenger and guide for Iron Duke Commando. He rescued Charlotte from a train full of prisoners heading for Kz1. They lived together and they were married in 1944 after the death of their baby.

Katsuyori, Captain (1920-1959)-*Descended from a famous Samurai warrior. Chosen to be one of the Grey Foxes by Emperor Hirohito.*

King, Admiral Ernest J. (1878-1956)-Appointed as Commander-in-Chief of the U.S. Fleets (Pacific and Atlantic) by FDR *in August 1941.* He was a graduate of the Annapolis Naval Academy and served on the staff of Admiral Mayo, commander of the U.S. Atlantic Fleet during the First World War. In 1922 he became a submariner and in 1930 learnt to fly. He was a strong advocate of naval air power but had a prickly personality.

King unsuccessfully opposed plans to land a U.S. army in North Africa *and prevented the USA from following an island hopping policy to reclaim territory from the Japanese as the first step in defeating Japan.* He saw the Pacific War as more crucial than the one in North Africa and Europe.

King, William Lyon Mackenzie (1874-1958)-Liberal Prime Minister of Canada during World War II. He was an adroit politician who supported an independent Canada within the

Commonwealth. He waited one week before leading Canada into World War II as Britain's ally on 10th September, 1939. A bachelor, he was interested in spiritualism. He declared that the Allies would win the war because the hands on his office clock on Parliament Hill in Ottawa were at the correct position to indicate success.

He welcomed the Royal family to Ottawa and became something of an uncle to Princesses Elizabeth and Margaret. He also helped the Norwegian, Dutch and Belgian royal families in exile, as well as the respective governments-in-exile for Great Britain, Czechoslovakia, Poland, Denmark, France, Norway, Holland and Belgium. King worked with Churchill, Attlee and Roosevelt in developing a co-operative strategy and *put Canada on a total war footing with compulsory conscription for all able-bodied men and women not working on farms or essential industries in November 1940.*

Konoye, Prince Fumimaro (1891-1945)–Member of Imperial clan of Fujiwara whose Princes were advisors to Emperors for 1300 years since first serving Emperor Tenji in the 7th Century A.D. He studied at Kyoto Imperial University. In 1916 became member House of Peers, formed his first government in 1937. Led the Japanese government modeled upon Nazi Germany and negotiated the Tripartite Pace. He was ousted by his Minister of War, General Tojo. *He became Hirohito's premier in place of the imprisoned Tojo when the 1944 coup took place.*

Kowolski, Kris-*Brilliant American mathematician in his mid-twenties, a recent graduate in Maths from MIT (Massachusetts Institute of Technology) assigned to work under Turing at Hamilton Hall in August 1941 as part of the American participation in the decoding of enemy signals using the Enigma decrypts.*

Khrushchev, Nikita (1894-*1944*)-Politburo member and strong supporter of Stalin by whom he was placed in charge of Moscow. He was a coarse, semi-literate peasant full of energy and a mouth full of gold teeth.

Kiwi-Nickname for a New Zealander

Lawrence, Charlotte-Fifteen-year-old daughter of the Reverend Reginald and Sophie Lawrence of Canterbury, Kent. Rescued from the train on way to KZ1 in spring 1941 by Marcus Jeffries. She kept a journal of her new life living as a 'cousin' to Marcus in Brighstone, Isle of Wight. She helped the resistance as a telephone operator and helped nurse her escaped parents back to health after Operation Magnet, the raid on Kz1. She lived with Marcus and fell in love with him, they married after losing their baby in 1944. She joined the Land Army siphoning what food she could to help feed a New Britain starved by sending the best food to Hitler's Europe.

Lawrence, T.E. (Thomas Edward) (1888 -1950)-Lawrence of Arabia was born in Wales and was a first class scholar at Jesus College, Oxford. His architectural thesis dealt with the effect of the Crusades upon European fortications. Before W.W. I he worked as an Archaeologist in the Middle East developing a taste for living like a Bedouin. From 1914 he acted as a spy in Syria and from 1916 led the successful Arab Revolt in Arabia against the Turks. After the war he attempted to create a single Arab state but became disillusioned by Arab factionalism and British political compromises and broken promises. He changed his name and joined the RAF as Aircraftsman Ross in 1922 but when it became public knowledge he joined the Royal Tank Corps as Trooper Shaw. *He ostensibly died in a motorcycle accident in 1935 but after surgery became a spy in the Middle East for Churchill. During W.W. II living in Jerusalem as Captain MacDougall (retired) he worked on bringing his old enemy Turkey on the Allied side and keeping the Arabs neutral. His code name was Sphinx.*

Le Meseurier, Felicity-Born in Montreal, Canada 9 February, 1919. Her mother was an American medical doctor Susan Van Dyke from Chicago, who treated her father, Henri Le Meseurier an officer in the Canadian army, while he recuperated from poison gas inhalation on the western front in a hospital in Scotland. He was a veteran of the Canadian victory at Vimy Ridge in 1917 where he became a lifelong friend of John Stafford's father,

Colonel Rex Stafford, of the Royal Hamilton Rifles. Consequently, Felicity knew John and his brother Alan, from the summer holidays they shared together as they grew up.

Felicity, an attractive brunette with green eyes was fashionable with an interest in art. At the outbreak of war she worked at Windsor Castle helping to store the art there for the duration. During the attack upon Windsor Castle she helped save Princesses Elizabeth and Margaret. She escaped Britain in the 'Great Evac' and received espionage training in Camp X, Oakville, Ontario.

Aged only twenty-one she joined Resistance Britain and participated in Operation Lion Heart. As a spy she worked as a Fashion Designer in occupied London moving in elite fascist circles. Despite living in occupied Britain, she married John Stafford on 21 May, 1941 at Battle, Sussex. Reporting to resistance leader C in London, Felicity is a fashion design assistant at the House of Mayfair on New Bond Street. Circulating on London's cocktail circuit she kept her ear to the ground for any information helpful to the Allied cause. She is a member of the board of Directors of the New British Red Cross organization which further increased her contacts with German and Fascist British officials.

Le Meseurier, Colonel Henri-*Born in 1894 in Montreal a major in World War One in the crack Canadian infantry Regiment the Royal 22nd 'Van Doos' (Vingt Douze), he served on the Western front in the Canadian Division. He became friends with John Stafford's father, with whom was with him at the Battle of Vimy Ridge in 1917. In the 1930s he was posted to London as an Intelligence military attaché. He asked John to spy for Churchill and Lord Beaverbrook in 1938. He was recalled to Ottawa to head the Canadian Military Intelligence department in September 1939.*

Lincoln, Francis-*Born 1901 in Halifax, Nova Scotia the son of a carpenter and lay Baptist Preacher, Samuel who was descended from a black slave who came to Canada on the 'underground railway' from the U.S.A. to find freedom in the 1840s. The* *escaped slave, Noah Richards, changed his surname to Lincoln when that American president freed all slaves in the United States. He decided however, to stay and raise his family in the country that had accepted him. Francis's mother could claim as an ancestor a black soldier, Slocum Archer, a descendant of a tribal prince from Nigeria, who fought under Cornwallis in the American Revolutionary War and came to Nova Scotia to receive the land grant given by King George III to all loyalists and to retain his freedom.*

Although bright, Frances had to leave school to support his family. He joined a boxing club and soon became a pugilist to reckon with. In 1932 he fought the Italian heavyweight Primo Carnera and won. He joined the British army, trained as a Physical Education instructor and was ordered to teach Commando recruits at Achnarry, Scotland in the summer of 1940. He received permission from the Commandant of the camp to join John Stafford's Troop which was ordered to Windsor Castle and stayed with John, Duncan and Aubrey in Red Dragon Commando in Wales, participating in Operation Lion Heart. Soft spoken but a tough soldier, his favourite weapon is the Bren gun, nicknamed Bertha. He was missing in action during the Afghan campaign.

His nickname was 'Mr. President'.

MacLeod, Duncan*-Became a Commando attending the training camp in Achnarry, Scotland in the summer of 1940 with John Stafford and Aubrey Hunter. Born in Edinburgh, Scotland in an upper class family in 1921, at the outbreak of war in September, 1939 he tried to join the RAF but failed the medical. He passed his first year pre-medicine courses at the University of Edinburgh but enlisted in the Royal Navy in May 1940 and was accepted, despite his short-sightedness which he kept from the medical examiners by memorising the chart.*

He was commissioned as a sub-lieutenant, serving on a destroyer in the Royal Navy and volunteered to be a Commando. He was with John Stafford, Aubrey Duncan and 'President Lincoln' at the Battle of Windsor Castle, at Portsmouth and in the Red Dragon

Commando in Wales. He was part of Operation Lion Heart. He wears brown tortoise shell glasses and his intellectual looks cover up a stubborn nature and wiry physique that got him through Commando training.

Margaret Rose, Princess (1930-2002)-Known in the '30's as Margaret Rose, second child of George VI and Queen Elizabeth, and younger sister of Princess Elizabeth. Born at Glamis Castle, Scotland. *Sent to live at Windsor Castle after the German invasion of France, with her sister, Princess Elizabeth. She survived the German paratroop attack on Windsor Castle and was evacuated to Wales, then Scotland, then to Canada for the duration of war. She attended the funeral of Winston Churchill in Australia in June, 1941 with Princess Elizabeth. She accompanied Princess Elizabeth on a state visit to Washington D.C. in 1943.*

Marshall, General George (1880-*1950*)-American army general. Appointed as Chief-of-Staff by FDR on 1 September, 1939 he oversaw the growth of the American army from two hundred thousand men to three hundred and seventy-five thousand re-organized and re-equipped troops by the spring of 1940. *Removed General MacArthur from his command in the Pacific in early 1942 and replaced him with General Eisenhower who commanded the 1st American army in Australia. Marshall supported the Chinese effort against the Japanese and General Bradley's campaign in Morocco and Algeria against Rommel, and eventually Spain, from 1941 on. Presciently he chose General Patton to head homeland army defence.*

Mescalyne, Jasper-Magician who began an extraordinary career aged nine. He was a master of illusions and after impressing military experts with a demonstration of making it look like the German battleship Graf Spee was coming up the Thames he was dispatched to Egypt and eventually concealed Alexandria by constructing a replica up the coast and made first the Suez Canal disappear then an entire army in the desert. *In 1944 he applied his talents to hiding the Allied forces in Morocco then went Afghanistan where he misled Rommel as to the location of the*

Khyber Pass into India gaining precious days for Montgomery to launch his offensive.

Michael, King (1921-   )-Son of King Carol III of Romania. In 1938, his father became dictator since the country was on the verge of civil war due to the instability caused by the pro-German fascist Iron Guard. King Carol travelled to Western Europe seeking aid and a military alliance, but was turned away empty-handed. The Germans, however, courted him. Faced with threats from Russia and Hungary, Romania sided with Germany, declaring war on France and Great Britain in May 1940. Hitler forced the Carol III to give up land to Hungary and he was forced to abdicate. Michael became king of Romania at the age of twenty, sympathetic to the allies, but forced to reign over a nation governed by pro-Nazis, doing what he could to help Jews and others persecuted by the fascists. *During the collapse of Germany in 1947 he led the fight against the fascists and communists to re-establish Parliamentary democracy.*

Mole, Marmaduke-Elderly butler of Dumbleton Hall who serves Adolf Hitler when he is resident in his English country home and attempts to teach his master English and various country gentlemanly pursuits such as fishing.

Montgomery, General Bernard Law, 1st Viscount *of the Pyramids* **(1887-1972)**-Descendant of a Norman Baron who accompanied William the Conqueror in his successful invasion of England in 1066. He was a World War I veteran who was the successful commander of the 3rd Division British Expeditionary Force in France in 1940. While Britain braced itself for invasion, he commanded the army in S. E. England. Although demanding and eccentric he got results and was affectionately known as Monty to his troops who responded to his concern for their welfare.

He defeated the German invasion at the Battle of Dover, September 1940 but was seriously wounded at the Battle of Hayward's Heath just as the German front seemed to be buckling, and the battle was subsequently lost and with it Britain. After recuperating in Gibraltar in 1941 he flew to Cairo to take command of the 8th Army in Egypt. After helping Bradley organize Operation Overlord he commanded the 8th Army in Afghanistan defeating Rommel' Asia Korps. He became Britain's most successful general since Wellington.

The actor Clifton James uncannily resembling Monty was approached by fellow actor David Niven to be in a 'film about the army'. Little did he know that he was to actually dress and act like the real Montgomery and was even given a fake finger to make up for the one he had lost in the Great War. His ruse was a great success misleading the Germans that the expected invasion would come to the north of Europe.

Mosley, Sir Oswald (1896-1980)-An admirer of Adolf Hitler who founded the British National Socialist Party in the 1930s whose members were known as Blackshirts since they wore black turtleneck tops, trousers and jackboots. Imprisoned at the outbreak of war *after occupation he was released and assumed a high position of power setting up the British SS.*

Mussolini, Benito (1883-1945)-Son of a blacksmith, he was named after the Mexican revolutionary Benito Suarez and became a socialist. He founded a socialist newspaper, was draughted into the Italian army (allied to Britain and France) in World War I and was wounded fighting against the Austrians.

He created the fascist Blackshirts who seized power and founded a corporate socialist Italy with himself as '*Il Duce*' (The Leader). His aim was to recreate Italy's ancient Roman Empire in the Mediterranean. Hitler used him as a model and Mussolini allied himself with Hitler and Japan to form the Axis Alliance. Mussolini over-ran Abyssinia (Ethiopia) in 1936. He declared war against the Allies in June 1940, when it appeared Germany was winning.

Nagano, Admiral Osami (1880-1947)-*One of the Grey Foxes organized by Hirohito.* Born in Kochi to a Samurai family, graduated from the Imperial Japanese Naval Academy and attended Harvard Law School 1913. He was a military attaché in Washington in the 1920s. Served as the head of a naval delegation at the 1935 London Naval Conference where Japan withdrew in protest since they were disallowed from achieving naval parity with Great Britain and the U.S.A. He was appointed Minister of the Imperial Japanese Navy in 1936 and C-in-C of the Combined Fleet in 1937. In 1941 he became Chief of the Naval General Staff. He supported the decision to wage war on the United States and Great Britain *but was persuaded by Hirohito to support his secret plan to negotiate peace terms if Japan overextended itself and was threatened with destruction.*

Napoleon IV (1902-1967)-*Leader of the Free French movement after leading a successful coup d'etat in Indo-China against the Vichy government on 2 December, 1942, the anniversary of Napoleon III's coup which secured him total power in France in 1851. Born 10 February, 1902, Charles Albert Louis D'Allaincourt used his mother's surname until 1942 but was actually the grandson of Napoleon III founder of the Second French Empire, who was himself the nephew of Napoleon I, creator of the First French Empire.*

Before the Prince Imperial died aged 23 at the hands of the Zulus during the Zulu War as an officer attached to the British Army, he secretly married a French Countess in South Africa, who gave birth to a son seven months after his death. This son, Bernard Josef, became father to Napoleon IV. He used his mother's surname, D'Allaincourt, to avoid being the centre of a Napoleonic political movement that would have been doomed to failure in the days of the Republic. He was a divorced captain in the French army who retired to the port of Nantes. He married Emma Rose Duvoisin who was poor but of a noble family. They sacrificed much to send his son to St. Cyr, the French Military academy. After graduating and joining the army as an Artillery Lieutenant, just like his ancestor Napoleon I, he served with the French Foreign Legion and was a military attaché to Washington in the 1930s before being posted to French Indo China in 1939. Although hating the Vichy Government he secretly contacted

400

Charles De Gaulle and the Free French Government in Montreal. He offered his services to General De Gaulle in November 1940 and bided his time planning a coup to free the South East Asian part of the French Empire from its collaborationist government.

Napoleon IV was pro-British, unlike the first leader of the Free French government-in-exile, the proud and prickly De Gaulle who resented pressure from Churchill and Roosevelt. De Gaulle was seriously wounded in Algeria and control of the Free French movement was taken by Napoleon IV. At the Casablanca conference with the full support of the other Free French leaders, Roosevelt and Attlee, General Bonaparte declared himself Emperor Napoleon IV.

***O-No, Chouku (1926-1971)**-Japanese princess a niece of Hirohito but averse to Japanese traditions. The daughter of the Japanese ambassador to Paris, despite her mother's protestations, was given a lavish western education and became a well known upper class rebel living a rebellious lifestyle within the rich and pampered circles of Europe. She met King Frederick and at first took advantage of him then fell in love with him, marrying him and becoming Queen Chouku, her first name meaning 'Butterfly child'.*

Orwell, George *(1903 -1954)*-Pseudonym for Eric Blair, who became disillusioned with the British Empire when working as a Burmese police officer in the 1920s, became a leftist writer and fought for Republicans in Spain, where he was shot in the throat. He condemned the totalitarian mindlessness of Stalinists and anarchists in the Republican cause. A Home Guard Sergeant during the Battle of London *he helped his platoon defend the St. John's Wood, London's telephone exchange for two days then ordered the remaining troops to go home, hide their weapons, uniforms and ammunition and join the nascent resistance movement when the battle was lost. He wrote articles condemning the fascist regime in the underground press. To protect his wife Sonia and child he took lodgings in Chelsea where he was arrested by the Gestapo in 1941. He had almost finished the play Animal State when he was taken to Kz1 where he became a mess steward* *escaping with Josef Comenici, eventually taking a Spanish freighter to Gibraltar. In Gibraltar he served in an anti-aircraft gun crew with Josef then was posted to Calcutta to work as a BBC broadcaster to S.E. Asia.*

Roberts, Field Marshal, Lord Frederick, Ist Earl Roberts of Kandahar, Pretoria, and Waterford (1832-1914)-Born in Cawnpore, India 30 September, 1832 went to Eton and the Royal Military College, Sandhurst, and Addiscombe Training College of the Honourable East India Company, appointed to Bengal Artillery in E. India Army in 1851. A 'soldier's soldier' he joined the Bengal Artillery at the age of nineteen and won the Victoria Cross during the Indian Mutiny in 1857 where he helped relieve Delhi. He and 6,000 British and loyal Sepoys were holding Flagstaff Tower. He tried to calm terrified horses to get artillery to safety and received a bullet near his spine, a leather pouch around his breast had slipped and prevented the bullet from penetrating deeply. He scouted out the weaknesses of the 30,000 mutineers and with a fellow officer took the Lahore Gate. He went on to help relieve Cawnpore. At Lucknow his excitable horse was shot in the head but survived and continued to be his mount.

He commanded the British relief force sent to Kandahar, Afghanistan during the 1878-1880 Second Afghan War became commander of the Indian Army then of the army in Ireland. From 1899-1900 he was made Imperial commander of the army in South Africa and captured Pretoria after setbacks against the Boers, until 1904 he was Chief of the Forces. Beloved of his troops he was nicknamed 'Bobs'.

Rommel, Field Marshal Erwin (1891-*1944*)-A veteran German infantry officer in W.W. I who was awarded the *Pour la Merite*. His post-war infantry tactics text made him world famous in military circles. Hitler appointed him as commander of his bodyguard. Rommel brilliantly led a Panzer division into France in 1940 and was promoted first to major-general *then to General and given command of the 6th Army Group during the invasion of Britain. His troops took the Isle of Wight and Portsmouth and* *linked up with the 4th Army Group at Hayward's Heath where the Germans won against Montgomery. In 1941 he was given the Afrika Korps in Tripoli with orders to destroy the British army in Egypt and take the Suez Canal.* He had great success until defeated at Alam Halfa and El Alamein by his nemesis Montgomery. Hitler promoted him to Field Marshal and recalled him to Germany *to lead the Asia Korps. His army swept all before him until he was confronted by Monty's 8th Army in Afghanistan. He was defeated in Operation Rose Garden by airborne and land forces. Shot by snipers he died in Kandahar. He was given a state funeral in Berlin.*

Roosevelt, Franklin Delano, President (1882-*1948*)- Born in New York to an aristocratic family of Dutch ancestry, he had a brilliant mind and incisive political instinct enabling him to be elected an unprecedented *four* times despite being a victim of Polio and unable to walk without help.

He was America's greatest leader, steering it not only during the grim years of the Depression but through the terrors of World War Two. Nicknamed FDR he was a fifth cousin to the popular Republican President Theodore Roosevelt 1901-1909. FDR was Secretary of the U.S. Navy in World War I and a successful Governor of New York from 1928-1932. As a Democrat president he helped unemployed Americans in the financial depression of the 1930s by establishing government work programs called the 'New Deal'.

He declared war against Japan, 26 December, Boxing Day, 1941, after Japan attacked Hawaii and bombed San Diego catching America by surprise.

Spencer, Lady Helen -Anne joined the WRNS in 1939 and become a first officer in the Wrens. In 1940 she was given a pair of French stockings by a soldier evacuated from France and she donated them to the fund paying for the construction of a new destroyer HMS Wren which made the news since nylons were impossible to obtain. *After working on the Admiralty's planning of Dunkirk and the Great Evacuations in 1940 she sailed for Capetown, South Africa where she delivering convoy sailing instructions by hand to each Captain to help* *keep routes secret. Transferred to Gibraltar then to Murmansk to supervise convoy plotters.*

Sphinx*-Codename for Colonel T. E. Lawrence and his band of agents in Asia and Asia Minor working on behalf of British interests with the tribesmen of the deserts and mountains of the Middle East, Turkey, Iraq, Iran and Afghanistan.*

Stafford, Alan*-Younger twin brother to John by five minutes, born in Hamilton, Canada 29 July, 1920. Identical to John except he is right-handed. Has a scar on his chin from an encounter with an ice hockey puck. More athletic than John, he was a champion junior tennis player for Canada and played at Wimbledon in 1939.*

He joined his father's old regiment the Royal Hamilton Rifles as a first lieutenant in September 1939 and was posted with John in the Canadian 3rd Division which sailed for Britain. He fought against the German invasion at Eastbourne and as the army withdrew west to Bristol. He volunteered for Commando training when the course was established in New Brunswick in January 1941. Alan was six-feet tall like his brother, has light blue eyes and straight red hair like John but prefers not to grow a moustache. He had more freckles on his face than John, and weighs ten pounds less. His disposition was easy-going.

Stafford, John*-Eldest son of Colonel Rex Stafford, Colonel-in-Chief of the Royal Hamilton Rifles and his wife Winifred (Lawrence) a distant cousin to Lawrence of Arabia. Older identical twin to his younger brother Alan by five minutes, born 29 July, 1920 in Hamilton, Ontario. Interested in history and archaeology in 1937 went to Munich for summer holidays staying with a Bavarian family. After graduation from Westdale Secondary School in June 1938 he went to Munich for a year study of german and fencing. He sailed to London en-route to Munich, where old family friend, Colonel Le Meseurier asked him to gather information while studying in Germany.*

After completing his studies and taking secret photographs of new Luftwaffe aircraft he travelled to Romania where he saved Prince Michael from a Nazi assassination plot. In Malta he learned to

404

scuba dive and with a friend in the Royal Canadian Navy thwarted Italian frogmen spying on a British battleship. Back in London John reported to Colonel Le Meseurier and began to fall in love with his daughter Felicity, a year older than himself.

While waiting to start his second year at the University of Toronto he joined the Royal Hamilton Rifles as a militia lieutenant and was commissioned in the regular force on September 4, 1939 as a second lieutenant. Shipped to England with his brother, part of the 3rd Canadian Division he volunteered to be part of the British Norwegian expeditionary force sent to Narvik, Norway in April 1940, to unsuccessfully stem the German invasion. He was awarded the Military Cross for successfully storming a German machine-gun nest and was promoted to Captain.

He volunteered for the newly formed Commandos and took the course at Achnarry, Scotland with the men who became his team in Red Dragon Commando: Sub-Lieutenant Duncan MacLeod, RN; Lieutenant Aubrey Hunter, Royal Australian Artillery and 'President Lincoln'.

With the Nazi invasion imminent he was given the rank of acting major and the two hundred men of A troop, 8th Commando. His orders were to drive to Windsor Castle and protect the princesses. They arrived in time to beat off a paratroop attack. He took his men to Portsmouth where they retrieved naval munitions from the docks. When Churchill ordered the evacuation John read his sealed orders and led his men to Wales and their new role in Resistance Britain as Red Dragon Commando. He was made an Officer of the OBE (Order of the British Empire) for rescuing Edward VIII and Queen Wallis from the Tower of London.

John's characteristics are light blue eyes, erect stature of 6 feet, solid build, quick smile, straight red hair and ginger military moustache. He is driven to succeed and is a good shot, especially with the long-barreled Webley and Scott target revolver his father gave him.

Stalin, Josef (1879-*1960*)-Born in Georgia the son of a cobbler. His real name was Loseb Dzhugashvili. He was feared by all but his family. On the death of Lenin in 1924 he consolidated his power in the Communist Party through terror and in the 1930s his paranoia made him stage show trials, secret murders and mass executions on a huge scale. His five year programs of collectivisation of farms and industrialisation modernising Russia could only be achieved by massive social dislocation including widespread political repression and planned starvation in the Ukraine. He originally trained as a priest but became an atheist Marxist joining the Russian Social Democratic Worker's Party in 1899 calling himself Kola inspired by the Caucasian outlaw in the book *The Parracide*. He worked as a weatherman in Tiflis. In 1902 he was arrested and exiled for the first of seven times. Under Lenin and Stalin's rule the lax Tsarist system of Siberian exile became crueller and more efficient. He was short, 5' 6" and walked ponderously since the second and third toes of his left foot were joined, his right arm was shorter than the left. He usually wore a simple tunic, baggy trousers tucked into his boots and an old army greatcoat. His matter of fact cruelty is encapsulated by one incident in the civil war that savaged Russia from 1917-1924, he sank a barge containing ex-Tsarist army officers advising Trotsky 'Death solves all problems. No man, no problem.'

Thomas, Dylan (1914-1953)-Welsh poet and writer who wrote screenplays for the Crown Film Unit in 1940. *He was evacuated in October 1940 and worked in Canada writing scripts for propaganda films and broadcasting poetry and short stories. He returned to Britain to his family in 1946* and achieved world fame for his poetry and notoriety for his wild life.

Tojo, Hideki (1884-1948)-Brilliant lieutenant-general and Minister of War in Prince Konoye Fumimaro's government then assumed control of the government after leading an army coup. Led the 'Strike South' group believing that the United States and Great Britain must be attacked while Japan was strong enough to defeat them. *He was arrested in a coup engineered by Hirohito who wanted a peace government in place to end the war.*

Turing, Alan (1912-1954)-Eccentric but genius mathematician, graduate of King's College, Cambridge, obtained a doctorate in the U.S.A. at Princeton 1936-38 and wrote a 1937 paper *'On Computable Numbers'* which became the basis of his mathematical explorations which led towards creating the prototype of the electronic digital computer. Worked at Bletchley Park decoding centre 1939-*1940 and established and headed their relocated HQ at McMaster University, Hamilton, Canada 1941-1945.* He masterminded the first computerized decoding machine, Cyclops which used thirty-four hundred vacuum tubes and scanned twenty-five thousand characters a second. It worked on his principle of calculating mathematical certainties and irregularities. He was a homosexual at a time when that was considered a crime in most circles.

Wallis, Sir Barnes Neville (1887-1979)-Inventor and aircraft designer, developed the Wellington bomber and the 9,000 pound skipping bomb used by the Dam Buster squadron, also 10 grand slam and 6 ton tallboy bombs, developed swing wing fighters in 1970s.

***Williams, Corporal**-Welsh Batman (servant) to John Stafford in Wales. Trained sniper in Red Dragons who accompanies John to Egypt, later is one of two snipers who kill Rommel.*

Wilson, Harold-Affable Labour Member from Manchester. A junior member of the British government under Churchill, then promoted by *Clement Attlee.* Wilson was famous for his Mancunian accent and pipe-smoking habit. He became prime minister himself *and established the British-Russian space program in 1963.*

***Stannard, Ben**-U.S. Army Major of the Ist Battalion Rangers unit set up in 1941 to emulate the Commandos and make amphibious raids. He was born in Niagara Falls, New York state in 1915, the son of a police Sergeant. As an Army Lieutenant in the U.S. embassy in London during the Battle of Britain he helped embassy staff escape to America when the Germans invaded. He* volunteered for the Rangers when they were formed in August 1941.

Wellington, 8th Duke, Arthur Valerian Wellesley-Attended Eton, joined the Royal Horse Guards. *As a subaltern he served under Freyberg in besieged Singapore. On becoming the next Duke of Wellington upon the death of his father he carried on the tradition of providing a flag to the sovereign on the occasion of the anniversary of the Battle of Waterloo on 14th June. He sent the tattered Union Flag (Union Jack) that flew over the war-torn port to Queen Elizabeth in Scotland in place of the flag bearing the Wellington crest.*

White, Horace *-Member of Resistance London who with Mr. Torrey met John and Felicity at the commando underground HQ. A large man he wore crumpled suits, loud ties,1 scuffed shoes and round wire-framed spectacles in need of a clean. He controlled various agents in London including Charlie Gates before he moved to Yorkshire.*

Patricia, White-*Young secretary at The London Chamber of Commerce , daughter of Horace White.*

Yezhov, Nicolai- *Commander of the NKVD, the Soviet secret police known as the 'poison dwarf' because of his shortness and bloodthirsty ruthlessness as Stalin's prime executioner organising the great purges of the 1930s.*

GLOSSARY

Fictional descriptions are shown in *italics*

Ack-Ack-Alliterative British term for anti-aircraft fire which Americans termed flak.

ADC-Aide-de-Camp, an officer assigned to assist a staff officer or member of the royal family.

Afghanistan-Ahmad Shah Durrani in the eighteenth century united Pushtan and other tribes to create Afghanistan. The First Afghan War began in 1839 when Britain replaced Dost Muhammed with Shah Shorja, the Afghans defeated the British army and in the retreat to India massacred everyone but one man. Russia and Great Britain were rivals to control the region this was known as the 'Great Game'. Britain invaded again in 1878 with an army under Lord Roberts after defeating the pro-Russian Shah's army and set up Abdor Khan on the throne in Kabul. His successor Amanallah Khan received payment from Britain and remained neutral in W.W. I. Assassination, civil strife with some reforms took place in the 1920s. Mohammed Zahir ruled from 1933 creating a parliament. *After W.W.II Afghanistan joined the Earth Government and developed a tourist industry attracting many Chinese and American tourists*.

Allies-Nations allied against Fascism.

Atombombe- German for atom bomb, pronounced a-tom-bom, *called F or Fission bomb by the Allies*

Axis-Another name for the Tripartite alliance of Germany, Italy and Japan *which expanded to become the with the addition of the Latin Fascist Alliance and Spain.*

Bandit-RAF codename for an enemy plane.

BBC-British Broadcasting Corporation, government national radio and television service. *Became the New BBC when the fascists took over Britain, the real BBC continued to broadcast radio programs from Canada.*

Black Douglas Commando-*Scottish Resistance unit named after* Sir James Douglas c. 1286-1330, who fought with King Robert the Bruce of Scotland against the English. In 1313 he captured the Castle of Roxburgh by disguising his men as black oxen and became known as 'The Black Douglas'. He fought with Robert the Bruce at Bannockburn and later set out to take that Scottish king's heart to Palestine in a silver casket. However, he died while fighting the Moors in Spain.

Blackshirts-Name given to Nazi SS troops or British fascists led by Sir Oswald Mosley, who wore black uniforms of turtlenecks and trousers or jodphurs and jackboots.

Bletchley Park-Site of the British Code and Cipher School 50 miles (80 km.) north-west of London under the guidance of MI6 was a secret residence of several hundred mathematicians and code experts whose job it was to decipher German and Japanese secret codes. The experts included such geniuses as Alan Turing, who created the first computer. *The decoders were shipped to Canada during the Great Evac and set up a new secret site at McMaster University, Hamilton, Ontario*

Blitzkrieg-German for 'Lightning War' the quick style of warfare using tanks, aircraft and troops in vehicles, used to great effect by the German Wehrmacht in 1939-1940. Shortened to 'Blitz' by the Daily Express during the Battle of Britain.

Bogey-U.S. air force codeword for enemy aircraft.

Bombe-Fast calculating machines designed to find contradictions in chains of letters and numbers millions of characters long, in order to decypher enigma codes. They were originally developed by the Poles and perfected at Blechley Park and *Hamilton Hall*. Weighing a ton each, they were seven feet long and two feet wide. They consisted of relay switches, a profusion of coloured wires and a dozen rotating drums making a noise like the ticking of a bomb. Bombe was a code name given it by the Poles who like ice creams of the same name. Two hundred and ten were built by the British *and Canadians*. Standard phrases such as 'Wetter fur die

Nacht' and 'Heil Hitler' and mistakes in enemy enigma messages helped Turing and his staff decode messages.

Bren Gun-best light infantry machine-gun ever produced, designed in Czechoslovakia and manufactured in Britain and Canada. Used by British Commonwealth troops in World War II it fired 500 rounds per minute from a detachable curved magazine that fitted on top of the breech, weighed 10.1 kg.

Browning - American small-arms manufacturer producing automatic pistols and belt fed machine guns used in Hurricanes and Spitfires.

C.O.-Commanding Officer

Commandos-British shock-troop unit set up in the summer of 1940 for amphibious attacks against German-held Europe. Volunteers were trained in Achnarry, Scotland in cliff-scaling, kayaking, amphibious operations, unarmed combat and living off the land. Units of Commandos of 200 men known as Troops *became the initial core of British resistance after the occupation in October 1940*, used in mainly amphibious and special military operations.

Commonwealth-British Dominions of Australia, Canada, New Zealand and South Africa given independence by the Statute of Westminster in 1931 remained in the co-operative organization called the British Commonwealth. After World War II many ex-colonies of the Empire, such as India, were granted independence and chose to join the Commonwealth and retain close links with Britain.

Concentration Camp- *Konzentrationslager* were set up by the Nazis in Germany (e.g. Dachau) to house political prisoners, the mentally ill and physically disabled but mostly proscribed groups such as Jews, Slavs, homosexuals and gypsies. The inmates lived in appalling conditions and were used as slave labour. Later, more concentration camps such as Auschwitz in occupied Poland were built for the mass extermination of about six million human beings.

Two were established in New Britain, on the Isle of Wight and the Isle of Man.

Cyclops-I changed the name from Goliath the analytical machine developed by Alan Turing, kept secret until recently since it could decrypt coded Enigma message in an hour that would take a standard modern computer a year to decode.

Desert Rat-Nickname for members of the British 8th Army which made its reputation in North Africa.

DSO-Distinguished Service Order. British award for bravery.

Dumbleton Hall-An English country manor house in Oxfordshire scouted out by the German Foreign Minister von Ribbontrop, a one-time wine salesman, in the 1930s as the ideal English home for Adolf Hitler once Germany had subdued Great Britain.

Earth Government-*Known as EG, the world government a stronger successor to the League of Nations was proposed in 1943 by the Free Nation Alliance as the post-war world government.*

Eagle-*First U.S.A.A.F. helicopter developed by Sikorsky used in every theatre of World War Two by American forces in great numbers. It used two rotors and was used to carry troops into the battlefield, to attack enemy positions, for reconnaissance and to take wounded soldiers to field hospitals.*

El Caudillo-Spanish term meaning 'The Leader', referring to General Franco.

Enigma-Name of German coding machine using rotors and electrical plugs which allowed for millions of permutations of letters and numbers. Thanks to the courage of Polish partisans an enigma machine was captured from a German army convoy in 1939 and sent to Britain. The Royal Navy captured code sheets from the German navy. Decoding experts at Bletchley Park were given the task of cracking the code and providing the results, known as Ultra, to Churchill. It took some years to completely crack the enigma code but it engendered the first true computers built at *Hamilton Hall, Canada.*

Erk-nickname for an RAF mechanic or fitter

E.T.A - Estimated time of arrival

Fission Bomb-Allied name for the atomic bomb, also called F-bomb developed in Operation Wyoming led by Robert Oppenheimer in North Dakota. The first F-bombs were not ready until 1945. Germany used its own atomic bomb for the first time in August 1944.

FACE-Acronym for Free Alliance Control Executive, the name given to the supreme command of FAN (Free Alliance of Nations). It comprised Admiral Pound RN, head of Naval Operations, General Arnold, U.S.A.A.F., head of Allied air forces and General Marshall of the U.S. Army, head of Allied armies.

FAN-Free Alliance of Nations, comprising Australia, Canada, China, South Africa, New Zealand and the governments-in-exile of Belgium, China, Czechoslovakia, Great Britain, Holland, Norway and Poland. The Washington Conference of January 1942 attended by delegates from the various allied combatants agreed to a unified command (FACE) by the Allies. Their aim was the defeat of Germany, Italy and Japan. FAN became the basis of E.N.O. (Earth Nations Organization) the hardier successor to the failed post-World War One attempt at World Government known as the League of Nations.

Fascism-Anti-communist and patriotic movement founded in Italy during World War I (1914-1918). Benito Mussolini became leader of the fascist Blackshirts and dictator of Italy. Their symbol was the fasces, a bundle of rods with an axe in the middle which was carried before important officials in ancient Rome. The word was used to describe the bellicose, anti-communist regimes of 1920s Italy and 1930s Japan and Germany. Sir Oswald Mosley established the British Union of Fascists in the 1932. At the outbreak of war he was imprisoned *but was released after the Germans entered London and became one of Lord Eastbourne's closest advisors.*

Fascist-Follower of Fascism.

413

Flak-American term denoting anti-aircraft fire which became universal, the equivalent of the earlier British term ack-ack.

Fuhrer-Leader, a German term coined by Josef Goebbels to refer to Adolf Hitler.

Gestapo-Secret police (Staatspolizei) in the Third *Reich*, organized in 1933 by Goering but came under the command of Heinrich Himmler in 1936, it was used to terrorise anti-Nazi movements.

G.I.-General Issue, the term for equipment issued to American soldiers which became their nickname.

G-Suit-Gravity suit, developed by Dr. Wilbur Franks, Canadian National Research team under Dr. Frederick Banting's direction. He developed a suit for fighter pilots to enable them to fly while undergoing up to 7-8 Gs of gravity while turning at high speed in a propeller-driven plane, and later of flying at high speeds in jets. The first G-suit was home-made and he tested it and subsequent suits in a Spitfire. Became the basis for space suits in the 1960s, the Germans used a captured suit as the basis for their fighter pilot suits *and later, space suits.*

Gen-British 1940s slang for 'General Information'

Geschwader-Aircraft

Ghurkas-Nepalese troops serving in the British Army, short in stature they are known for being loyal and courageous. They use the Kuri knife to great effect terrifying their opponents, they fought on the Western Front in W.W. I and in all theatres in W.W. II. They also fought in the Falklands Islands War of 1982. Originally recruited after the British tried unsuccessfully to take the Himalayan country of Nepal. So impressed were British officers by the courage of the defenders of the city of Gorkha they recruited Nepalese for their army and called them Ghurkas.

***Great Evacuation (Operation Magneto)**-The evacuation of the armed services, government officials, scientists and the British gold reserves to Canada by sea. Evacuees included governments-in-exile of the occupied nations in Europe and their royal families*

(Netherlands, Belgium, Norway), Princesses Elizabeth and Margaret and their grandmother, Queen Mary.

Gross Deutschland-Nazi term referring to the German Anglo-Saxon empire: Denmark, Great Britain, Netherlands and Norway.

Grey Foxes- *Secret group of supporters organized by Emperor Hirohito to be in place to negotiate a peace if the war turned against Japan. It included family members such as Prince Konoye, Prince Kotohito Kanin, Chief of the Army General Staff to 1940; Admiral Nagano, Chief of the Naval General Staff, naval officer Oka, a member of the Satsuma clan and General Anami Korechika. Hirohito asked them to be ready to act on his orders to take over the government and begin peace negotiations if his Prime Minister was close to destroying Japan with his megalomania. Korechika was the Emperor's aide-de-camp until 1933. After serving with distinction in China he was on the General Army staff HQ in Tokyo. He did not support the 'Strike South' faction and was assigned the task of finding Generals willing to follow the Emperor against Tojo. Prince Konoye is to be Prime Minister and Nagono to be War Minister if the Emperor's coup is undertaken. The codeword for the coup is 'Three Storks'.*

Hamilton Hall-*Centre of code decrypting by Alan Turing and his team of code-breakers,* a building located at McMaster University, Hamilton, Ontario in the centre of Canada close to Toronto. *Its team members were brought to Canada in the 'Great Evac' and others added to it such as Kris Kowolski, an American mathematician. Their work engendered the first computers.*

HMCS-Her (His) Majesty's Candadian Ship

HMS-Her (His) Majesty's Ship.

Hong Kong-British Crown Colony on Chinese coast overrun by the Japanese army *4-19 August 1941. Thanks to U.S. aircraft carriers being allowed to serve under the Royal Navy Ensign in a secret deal between Attlee and Roosevelt, thousands of troops and supplies were successfully evacuated from Hong Kong and used to reinforce Singapore, Ceylon and India.*

415

Horsa-*Troop carrying glider used by British Airborne Division. Towed by transport or bomber planes and let loose to glide to a landing.*

House of Mayfair-*Haute couture fashion house on New Bond Street in fashionable Mayfair in London, where Felicity works for Jonnie Hawker as a costume designer.*

HQ-Headquarters

Jerry (Jerries)-Nickname for German soldier(s) used by British and Commonwealth troops.

Junkers 88 (Ju 88)-Versatile, high-speed, two-engined German bomber. It had a crew of four. *The See (Sea) version was developed for use on aircraft carriers.*

Kampfwagen-Literally German for 'war-wagon', an open top staff car.

Kiwi-Nickname for a New Zealander after the ubiquitous national flightless bird known as the Kiwi.

Knot-measurement of a ship's speed, the rate at which a ship travels one nautical mile, (1.15 British statute miles). A ship travelling 30 knots an hour would be travelling over 30 miles per hour (50 kilometres)

Konzentrationlager-German for concentration camp, known in short form as Kz.

Kraut-American derogatory slang term for German referring to the German penchant for eating saurkraut (pickled cabbage).

Kriegsmarine-German navy

Lee-Enfield-Standard British Commonwealth bolt action infantry rifle .303 calibre. Its magazine held 10 bullets and could be fired quickly; 1914, the German army when confronted by the small professional British army using Lee-Enfield rifles were convinced that they were facing machine guns.

Liebel-German for butterfly, name given to the single rotor helicopter used by the Luftwaffe .

Leibstandarte-Hitler's personal bodyguard of elite troops formed in 1933.

Limey-Slang term for Britons used by Americans, based on fact that Royal Navy captains in the eighteenth century had their crews eat limes and oranges to fight scurvy.

Lord Mosley Hospital-The King Edward VII Hospital for Officers St. Agnes was founded in 1899 by two sisters Agnes and Fanny Keyar who offered their Grosvenor Crescent home to help wounded officers returning from the Boer War convalesce. *In 1941 the hospital was renamed after Lord Mosley founder of the British fascist party who became leader of the one party House of Lords.*

Lorry (Lorries)-British term for a transport truck.

Luger-German officer's pistol with a bullet magazine in its grip, a so called snail magazine which could be pulled out for reloading.

Luftwaffe-Term for German Air Force, its aircraft had black crosses edged with white on wings and fuselages, swastikas were painted on their rudders or tails.

M4A1-Famous American half-track (front wheels and back caterpillar tracks) armed with an 81 mm. mortar, one rocket launcher, and .50 mm. Browning machine gun made by the White Motor Company. Used as a command and scout vehicle in every theatre. Capable of 45 mph. 20,000 were manufactured.

MP-38-Popularly known as a Schmeisser machine-gun, a 9 mm maschinen pistole used by the Wehrmacht and *New British gendarmes.*

Mauser-German infantry rifle.

Met-Nickname for meteorological or weather report used by RAF.

Mile-Ancient Imperial (British) measurement of distance of 5,280 feet (1,780 yards) equivalent to 1.8 kilometres. *The New British*

Government changed all road signs to kilometres but these were changed back to miles after freedom was restored. There were celebrations in many cities, towns and villages when the last signs were replaced in the late 1940s

NADO-*North Atlantic Defence Organization proposed at meeting of FDR and Attlee on the battleship HMS Iron Duke off the coast of Newfoundland in August 1941. The United States, Great Britain, Canada and the European Governments-in-exile became signatories in a ceremony in Washington, D.C. on 3rd September, 1941.*

NAFFI-Acronym for Navy, Army and Air Force Institutes, a charity which provided snacks, tea and coffee with social events for men and women in the armed forces where they could buy subsidised refreshments and enjoy dances and social evenings.

Nazi-Member of the Nazi party led by Adolf Hitler, which gained power in Germany in 1933 and created the Third Reich, in which Hitler was dictator as Reichzchanzler (Reich Chancellor). A police state was created and submarines, tanks and aircraft built in defiance of the Treaty of Versailles. Revenge for the loss of World War I and the humiliating peace treaty was the motivation for Nazi foreign policy, which wanted to make Germany the supreme world power by manipulation, coercion or brute force.

The party believed in the mythical supremacy of the Aryan race, supposedly exemplified by the 'master' race (Nordic-Germanic peoples) over the Slavs and Jews. The Nazi party was vehemently anti-Communist but cynically the Third Reich made an alliance with the Soviet Union in 1939 and carved up Poland between them.

NCO-Non-commissioned officer in British and Commonwealth army such as lance-corporal, corporal, sergeant, sergeant-major.

New Scotland Yard-London police headquarters, a red and white brick Victorian building in the Neo-Gothic style on Victoria Embankment SW1 build on the site of the Scottish ambassador's residence. *After the occupation it housed the central offices of the*

SD and gained a sinister reputation. Often referred to as Scotland Yard or simply the Yard.

Nip-British wartime term for Japanese from *Nippon* meaning Japan. 'Jap' was a common derogatory nickname for Japanese used during W.W.II.

Nippon-*Name for Japan meaning 'the origin of the sun' Japan. The country is comprised of over 6,000 islands the largest of which are Honshu in the middle, Hokkaido to the north and Kiyushi to the south.*

Number One-Term used in Royal Navy to indicate the Captain's second-in-command, usually a lieutenant.

Panzer-German for Panther, short form for panzerkampfwagon panther fighting vehicle, also known as PzKw.

PIAT-An acronym for Projectile Infantry Anti-Tank, the British and Commonwealth version of the American Bazooka using two men, one to aim and launch the rocket the other to load.

PM-Prime Minister

Pound-British paper unit of currency, decimalized in 1941 by Fascist government, the ancient system of 12 pennies to each of twenty shillings making up the pound was reintroduced in 1945 a year after New Britain was liberated.

Queen Alexandra's Royal Army Medical Corps (QARAMC)- Founded in 1902 by Queen Alexandra wife of Edward VII. Florence Nightingale and her Russian equivalents established military nursing on opposite sides in the Crimean War in 1854, Nightingale's determined assault on bureaucracy and reactionary British army administrators by 1888 saw the creation of nursing sisters being attached to military hospitals and in 1881 the founding of the Army Nursing Service. On the death of Queen Alexandra in 1925, her daughter-in-law, Queen Mary the wife of George V, became President of QARAMC until her death in 1953.

Quisling-Term used to denote a collaborator with the enemy. Named after Vidkun Quisling, the leader of the Norwegian Fascist

Party who became Prime Minister of Occupied Norway and an ally of Nazi Germany.

Radar-American term which became the widespread name for RDF (radio direction finding), a method of detecting aircraft devised by a Scottish scientist Robert Watson Watt. Radio signals sent by a strong transmitter were reflected by an aircraft up to a range of 100 miles and bounced back to a radio receiver screen. By 1936 the system was practical and a chain of RDF or radio location stations were secretly set up under the title, Chain Home Network.

RAF-Royal Air Force

Recce-Short form of 'reconnaissance'.

Red Devils (Rot Teufelen)-German nickname of members of the British and commonwealth Airborne soldiers who were given red berets and the Airborne Division winged badge when they passed their jump training.

Red Dragon Commando-British army detachment of Resistance Britain assigned to wage guerrilla war in Wales. They adopted the badge of Wales, the Red Dragon.

Reich-German word meaning empire.

RN-Royal Navy.

SAS-Special Air Service founded in 1940 in Western Desert by a Scots Guard subaltern, David Stirling, a member of No. 8 Commando Brigade (Layforce). He recruited sixty-five men for parachute raids but they achieved success using the tactics of the Long Range Desert Group on motorized patrols deep behind enemy lines using heavily armed jeeps. In early 1943 his group was renamed the SAS, he was captured and Paddy Mayne took over 1 SAS while David's brother, William, started 2 SAS.

Savoy Hotel-One of the premier hotels in London built in 1889 next to the Savoy Theatre overlooking the Thames River. It was the first to have lifts (elevators) and electricity.

SD-Initials of Sicherheitdeinst, the SS secret police.

Short Sunderland Flying Boat-Large Royal Air Force flying boat effectively used by Coastal Command in anti-submarine work and to ferry officials. Originally designed as a civilian airliner, its long range of up to 2,980 miles made it ideally suited for ocean patrols.

Sieg (Victory) Rockets-German rockets developed to deliver high explosive, gas or germ filled warheads.

Sikorsky H-2-*U.S.A.A.F* helicopter developed by Josef Sikorsky, had *two rotors: one above the cockpit and one above the tail, capable of carrying twenty fully equipped troops. Eventually used in every theatre by the U.S.A. to move troops, supplies and as flying ambulances.*

Spiritual League of North America-*Organization of witches, shamans and clairvoyants whose purpose is to use spiritual means to defend North America. Headed by the Druid Owen Gryffyd.*

Storm Band Leader-officer rank in the SS

SOE- Special Operations Executive set up *in Canada* to direct resistance movements across occupied Europe

SS-Initials for Schutzstaffeln ('Protective Squadron') formed in 1925 by the Nazi party after the failure of the Munich Beer Hall Putsch (Coup d'etat) in 1923. Under Heinrich Himmler it grew into an elite force of 500,000 men which regarded itself as a racially pure, 'Aryan', force. It formed many divisions of well-trained, fanatical troops known as the Waffen SS. *The Saxon Division was raised in New Britain by Sir Oswald Mosley.*

STAFFEL-Luftwaffe squadron

Supermarine Spitfire-Beautifully designed RAF fighter plane with eight .303 machine guns, four in each elliptical wing; able to reach a top speed of 448 miles per hour. Its versatility made it more than a match for the Me 109.

Thermobaric bomb-Developed by the USA it used intense heat and pressure to destroy up to one square mile. Used to blast enemy harbours and other military targets.

Third Reich-The Third German Empire (First led by Frederick Barbarossa, Second led by Kaisers Wilhelm I and II), founded by Adolf Hitler and the Nazi party. His dream was for it to last a thousand years, make Germany the predominant world power and eradicate the Jewish race.

Three Storks-*Code name for coup to take place on Emperor Hirohito's command, replacing Tojo's supporters with officials loyal to the Emperor and willing to open peace negotiations with the Allies.*

Tommy Gun-nickname of American Thompson machine gun made famous by 1920s Chicago gangsters. Their original round magazines of bullets tended to jam so rectangular magazines replaced them in 1942.

U-Boat-Short form of German Unterseeboot (Submarine)

USAAF-United States Army Air Force. Became the United States Air Force *after World War Two.*

Valhalla-the Hall of Feasting to which warriors were destined to go after death in Nordic Myths idealized in Nazi belief.

V.C.-Victoria Cross, the highest British Commonwealth honour given for bravery in the face of the enemy. Established in 1854 by Queen Victoria in the Crimean War, medals are made from the melted cannon of captured Russian guns in the shape of a Maltese Cross. The inscription is 'For Valour.' Canada recently changed the inscription of any future Victoria Cross awarded by the sovereign to bear the Latin equivalent 'Pro Valore'.

Walther PP-Snub-nosed German pistol issued to police forces, holds six 9 mm bullets in a magazine contained in the butt. Used by SS forces including Otto von Darmstadt.

Webley-British small arms manufacturer of revolvers, etc.

Wehrmacht-German Army

White Eagle Lodge-Group of spiritualists witches and clairvoyants who were asked by the government to spiritually defend Great Britain in 1940. *Most of them were evacuated and under the leadership of Owen Gryffyd, recruited North American members with a mandate to make spiritual war upon the Axis powers.*

WRAF-Women's Royal Air Force, pronounced RAFS. Over 180,000 WRAFS served during W.W. II in air force stations as barrage balloon operators, radio and radar operators or secretaries, in command centres as photograph interpreters, plotters, also as mechanics and nurses. Several were killed in the Battle of Britain.

WRENS-Women's Royal Naval Service. A popular destination for women volunteering for service due to the smartest uniform for women in the armed forces. However, the first 1,500 recruited in 1939 had no uniforms until 1940. Wrens were Ratings who became Leading Wrens after one year. They did carry out combat roles but served in shore establishments as radio operators, secretaries, plotters, mechanics or inspecting vessels in harbours. They often worked twelve-hour shifts with no meals when working 8 pm-8am. Make-up was allowed but no nail polish, shorter hair was the order of the day and shoe laces had to be laced straight across. By the end of the war there were 100,000 Wrens. Officers were graduates of a three week course and were allowed the luxury of wearing black silk stockings. The official naval tailors, Grieves, measured entrants to Greenwich naval school but did not complete their uniforms until the entrant was passed by the board.

Yank-shortened form of Yankee, used by British and Commonwealth soldiers to denote an American.

Yard-Imperial British measurement of distance, equivalent to three feet (36 inches), 1,760 yards to a mile.

Zulfiqar-The fabled sword or scimitar presented by the Prophet Mahommet to his son–in-law Ali at the Battle of Uhud. Ali used it to kill the great Meccan warrior Amr Ibn Abdawud, who had the strength of one thousand men. Ali is said to have cleaved Abdawud's shield and his body into two. Mohammet is supposed to have said, "La fata illa Ali, la saife illa Zulfiqar' (There is no hero but Ali, and sword except Zulfiqar). The sword is shown in Arabic art and many replicas were hammered out by sword makers in the Middle East.

Author photo
Cannon Street Tube Station, London
Photo Ruth Oldham ©. 2007

ABOUT THE AUTHOR

Robert Oldham was born in Epsom, Surrey, England in 1950 and came to Canada in December 1963. He obtained a B.A. in History at the University of British Columbia and a Master of Library Science Degree in 1978 from the University of Toronto. He has been a librarian since 1979.

His short story 'Smashing Time' was short listed for the Commonwealth Short Story Competition in 1997. He has published two mystery short stories and a biographical piece on General Harry Crerar. He contributed to *Berkswell Royal Year 1993/94* and his poems have been published in *otobe/ingland*, *Quarry*, *Acta Victoriana* and the Coach House anthology, *This Is My Best*. His articles have been published in *Monarchy Canada* and the *Canadian Library Journal*.

Besides writing, the author enjoys acting and has performed in *Forget Me Not Lane*, *Midsummer Night's Dream*, *Hamlet, Evita, The Elephant Man* and the *Madness of King George III*.